Praise for works by
CHRISTINA SKYE

TO CATCH A THIEF
"Fast-paced action, vivid detail, a touch of the paranormal, and hot lovemaking will please readers of adventure romance, while fans of Skye's Draycott Abbey and Code Name series will enjoy this clever union of the two."
—*Booklist*

CODE NAME: BIKINI
"A fun, antic read."
—*Publishers Weekly*

"Fast-paced action, flashes of humor, and futuristic flavor typify this romantic action-adventure. Fans of the Code Name series will enjoy this delicious addition."
—Kristin Ramsdell, *Library Journal*

CODE NAME: BLONDIE
"Romantic thrills and adventure from the expert."
—*RT Book Reviews*

"Skye is terrific at writing fast-paced adventure romances...a tantalizing addition to the compelling Code Name series."
—*Booklist*

CODE NAME: BABY
"Thrilling...fans should eagerly await the next in the series."
—*Publishers Weekly*

THE DRAYCOTT LEGACY
"Christina Skye's delightfully haunting Draycott Abbey tales...pass the test of time, as they remain some of the better romantic fantasies available."
—Harriet Klausner

Also available from

CHRISTINA SKYE

and HQN Books

CODE NAME
Code Name: Bikini
Code Name: Blondie
Code Name: Baby

DRAYCOTT ABBEY
To Catch a Thief
Draycott Eternal
The Draycott Legacy

And coming in December 2009
Bound by Dreams

CHRISTINA SKYE

DRAYCOTT EVERLASTING

HQN™

Recycling programs for this product may not exist in your area.

ISBN-13: 978-0-373-77415-9

DRAYCOTT EVERLASTING

Copyright © 2009 by Harlequin Books S. A.

The publisher acknowledges the copyright holder of the individual works as follows:

CHRISTMAS KNIGHT
Copyright © 1998 by Roberta Helmer
First published by Avon Books in 1998

MOONRISE
Copyright © 2009 by Roberta Helmer

www.HQNBooks.com

Printed in U.S.A.

CONTENTS

Christmas Knight

PART ONE

The Wish

Fire at morning,
fire in rain.

PROLOGUE

Glenbrae House
Glenbrae, Scotland
Early summer

HOPE O'HARA CLENCHED her fists to keep from trembling.

Scotland. Brooding and magical.

Green hills rippled before her, densely wooded above a pristine loch. Sunlight cast a glow over sharp slopes, chasing away wisps of early morning mist.

High hills full of legends and ghosts.

A tremor raced through her, swift and sharp. Suddenly Hope had the sense that something rare and momentous was about to happen, something meant only for her to see and share.

Sunlight shifted.

Mist swayed.

Since her eighteenth birthday her uncle had urged her to visit this green glen. Hope was sorry her visit had come only after his death. There had always been some delay or prior commitment. And then it had been too late.

Her eyes blurred for a moment as she remembered her uncle's noisy laughter and interminable bad jokes. During a book research trip Dermot O'Hara had fallen in love with Glenbrae, assuring Hope that she would, too. How right he had been. She only wished he were here to share it with her now.

No regrets, girl. His booming voice seemed to sweep out of the shadows to comfort her. *Get on with living.*

When Hope saw the rugged tower house that loomed beyond the banks of the loch, her pulse tripped. Against all logic or explanation, each stone felt familiar. Just as before, she had the sudden sense that time was reaching out to her, offering all its mysteries.

If only she were brave enough to take them.

A beam of Highland sunshine peeked through the racing mist, burning over the tarnished letters on the front door.

Glenbrae House.

So beautiful. But why was it somehow…familiar?

A chipped flagstone path ran past the first early roses, an explosion of pink, peach and fuchsia. Below the thatched roof, sunbeams lit hundreds of fragile leaded-glass panels. It was like a dozen other old buildings Hope had seen since coming to Scotland two weeks before. All had been full of broody atmosphere tinged with magic.

But Glenbrae House was different. Personal, almost. She felt as if she were at home.

As if in a trance, Hope walked closer, feeling her heart race. The original house was thirteenth century, the estate agent now waiting in the car had explained, a traditional Scottish tower structure built for a local branch of the MacLeod clan. When the family fortunes had declined in the last century, a band of pre-Raphaelites had bought the property and turned the lower floors into painting studios.

They had felt the magic, too. Hope had seen some of their luminous illustrations of Glenbrae's weathered gray walls exploding with summer roses. Warriors rode through the deep woods, and faeries seemed to peek from beneath green bowers.

Legends lay everywhere. Magic touched every shadow.

In silence the house called to her.

How could she resist?

She brushed back a vine and pushed open the front door, half expecting to see ghostly figures drift past her shoulder. But her footsteps echoed through the empty rooms. Only dusty motes danced over the scuffed wood floors.

Lonely, the house seemed to whisper. *So lonely.*

But it took little imagination for Hope to envision bolder days when hardened travelers in heavy kilts gathered by open fires that blazed in the great hall. Here battles were plotted and history planned. Even the smoke on the stones whispered to her, holding cherished fragments of Scotland's stormy past.

Ghosts, some would call them. But Hope had never feared ghosts. Since childhood she had walked with ghosts, and history had been her greatest love, along with the beautiful books that captured its legends. And right now she stood shivering, breathless, drowning in history.

Because every corner of Glenbrae House felt like home.

The house seemed to shift and whisper, breaking the silence. Perhaps because she had become accustomed to the sounds of loneliness at an early age, she found herself listening to those low whispers. The shadows did not scare her, nor did the grime she saw.

She had once been awkward and quiet. Even as a child she had been too grave to suit those her own age, and she still didn't fit in. While others her age were busy lining up stock options, mutual funds and a collection of summer homes, Hope was still wandering. Six months in the Aegean and a season in Milan. Even a year spent teaching basic English in a lonely mountain village in western China.

Always searching. Always looking for magic and the right place to put down roots.

Now there was no family to hold her. Mother, father, uncle—Hope had lost them one by one. She only occasionally remembered her mother's breathless laugh or her father's slow smile. A boating accident had caught them during a summer storm on the Aegean the year that Hope turned thirteen. She had been convinced she could not survive, but she had, largely through the unswerving optimism of her boisterous uncle. Dermot O'Hara had soon become father and mother, guardian and friend. He had made her laugh and he had taught her to dream.

And Hope dreamed now.

Of sunny rooms and Christmas carols on a snowy night. Of a house that would soon become a home.

Not that the job would be easy. Glenbrae House had stood empty for almost twenty years, and sunlight dappled the chipped, gouged floors. Marks of disrepair were everywhere.

In the great hall, high, cantilevered beams bore tracks of soot from centuries of peat smoke. But instead of grime, Hope saw hard-eyed warriors who warmed their hands by the roaring flames.

The great house whispered, teasing with ancient secrets. Outside, the wind rustled the hedges and shook the rose shrubs as springtime fragrance spilled through an open window, heady and rich. Around the loch, wildflowers dotted the hills and danced in the sun. It would be hard work to bring the grounds back to their pristine beauty, but Hope had never been afraid of hard work.

Of other things, but not work.

She stared out the window at the shifting silver water of the loch, feeling Glenbrae's beauty seep into her weary, wounded soul.

She had traveled long enough. Maybe here along the rocky banks of Loch Glenbrae in a fortified thirteenth-century stone tower house with eight-foot-thick walls and a roof that probably leaked, she could finally put down roots.

With her uncle's death had come a small legacy and the promise of more in the future. Hope knew he would like nothing more than for her to be settled here between the peaceful green hills.

Above her head, a bar of sunlight swept the turret stair. Her breath caught as light brushed the dim outline of a painting worked over the plaster at the turn of the stairs. A warrior in flowing hauberk and chain mail glared down at her, pride and arrogance set in every angular feature.

A MacLeod, no doubt. A warrior by the look of him. A man of duty and granite honor.

With the changing light, he seemed to waver, an apparition from a Highland dawn.

Somehow, he, too, seemed familiar.

Hope told herself it was imagination, run amok after hours of travel over pitted roads. But the loch-gray eyes seemed to follow her movements, questioning her right to enter his shadowed domain.

She stood rooted to the spot, fighting the challenge of that keen gaze.

Even as her logic counseled her to flee, her heart stirred. She was crazy to be here, crazy to spin fantasies of belonging in a house at the edge of nowhere. The repairs alone would cost a fortune. But Hope felt linked with this house, as if she were no longer free to leave the beautiful old halls so much in need of tender hands and loving repair.

She stretched trembling fingers to the dim painting, half expecting to feel warm skin and rigid muscle through the cold textures of plaster and paint.

But there was no warmth, of course. No life behind the cold eyes.

Yet still the painting held her.

"Let me go," she whispered.

Around her the shadows moved. The room carried the echo softly.

"Then at least give me your whole name. Which MacLeod are you?" Softly, her words swept the empty room.

WhichMacLeodwhichMacLeodwhichMacLeod.

A car horn blared outside. Hope shivered and turned toward the door.

The agent had another house for sale on the far side of the valley. Something new and tidy, closer to the village and in need of little upkeep.

Yes, that was the sensible thing. But she didn't want to be sensible.

Wind scurried over her shoulder, tugging at her hair. Threadbare lace curtains fluttered at a broken window.

Then the front door slammed shut, closing her in, shuttering the room in darkness. With a gasp, Hope spun around. Light played over the figure above the staircase, where the keen, misty eyes glinted, filled with challenge—and just a hint of humor.

"Very funny, tough guy. Just don't think you're going to scare me into leaving."

The scent of roses filled the air, and Hope imagined how the house would look filled with candles and warmed with laughter. She knew from personal experience that there was no inn within thirty miles of Glenbrae. And she would have all these empty rooms...

An inn. A period inn that clung defiantly to its history and authenticity. Tartans on the walls. Laughter amid shadows and crackling fires on a gusty night, a haven for weary travelers.

Her breath caught. She rubbed the bank check in her pocket, the first installment of the legacy from her beloved uncle.

Don't talk to me about miracles, girl, Dermot O'Hara had always said. *Go out and make your miracles happen all by yourself.*

Hope could work a miracle here. This ruined, beautiful house in a quiet corner of the Highlands was a place to make dreams and put down roots. And maybe here she would finally heal from the heartbreak of losing her family.

Wind whispered down the high chimney, stirring the fine hairs at her neck. Almost like a greeting, Hope thought.

She sent a saucy glance to the painting. The warrior's eyes seemed to glint back at her, bright with challenge.

Hope laughed softly, swept by a sudden illogical sense of adventure. "Better make some room, MacLeod. Looks like you're going to have to share."

CHINTZ CURTAINS TWITCHED at the front window of a tiny cottage just beyond the loch. Three white-haired heads bobbed at the leaded panes.

"I told you so! See how she's following the path." Perpetua Wishwell, the eldest of the three sisters, pointed over the glen. "Look, she's going inside."

Her sister, Honoria, the middle sister and the plumpest of the three, gave a quick laugh. "She's taken down the sales sign. She's going to stay. I can almost feel it."

"She looks very nice." Morwenna Wishwell gave a thoughtful frown. "American, do you think?"

Honoria nodded briskly. "From a place called Chicago. I think she's the one we've been waiting for."

Morwenna toyed with a silver pin of a cat staring up at a full moon. "It's the correct planetary alignment. The moon in Libra—a very good time for establishing roots and turning a house into a home. What do you think, Perpetua?"

The tallest of the three, Perpetua tapped one finger against her rather pointed chin. "She looks too slender. Too young. What if the house proves too much for her? The past hangs heavy there. And we all know that the thatched roof leaks terribly. She might not be up to this."

"She is," Honoria said quietly.

"What about the dilapidated kitchen? One sight of that stove would make a strong man run for cover. And we still don't know her name."

"Hope O'Hara," Honoria answered quickly.

"Irish?"

"Irish, German and Spanish," her sister corrected.

"Even some obscure Russian ancestor who settled in a place called Duluth."

"Never mind Duluth." Perpetua frowned. "If you ask me, she's too fragile to tackle the manor. One good wind will knock her down."

"Nonsense," Honoria snapped. "I've done her chart. She *belongs* in the manor house. I did her transits after I got her birth date from that nice young man who was driving the loan car for the estate agent."

The shrill blast of a horn cut through the air.

The sisters pressed closer to the window. Morwenna murmured a low, inaudible phrase and stroked the silver cat pin. "She is very vulnerable right now. She's lost her uncle, I believe. And her parents, too. But there's something else…something physical that troubles her deeply."

"What sort of trouble?" Honoria demanded.

"I can't see."

"Hmm. What she needs is a vacation," Honoria said sagely.

Morwenna's eyes turned speculative. "What she *needs* is a man."

"A man?" Perpetua's eyes narrowed, almost catlike.

"A man of honor, of course. An ally and companion. Someone who doesn't mind hard work. Restoring Glenbrae House is going to be a labor to task Hercules, believe me."

"Unfortunately, Hercules is unavailable at the moment." Perpetua smiled faintly. "But hard work would mean nothing to the right man. A man who doesn't know the softness of a woman's laugh or the heat of her skin. A man who has been too long from home, too long on the move."

"You have someone in mind?" Honoria said eagerly.

"Possibly." Perpetua's head tilted. Light gleamed over her snowy hair. "Yes, quite possibly the perfect man."

Morwenna sat up straighter as an image swept into her mind. "Not *him*. The man's dead inside."

No answer.

"Perpetua, you're not listening to me. Ronan MacLeod is a *soldier*. Any woman in his life will be merely a night's diversion."

"That might change," Honoria said slowly. "With the right woman beside him. Someone to soften the past."

"It would take a ton of steel wool to soften *his* past." Morwenna shook her head. "All he has known is war and loss since the first moment his father put a bow in his hand, cuffed him and told him to meet his mark or he'd see that the whole village went hungry that night."

A frown crossed Perpetua's smooth brow. "A crude man, Angus MacLeod. Such a pity the mother died so young. But that changes nothing. Ronan MacLeod is the one."

Morwenna's fingers moved restlessly. "He's as hard as the steel of that weathered broadsword he values more than life. And the things he's done…"

Perpetua shrugged. "He is a man of honor. On that, you'll agree."

Morwenna nodded reluctantly.

"And he is capable of the most arduous campaign."

Another nod.

"Then it's settled. Ronan MacLeod will do very well for our Miss O'Hara."

"But they'll be like oil and water. He's positively medieval. And she's so—modern."

"I think we should have a look," Perpetua said abruptly. In silence their fingers linked. "In and out quickly, mind you. We don't want him to sense anything," Perpetua whispered.

She raised her hands to her sisters. The thrush song faded away and silence gathered, deep and oppressive. Around them the room receded as the shadows thickened.

A figure slowly took shape in the semidarkness. His eyes were hard, the flat gray of a mountain loch in winter. Sunlight gleamed from the plate armor at his chest and his dented broadsword. Behind him stretched muddy paths and the thatched roofs of a country town.

Glenbrae Village, as it had been in early spring, seven centuries in the past.

Perpetua murmured in satisfaction. "Careful," she cautioned as their thoughts began to link and expand outward. "If he senses us, he'll put up resistance, and that will make our next contact much harder."

Honoria frowned. "He's smarter than he looks. And he's more dangerous. Dear me, maybe we *should* reconsider our plan…"

RONAN MACLEOD SLID from his weary horse and rubbed the back of his neck. Endless hills stretched before him like restless seas, rich and green.

Endlessly different from the landscape he had known for the past years as a Crusader in the burning sands of the East. "Do you sense that we're being watched?" he asked his page.

"Aye, my liege. The whole town has come to watch the King's Wolf ride in."

"Not that," MacLeod said slowly. "Closer. And yet not close at all. It is most…strange."

The page shrugged, well used to his master's flights of fancy. "I see nothing but muddy streets full of curious villagers, my lord."

Ronan MacLeod surveyed the rugged green slopes. Long years of warfare had given him an instinct for danger he had learned never to ignore, but the muddy streets posed no threat that he could detect. There were no armed Saracens crouched behind the half-timbered walls. No plotting courtiers hid behind the baker's ovens.

Yet still the odd sense of uneasiness persisted.

He smiled bitterly at the grim little hamlet before him. Who would not feel unease in such a place? Glenbrae looked primitive and rude after the colorful cities he had passed in the East on his way to the Crusades. He had heard the bells of Paris toll from the greatest of the cathedrals. He had eaten the finest of roast swan with his fellow knights in Champagne and Burgundy. He had hawked on the slopes of the Pyrenees and savored the colors of a hundred kinds of silk in the teeming markets of Damascus. Through it all, he had fought for a king and felt a thousand times as if he were drowning in the blood of war.

Now Ronan MacLeod had come home—home to a narrow, muddy little hole in the hills known as Glenbrae.

If one could call a dozen stone cottages huddled in the shadow of a glen home.

He pulled a roll of parchment from beneath his hauberk and fingered the red ribbon threaded through the document. From the ribbon hung a wax seal with the image of his sovereign lord, Edward. "For loyalty in right trusty service in many hours of dread, I, Edward, by God's grace King of England, do entrust this deed conveying all revenues and rights of fee for the village of Glenbrae. By royal grant may Ronan MacLeod, my faithful man, collect wod-penny, agistment, foddercorn and chiminage, from now to his hour of death."

Fine words for a village clinging desperately to life, one step away from starvation.

MacLeod rubbed the only coins in his pockets, two silver French deniers. As they clinked hollowly, he tried to find excitement and satisfaction in a body hardened from months of travel and years of war.

He did not look up as three dirty-faced children scrambled over the pitted street and stumbled to a halt before him. "'Tis the knight," one muttered in the rippling Gaelic of the far North.

"Aye. Blackhearted, he is, so my da says. And the knight does eat the hearts of wee children to break his fast." The boys drew closer together, their eyes huge. At any second they expected the hard-faced Crusader to pounce upon them with his sword.

Ronan stared back, fingering his belt. Word of his hair-raising exploits in battle had spread along every dusty road from Damascus to Ghent. Even the court in London buzzed with the tales. And with each telling, the deeds became darker until the man called MacLeod became a monster with no shred of human feeling left.

Such tales had suited him full well, in truth. He seldom had need to raise his sword because his own black reputation had already done the work of conquest for him.

The scar that ran across his forehead usually did the rest.

The King's Wolf, so he was called. A soldier who acted first and spared no time for regrets. A man who would master any woman foolish enough to tempt his embrace.

In spite of his grim reputation, the women had always found him, all too eager to taste the passion of a hardened soldier.

At first MacLeod had been happy to oblige. He had kissed them, stirred them, ridden them to noisy pleasure. He had seen the calculation in their eyes and felt it answer something in his own tortured heart.

But the novelty had faded. He began to feel defiled with each cold encounter, and the bitter taste in his mouth drove him to an uneasy abstinence. It had been longer than he could remember since he had touched a woman's cheek, cupped the curve of a hip or breathed the fragrance of roses in silken hair.

MacLeod scowled at the frightened urchins huddled before him. "Begone," he growled, tossing down a rumpled bit of linen in which he had wrapped a pigeon pie. Warily the boys studied the castaway food, suspecting some subtle treachery. The youngest of the three, little more than a bundle of bones, snatched up the pie and ran away, followed by his shrill companions.

A fine homecoming indeed, the warrior thought darkly. Across the muddy road, he watched a pickpocket slip clever fingers into the leather pouch of a well-fed merchant. From the roof above rang an incomprehensible shout as brown sludge descended from a chamber pot, spraying the street.

Home. MacLeod began to wonder if the heathen East did not have its attractions after all.

There was no escaping the curious gaze of the villagers busy about their work. He saw how the fathers stiffened at his approach and nudged their daughters out of sight. Even here the legends had spread.

But it mattered not. He was their lord. They would obey him and offer him the respect he deserved. Whether they gave him any warmer sentiment was of no importance.

His young page shuffled restlessly.

"What is it, Will?"

"The manor house—it's just over that hill. You wished to arrive before nightfall."

In truth, the Crusader could summon little excitement for his new house or anything else. He had learned young that enthusiasm was an emotion best left to women and fools. But he felt a shred of sympathy for the weary boy beside him, who had been traveling for long, chill hours without complaint. "Do you know the way then, whelp?"

"Just past the wheelwright's shop. I was told there is a path that leads through the orchard. The house is just beyond."

"Then let us go and discover this fine grant the king has made to his best assassin."

Four men in tattered tunics sat along the path, their fishing lines angled into the clear water. At the sight of MacLeod, they scrambled awkwardly to their feet.

MacLeod recognized the fear in their eyes. Yes, his legend had certainly spread here.

He rubbed his jaw and studied the layout of the pool. "Is there someone to organize the villeins for work here?"

His page's head bobbed. "The abbot has a way with the locals. Anything you want, he can arrange."

"Then we'll start here," MacLeod said firmly. "We'll add an outer ring of water and a new set of dikes. I'll have sluice gates to control the flow of pike and eels. Tell the abbot the men of Glenbrae may fish here on Mondays. On all other days the pond is open only to women who are with child." His face hardened. "From the looks of those I saw on the road, most will have little hope of living through the winter otherwise."

The page nodded. He, too, had seen the gaunt faces and undernourished bodies. "Shall I tell them it is at your order, my lord?"

"No. Tell them it is the command of their sovereign. Let King Edward take the credit and their gratitude."

The page made no protest, well used to his master's eccentricities. As they trudged on, villagers gathered silently along the muddy path. The men looked apprehensive, and the women did not meet his gaze.

Not that MacLeod expected anything different. He was a native son gone too long among the Sassenach enemy. By the people of Glenbrae, he was neither trusted nor remembered.

Up the hill the warrior saw the dark stones of a grand tower house. Wooden shutters covered the dozen windows on the lower floors. Where the shutters lay open, MacLeod swore he saw true glazed casements, a sign of wealth beyond what he had expected.

Smoke curled lazily from the tall brick chimney, and the warrior felt a sudden tug at his heart. He had never had a proper home. After the long years of war, all he could remember was dusty roads and the sight of the next hill rising before him.

Yet the prickling sense of uneasiness did not leave him, even here in the shadow of the grand tower house by the loch of Glenbrae. Home or not, something waited.

And MacLeod sensed dangers yet to come....

SUNLIGHT STRUCK Perpetua's heavy amber pendant as the images from the past swirled around her and slowly faded. She stood up, color spilling over her plain gray dress. "Oil and water, no doubt about it." Mischief lit her striking green eyes. "But the fireworks between them should be absolutely *delicious*."

CHAPTER ONE

Glenbrae House
Late November, seven months later

HOPE LISTENED TO A thrush trill. Outside her window the last hardy roses burned in glorious color, their sinuous vines coiling up Glenbrae House's stone walls.

Blue and white porcelain gleamed on the mantel above the fireplace, and bright chintz chairs warmed the corners beside the window. Sunlight glinted off the polished floor, just as she had pictured it on her first visit.

The inn she had dreamed of that sunny afternoon was finally nearing completion. Unfortunately, luring paying guests to the quiet valley had not turned out to be so easy.

Hope frowned at her easel. Her latest attempt to reproduce the figure painted on the stairwell was faring no better than her other efforts. The man's face was too flat. Too cold. With no hint of life.

Even now, months after moving into Glenbrae House, the brooding image on the stairwell continued to fascinate her. Hope decided he was a medieval warrior sent on the king's service. Something covert, no doubt, involving jewels or secret documents to be transferred to a safe hiding place out of reach of the king's enemies.

With eyes like that, the man knew the weight of dangerous secrets. He bore the hard responsibility of human life and death. Each hard choice was marked on the canvas of his proud face, hidden in the depths of his shadowed eyes.

Hope sighed and put away her brushes. For the past weeks, every picture she painted seemed to incorporate the medieval figure above the staircase. Even her dreams were touched by images of a broad-shouldered figure with keen silver eyes. Sleeping hadn't been easy, to say the least.

Considering the sad state of her finances, sleeping wasn't likely to get any easier. Not without a genuine, honest-to-goodness miracle.

But Scotland seemed to be a place for miracles.

A door slammed downstairs. Footsteps tapped over the polished floor from the kitchen, and a voice called up, "I have the chocolate tea cakes. And the Wishwells have sent over more homemade wine."

A delicious aroma of chocolate and roasting almonds drifted up the stairs. Hope remembered that she hadn't eaten since breakfast.

She stretched, then slid her brushes into a glass of clean water, studying her mysterious subject. "Gotta go, MacLeod."

For a moment she could have sworn a gust of wind swept over her neck. Impossible, of course. The windows were sealed and the room was comfortably warm.

Too much imagination, she thought wryly. That was another thing that Scotland's brooding landscape seemed to foster.

"Coming right down, Gabrielle," she called.

Her bank account might be at rock bottom, but thanks to the generosity of her neighbors and the skill of her young Parisian chef, they would always eat well. Baskets of tomatoes fresh from the vine had appeared at the front door all summer, followed by armloads of cheese and homemade delicacies. None of her neighbors would accept a pence in payment; by same baffling, unspoken knowledge, all of them knew of Hope's financial predicament.

At first she had tried to refuse, only to discover that the "extra" produce was left anyway. The more she refused, the more was given. Even now the quiet generosity of the Highlanders left her in awe.

If only she had as many paying guests as she did vegetables from her neighbors' fields…

She sighed, walking to the window. The last of the hollyhocks peeked among the hedges. The magical scene almost helped Hope ignore the way the thatched roof tilted.

The expert she had called in several months ago had told her that even the best thatch had to be replaced every twenty years, and Glenbrae House's roof had not seen replacement for half a century. Unfortunately, bills for a dozen other repairs already awaited payment, from hinges for the leaded windows in the study to new plumbing in the guest rooms and carpeting for the front salon. All bad enough.

Now a new roof. Where would it end?

Hope shoved a strand of chestnut hair off her forehead and followed the scent of tea cakes to the kitchen. Today her French chef sported computer-chip earrings and a huge necklace made of silicon wire.

"Nice earrings," Hope said, settling at the broad table and gratefully accepting a steaming cup of Earl Grey tea from her young chef. Although barely twenty-one, Gabrielle was an extrovert with a world-class network of contacts stretching from the Arctic to the Amazon.

"In *honneur* of the Glenbrae Investment Club, I try out some new recipes for their favorite food."

"Zucchini again, I take it?"

Her chef nodded happily. "Curried zucchini soup. And the corn bread with the so very hot chilies, from my friend in New Mexico."

It was a lucky thing that their spry septuagenarian neighbors had stomachs of iron and opinions to match. They liked their food hot and their arguments noisy. Most nights their investment meetings turned into loud and personal shouting matches, though somehow no feelings seemed to be hurt. Hope seemed to know exactly when to interrupt with pitchers of fresh lemonade and Gabrielle's steaming soup, flanked by wedges of hot corn bread.

"They make much money, these investors of Glenbrae?" the Frenchwoman asked, setting down her cup of tea.

"Rich as Croesus, I believe. Last month they received dividend checks that made me drool. They keep insisting that I should let them establish an account for me."

"And why do you not?"

"You know very well why, Gabrielle." Hope studied the cozy kitchen, where sunlight glinted off hanging copper pots and herbs strung from beams in the ceiling. "I have no money for anything extra. This beautiful old house is all the gamble I can afford. And if I don't have paying guests soon, even this gamble will be lost."

The young Parisian slid off her white toque and tapped her jaw. "I have been thinking about this and then the perfect idea comes to me. It is a thing that will make Glenbrae House as popular as the beautiful Draycott Abbey. I visited only last year, you know. Marston, my butler friend there, tells me the tourists come every week by busloads."

"Draycott Abbey. That's in England, isn't it?"

The silicon chips danced madly as Gabrielle nodded. "All granite and glass, a most beautiful place. Marston says it draws visitors like a magnet, mainly because of its ghost."

"Ghost?"

"A very eccentric and dashing figure with a reputation most evil. The tourists love it because he walks the battlements."

Hope hid a smile. "Did you actually see him?"

"No, but some have," Gabrielle said defensively. "Very many of them."

"That's all very well for Draycott Abbey, but we don't

have any historic treasures here. Even the history of Glenbrae is sketchy."

Gabrielle smiled shrewdly. "But you have other things just as good as history. Soon you will have the tourists in busloads, too. Just like Draycott Abbey." Gabrielle slid another slice of cake onto Hope's plate. "And it is only one little lie."

"Giving me more cake isn't going to change my mind." Hope sighed. "I should at least be starving by now, considering that we're perched on the brink of complete ruin."

"Good day or bad, one must eat," Gabrielle announced with Gallic pragmatism. "Hours pass and you eat not one scrap. Always you work, you pace, you paint." Gabrielle toyed with the chunky silicon earrings at her cheeks. "But now I see the answer most perfect."

All Hope could see was an endless future of rising debt and leaking thatch. She moved her spoon, drawing crosses in a butter-light ridge of icing. "I'm afraid to ask." As a cook, Gabrielle was a genius, but her common sense was noticeably weak.

So Hope refrained from reminding her friend that her prior efforts to forcibly detour tour buses past the inn had resulted in a massive traffic jam and a threatened civil action by the county constable.

"No more problems with the police, I assure you." The chef's dark eyes gleamed. "*Pigs,* that's what they are. But now from miles around people will fight to spend the night beneath our roof. All it takes is one small addition, one thing every tourist wants."

"Free breakfast?" Hope added a row of dollar signs to the buttercream crosses.

"You are too practical. What people want is excitement, passion. Danger mixed with romance."

"Don't tell me you're hiring Tom Cruise to work in the kitchen. Or maybe Mel Gibson. I doubt that I could afford either one for a sous-chef."

"It is a joke, no? I do not hire these men. Me, I find something much better for you than any man. I find you—a *ghost*."

"I've sensed magic and stirring history in Glenbrae, but never any ghosts."

"It is the perfect thing to make the tourist's heart drum like thunder, *non?* First, they hear the *bang-bang* in the night."

"That would be the water pipes going," Hope muttered.

"Then they see a shape, all cobwebs and mist, gliding up the stairway."

"That would probably be our dust motes."

The chef ignored her. "Now they are frightened, trembling. They clutch their hearts and race forward, desperate to see more. Then they hear the throb of laughter, low and terrifying. Closer it comes, rippling down the stairs." Gabrielle's voice rose. "Now they shiver with fright, eager to tell all their friends about the haunted-house tour in Glenbrae. Soon you will be very rich."

"I don't know about that…."

"You Americans love the thought of a ghost in the bedroom, *non? Voilà,* in a week you have more visitors than beds to hold them and no more problems of money for you."

Hope sat back slowly. "You're saying that Glenbrae House needs a ghost in the bedrooms?"

"Of course not." Gabrielle smiled sagely. "What we need is the *idea* of a ghost, one to summon only while the guests are here."

"Out of thin air, I suppose."

"But no. Out of the old curtains, of course." Gabrielle sat forward eagerly. "And just today in the village I meet a friend whose specialty is *Macbeth.* I am certain he can help us."

"Really, Gabrielle, I don't think you understand—"

The Frenchwoman strode to the side door leading out to Hope's herb garden. "You will please to come in now, Mr. Jeffrey."

A gangling youth in a rumpled white shirt and threadbare

flannels rose from behind the ragged hollyhocks and rocked anxiously from foot to foot. "Don't blame Gabrielle," he said, picking up the conversation as if he'd been part of it all along. "This was all my idea. I've been doing some amazing lighting effects for the drama project I just completed. 'New Concepts in *Hamlet* and *Macbeth*.' Might even be put down for an honors when I'm done." He frowned, as if thinking of something unpleasant, then shrugged. "Not that any of that matters. The thing is, with backlighting and a double-colored floodlight, angles can be made to recede and corners can be blurred."

Hope didn't see the connection. "They can?"

"Of course." His cultured voice burst with enthusiasm as he ambled into the kitchen. "Special effects are everything today. You take a pinch of dry ice here and some chemical smoke there." He waved one hand. "*Voilà.*"

"Then you have a fire hazard on your hands?" Hope said dryly.

Jeffrey slid into the seat opposite, eyeing Gabrielle's last wedge of almond cake. Hope was fairly certain she heard his stomach rumble. She decided that he could use a good meal, since he looked dangerously thin. "Be my guest," she said, sliding the plate closer.

She had to appreciate his bitter effort to resist. "Oh, I couldn't. We barely know each other, and Gabrielle made it for you, after all." He looked at Hope's chef with doglike devotion.

Hope filed that look away for future reference. "But I insist. I couldn't eat another bite."

Hunger finally won out over good form. Half of the slice was gone within seconds, the other half consumed more slowly, while the young drama student's pale blue eyes closed in silent rapture. He scraped the last piece of icing off with his thumb, then linked his fingers eagerly. "It will work. Trust me, I'm an expert at ghosts."

"You're a parapsychologist?"

"No, a lighting specialist. Our test performance of *Macbeth* went off without the slightest hitch. Mr. Willett-Jones said I was the best thing since dry ice."

"Mr. Willett-Jones is your professor, I take it?"

"Hardly. He's the drama critic for the *Observer*. It's a small paper, but it has a good deal of clout in dramatic circles."

Hope wondered if Jeffrey's parents knew about those "dramatic circles." Or if they cared. The boy looked as if he was wearing his last shirt, and he clearly hadn't eaten properly for quite some time.

"Jeffrey is good, I swear it," Gabrielle said firmly. "When he makes the lights follow his ghost onstage, my skin creeps most terribly. Even I believe it is real." From the sternly pragmatic Gabrielle, this was praise indeed.

As the two stared at her, Hope had the perilous feeling she had lost the argument before it had even begun. "I'm afraid it's out of the question. I won't lure visitors to Glenbrae under false pretenses."

"You don't understand." Jeffrey rocked forward on bony elbows. Though worn, his shirt was custom-made, with fine hand seaming inside. "*All* these old wrecks have ghosts. Glamis has dozens of them, and Windsor is chock-full of odd knocks and bangs." Jeffrey looked very pleased with himself. "I remember my mum always used to say—" His smile abruptly faded.

"Even if I wanted to try it—which I don't—there's no way your scheme could work," Hope said quickly. "It wouldn't be convincing."

Jeffrey roused himself from his reverie and jammed long fingers into his hair, frowning. "Wrong again. Gabrielle showed me around this morning while you were working, and I've got the whole place mapped out. I already have a list of the materials I'll need."

Hope swallowed. "Materials?"

Gabrielle beamed. "He is very organized, you see."

Jeffrey tried to hide a flush at her praise. "All your visitors will see is a lovely hint of ghostly garments drifting down the stairs. Add some wonderfully maniacal laughter and it's guaranteed to bring down the house."

He moved closer to Gabrielle. Together the two stared at Hope.

"Now, just wait a minute. Even if this apparition *did* work, how would you get the word out? You can't post a sign in the village announcing that Glenbrae House now has a resident ghost."

Gabrielle cracked eggs, then added vanilla and cream for a rich chocolate sauce. "Just today Jeffrey and I pass a group of tourists on the way to hike in the hills. I hear them complain there is nothing to see in Glenbrae. But I explain very carefully about the secret of our little village."

"And just what is that?"

"The secret ghost of Glenbrae House, of course."

TWENTY MINUTES LATER, shadows filled the great hall.

Plumes of smoke drifted along the oak banister. Only the wood paneling and stairway were visible in the semidarkness.

"Not like that. Slower. *Glide.*" Jeffrey's voice was muffled as he crouched behind a velvet sofa, toying with a complicated electrical panel. "You're supposed to be terrifying, remember? A bloody apparition from beyond the grave."

Hope tugged at the microfiber shrouding her head and did her best to glide. "There's no way that this can work, you two. I wouldn't fool a blind man."

"But you are wrong," Gabrielle said. "In the darkness your sleeves glow like fire itself, and you are the picture of a ghost. Just keep coming. Jeffrey has run the wires under the carpet so you will not trip."

"There's another problem." Hope paused on the stairs.

"All this electrical equipment and wiring you mentioned is going to cost a lot of money—money that I just don't have. I can't afford to pay you, either. Maybe it would be better if we forgot the whole idea right now and—"

"No problem," Jeffrey said eagerly. "I have a van full of equipment on loan from the university until the end of term, free and clear. It's almost as if fate has stepped in. Actually, I think Glenbrae House was *meant* to have a ghost."

Hope closed her eyes and prayed that Glenbrae House was not *meant* to have a lawsuit filed by an irate tourist.

As Jeffrey worked over a different row of buttons, the light intensified. Hope's diaphanous gown rippled.

"Now start the tape recording, Gabrielle."

A bloodcurdling howl erupted from the floorboards outside the kitchen. The effect of the shriek, combined with the ghostly illusion, was quite remarkable.

"I'm going to hit the lights. Hope, you can start moving along the landing."

Dutifully Hope stepped forward, awaiting her cue. In the sudden darkness she could almost imagine the hushed silence of the house as it had been centuries before, lit only by candles and overseen by its stern-eyed master, the MacLeod.

An odd prickling sensation ran down her neck.

"Go," Jeffrey ordered in his best stage director's voice.

Hope glided down the stairs as Jeffrey had instructed, her hands floating out beside her.

"Perfect. Gabrielle, hit the third button."

A pale gleam emanated from the ceiling, taking shape at the curve of the stairway, where two long sleeves, a ghastly fluorescent head and a trailing gown drifted over the steps.

No wind touched the room.

No noise marked the apparition's descent.

Hope finally reached the turn of the stairs, feeling her way with her fingers in the darkness. She could barely breathe beneath the cowl Jeffrey had draped over her head, and she could see almost nothing. At the third step, something caught the hem of Hope's ghostly gown, and when she grappled for the wall, something pricked her finger hard.

She bit back a hiss of pain. "Jeffrey, I don't think—"

"Great. Just fabulous. Now do the rest, the way we rehearsed."

"But I still don't think—"

"Go on."

Sighing, Hope raised her arm. As the lights changed, her ghostly shape took full form in the darkness. Then the silence was split by a shattering scream, and the ghostly head separated from its body and flew toward the ceiling, accompanied by ghoulish laughter.

Outside, the front steps creaked. "Miss Hope?" The oak door opened slowly. "Is anyone here?" A white-haired head appeared in the gloom of the front hall.

Wildly Hope clutched at the yards of fabric trapping her face. She tried to answer, but every sound was muffled by her costume. After a moment she recognized the voice.

Morwenna Wishwell. An inveterate meddler, but a wonderful neighbor.

With sickening clarity Hope envisioned her first lawsuit: a spry old lady shocked into an early grave by the sight of a headless apparition flittering over Glenbrae's oak banister.

CHAPTER TWO

HOPE STRUGGLED DOWN the stairs, expecting disaster.

Jeffrey's curse was interrupted by a boom as one of the speakers toppled behind the sofa. Static filled the air, and high overhead the lost soldier's "head" reappeared, floating like a grinning pumpkin.

Why didn't Gabrielle just turn on the lights?

"Dear, dear me." Morwenna halted in the foyer. Her breath caught in surprise. "First a head and now a torso. I see this lovely old house finally has a ghost of its own. How perfectly *wonderful*."

Hope continued to pull at her hood, staggering forward and fighting to be heard above the static that rumbled through the hall.

Then the lights came on, and Jeffrey and Gabrielle ran to Hope's side. "Are you all right?" Jeffrey demanded.

Hope finally managed to tug off the hood that was threatening to choke her. "Just barely." She wobbled down the stairs toward the visitor. "I'm sorry about that."

"Oh, no problem, my dear. Most enjoyable, it was."

Hope frowned. "You weren't afraid?"

Morwenna smiled benignly. "Was I supposed to be?"

"Yes, actually." Hope rubbed her stinging wrist. "And that proves my point. I've been telling Gabrielle and her friend that this ghost idea won't work."

"On the contrary, my dear." Morwenna tapped her jaw thoughtfully. "Anyone seeing you there in the dark would have been certain they were looking at a class-one apparition. Of course, anyone with *real* knowledge of the subject would have been looking for the related signs of paranormal activity. Temperature change, for one. Pervasive fragrances and unusual auditory stimuli—that sort of thing."

Just then a bloodcurdling scream blasted from Jeffrey's carefully prepared audio system.

Morwenna chuckled. "Not bad," she said calmly. "Perhaps a touch heavy-handed, but effective nonetheless. Just last month while we were visiting Warwick Castle, my sisters and I saw a wonderful apparition cross the herb garden. He had a most impressive shriek, but not nearly as good as yours, I'm bound to admit. Was your tape sound-enhanced?" she asked Jeffrey.

He blinked in shock. "Er, I rigged up auxiliary speakers and sound tracks with extra feedback. Two speakers behind the bottom step."

The old woman's eyes twinkled. "How very clever. I think that another pair added at the entrance hall might give you a very nice rebound effect."

Jeffrey looked stunned. "Where did you study stage acoustics?"

"Oh, here and there, my dear boy," Morwenna answered. "And I don't mean to intrude, but the mail-delivery woman was in a rush to get home to see her sick daughter, so I offered to bring this letter up to you. I hope that was all right?"

"It was very kind of you, Miss Wishwell. May I offer you a cup of tea? Or perhaps something stronger?"

"Some other time, I think. My sisters will be wondering what's happened to me."

Hope barely heard as she scanned the return address of the overpriced Chicago law firm that had handled her late uncle's estate. She prayed this was the rest of the money she had been waiting for, the final part of her uncle's bequest that had been tied up in court for over a year now. Eagerly she tore open the heavy envelope. But a moment later the words blurred before her eyes.

She sank down in a chair beside the door, the letter falling unheeded to her feet.

Morwenna touched her shoulder. "Nothing bad, I hope?"

It was worse than bad. The law firm informed her there would be no more funds. And as a result of her uncle's poor planning, *she* now had a whopping bill that she owed the U.S. government. Hope suspected it was because of his law firm's inept miscalculations.

Either way, she was ruined.

Hope blinked hard, fighting back tears.

"You had better drink this, child."

Numbly Hope accepted the glass pressed into her fingers. The elderberry wine Morwenna must have fetched from the sideboard went down like kitchen grease. She would have to sell the few good antiques she had managed to acquire for the manor. Like it or not, the books in the library would have to be sent to auction. But none of these measures would stave off ruin for long.

Morwenna's kindly eyes seemed to bore right through her, picking out her secret worries. "Things are never as bad as they seem, my dear. The inn will catch on, and this ghost of yours is quite wonderful. It's been too long since we've had any visitations here on this side of the valley. The last one was—" She cleared her throat. "Dear me, I mustn't run on." She smoothed her shawl as she stood up. "Are you sure that there's nothing I can do? We still have a spot for you in our investment club."

Hope shook her head. Her problems were beyond the help of mutual funds or slow-growth portfolios. Besides, she had no money to commit.

Suddenly Morwenna's fingers tightened on Hope's wrist. "My dear girl, you're *bleeding*."

Hope looked down in surprise at the line of blood trailing over her wrist. "It must have happened when I tripped on the stairs." She summoned a smile. "I'll be fine."

Morwenna looked as if she was going to say something, but shrugged instead. "I suggest you try a bit more gain on the bass, young man. You'll find that it enhances the resonance." She waved at Jeffrey, then disappeared outside.

"Who was that?" he asked.

"One of our neighbors," Gabrielle explained. "A very clever lady. If she suggests some electronic change, I suggest you do it."

Jeffrey rubbed his jaw. "That's the odd thing. I was considering that even before she mentioned it. But how could she know so much about sound systems?"

Gabrielle studied the white-haired figure on the gravel drive. "She knows very much, that one. So do her two sisters. And now," she said sternly to Hope, "you will tell us what was in that letter."

"More bills, this one from the IRS. They're not the sort of people to accept excuses."

Gabrielle frowned. "This is bad, no?"

"As bad as it gets." Slowly Hope picked up the letter and slid it into her pocket. "I…I'm going outside for a while. Then I think I'll try to get some sleep."

Gabrielle and Jeffrey exchanged a look, but said nothing. "I'll bring you some lemonade if you like," Gabrielle said helpfully.

"That would be nice," Hope said.

But what she needed was a way to escape the ruin that was staring her dead in the face.

What she needed now was a genuine miracle.

"I'M TELLING YOU, she looked as if she'd seen a ghost. And I don't mean the apparition that those clever young people conjured up on the stairway." Morwenna frowned as she paced briskly back and forth in the tiny, beamed kitchen of the cottage she shared with her white-haired sisters.

Perpetua, still regal at seventy-four, smoothed back a stray hair. "We'll have to intervene."

Morwenna ran her fingers over the silver pin at her collar. "Once the plan is launched, it would be too late for her to protest. It will only take me a few minutes to do the calculations." She sat at the desk and began keying codes into a sleek laptop computer.

Perpetua sank into a chair beside the preserves bubbling on the fireplace, and a white angora cat with pale green eyes jumped onto her lap. "Well, Juno, what do *you* say? Do you think our Miss O'Hara needs a miracle?"

"And what will she do when she *has* it?" Honoria said, with her usual astuteness. "People always say they need a miracle. They plead and plan, but when they have one standing in front of them, they haven't the slightest idea *what* to do with it. Why, I remember that nice man, Mr. Schweitzer. A little absentminded, but then we all are at times." Her eyes took on an unfocused, dreamy appearance. "I'll never forget how we had to—"

Perpetua's rocker creaked softly. "No more nostalgia, Honoria. Hope O'Hara needs our help, though she is too proud to admit it." She opened a large, leather-bound book and ran her finger down the page.

Somewhere down the hill a thrush trilled in the late afternoon sunlight, and the sound spilled through the silence of the glen, full and rich.

"It has to be now." Perpetua slammed the volume shut and stared at her sisters.

Morwenna nodded as she shut down the computer. "If we miss the transit tonight, it will be six months until we have another chance. We all know that Ms. O'Hara might not be able to hold out for that long." She bit her lip. "It's very risky."

"Last week I tripped on one of your shoes and nearly

broke my neck on the stairs," Perpetua said. "Don't talk to *me* about risky. It's now or never, I'm afraid. What do you say, Honoria?" Both turned toward their silver-haired sister.

"Your calculations are correct." With a sigh, she rubbed red-rimmed eyes. "The transit will be operative until 2:00 a.m., but no longer. The next window won't appear until mid-May."

Silence hung. The wind rattled against the snug casements and grumbled across the glen.

Morwenna sighed. "Tonight, it is."

Lightning flickered far to the north.

Outside, the first fat drops of rain struck the flagstone path.

"If we do not act now, our young friend will run out of time and maybe even out of dreams," Perpetua said. "It is time for the vote."

All movement stilled. The powerful word had been uttered.

The three women stood, hands raised. As quiet as sunlight, they moved closer. "Shall we find a man for Hope O'Hara?" Perpetua asked.

Light changed and swirled in front of them.

A figure slowly took shape in the semidarkness. Light gleamed from the armor at his chest and brushed his dented broadsword as he sprawled in a chair by a cold hearth.

Even at rest, his eyes were hard, lined by months in the blinding desert sun.

Honoria frowned. "He looks dangerous. Dear me, maybe we should reconsider...."

Perpetua shook her head. "We have to do this. Dangerous or not, he is exactly what she needs."

Morwenna nodded. "A flawed miracle is better than no miracle at all. It is time for the vote."

Honoria nodded with a sigh. "Then let it be done."

"Look." Morwenna pointed at the misty image. "He's vulnerable now. There won't be a better chance than this."

The three women stood, hands raised. As quiet as

sunlight, they moved closer. "Shall we find a man for Hope O'Hara?" Perpetua repeated.

All three nodded as one as they tightened their circle and then stood still.

The firelight flickered. Light shimmered and swirled. Outside, clouds brushed the high cliffs. Then time wavered and seemed to stand very still....

HOPE WANDERED to the open window, listening to a distant peal of thunder. Tax worries from her newest financial blow had made sleep impossible, and she slipped on a paisley shawl, intending to raid the kitchen for Gabrielle's hot milk and fresh cookies.

At the top of the stairs her skin began to tingle. Strange, nervous energy brushed her neck, almost as if life were about to hand her an unexpected gift.

She stopped at the foot of the stairs, watching moonlight play over the hard features of the manor's ancient owner. "What am I going to do?" she whispered. "How am I going to save this beautiful old place? That's what you want from me, isn't it?"

The lace curtains stirred at the open window. Somewhere in the darkness a nightingale piped in solitary splendor.

As moonlight pooled through the open shutters, light glanced off the warrior's face. His gaze seemed to cut through her, proud and commanding. There was a touch of light at one shoulder, and Hope had the sharp impression of a crouching form that might have been an animal.

An animal no more wild than he, with his cloak flying out behind him and his eyes dark as a hunter's. In that moment sadness filled her, pain for a warrior she had never seen and a hero whose name she would never know. Just as on her first visit to this house, the portrait called to her and Hope reached out to the man, out to the animal glinting at his shoulder. Her fingers opened, curved to touch the ornament at his surcoat.

"Who are you?" she whispered. "Tell me your secrets."

His face danced before her, a thing of restless beauty sculpted from moonlight and shadow. His eyes glittered with pride and the habit of command.

In the moonlight she almost felt his heat and the play of his breath, so close he seemed.

"Give me an answer," she whispered. "Heaven knows, Glenbrae House needs help from someone tonight."

Above her head moonlight played through the lace curtains and shimmered along the polished wooden steps. Hope drank in the sight, realizing just how much she had come to love this old house. How could she bear to lose it?

As she walked into the bar of moonlight, something sparkled on the floor before her. Bending, she ran her hand along the hand-carved wainscoting, only to feel a jab at her finger, just as she had felt earlier during her rehearsal on the stairs. When she tugged aside an uneven piece of wood, she found a circular piece of metal half-hidden in the shadows. Dark patches of tarnish clung to the deeply etched grooves as she carried it to the window.

Moonlight met the snarling face of a wolf, his powerful body crouched to attack. The raw beauty of the piece left Hope stunned. She felt the aura of power clinging to the old ornament, and her breath caught.

The figure was hard and uncompromising, just like the portrait behind her. Surely this was a man's design, never worn by a delicate female. No woman would feel comfortable wearing a symbol of such blatant male power.

Hope shivered, half expecting to see an arrogant male face glaring at her for touching this treasured ornament. As she turned, moonlight swept the old painting and the knight's long cloak seemed to blow about his powerful body. Suddenly the circular shape at his shoulder was very clear.

A crouching wolf, just like the one in her fingers.

Hope cradled the heavy brooch, feeling the metal warm

to her touch. Its beauty was hypnotic, pulsing with powerful images of the man who had worn it above one shoulder. Like the portrait, the brooch belonged here at Glenbrae.

But perhaps it would have a special use.

An idea came to Hope in a blaze of inspiration. A design of such power and beauty would be worth a great deal to the right person with an eye for history, and she knew just that man, English collector Winston Wyndgate.

Her fingers tightened on the silver oval. Perhaps Glenbrae House had just given Hope her miracle.

The wind whined past the house as Hope snuggled into a thick down coverlet two hours later.

Moonlight and stars were gone now, trapped behind angry banks of clouds.

She should have closed the shutters, but there was a rare magic in the sight of a storm churning over the Scottish countryside.

She willed herself to relax, fighting tangled thoughts of border raiders and dour Highland warriors. Worst of all was the image of a silver wolf that howled its pain to the night sky.

After her discovery on the stairs, Hope had pored through Glenbrae's extensive library for any clues to the dating of the exquisite silver brooch, but her search had been fruitless. Though she found pages of simple necklaces and religious pieces, none showed the dramatic sculptural detail of her wolf.

There was no question the brooch was old and very rare. Its striking artistry would only add to its historical value. She prayed that its sale would keep her solvent a while longer.

But there was still the problem of luring visitors to Glenbrae, of course. At first she had been convinced that a stay in a rugged Highland tower house offered the perfect adventure for sophisticated travelers. In fact, when she had initially approached travel companies in Britain and the U.S., she had received enthusiastic support.

Only later did Hope discover she was expected to slip them a healthy "facilitation fee" before referrals would appear. By the time she understood the bald hints, Glenbrae House's renovation had emptied her bank account. Without paying guests, she had no money for bribes to buy referrals. Without bribes, she had no guests.

Catch-22.

Outside came the bang of loose shutters. Tree branches whipped angrily in the rising wind.

Storm or not, there was magic in this quiet glen, and Hope was determined to find a way to hang on. She prayed her brooch was the answer as she drifted off into a troubled sleep.

Hope tossed restlessly. She dreamed of fighting her way through corridors filled with unsmiling IRS agents. And silhouetted in the background was a warrior, one hand on his sword hilt as he stood guard over his rugged domain.

A shutter banged angrily in the wind. Lightning streaked in angry fury above the hills.

A branch tore away from a tree. Hope sat up sharply, suddenly wide-awake. The rain hammered in earnest now, drumming against the roof and windows. A bulky black shape flew past her window and hung flapping from a tree branch.

It was the last tarpaulin she had spread over the damaged roof. So much for her temporary effort to repair the hole in the thatch.

She jerked on a sweater and jeans and ran for a flashlight, regretting that Gabrielle and Jeffrey had decided to spend a leisurely evening in the village. By the time they returned, the six upstairs rooms could be awash in rain and damaged beyond recovery.

Rain pounded at her face as she shoved open the rear door and raced outside to get a ladder. Gasping, she hefted the heavy frame against the house. With water sluicing down her cheeks, she wobbled up the rungs while the tarpaulin snapped angrily in the wind.

At the top of the ladder, she crawled onto the wet thatch. The remaining length of canvas was already flapping free above the roof hole. Blinking against the rain, Hope tackled the cloth, blindly fighting the wind.

A tree branch tore free and sailed past her head. Hope ducked just in time, barely avoiding a direct hit. Below her the hillside stretched black and ominous.

Don't look down, she thought hysterically. A few more gale-force gusts and she would be tossed off the roof. Breaking her neck seemed a real possibility.

Hope heard the faint cry of an animal, all but drowned out by the drum of thunder. Lightning arced again, outlining the streaming reeds. Frantically she twisted a heavy rope over the slapping canvas.

As she glanced up, she was struck by a sudden sense of unfamiliarity about the landscape. The hills seemed— wrong. Trees rose where there shouldn't have been trees, and the curve of the path lay like a dark snake, angled higher than it should have been.

Wind tore at her hair and pebbles stung her cheeks.

She swayed dizzily, telling herself that Glenbrae House was exactly as it had always been. Only the darkness made the surroundings look unfamiliar.

Balanced precariously, she lashed the last rope down over the ragged thatch, again struck with the dizzy sense that something was wrong. Out in the darkness she heard a sharp cry that might have been the neigh of a horse. Squinting, she made out a black shape racing through the trees above the orchard, the form almost like a man on horseback.

Hope fought back a wild laugh. Either the rider was mad or *she* was hallucinating.

The figure grew larger, silhouetted against the steep gorge bordering the mouth of the loch. No one could jump the chasm and survive, Hope knew. Not even in broad daylight.

On a night like this, it would be suicide to try.

Surely he must know that.

On he came, the thunder of hooves clearer now. Against the storm, man and mount gathered speed, and Hope watched terrified as they raced toward the high stones leading to a sheer drop.

And certain death.

She closed her eyes, afraid to look. Any second she expected to hear the animal's shrill scream of terror.

As the storm raged on, she opened one eye and in a ghostly flash she saw horse and rider soar over the wall of stone, out above the churning waters at the far side of the loch.

The landscape seemed to change, shifting beneath them. Hope clutched at the rain-slick rope, blinking back tears. Only by a miracle had they survived. The man might be crazy, but he had rare courage to make such a leap, enough perhaps to help her finish lashing down the canvas....

The wind gusted around her, angry and furious, whipping her hands free. The next thing she knew, she was falling, slammed blindly down toward the roof's yawning hole.

The sound of her *own* terror rang in her ears.

PART TWO

The Gift

Night cannot hold,
Nor forest gain…

CHAPTER THREE

A TRUE STORM FROM HELL, MacLeod thought grimly.

Demon winds fought the night, wild beyond any he had known.

Dirt and branches slapped his face. He cursed, trying to hold his mount steady as it danced skittishly beneath every burst of thunder.

He had left the village hours ago, only to wind blindly through the bracken-covered glen. Now, for some reason, every stone and slope looked foreign to him.

In truth, the hard ale he had consumed at his meal may have been to blame, but somehow MacLeod did not believe it so.

His horse sidestepped wildly as lightning struck only yards away. Where was the infernal track back to Glenbrae?

"Soft, my beauty," he murmured, gentling the great bay with a touch. "We'll be inside and there you'll find dry straw beneath you instead of this cursed mud." As MacLeod spoke, the rain-slick bank gave way. His mount foundered before finally kicking free and plunging forward.

Darkness and more darkness stretched before them.

Well did the warrior regret leaving his pallet. Even more did he regret the strange sense of need that had pulled him from his snug tower house out into the gusty night.

But a knight of St. Julian did not turn away from anyone in need. The storm had called to him like a silent cry for help, and a terrible force of urgency churned inside him even now.

With his bay saddled, he had plunged across the glen,

ignoring the worried looks of his groom and page. Rain lashed him in sheets, dimming his view to little more than the muddy slope before him.

There were cliffs all about these glens, MacLeod knew. Every bend hid sheer walls and dizzying drops. But worry gained strength as he rode, and he could not turn back until he had an answer.

Somewhere below he heard the roar of water. The byrne was angry, awash in the storm. The ground seemed to dip and the trees whirled around him.

Wrong, he thought. All infernally wrong.

Over the shriek of the wind, he heard a scream of terror. He could have sworn that the trail changed, flattening before him.

He gripped the reins, peering into the sheeting rain as lightning flared overhead. Another scream confirmed that his instincts had been true. Danger lay nearby in the night.

The old wound burned at his knee as the bay reared, mud flung up beneath the powerful hooves.

Down the slope and a league beyond, darkness veiled the cliff face. Fighting a sense of dread, MacLeod struggled to turn his mount, but the bay was at the gallop, wild with fear.

While the wind keened, man and rider leaned into the jump, out over the deadly stone face combed by rain and mist. Into the darkness they plunged, across the heather and the wild byrne.

Another cry reached out to MacLeod even then....

HOPE SCREAMED WITH PAIN. Her fingers burned as she clawed at the roof edge, losing inches with each passing second.

Thank God, the rider had come from the cliffs, answering her call.

He rocked forward into the wind while his anxious bay sidestepped nervously along the narrow trail. A branch swept past his head, and he ducked at the same moment he saw Hope and called out.

She did not understand, his words lost against the boom of thunder. Wind whipped around the steep, angled roof and tore the rope from her fingers. As she grabbed for a handhold, the horse reared and its rider again shouted a harsh command.

Desperately Hope clawed at the soggy reeds, which shredded at her touch. Her foot sank through a rotting beam and swept her out into cold, empty space.

She pitched down the wet reeds, a captive of the rope lashing down the tarpaulin, her scream drowning out the man's angry shout. Rain slammed into her face, and time seemed to go on forever. As if in a nightmare, she plunged toward the ground, spinning blindly.

The great horse neighed shrilly as its rider kneed forward.

Instead of hard earth, Hope felt the impact of warm muscle halting her descent. Her breath shuddered as she toppled forward, clinging to the terrified horse. Her whole body throbbed, but she was alive.

Breathless, she turned to study the man whom she had to thank for saving her life.

His long black hair blew about his face, as wet as her own. Darkness veiled his features, permitting only a glimpse of piercing eyes and tense jaw. But the strength of his body was unmistakable. She blushed to feel his thighs strain where she straddled him.

He muttered a low phrase to the horse, the words snatched away by the wind. The sounds seemed to gentle the creature, and Hope, too, felt curiously calmed by the soft rhythm of his speech. Though the language was unclear, she decided no man could be a complete villain if he could calm an animal with such gentle confidence.

Above their heads the tarpaulin swept free and a four-foot section of packed reeds hurtled toward the ground. As the wind howled, a plank of solid oak flew past, grazing his head before it slammed into the beech trees beside the garden.

The rider cursed and kneed the horse away from the unstable roof, struggling to control the frightened mount.

Hope understood exactly how the horse was feeling. She sat rigid, aware of the stranger's locked thighs and the hard hands clenched around her waist. Another plank spiraled past and she twisted, measuring the distance from the roof. More debris rattled down the high-sloped eaves, and the man behind her hissed out some kind of order.

Hope pointed toward the roof. "We've got to go," she shouted. "That whole edge of the roof could collapse any second!"

Another section of reeds and oak gave way with an explosive crack.

Hope cried out in pain as wood chips pelted her forehead. The man in black gripped her shoulders, struggling to hold her upright while he calmed his skittish mount.

Consciousness came and went.

Dimly she felt the rider's hands circle her shoulders and explore her cheek. Even that slight touch was an agony.

Hope swept his hand away, feeling consciousness blur. The cold ate into her, numbing body and mind.

Deeper she slid. Down and down again...

Finally, even the rider's callused hands could not hold her back from the darkness.

RONAN MACLEOD SPURRED his horse toward the back of the house, cursing the rain that blocked his vision. Only by the back stone fence did he halt, sliding to the ground with the motionless woman still locked in his arms. He stumbled twice in the soft mud by the gate, with no light to guide him beyond the lightning that split the night sky.

But MacLeod did not expect to find light for his path. Candles were precious and not to be left burning in an unoccupied house.

He scanned the roof, frowning. In the darkness the slope seemed wrong.

But his mind was hardly clear, and his heart still raced from his miraculous escape over the cliffs. No doubt the change was a trick of the glen.

He frowned at Glenbrae House, rising tall and rugged against the rain-veiled slopes.

Home, he thought.

Even if something about it *did* seem strange. Maybe the windows. Maybe something more…

He looked down at the woman in his arms. An odd creature, she was. Her garment was bizarre and her scent was of no flower he had ever smelled before. Even her broken speech had made scant sense to his ear, not that he could hear against the fury of the storm while wood and thatch rained down in the hellish winds. His own strength was nearly spent, and his knee ached like a thousand demons from his mad race through the glen.

But even in his exhaustion, MacLeod realized there was something unnatural about the shrill keening of the wind. The hillside looked different, the trees bent low, whipping wildly. And they seemed more dense than they should be….

He shoved the thought from his mind. He had a life to save. A woman's.

When he had first seen her balanced on the roof in strange leggings and tight tunic, he had thought her a man grown. One touch of her soft thighs and rounded breasts had taught him the full measure of his mistake.

Aye, a woman. A creature of fire and spirit who balanced against the devil's own wind while her hair tossed in soft folds around her ivory cheeks.

By the honor of St. Julian, what was the mad creature doing in men's garments and scrambling on *his* roof in this mother of all storms? Was she there to cast some pagan spell against him?

He ducked as a branch whizzed past his head, sweeping all questions from his mind. MacLeod realized that he had *two* lives to save this night.

He staggered up the stone steps and pushed open Glenbrae House's heavy oak door with his boot. The storm seemed to prey on his strength, challenging every fiber of his determination. Sweat beaded his brow as he inched through the darkness toward the stairs. He would need a place to settle the female in safety and help to undress her.

He shouted for his page, surprised when he heard no answer in the silent house. Where had the boy gone?

With his arms aching, he climbed the stairs in the tower. He would settle the female in his own bed.

And there he would sleep for a fortnight, the warrior thought wryly.

CHAPTER FOUR

"CAN YOU SEE ANYTHING?" Gabrielle hunched toward the windshield of Jeffrey's small Mini. The wind drove clumps of grass and mud into the glass.

"Bloody little in this soup." Jeffrey muttered an oath and rolled down his window to clear away a section of rose branches. "How much farther to the house?"

"Just beyond the next turn, I think, but everything looks so odd. There has never been such a storm all my weeks here."

"A good thing, too. Buckle your seat belt," Jeffrey said sharply as they slid down a muddy bank and the car tipped sideways.

Gabrielle obeyed, unable to shake the feeling that something about *this* storm was like no other.

SAFE, HOPE THOUGHT, caught in the netherworld between sleep and waking.

Something warm pressed at her chest. The sensation was extraordinarily pleasant, and she let her mind drift through waves of gentle heat. She was imagining busloads of wealthy, paying tourists when something tickled her nose and drew her slowly back to consciousness.

She opened her eyes to a dark room. Rain skittered down the windows.

She sat up groggily.

There was work to do, a roof to check. Just as soon as

she could burrow out from beneath the warm covers and the man's hand that cupped her shoulder.

Man's hand?

Hope gave a strangled cry and went rigid.

It was no hallucination. There was a very definite male body sprawled on the bed beside her. A callused male palm lay curved over her shoulder.

She wriggled slightly and felt a counterpoint near her waist. Sweet heaven, the weight at her hip was a man's thigh.

A very naked thigh, by the feel of it.

Heat filled her cheeks as she tried to break the intimacy of the touch. *Get a grip, O'Hara. It's just a man's body. There has to be some perfectly logical explanation for how he got here.*

Her hair fell slick and damp against her neck. Suddenly it all came back to her—the climb to the roof, the storm… her fall into a stranger's arms. Her unknown rescuer must have carried her inside after she blacked out.

Probably he had been exhausted himself and had passed out on her bed immediately after.

A distant bolt of lightning illuminated the room, giving Hope her first real glimpse of the body sprawled against hers. A pale scar slashed across his right temple, and dark hair framed a face full of shadows. Long lashes lay in dark curves against his cheek, softening the lines of his angular face.

He seemed totally comfortable in her bed, sleeping beneath the eaves while the storm growled. She could almost feel his exhaustion as his chest rose and fell.

She had needed a miracle several hours ago. His appearance had been an answer to her prayers. But where had he come from, and what was she supposed to do with him now?

He slept on, oblivious to her intense scrutiny, muttering occasionally beneath the down covers. As thunder hammered over the roof, he slid closer to Hope. One hand hitched around her waist, hot and heavy.

Definitely time to leave, she thought.

As she inched away from him, one of her stuffed pigs gave a loud *oink,* but the stranger gave no sign of waking. He must have been exhausted long before he reached the edge of her roof. By the look of it, nothing short of cannon fire would wake him.

Something cold and wet trickled down Hope's forehead, and she reached up, feeling the solid outline of a metal glove. A gauntlet?

She frowned at the antique contraption lying just above her pillow, dripping rusty water onto her best moiré coverlet.

What sort of man galloped around at midnight in a medieval costume—especially during a gale? Whoever he was, she wasn't about to have her first real conversation with him while he lay thigh to thigh beside her on the bed.

As she struggled to sit up, her sweater tugged tight, caught somewhere beneath her rescuer's waist, the culprit a row of metal prongs at one side of his ribs. Hope eased her fingers beneath his chest and tried to work her way free.

Murmuring, he flung his arm sideways. Hope winced as his fingers opened at her throat. His touch softened as he traced her shoulder and then moved to cup the swell of her breast.

Rescuer or not, enough was *enough.*

Slowly his fingers opened in sensual exploration, tracing her breast through the wool sweater. He muttered a sound of approval. Hope twisted sideways and managed to wriggle free of his exploring fingers. But she got no farther, held tight by the devilish row of metal prongs.

Scowling, she searched for a pocket, hoping to find a wallet or personal identification buried beneath his bizarre archaic costume. But when she worked her hand beneath the stiff, nubby fabric, she found neither pockets nor wallets. There was no glint of a watch at his wrist nor any sort of jewelry.

Hope glared at his inert form. If the man hadn't been sleeping so deeply, utterly lost to the world, she might have been panicked by the intimate pressure of his hard body. As it was, all she felt was growing irritation at her inability to pull free. The offending prongs holding her sweater were bent and uneven, covering some sort of metal plate which he wore beneath his long black tunic.

She didn't want to meet his dresser, she decided wryly, working her sweater up and down over the curved pieces of metal.

But to no avail. She was caught fast. *Blast* the man and blast the storm! She needed to check on the roof.

He shifted against the pillow and her worn pig grinned, caught beneath his broad cheek. Desperate, Hope closed her eyes and gave one last tug.

This time she pulled free—along with most of her sleeve, sliced through by the sharp metal studs. Hope scowled, watching her best mohair sweater self-destruct cleanly from wrist to shoulder. The man was going to pay for that, she swore, rising to her feet.

Quickly she stripped off her damp jeans and the remnants of her sweater, keeping one wary eye on the stranger in her bed, then pulled on dry jeans and a champagne-colored cashmere sweater.

Rescue or not, if the man ruined *this* sweater, she'd boot him right back out into the rain.

As lightning flickered in the distance, she stared at the stranger who had leaped the cliffs, charged through the storm, and saved her life. A man of action, a man of little fear, she thought, studying the rise and fall of his chest. He curled one big palm around her old toy and slid it closer to his cheek.

A crooked grin played over her lips at that simple movement. It was hard to be afraid of someone who was cuddling up with a toy pig.

An unexpected sense of protectiveness swept over her.

That worn and frayed pig had been a gift from her uncle on her twelfth birthday, the year before her parents' death.

The hero pig, her uncle had called the battered creature.

The hero in her bed looked almost as battered, Hope decided. Moonlight played over the scar snaking along his right brow, and the line of his jaw was softened now in sleep, but the power of his callused hands was proof enough that he lived by his strength.

The clock on the desk read 3:45 a.m. as Hope crept toward the old armoire by the window and tried the telephone. As she had feared, the storm had downed the wires. It might be hours before service was restored, and she wasn't going to spend the time cuddled in her bed with a complete stranger.

She searched the armoire until she found a flashlight, which she covered with a lacy camisole to filter its light, then made her way in silence toward the door.

Gabrielle and Jeffrey should be back by now. She would bring them with her as backup when she woke her rescuer. Then she would ask him a few questions and decide whether he would be staying or leaving.

Perfectly logical, she decided.

Well satisfied, she smiled and reached for the door latch.

She was still smiling when something spun her backward and pinned her hard against the wall.

CHAPTER FIVE

HIS EYES SNAPPED WITH fury. Hope could feel the muscles standing rigid on his forearms.

"Wh-what do you think you're doing?" she hissed.

His hands tightened. Hope felt cold metal against her neck.

That's what you get for letting a stranger into your bed, she thought wildly. *Death by strangulation with a medieval metal gauntlet.*

Who would ever believe it?

"Listen, friend, there are two brawny men downstairs," she lied breathlessly. "In five seconds I'm going to shout for them to come up here and turn you into tuna salad."

He looked at her mouth, frowned, looked again. "Shout?" The sound was low and rough.

"That's right, shout." The man could barely talk, Hope thought. Come to think of it, her own throat wasn't feeling so good. Probably they were both coming down with a fever after being trapped out in the rain.

She shoved away any thought of compassion. It was fortunate that this man had been on hand to save her life, but if he expected something extra for his chivalry, like time in her bed, he was going to be sorely disappointed. "Well?"

He didn't move.

Hope kicked at his knee. "Let me go."

He sidestepped coolly.

"N-now." Fear raced, making her heart pump. If he heard the break in her voice or saw the pallor of her cheeks, he gave no sign of it.

Hope shoved angrily at his chest, but the motion was as useful as cobwebs hitting granite. In all honesty, the man didn't seem violent or intent on robbery. He simply looked angry and confused.

Not that Hope was about to take any chances.

"You can let go now."

No movement.

"You're *hurting* me."

His hands loosened, but he remained in front of her, an unshakable wall of chain mail and muscle between her and the door.

Hope stiffened as his hand slid onto her hip. "That's one bad idea, Galahad." Her hands clenched on the flashlight. As a weapon, it had limited value, but she wouldn't go down without a fight.

His hand closed over the flashlight. Frowning, he pulled the gray metal handle from her fingers and studied the tool suspiciously.

What was going on? Hope thought irritably. The man looked as if he had never used a flashlight before.

The handle jerked as he brushed a button and sent a powerful beam through the darkness. With an incomprehensible curse he dropped the flashlight and glared as it rolled across the floor, then ricocheted off a chair leg.

Correction, Hope thought. The man looked as if he had never *seen* a flashlight before.

She glowered as the glass face shattered at her feet. Being around this man was getting *expensive*.

"That flashlight cost a lot of money," she snapped, shoving vainly at his rigid arm.

No answer.

Hope gritted his teeth. The man was starting to make her

seriously nervous—and he didn't appear to understand a word she said.

"You might enjoy acting out captor-captive fantasies, but I don't find the idea particularly entertaining. Where did you get that costume, by the way? Wide World of Wrestling?"

Still no answer. Hope shoved at his hands. "I don't want to hurt you, but I will. I'm a fifth-degree black belt," she lied again.

He didn't exactly grovel in fright. In fact, his face registered no emotion whatsoever.

"Scram, will you? I've got *work* to do."

His jaw tensed. Something flickered in those keen, loch-gray eyes. "Work?"

Did he think that the floors cleaned themselves after a rainstorm? "Work, as in manual labor. Right at the top is checking the eaves—provided I still *have* any eaves left to check."

"Eaves?"

"The place where I nearly broke my neck when I fell in the rain." Nobody's memory could be *that* bad, Hope thought. Maybe he was high on drugs.

Just my luck, she thought miserably. She'd asked for a hero and instead she'd gotten a drug addict. "Eaves. As in roof." She pointed over their heads, making one last attempt to communicate.

"Ah. Roof." He pointed to the ceiling, too. "Up there." He touched her damp hair. "You are not a man."

"Surprise, surprise."

At least he seemed to speak English. Still, Hope decided that the sooner he left, the better. Her bedroom was beginning to feel decidedly cramped, and the hard thigh crowding her hip didn't add to her comfort.

"Give me some space, here." She shoved at him with her bent knee, but only managed to slap their bodies together. She winced as a metal prong jabbed her thigh. "Ouch! That circus costume of yours is dangerous."

Something flashed in his eyes. Hope didn't want to know what it was. He looked even more angry and confused than before.

"Listen, I'm going downstairs to work. I don't suggest you try to stop me." Would stomping on his instep work? she wondered.

"You perform...work here?" This time the words were rough but audible. He seemed to have a heavy accent that Hope couldn't place.

French? German?

"Of course. Just because I'm a woman doesn't mean I'm a wimp. Right now I need to see how much of the attic is buried beneath rainwater," she said grimly.

"Why?"

Hope counted silently to five. "Because this is my house, Jack. Taking care of it is part of my job description."

"My name is not Jack." Belatedly her last words seemed to register. A frown cut across his brow. "*Your*...house?"

"That's right. Do you have a problem with that?"

"You...work in this house?" he said slowly.

"Not this house, *my* house," Hope corrected. "At Glenbrae House I pay the bills and hire the help. I even wash the windows when necessary. Someone's got to keep this beautiful old wreck in one piece."

"Glenbrae...House." He swept a piercing look through the room. The glass glinted, dark with rain, holding their reflections just above the trees dimly visible in the orchard. "I did not give you hire," he said.

No kidding. She wouldn't work for this specimen in a thousand years.

"Who has brought you here? Will? My bailiff?"

Hope stared at him. The man was having *real* problems with his English. Maybe the bump on his head had done more damage than she'd realized. "Not anyone. And believe me, I've never seen you before in my life."

"Nor have I seen you. But if you have hire at Glenbrae House, it is by my grace."

A strand of black hair curled over his forehead, just above an angry purple bruise. Hope realized the bruise had come in his effort to rescue her.

Forget it, she told herself. She couldn't afford to be generous or grateful when he was intent on taking advantage of her. "No one hired me," she repeated. "I own this place."

His whole posture changed. "Glenbrae is mine by grant of the sovereign, with all wod-penny and chiminage. Mine." The words were rough but unmistakable.

His confidence unsettled her. Could her purchase have been a mistake? As an American, she was hardly an expert in the complexities of English entails and leaseholds. What if her lawyer had overlooked some technicality? Worse yet, what if someone else held prior right to the land?

Impossible, she told herself.

She took a long, slow breath. The man looked more disoriented than she'd thought. His body was rigid and his fingers were now clamped on her neck. She was going to have to set him straight about a few things.

"Two things," she muttered. "First of all, you're— strangling me."

He frowned. "Strangle?" The keen eyes narrowed, and then he released her throat. But his hands settled tensely around the back of her neck.

At least it was a start, Hope thought. "The second thing is a little more important. There's one problem with what you just said about owning Glenbrae House. It's already owned—by *me.* I hold clear deed and title, duly authorized by all relevant authorities. It may not be a royal grant, but I assure you it's every bit as legal."

For an instant more confusion filled his eyes. "Show me this deed," he growled.

"With pleasure." Hope smiled icily. "Just as soon as you take your hands off my neck."

He looked down at his clenched fingers, then shrugged and stepped back. "If you flee, I will track you."

"Don't worry, buster, I'm not going anywhere."

He scowled. "Enough talk. Show me your right of ownership."

Hope fumed at his arrogance. "I'm supposed to prove ownership to a man who goes around dressed in armor and a sheet?"

"My covering is called a surcoat."

"I'm *so* glad to know that. You must be a big hit on Halloween.

"Halloween?"

Hope shook her head. "Do you always dress like that?"

"It is customary."

Customary where? she wondered. In the medieval fair where he worked as an entertainer? If so, why didn't he just admit it?

She moved to the door, careful to make no quick movements that might provoke him. Given his unpredictable moods, she couldn't be too careful. "Forget the deed. My leaking roof is more important."

"Fetch your legal writ. Then I will see to the safety of the roof."

"I don't recall asking for your help," she said tightly.

"It is well you did not, for you growl like a Bedouin rug dealer cursing his camel. You would keep any man with wits to ten paces."

"Where does that leave *you?*"

"But I am not a Bedouin rug dealer," he said calmly. "And you…interest me. Even if you are a witch."

"If I were a witch, you'd be a toad right now." Hope took advantage of the distance between them to aim a fierce kick at his shin.

He gave no notice that he felt anything.

"Because you saved my life, I'll feed you one hot meal. After that, you're out of here."

"Out…here?"

"Gone. Departed. *Hasta la vista,* baby."

"I am no infant." His brow rose. "And where am I to go?"

"That's your problem. Go wherever you want. Home— or back to whatever fair it is you work at."

He slanted her an imperious glare. "I have seen fairs. They are noisy things of no interest to me."

Hope swallowed hard. When would Gabrielle and Jeffrey get back?

She thought of the small, battery-operated stun gun tucked in a drawer in the kitchen. Her uncle had insisted she take it on her first backpacking trip through Provence as a college student. Hope had only needed it once, when a drunken pair of American football players had decided it would be amusing to toss her fully clothed into the Seine.

In the end she had talked her way out of that confrontation. She would talk her way out of this one, too.

Then rescue or not, it was goodbye, knight errant.

The deed was exactly where Hope had left it, hidden inside a wall safe in her study. She might be naive, but she wasn't totally stupid, and she didn't keep her important papers lying around for someone to snatch.

The stranger watched curiously as she removed her fireproof protective metal document box and carried it to her desk.

Light brushed the peach moiré walls with warmth from floor to beamed ceiling, but there was little else to see. Hope had moved all her antiques to the guest rooms, keeping for herself only a simple pine desk flanked by high bookshelves.

His breath caught as he turned to study the walls. "So many books," he whispered.

Hope shrugged. "I like to read. It's not exactly a crime."

"Most unusual." He moved to the wall, frowning. "You are a cloistered woman?"

"A what?"

He spoke slowly, as if answering a child. "A female of God, wedded to the church."

Hope had a sudden inspiration. "I might be." Maybe that would keep him from inflicting any more bodily harm.

"Only in the cloisters or at court have I seen so many volumes in one place." He ran his fingers gently over the spines. "These are religious books that you read?"

Couldn't he tell? "Let's say they're a—a mix. The Church encourages broad-mindedness these days."

"Indeed. Shakes-peare. Ag-a-tha Christie. Tom Cl-ancy." He read the words in slow, halting tones.

Hope wondered how he could stumble over such famous names. The man would have to be from Mars not to have heard of Tom Clancy.

His fingers moved with gentle reverence down row after row, and then he turned back to her. "You have added these books." It was almost an accusation.

"Some of them. A few were here when I came." Hope shrugged. "There's not much else to do for recreation in Glenbrae."

He traced the scarred pine surface of her desk, then raised a fragile Venetian glass paperweight to the candle. "How come you by this?"

Why was he so surprised? It was hardly a priceless antique. "It was a gift, if you must know."

"Ah." He nodded. "From the king, was it?"

He must have meant the queen, not that it mattered. Hope had never been any closer to royalty than a quick taxi ride around the gardens at Windsor. "Not from the king, the queen or the thane of Cawdor."

"You know the thane?" He looked shocked.

Hope sighed. "Not in this lifetime. And that gift you're holding came from Venice. A friend brought it back for me."

Something flickered in his eyes. "Venice." He pronounced the word in four lyric syllables. "Truly a place of water and song. Flowers everywhere, and such color that a man might think he is dead and reborn in heaven as a saint."

"You've been there?"

"To heaven?"

"No, to Venice."

He shrugged, his gaze locked on the globe. Light refracted onto his face in blocks of color as he shifted the glass gently between his big hands. Each movement was impossibly careful, impossibly sad.

What had happened to him in Venice?

Hope could not tear her gaze away as haunting memories swept across his face.

Forget it, she told herself. Compassion could get a woman into a load of trouble these days. The man was probably wanted for wife beating or three counts of homicide. If not, then he was certifiable.

Either way, the sooner she got him out of her house, the better. "Turn around," she said flatly.

His black brow climbed. "Turn away? Why should I do this?"

"Do you have to question *everything* I say?"

"It is my right," he said coldly.

Not that again, Hope thought. "I'm waiting," she said pointedly.

"Why am I to turn?"

"Because there is a code for the lock. I'm not about to let you or anyone else know what the numbers are."

"Code?"

He could play dumb, but she wasn't buying it. When he didn't move, she crossed her arms over her chest. "Every minute you wait, more rain comes flooding through the roof."

He seemed to consider her words. Thunder rolled outside and he ran a hand across his forehead. Sweat covered his brow as he swayed back against the wall, his hand moving down to cup his right knee.

"Are you all right?"

He stiffened, all trace of confusion vanished. Though he was pale, his features were implacable. "I will turn away," he said imperiously. "You may have your secrets—for now." When he moved, Hope saw that he favored his left leg.

"Be quick, for I grow impatient," he growled, his back turned.

She had the strange impression this was the first time he had ever obeyed an order.

Quickly, she dialed her code, then removed a parchment wrapped in a velvet bag. "You can turn around now." She held out her deed. "Look for yourself. Everything's in order, right down to the seal."

He studied the parchment warily, frowning over the red wax seal. Or maybe it was the language of the document that bothered him. Hope had had more trouble than she cared to admit when she'd tried to decipher the flowing, archaic script.

His finger slid across the page. "The language is most strange."

"You can say *that* again."

"Why would I wish to?"

Hope sighed as he continued to read. His face cast a shadow across the parchment.

Abruptly he raised his head. "What sort of joke is this?"

Hope was fast losing all her patience with these nonsensical questions. "No joke, Galahad. Believe it."

"I believe nothing. Who are you truly, a spy sent to watch the village? One of the bailiff's hirelings? Or are you sent by a local coven?" He made the quick, wary sign of the cross as he spoke.

Hope had had enough of his interrogation. "I'm Hope O'Hara, just as the document says. I'm still waiting to know who you are."

"I am Ronan MacLeod." He seemed to be waiting for her reaction.

"Is that name supposed to *mean* something to me?"

"I am a knight of St. Julian, liege of Glenbrae House and all its lands. Others have different names for my position."

"Oh? Like what?"

His jaw hardened. "Some call me the King's Wolf."

A wave of cold air swept over Hope's shoulders.

Hope thought of the hard-faced warrior who stared down from the shadows of the stairwell, silent and eternal guardian of Glenbrae House. On his shoulder had been an animal form.

A wolf?

As dim light poured around him, Hope felt an eerie sense of recognition. Yes, there was a definite resemblance, even by the flickering light of her candle.

His name was MacLeod. Was he a distant descendant, someone who carried the blood of Glenbrae's ancient guardian? Or was he born from muddled bloodlines, through an illegitimacy hidden centuries before? Either possibility would explain his possessiveness about the house, she realized.

But not his *weird* style of clothing.

The sense of déjà vu persisted, gathering force. A tingling crept up her spine, as if she had walked into a mystery greater than her understanding. The howl of the wind and the rain slashing at the window only added to her strange sense of being caught out of place and time.

Yes, the resemblance was uncanny. The original frescoed image was blurred with age, but the jaw was nearly identical. And those eyes had the same cocky, arrogant glint…

Get a grip, Hope thought in disgust. The King's Wolf died centuries ago. And if he were still alive, he would hardly be the kind of fellow you'd want to meet for friendly conversation—especially if it involved a land dispute.

According to her limited knowledge of Scottish history, most Scotsmen solved such disputes with their hands—or with a sword.

Whether he was a descendant or not, Hope wasn't going to argue with the man. She was too exhausted to argue—and he was in no fit shape himself, judging by his pallor. His shoulder was braced against the door frame, and she realized he was fighting to stay on his feet.

Then again, maybe the title he had used was hereditary. "Is that title you mentioned passed down from father to son?"

"I have no son," he said gravely. "The title is mine, as anyone in Glenbrae will tell you."

Hope shook her head in disbelief. "You expect me to believe that you own this house and its lands?"

"I care not what you wish to believe, woman." He closed his eyes for a second, breathing heavily. When his eyes opened, they showed the strain of his effort to stay upright.

Perhaps the head wound was serious. Perhaps he would keel over right in front of her, Hope thought uneasily.

Before she could answer, he held out the deed, scowling. "You will explain *this* to me now." He tapped the lines at the bottom of the page.

"Explain what?"

"The number written here." His eyes burned, half in confusion and half in anger. "What does this mean, one-nine-nine-eight?"

CHAPTER SIX

HOPE JUST STARED AT HIM, fighting a sense of sharp uneasiness. "Exactly what it says. 1998."

"But what does this *mean?*" he snapped.

"It means the year." Sweat mottled his brow. Hope wondered if he was about to lose consciousness.

"No more lies!" he thundered. "By St. Julian, it is the reign of our sovereign lord, King Edward. As well you know."

Hope's pulse hammered. Edward, as king? Prince Charles certainly wasn't going to like hearing that. Was this some clumsy joke?

Lightning flashed, rattling the tiny, leaded windowpanes. For one ghostly instant Hope saw the trees bent flat against the darkness, their boughs like skeletal fingers before the wind.

But the stranger did not notice. He stood frozen, his fists locked over his strange tunic while his pallor increased by the second.

Hope took a step away from him. The expression on his face frightened her almost as much as his wild accusations. "Just calm down. I hate to be the one to tell you, but this Edward you're talking about is dead." Hope's history was weak, but she knew that much.

His hand plunged to his side and came up empty. Hope recalled seeing a dark bundle beside the bed. He must have left the sword beside him as he slept.

"Dead? When?"

She did a rough calculation. "I'd say about seven hundred years ago."

RONAN MACLEOD FELT his whole mind scream. What was she doing in his house? Was she a spy, a witch or a madwoman?

He frowned down at the document in his hands.

The year was 1998? Seven centuries into a future he could not even imagine? No, her words were impossible.

The script blurred before him as he fought a wave of exhaustion. The storm had drained all his energy and he could barely stand. But he dared reveal no weakness before this cunning spy. He had seen the vermilion tents of Sultan al-Ashraf Khalil stretched across the plain of Samaria, bright as blood. He had watched the Saracens storm Acre, raze the great towers, and run down terrified women. Nothing could blot the pain of those hellish nightmares.

In his soul he'd known only hard penance would bring him solace after his years of forced loyalty to a hated English king. Still, he had saved his village and all its people from the sword. Their safety had been the price of his unwilling service, though by the king's order, none could know this. After the life he had led, what pain could being branded a traitor hold for him?

But this night's adventure strained his very reason. By St. Swithin and St. Julian, had he lost his immortal soul or simply lost his reason?

Even now this woman's beauty tasked him, a torment to his senses. There had been no woman for too long.

"A lie," he growled, closing his free hand around her neck. "The date—tell it to me now."

She trembled. It pleased him that she finally recognized her danger. He did not relish harrowing women and children, but he vowed to have this trickery ended.

She shoved at his hands. "Let me go, you oaf."

"Not until I have the truth from you."

"What part of twentieth-century English don't you understand? The year is one-nine-nine-eight. Two years away from the new millennium."

Her moss-green eyes glinted as she strained against him, and MacLeod cursed, twisting to avoid hurting her. But he would not release her. Not until her answers were believable.

But even as he made his resolve, her volatile eyes continued to haunt him. She shoved and fought, sputtering like no woman MacLeod had ever known, argumentative as a drunken cloth merchant. And what manner of clothes were these exotic things she wore? Soft, sleek leggings hugged her slender thighs, making his breath gather in his chest like a hot desert wind.

In disgust, MacLeod felt his body harden. Even her scent seduced him, an unfamiliar blend of cinnamon and wildflowers.

He looked away, cursing his desire. She was a spy—or worse. Her beauty was part of her treachery. The date she gave was a joke from a jester's tale. No mortal could gallop through time and leap centuries in a heartbeat. Either she was sent by the bailiff to report on Glenbrae's new laird, or she was part of some new scheme of Edward's, meant to test MacLeod's loyalty.

There could never be enough testing. The king was a suspicious man, and his courtiers were far worse. A Highlander would never be welcomed in an English court. Only his sword was needed—and then only when the king chose his next victim.

Something bleak filled MacLeod's eyes.

No matter. He would wring the truth from the spy before dawn streaked the eastern sky or he would forsake his honor as a knight. She would soon learn the price of treachery.

"These lands are my demesne, woman. You hold this lie at your peril."

"Glenbrae House is mine." Her eyes flashed in fury and outrage. "I'll fight you in court if I have to. My purchase was made without liens or limits on the date you see on that sheet of parchment you're crushing."

Clever, she was. Bold as a Saracen, too. MacLeod turned to the window, his mind raging. So she did not accede.

Very well. MacLeod had faced treachery too many times to quail before it now.

Outside, the wind gusted. Darkness swallowed the hillside while rain slid down the fine, leaded panes.

As he watched, the drops blurred and the room grew hot. "End these tricks, witch." He released her throat; the parchment slipped from his fingers. His hands were shaking, and he shaped them into fists. "You'll nae win against me."

Suddenly the walls began to spin. MacLeod fought a gray tide of dizziness, feeling the floor pitch.

But his struggle was in vain. She was a worthy foe, this woman with green cat's eyes and hair like windblown silk. Her power was great.

Crusader, he was, sworn enemy of all evil. Why did duty and honor suddenly seem so distant and unimportant?

"Are you...all right?"

Her husky whisper fascinated him. The Scotsman swayed, unable to stand, unable to bear the worry in her voice. Darkness clawed at his reason, opening soft arms of treachery.

And then for Ronan MacLeod, reason was no more. Pain was no more. All the world lurched and slid away into shadow.

"HE JUST COLLAPSED," Hope said breathlessly, one arm beneath MacLeod's shoulders as Gabrielle and Jeffrey appeared, soaked, in the hall.

"Who is he?"

"Never mind who. *What* is he?" Jeffrey asked suspiciously.

"Just help me get him into bed," Hope said.

"Where do you want to take him?"

"To the Blue Room, I guess." Hope struggled beneath the man's weight. "He weighs a ton, and I'm going to need your help."

"Where did he come from?" Jeffrey grunted as he shouldered his share of the stranger's weight.

"From the orchard, as near as I could see. And before that, from the cliffs to the north."

"He could have been killed," Jeffrey muttered.

"That's what I thought. But I was having my own problems at the time—the roof gave way and I nearly broke my neck."

Gabrielle scowled. "You should not go alone to the roof. It is too dangerous."

"But nothing happened. He came riding out of the storm and caught me."

"Riding? Riding on a horse?" Jeffrey glanced uncertainly at the stranger.

"Saddle, bridle and all. And his timing was perfect," Hope said.

There was a sudden whirring at the door and something swept past her shoulder. "There you are, Banquo." A gray parrot soared into the room, long wings spread. "I thought you'd been caught out in the storm."

"It would serve him right," Jeffrey muttered. "Always shrieking nonsense."

The gray parrot tilted his head and fanned out his thoroughly sodden feathers. "Thunder and lightning. Thunder and lightning."

"You're got that much right," Jeffrey muttered. "Though I still contemplate a nice bowl of parrot stew."

"Shame on you," Gabrielle scolded. "Banquo is one of the family, and you'd better remember that. He's been here at Glenbrae as long as Hope has."

"Maybe that's why he's so arrogant." Jeffrey shot a dark look at the parrot. "You're not out of the woods yet, Banquo." Then his eyes narrowed as he studied the stranger. "Any explanation for all this chain mail?"

Panting, Hope helped Jeffrey negotiate the landing in

the new section of the house. She refused to consider taking the steep old tower stairs with so much weight to carry. "Beats me. All I know is he saved my life." She frowned, remembering the man's strange accusations. "Even though he was acting very odd before he passed out...."

"If you ask me, anyone who rides around in a storm wearing chain mail and plate armor has to be more than a little dim," Jeffrey muttered.

Hope still couldn't forget that the unknown rider had saved her life. She wished she had more answers. He had been angry and imperious, but his confusion had been equally clear. "What were the roads like?"

"Don't ask. The electricity is out all the way to Glenbrae. There were no lights and no other traffic." Jeffrey laughed darkly. "The car stalled twice in the mud and we were damned lucky to make it back in one piece. But enough of our woes. Why were you on the roof?"

"Trying to keep the attic from flooding. Not that I was very successful." Hope caught a breath as they reached the top of the stairs. MacLeod twisted and muttered hoarsely, but did not wake. "The corner of the eaves gave way and that's when Sir Galahad appeared—horse, gauntlets and all." Staggering, she took the last wobbly steps into the blue bedroom. It was one of her favorite rooms, with high oriel windows overlooking the orchards. Banquo flew off to preen his feathers on the sill as they deposited their burden facedown on the bed.

"Did he tell you his name?"

"We didn't get around to detailed introductions," Hope said, tugging at the man's loose black garment. "All he said was that he was a MacLeod. Hardly surprising, in this part of Scotland." She didn't even want to think about his insistence that Glenbrae House was his. She stared at the wet cloth clinging to his muscled shoulders. "Bring the candle closer, will you, Gabrielle? I can barely see."

Light flickered, gilding the stranger's body as Hope pulled away the black outer garment.

"The man has a strange fashion sense, that's for certain." Jeffrey shook his head at the heavy armor beneath the long tunic. "You're going to need help getting all that metal stuff off him. Amazing how authentic they can make this fake stuff, right down to the dents and rust. Do you have any idea how heavy armor was?"

"I think we're going to find out," Hope muttered. Together they tugged the metal plates over the man's torso. Both of them were sweating by the time the job was done.

"Big, isn't he?"

"Too big," Hope murmured.

"But with a very nice body," Gabrielle added, peeking over Hope's shoulder.

Hope hid a smile as Jeffrey's scowl deepened. In all honesty, she had to agree with Gabrielle. Their sleeping visitor filled the bed, and even then his feet hung over the edge. Hope was about to start on his shoes—some kind of free-form leather boots—when her gaze rose to his back.

Candlelight outlined rows of ridged muscles and black hair that waved along his shoulders. But Hope's breath caught as she looked lower.

There the marks began. Old wounds covered his neck and shoulders, slashes that might have come from a knife or a broader blade. Hope counted six scars alone between his shoulder blades.

"My God, the man is a walking checkerboard," Jeffrey whispered. "Maybe he's a soldier home from some kind of secret mission."

"Riding a horse?" Hope countered unsteadily.

Jeffrey shrugged. "Hey, you never know."

"He saved my life. I know that much." As Hope stared at the old scars, the room blurred, and she turned away, unable to bear the sight of the jagged marks. "I'll leave him to you, Jeffrey. You can take off the rest of that metal stuff and put him under the covers. Irritating or not, he deserves a good night's rest."

"I'm glad he's already asleep. I wouldn't want to tangle with him while he was awake." Jeffrey clicked his tongue. "But I still don't understand what he was doing out in the storm in complete medieval armor."

Hope didn't know either. And by the look of the man dead asleep on the bed, she wasn't going to find out until morning.

Lightning flickered over the steel-gray hills. Wind gusted down the glen, rushing through the orchard and wrapping around the old house.

Hope finally drifted into sleep, dimly aware of disturbing dreams, while in a room nearby, the stranger twisted and threw pillow and covers from the bed.

Downstairs in the kitchen, Banquo settled on his perch and hopped from foot to foot. "Mark, King of Scotland," he muttered, one eye on the dark window. "Mark the night." With a shrill cry, he tucked his head beneath one wing and spoke no more.

And in the rushing darkness at the foot of the glen, a light flashed twice, then abruptly disappeared.

HONORIA GLARED at the rain streaking the windows. "It's begun, hasn't it, Pet?"

Her sister rocked on before the fire, strangely calm. "Almost certainly. I can't remember a storm of this magnitude anytime in the past fifty years. Maybe even in this century." Perpetua's eyes narrowed. "Done well and fine, it is. The MacLeod has finally come back to Glenbrae. And now the rest begins."

"What do you see, Pet?" Morwenna's face glowed with excitement in the firelight.

"Clear, it is. How it begins—and how it will end." Rain struck the windows, as if to underscore her words. Her eyes slid half closed as she focused on inner visions. Drawing a deep breath, she began to chant.

> *"Fire at morning, fire in rain.*
> *Night cannot hold, nor forest gain.*
> *The page is turned, the mystery clear.*
> *The ghost of Banquo no more to fear."*

Morwenna heaved a sigh of delight. "I do so love a good mystery. We'll have one now, all of us. The King's Wolf is back and he'll set everything topsy-turvy." She hugged her arms to her chest. "I can barely wait. And your poetry is wonderful, Pet."

Perpetua closed her eyes and chuckled. "Aye, the MacLeod is back. He's brought the poetry with him. He's her miracle, sure enough. Now Hope O'Hara's going to have to figure out what to do with him."

AS DAWN TOUCHED the glen's eastern slopes, Ronan MacLeod thought neither of destiny nor mystery. Instead he was remembering a pair of upturned eyes and a full, expressive mouth. They would be soft, those lips, sweet with a hint of raspberries. They would open, clinging to him as she sighed and urged him closer to...

Scowling, MacLeod stood up sharply.

The floor spun and his legs shook. By the Holy Bones, he was mad. He had a queer memory with images that did shake his very reason. First was a storm from hell itself and then a leap that had carried him from the cliffs into bleakest death.

But instead of death he had found a woman, her face like dawn and her smell a thing of springtime and youthful dreams.

More poetry, the Crusader thought in disgust. There was no woman, only a nightmare wrought by his exhaustion.

Stark naked, he stretched and studied the curious piece

of furniture beneath him. He would have called it a bed, but it had far too much padding, even with half the drapings tossed aside. In the future he resolved to sleep on the floor. Such softness was for women and sick old men.

He wound his long length of patterned wool about his waist, belting it tightly. By habit he slid his sword into its leather sheath, then strode out into the hall, looking for the garderobe.

No one was about. All was gray in the quiet of predawn.

By honor, why was the house yet so still? Where were the servants stirring at the fire and horses neighing in the fore-court?

Then MacLeod froze, feeling the same uneasiness as he had felt in the storm.

Something was wrong.

He found his way to the tower stairs at the end of the house and stared down into the gloom. The tower was the same, as were the broad stone steps leading downward.

But as MacLeod reached out with his left hand, he swayed and nearly fell. By all the saints, who had moved the stair rope? It always hung on the left, giving him full use of his right hand, which was his sword hand. Whoever had ordered this change would soon answer to him.

He searched in the gloom and found a rope strung down the opposite side of the stone staircase. But instinct whis-pered that this was no simple mistake.

He ran a hand over his forehead and felt his fingers tremble. A sense of treachery wrapped around him. Had his nightmares been real after all?

He strode down the hallway and jerked open the first door, watching shadows flicker over odd pieces of furniture in unfamiliar colors. Square wall designs glinted, covering patterns of cloth in stitches he had never seen. Books lay everywhere on neat shelves, more leather and paper than MacLeod had ever seen in one place before. Beneath the

books, fragile bowls of colored glass held flowers for which
he knew no names.

All unfamiliar.

Darkness clawed at his reason.

To the next room he went, and thence to three others, and
each room told the same tale. Strange, all strange. Colors and
shapes confounded his senses. Objects fought against his
very reason. Was it to hell he'd come or a haven meant for
madmen?

He stood in the last doorway, one shoulder pressed against
the cold wood. Even the smells were wrong. No woodsmoke
drifted. No herbs and dried rushes covered the floor.

Strange, all strange.

He closed his eyes, making the sign of the cross for
protection.

The house seemed to mock him, for it was the same yet
not the same. Dizziness twisted his mind, and he knew if he
moved from the door, he would fall.

Seven centuries gone past?

No, it was purest madness. But the evidence was before
him now, glinting in every shadowed room. How could he
fight the terrible proof of his eyes? This was the same house
he had left before the storm—yet now its differences were
stark.

Rain struck the roof. MacLeod stiffened as fingers softly
brushed his arm. He wanted no more contact or dialogue
with the spy. How had she wrought such changes here in a
single night? Glenbrae House had been his first home in
decades, a place where he had hoped to find contentment.

Now all hope of that was vanished.

"I'm sorry. Truly I am."

She was a flawless performer, MacLeod thought. There
seemed to be genuine regret in her voice.

"Sorry for what?" he said bitterly. "That you have failed
in your mission to shake my hold on reason?" He laughed

tightly. "Edward makes no reward to those who fail him, as you will learn soon enough."

"You really believe that Edward is still king, don't you?" she whispered.

MacLeod stared off into the gray clouds where lightning flickered coldly. "So he was when last I saw him, in the flesh at his court but two weeks ago."

There was a soft catch in her throat. "I...don't know what to say."

In truth there was nothing left to say, the Crusader thought grimly. Either the woman lied or he had lost all reason, and he refused to accept the second possibility. "The bailiff sent you here to cozen me."

"There is no bailiff at Glenbrae House."

MacLeod laughed darkly. "Then perhaps the king selected you as my wife. He has threatened often enough that he might, if I did not choose on my own. Have you come from the court to tie the knot about me?"

Her voice hardened. "I don't know any kings. Even if I did, I would marry for no reason but my heart's desire."

"Spoken like a woman." MacLeod sank back against the door frame. The rain seemed to streak inside his eyes, blinding him. No, this tale of hers could not be true. She had been sent to befuddle him with her heady scent and expressive eyes, a seasoned spy in Edward's employ.

But what if her words were true...?

Then all the world he knew was gone. All the people he trusted were turned to dust. And he had no home left, no king to serve and no village to protect.

The thought was a dagger to his flesh.

"What magic have you worked?" he whispered hoarsely, burying his fingers in her hair and hauling her against his chest. "Speak me the truth now, witch, before I squeeze the last breath from your lips."

CHAPTER SEVEN

HOPE SAW THE ALARM harden his mouth and fill his eyes, overshadowing the anger. She had come from her room, wakened by the sound of slamming doors and muttered oaths, only to find her visitor struggling to stay upright. If not for the fear in his eyes, she would have sworn she was dealing with a madman.

"Tell me," MacLeod repeated roughly.

But his fear held her, tempering her own anger. "I'm no witch. I doubt such creatures exist. I almost died in the storm, remember? If I could make magic, I would have used it, believe me."

"Perhaps weakness was your greatest trick."

Sticks and gravel rattled at the window. The house creaked around them, rocked by lashing winds.

Hope stared deep into his eyes, looking past the worry and the anger, willing him to believe her. "These things I have said are true. Hurting me won't change that."

He looked down at his hands, now locked around her wrists. "Hurting you was not my purpose." He closed his eyes, a shudder working through his body. "Nothing I do is as I plan. Why is it all so different?"

"Different in what way?"

He made an angry, impatient sound. "In every way. The colors are too bright. The smells are flat, too sweet. You have glass everywhere, too many books. And the colored walls…"

He fought for control. Then, very gently, he ran his hands over her wrists. "I ask your forgiveness for any harm I have given. It shames me, and I will undertake penance for giving you pain."

He was deadly serious, Hope saw. "I'll be fine. Just don't plan on trying anything like that again."

Gravely he pulled his sword from its sheath and held it out to her. "If I do such a thing again, I order you to use my sword against me."

The man is serious, Hope thought. "You want me to— attack you?"

"I will not oppose the blow. Deal with me as you must. If a man cannot wield control over himself, he is no more than a dog."

The conviction in his voice shook Hope. He would let her strike him down and never oppose her blow, if he thought himself at fault.

Men weren't supposed to act this way. There was something seriously wrong here.

"Take the sword," he ordered.

Reluctantly she gripped the leather-wrapped hilt. As the stranger released his hold, the weapon nearly plunged from her fingers. "You didn't tell me this thing weighed a ton!"

"You will need two hands," he said gravely, shaping her other hand around the hilt. "Hold it so." He moved her fingers so that they lay tightly on the handle underneath his. "Now lift your arms together and swing in a free arc. That will give power to your movement."

Hope felt hysterical laughter rise in her throat.

This couldn't be happening. She was not standing in her hallway in the gray light of dawn, discussing sword technique with a man who looked like he could have given Braveheart Wallace fighting lessons.

But the sword was cold and heavy in her fingers, all too real. So was the man's body pressed against her side.

"I—I'll remember that. About using two hands." She eased away from him and held out the sword.

His dark brow rose. "You trust me?"

Hope considered the question carefully. "No," she said. "I know nothing about you."

His eyes hardened. "Then keep the sword."

"There is no need. For now, your eyes tell me all I need to know."

"Are you a seer to read them?"

Hope stared at his well-used sword. "It doesn't take a witch to read what's in your eyes."

"And what is that?"

"Pain. Confusion. And…fear."

His whole body stiffened. "I am a knight sworn to the cross. A knight does not know fear."

That strange talk of knights and honor again.

Hope shrugged. "I know nothing of knights or what they said in public. But in the silence of the night, even a knight would be only a man. And there he would face his fears alone."

He took his sword from her and slid it into the leather sheath on his hip. "You speak of men. Have you known so many?"

"A few." Hope shrugged.

His fingers opened, guiding her face back to his. "Finish."

"None of them was like you. You jumped the cliffs when I needed a rescuer. You…saved my life."

"I did no more than my duty." He stared down at the mottled marks on Hope's wrists, his jaw tense. "And then I did this. A knight may not bring pain to a woman. It was my vow, and I have broken it. Perhaps the stories about me are true."

"Stories?"

"It is said that I have no heart beneath my steel. That I can be cut, but I do not bleed."

A terrible bleakness filled his eyes. Hope remembered the wounds across his back and shoulders and was certain he had known pain enough for twenty men.

But if he had shed tears, it had been in solitude and in grim silence. He might be half crazy, but he was more of a hero than any man she had ever met before.

She saw him run one hand over his knee and shift to his other leg. "Is your knee bothering you?"

He shrugged. "It is an old and familiar pain."

Hope wanted to laugh, but there was nothing to mock. There was no bravado in his speech, only simple truth, coupled with a disturbing resignation.

He hurt, she realized, and he hurt often. It was no more than what he expected of life. In his eyes, his endurance entitled him to no special respect.

Hope wasn't sure whether he deserved a medal or a referral to a good psychiatrist.

She was about to ask more about his knee when a door opened at the back of the house and footsteps echoed up the stairwell.

Her rescuer went very still. "Who enters without permission? Your maidservant?"

Hope blinked. "I have no maidservant."

"Stay here," he ordered. "I will see to the intruders." He drew his sword and moved toward the stairs.

The crazy man was going off to fight on her behalf, Hope realized. With a gasp, she ran after him. His sword could do serious damage from weight alone.

When she reached the stairs, Jeffrey was staring down the battered blade of the broadsword.

"Halt or I drop you where you stand."

"I give up. I'll say uncle or anything else you want." Jeffrey raised his hands. When he saw Hope, he gave a weak smile. "Tell him the natives are friendly, will you?"

"You can put down your sword." Hope bit back a ragged laugh, giddy at the absurdity of the whole scene. "This is one of my friends."

"A friend? Is he your lover?"

"What?"

"Lover," MacLeod said impatiently. "Does he share your bed?"

"What makes you think you can ask—"

Glowering, Hope's rescuer closed in on Jeffrey, sword leveled. "What say you to my question?"

"Er—lover? No way."

"Thank you for the compliment, Jeffrey," Hope muttered.

The young man's face flamed. "That is— We're not— Of course, I didn't mean to say that I don't think you're—"

MacLeod made a sound of disgust. "Are you one of the bailiff's men?" he demanded. "Or were you sent by Roulfe of Montaine? I should never have trusted him after he stole my horse in Genoa."

"Never been to Genoa," Jeffrey said quickly.

"You dress surpassing strange." He brushed his sword over Jeffrey's torn blue jeans and dripping blue anorak. "Are you jester to a troupe of traveling players?"

Hope sighed. "Just let him past, will you? Can't you see he's soaked?"

"So I have seen. Why?" MacLeod demanded suspiciously.

"I heard a noise outside. When I went to check, I found the tarpaulin dangling from a branch next to my window."

"Tar-pau-lin?" MacLeod repeated.

Jeffrey shot a questioning look at Hope.

"There seem to be some gaps in Mr. MacLeod's memory," she explained.

Gaps at least big enough to drive a tank through.

"My memory is sound," MacLeod said.

Hope ran a hand through her tousled hair. "He's convinced that Glenbrae House is his."

"And so it is," the stranger said stiffly. "Glenbrae and all the demesne lands around it."

"We're still debating that particular point," Hope murmured to Jeffrey. "In appreciation of his help, I've promised him a hot meal. Then he's on his way home."

"*This* is my home."

Jeffrey's brow rose. "Uh-oooh," he said slowly. "But how could he be—"

"You can vouch for this man's loyalty?" MacLeod demanded suddenly.

"Of course. He's my friend."

"But not your lover?"

"That's still none of your business."

"The answer's no," Jeffrey said decisively. "Definitely not lovers."

From somewhere below them came the clatter of pans. The aroma of brewing coffee drifted up the stairs.

"Truce." Hope waved an imaginary flag. "No more arguing until after breakfast."

"You will all come and eat now," Gabrielle called from the kitchen. "There is oatmeal, nice fat sausages and the buns with cinnamon icing. The electricity runs again, thank the good Lord."

Jeffrey headed for the stairs at a trot. Hope looked at MacLeod. "Well?"

He shrugged. "I will eat. Then there are questions to be answered."

Hope looked at his sole garment, a broad length of wool belted around his waist and tossed over one shoulder. "Aren't you going to change?"

"To change what?"

Hope tried not to look at his legs—and failed. "Your clothes."

His brow rose. "What need have I for that? When I fight, I wear my armor. If not, I wear this."

"Fine, fine. Let's just eat."

As she followed him down the stairs, every movement stirred the planes of muscle beneath his wind-burned skin.

There was beauty to his strength and a grace to his powerful stride.

He turned and saw her staring. "Why do you look at me?"

Hope swallowed. "Your back—the marks. How did you get them?"

He shrugged. "A warrior fights."

"That's not an answer."

Something glinted in his eyes. "It is all the answer I choose to give."

But MacLeod halted at the kitchen door, frowning. He seemed to be fighting for composure as his gaze flickered from one corner of the room to another. He fingered his sword, staring at the single lamp that burned near the window. "By all the saints, what chaos have you brought to my house?"

"Now, wait just a minute," Hope snapped, as she sat at the table.

He ignored her, studying Gabrielle warily. "You are the maidservant here? What is the year?" he demanded.

She poured a cup of coffee and held it out to him. "Try this. My coffee will restore your memory," she said sympathetically.

He took an experimental sip and his face twisted in a grimace. "What manner of poison do you give me to drink?"

"Double hazelnut espresso."

"Have you no good ale when a man breaks his fast?"

Gabrielle simply stared.

"No matter. What year is it?"

Gabrielle looked at Hope. "Is this a game he plays?"

"No game," MacLeod said, deadly serious. His eyes were locked on the lamp glowing beneath the window. "Unless it is a game from a nightmare. Tell me the year."

"It's 1998, of course."

A muscle moved at his jaw. Otherwise he stood rigid, frozen.

Reeling inside.

Again that impossible number. They changed his house, and then they set out to becloud his brain. Even the drink they gave him carried the bitter hint of poison.

MacLeod saw their lips moving but could not understand their meaning. They spoke in blurred sounds that were almost a foreign tongue.

"I am going out." At least in the fresh air he could think clearly. It was dangerous to stay inside any longer. The room held too much color and heat, too much light from a globe where no light should come.

Hope pushed back her chair and stood up. "I'll go with you."

"There is no need."

"You'll get lost. You're in no shape to be wandering around alone."

He could not have her following him. The turmoil inside him was not for others to share.

He schooled his face to a glare. "I need to wash, woman. Do you mean to follow me even there?"

Color filled her cheeks. It only made her more beautiful, MacLeod thought bleakly.

"No." She looked away. "Of course not. But you'll need soap, a towel. But we have a perfectly good shower inside."

The Scotsman turned away. The concern in her voice hurt him more than anything else. He had never known concern from a woman, never experienced uncomplicated human tenderness. It had been heat and anger and rough conquest on both sides, never tenderness and concern.

Now he heard both in her voice. Now, when they could mean nothing to him.

They made his breath tighten. They made him want her as he had wanted no other woman, spy or not.

He cursed softly, moving to the door. The cold water would check his passion and clear his head.

Maybe then he would find some answers.

CHAPTER EIGHT

MacLeod STRODE THROUGH the glen, half blind.

Around him the trees whispered, their dark leaves hung with beads of rain. But he did not notice. Only at the edge of the meadow did he stop and draw a shuddering breath.

The air was heavy with the tang of pine sap and heather. Even that smell seemed wrong, with an edge of something he could not name. He stared at the glen, really seeing it for the first time. *Pie Jesu,* the changes were legion. Why had he not noticed them before?

There should be no roses in a dark tangle at the base of the slope. There should be no neat plots of climbing beans and green herbs beyond the kitchen wall. To the north, where mist clung to the dim cliffs, the trees were too thick and the path was set at the wrong angle. Mounds of stones rose where no stones had lain, and new hedges ran in neat, clipped rows.

Nothing as he remembered.

Not the land. Not the house.

MacLeod raised an unsteady hand to the weathered stone fence beside him. Thank the saints, this was the same. He had helped to raise these stones as a boy of eight, and he still remembered that day of woodsmoke and laughter, the sweat and tall tales that always came when MacLeod men gathered together to work. Yes, the fence stood unchanged, as if it had been raised only yesterday.

But it had not been yesterday. Seven centuries and half

a lifetime had passed since he had been an innocent boy of eight.

His mind howled in outrage.

It could not be. It could not....

Yet how could he deny the strange shifting of earth and sky during the storm? How could he deny the truth of what he saw right now, familiar stones, familiar loch, yet all of it so completely wrong?

His hands clenched on the rough stone. The pain would harden him against the questions he could no longer escape.

MacLeod thought of all the changes he had seen inside the house: books that nestled in every corner instead of hidden safely away in locked chests. Bits of paper left lying about as if they were not precious materials. Finally, he thought of the stair rope strung on the wrong side of the entry tower and the kitchen filled with strange metals, colored baskets and too-bright fabrics.

Wrong. All wrong.

In the light of day there was no escaping the dark truth.

He leaned against the stone fence and drove his fists against his eyes as if pain could chase away his questions. But the mocking images remained, proof unshakable that what he feared was true.

Time changed. Time broken. His world...

Gone.

He sank blindly to one knee. What spell had cast him into this strange future? By whose hand had he been brought to this time?

He had no answers.

His jaw hardened as he drew his sword, trusted companion over so many years. With the sun glinting along the great blade, he drove the steel into the earth, fighting to understand what lay around him.

The year was 1998.

Centuries had fled past in a blur, wars fought and

kingdoms lost. The treachery and intrigue of his age were now
no more than words in dusty old books, like those lining
Hope O'Hara's shelves. In this age other wars were fought
and other campaigns planned, in which he had no part.

Time come and time gone.

The changes of this new world battered at MacLeod's
mind. If it was true, he was finally free. His forced loyalty to
the hated English king was at an end. Edward and all his court
were no more. He had heard all his life about witchcraft and
magic, but what conjurer could manage such vast changes?

MacLeod bowed his head, touching his forehead to the
cold silver of the sword's pommel. There in the glen he
struggled to understand, struggled to hold on to some shred
of the only world he had known.

But emptiness and a killing sense of loss lay around him.
Tiny beads of rain brushed his face while the pungent smells
of autumn drifted. And in that moment of reeling shock,
death seemed welcome.

But death would be no release. His father had taught him
that.

MacLeod stood slowly. His shoulders straightened. He
remembered Angus MacLeod's face when the English had
marched through the glen. Even while the old man lay half
dead after battle, hate and pain had forged his eyes to beaten
steel. "There will be a purpose in their coming," he had
whispered while death yawned before him. "Go with them.
Learn their ways and their strange tongue. Listen and mark
well all their secrets. Then return home. That will be your
purpose today. Not more death."

The old warrior had died then. Edward's brutish soldiers
had found Ronan hunched over his father's lifeless body. In
spite of his father's words, the boy of twelve had bitten back
tears and fought like a man. More than a few scars on his back
bore old testimony to his rage against the English invaders.

But in the end Ronan had failed. There had been no hope

of victory in that icy glen. Bloody and defeated, bound by ropes and steel, he had done as his father bade and gone with his enemies. There had been no choice.

"What purpose do you hold for me in this?" he whispered now to the God he had served so well in the East. But God seemed lost to him here, where mist veiled the trackless hills. Perhaps God had forgotten all about him.

Down the glen, the wind seemed to carry his words through the tall pines. For a second Ronan almost imagined the weight of his father's hand on his shoulder and the sad, cruel keening of the pipes.

Tears burned at his cheeks. Tears for warriors gone and dreams shattered. He had traveled far to find a home, only to find it stolen. But why?

Again there were no answers.

Blindly he made his way along the rocky slope. He had to believe he had been brought here for a purpose.

Behind him pebbles rattled hollowly over the bank.

MacLeod's fingers locked on his belt. Even here the woman came, fearless just as he had known she would be.

He made a low, savage sound. He could face no one now. The strangeness was still too raw, leaving him with anger that roiled to find a victim. "Go away."

"No. Not until I have some answers."

He cursed softly. He wanted the same thing she did, but there were no answers to give. He tugged at the wool girding his waist. He did not trust his control, and the last thing he wanted was to hurt her.

Better to make her go, and this would be the fastest way. "Stubborn creature. I ask you to leave." The cloth loosened at his waist.

"And I'm asking you for answers."

"There are none. But if you wish to stay, you are welcome to watch me bathe."

He pulled the cloth free. As he had expected, she

gasped, a soft sound lost in the swirl of the water as he met the loch.

The current was as cold as an assassin's heart. Ignoring the chill, MacLeod strode deeper. He heard a strangled cough and swift footsteps that crossed the bank. So she had gone.

He knew a moment of regret. What was he to do now? What sort of life could this strange, hostile world hold for a warrior such as he?

All he wanted was to go home.

"I'm not leaving, you know." A twig snapped. "Not until I have an explanation."

She sounded angry.

She sounded frightened.

The Scotsman's lips curved in bitter humor. By honor, so was he.

But even frightened, she would not leave. He was beginning to see the steel in her. It was clear that she cherished his house, and she did it without the help of any man. Extraordinary that the woman was a fighter just as he was.

But this was one fight she would lose. MacLeod was determined to be alone.

He strode out deeper, his teeth chattering as he welcomed the cold currents in a headlong plunge. Exhilarated, he let the icy water clear his muddled thoughts.

So he had lost his time and his world. At least he was alive. With luck he could find a way back. And if not...

If not, he must adapt as he had adapted before.

God's hand was in all things, even the most insignificant, so the Church said. MacLeod took refuge in that thought now.

He had survived before and he would survive again.

As a boy, he had plunged into this same loch. Already lanky at the age of eight, he had splashed and made mayhem in the cove while his three sisters mocked and ambushed him in turn. Three beauties, they had been. Strong-willed just as Hope O'Hara was.

But Ronan had seen their laughter fade. He had seen the English take them, and even now he remembered their screams and the curses, so abruptly silenced. Tied with rope and marched over the hill like cattle, taken God knew where. And nothing he or any other MacLeod man could do to save them.

No more laughing then. No more sparkling eyes.

The dark memories clung as he broke the surface. Sputtering, he threw back his head. Did the English still fight the clans now? he wondered. Were the stones of the glens still dark with Highland blood?

If so, God help them.

When he turned, the woman was still on the bank, her shoulders stiff as steel. "I'm not leaving. You may be stubborn, but I'm more stubborn. If you swim away, I'll just follow you."

Humor warred with irritation. For such a small woman, she would task a Norman sausage butcher, so she would. "What answers do you want of me?"

"Why you left, for one. Make it the truth this time."

Did he know what the truth was? And could she bear it if he told her?

MacLeod studied the rocky bank. The truth was, he felt no comfort being near her. The truth was that he didn't *want* to feel her beauty eating into his very soul. He had enough trouble struggling to control his reason without *her* to assault his senses.

"One man's truth may be another man's lies. They may hurt more than you know."

"I'll risk it."

"Perhaps I will not." It was too soon to speak of what had happened. He needed time to understand for himself first.

But she sat down on the bank, her eyes unflinching. "I'm here to stay. A little naked skin isn't going to scare me away."

He drew a harsh breath. "It would be safer if you left."

"Safer for whom?" She danced on the edge of a flame, he thought. And like most women, she was unaware of her danger.

But she could be bested.

He stood up slowly, water lapping at his chest. "You still choose to stay?"

Her cheeks flamed, but she did not move, fully resolute. MacLeod could not help but admire her. By heaven, she was a stubborn sort of female.

So be it. She would see where her stubbornness led her.

Her eyes flickered toward his chest—then lower. When he realized where she was looking, his mouth twisted in a hard grin. So the lady was curious, was she? If so, it would be her undoing. "Are you so anxious to inspect my limbs?"

New color swept into her face, but she stared him down. "I might be—*if* you had anything worth looking at, which you don't. In fact, I've seen better muscle definition on a sumo wrestler."

MacLeod had no idea what a sumo was, but he recognized an insult when he heard it. His dark brow rose. "You wound me."

She snorted. "Even a Mack truck couldn't wound *you*."

"What is—"

"Never mind."

Ronan MacLeod suddenly knew she was lying. Perhaps it was because her cheeks flamed red, like a choirboy's in a brothel. Or perhaps it was the way her eyes kept slanting toward the water where it lapped at his waist.

Curious, the woman was. He did not displease her. But she was a complete innocent, judging by her restless, uneasy movements.

The knowledge sent heat coursing to his half-frozen limbs. "You have studied many men?"

She crossed her arms, all defiance. "Enough to know what's good when I see it."

"And how many men is that, Hope O'Hara?"

She looked out over the water, her voice low and breathless. Was the memory of a man's heated touch with her even now?

Something like envy tightened his throat.

"Dozens, that's how many."

As a liar, she was appalling. But as a woman, she was entrancing beyond measure. MacLeod's curiosity grew. "And you took these men as lovers after you made your…observations?"

"That's none of your business."

"Perhaps not." His lips pursed. "You found them pleasurable?"

More color snapped across her cheeks. "Absolutely. Let me tell you, I had *huge* pleasure. *Incredible* pleasure."

"You observed them in groups, did you? Was it three at a time? Four? Twenty?"

She glared at him. "I don't remember." She shifted from side to side, frowning. "It was a while ago."

"How long past?"

"Two years—three. I forget."

He grinned. He couldn't help it.

"And what is that silly smile supposed to mean?"

"If they had been MacLeod men, you would *not* have lost the memory so easily."

"Says you. All men get boring after a while. All those nights. All those amazing bodies." She gave an airy wave. "Who can even keep track?"

For a woman who was as skittish as a colt on spring ice, she claimed the worst sort of depravities. She could not even lie without flushing the color of new roses. Yes, she was a pitiful liar.

And he was charmed beyond description.

She dressed like a man, worked like a man, thought like a man. She even knew how to *argue* like a man. MacLeod bit back a laugh. She was a woman to make a man's temper climb and his pulse race. He only wished he had met her in his own time.

The wind ruffled her strange, boyish cap of chestnut curls, sending fresh color through her cheeks. Though her leggings were odd, they hugged her slender legs most pleasantly.

The thought of her body was an instant mistake. Even in the icy water he was not immune to desire, MacLeod discovered. But there could be no future between this woman and himself. He might be tossed back into his own time at any moment, as swiftly as he had come. By all honor, this sudden heat singing through his limbs could come to naught.

His reason knew that.

His body did not.

And soon she would see the evidence of his desire most clearly.

She wriggled restlessly. "Stop staring at me."

"If you wish." But he could no more master his urge to stare than he could walk on water. In this chaotic, unfamiliar world, she was life and color to him.

Sand swept around his feet, mottling the crystal water. Like those tiny, swirling grains, he was tossed adrift, his future unclear. Somehow he sensed that she held the clue to the mystery of his arrival here.

"Why did you leave the kitchen? What were you so afraid of?"

"I saw things I did not wish to see."

"What kind of things?"

"Do you hound a man always, giving him no peace?"

"I have to know. In a way you're my responsibility now," she said tensely.

A MacLeod was no one's responsibility but his own, by heaven. Especially not a woman's. "I have no answers to give you, woman! All is loss and confusion." MacLeod closed his eyes. He heard water gurgle past, relentless as time in its passage. "Mad, that makes me. A very fool. Laugh at me as you will."

Her eyes darkened. "I'm not laughing."

"Do you believe me then? Do you accept that Glenbrae is mine?"

She shook her head slowly. "How can I?"

But he wanted her to believe him. It hurt to feel how much he wanted that. MacLeod hit the water hard and sent silver beads flying. "Is it the truth you want? I am fit of mind and body, this is my truth. I have finally come home to the glens—only to find I've come centuries too late. The year, *my year,* is 1298." He glared at Hope. "Hold your sides and laugh. *I* would did I hear such a wild tale."

But she did not laugh. "You know it can't be true. People don't leap through time. Einstein said it was possible, of course. Theoretically."

MacLeod stiffened. "Then take me to this Einstein. Maybe he can send me back."

Hope made a soft, exasperated sound. "Einstein is dead."

Another blow. "He was a great magician, this Einstein?"

"No, he was a nuclear physicist."

Again she spoke in riddles. "I understand none of this," he said harshly. "Why do you raise possibilities, only to destroy them?"

Her head tilted. "Maybe you're confused from the storm. After all, that plank did crash down on your head after you caught me...."

"'Tis no dream I am having, woman! I *know* the year and I have all my wits sound in my head. The loch, the glen, even that house on the hill—all were present and real when I left in the night. Only their age has changed."

He dared her to throw back her head and roar at his misbegotten story.

But she did not. Her expression only grew graver. "I'm worried about you."

"I do not need your pity."

Her head tilted. "I said 'worry,' not 'pity.' There's a major difference."

Not to him. He had never known a woman's worry, nor her concern. Feeling them now left him in greater confusion.

The Scotsman muttered a rough phrase in Gaelic. "What I say appears impossible. Yet I also know I am here beside you, locked in a time that is not my own."

She made no answer. MacLeod knew that there was no answer to give. He could not fault her for the disbelief in her eyes.

Arguing, too, was pointless.

He turned away, his knee throbbing from the cold. To distract himself, he bent low, scooped up sand from the loch's bottom, and scrubbed his back.

"What are you doing now?"

"Washing."

"That's the stupidest thing I've ever heard. You're turning blue in there."

"It is my choice. Besides, the water is bonny." He tried to ignore how his jaw clenched against the chill seeping into his bones. "'Tis the company which does naught for my temper."

"Don't be an idiot, MacLeod. Come back to the house."

He slung another handful of sand onto his shoulder. What answers were there for him in the bright, strange rooms? "I will stay here."

"And freeze to death, no doubt."

"I can freeze as I choose," MacLeod thundered. "This is my land. At least it *was* my land," he added grimly.

"You'll be lost by dark. Or maybe you'll break your neck when you fall off the cliff."

"Sorry I am to bother you, lady. When next I ride through time, I shall try to choose a more convenient hour and place to do it."

"That's *not* what I meant."

"No? You do not hear a word I say. You do not listen because it makes you uncomfortable. You look at me and feel pure terror. I can see it clearly in your eyes."

She blinked. Again the fear was there, just as he had said.

MacLeod finished scrubbing his back, then turned to wash his chest. The air between them shimmered with tension.

He dropped the last of a handful of sand. "I'm coming out now."

Hope glared back at him, her body rigid.

"Very well." MacLeod waded toward the bank. "If you wish to fill your eyes with all of me, then remain."

Two bright spots of color raced into her cheeks. "You'd like that, wouldn't you? You enjoy being a bastard."

"I am wedlock born, woman. Were you a man, you would regret those words."

"I can hardly contain my terror, Your Worthiness." His patterned wool sailed through the air and struck him full in the face.

MacLeod barely managed to catch one end before the whole length tumbled into the water. Cocky wench.

His throbbing leg, empty stomach and growing frustration made him more reckless than usual. Since she thought his behavior crude, let him convince her of the fact now.

Grinning, he tossed the bright fabric over his shoulder, where it fell to one hip. His gaze never left her face as he strode from the loch, up the bank and directly toward her, naked as the day God made him.

Now let us see who would stay and who will bolt, the Crusader thought.

CHAPTER NINE

HOPE TOOK A STRANGLED breath and fought to keep her gaze on MacLeod's face.

It was a magnificent face, she admitted. Angular and sharp, his cheekbones were washed with color. Pride shimmered in his eyes, and his long hair lay slick and dark down his neck.

He could have been the twin of the man in the painting above the stairs, she realized. Was it possible his fantastic story was true? How else could she explain his confusion, his strange garb and his uncanny knowledge of the house?

Even now he stood with rigid arrogance, lord of his lands. Only they weren't *his* lands, they were hers, and he was going to have to accept that—along with the true date.

Her head began to pound. There was no sense trying to understand the inexplicable. Meanwhile he seemed just as confused as she was.

The water slapped gently at her feet. In spite of her irritation, Hope was drawn to the man, touched by his uncertainty and pain.

Unconsciously her gaze strayed lower, past the taut stomach ridged with muscle, past the snug hips, down where water hung in tiny beads that glittered below his navel.

Bad idea.

The man was gorgeous. Drop-dead gorgeous. And there was something heartbreakingly *lost* about him, even in his anger.

Hope didn't like the wave of heat uncurling through her chest. So what if he was good-looking? She considered herself a liberated twentieth-century woman. She knew how the human body worked and she understood the mechanics of sexual arousal in precise detail. But seeing a man of such stunning endowment up close was a shock. He was so alive, so complex.

So confused.

Something blocked her throat. *The only one confused here is you,* a voice warned. Ronan MacLeod was about as helpless as a gorilla on steroids. Almost as ill-tempered, too.

You can't afford to be protective, she thought. *Not when you know next to nothing about the man.*

Yet she continued to stand, continued to stare. Hope had to admit she was enjoying the view, every muscled inch of it, even if he was freezing to death in that icy water.

"Do you find the sight of me pleasurable, woman?"

Hope swallowed. One second the man was confused, the next he was all rottweiler.

"Not particularly." As a lie, it was spectacular, but he didn't have to know that. She spun about and started for the house. "Go on and freeze, if you insist. Drown in the loch. Get lost in the peat bog." With every word her heart hammered harder. "Break your neck up there on the cliffs. It makes no difference to me," she said unsteadily. "I don't c-care a bit, understand?"

In one pace he caught up with her and pulled her around to face him. "*Pie Jesu,* you are crying."

Emotion left her trembling. "So what if I am?" She fought vainly to pull away.

"You are crying for me?" MacLeod asked.

"Don't let it go to your head. I'd cry for anyone who looked as lost as you did when I came out here. And it doesn't mean a thing, understand?" Hope ignored the feel of his hands on her shoulders. She ignored the damp wool crushed against her chest and the rigid wall of muscles beneath. "I m-might as well be crying for a lost puppy or a bird with a broken wing. And as for that *ridiculous* story you told me about being lost in time—"

The madness seized MacLeod before he could control it. All he knew was that she was trembling against him and that the tears on her cheeks were for him.

For *him.*

He pulled her against him in midsentence. A hardened soldier, he knew when to argue and when to storm enemy terrain.

He stormed now.

He breached every defense. Hands rigid, he caught her shoulders and lifted her face to his. She was still arguing when he slid his fingers into that piquant cap of shining chestnut hair and kissed her.

Her scent filled his senses, spring meadows after soft rain. Closing his eyes, he sealed his mouth to hers, hunger driving away all subtlety and restraint. He had to have the taste of her, deep and long. He had to have her against his mouth *now.*

She shivered—and then her lips opened. In that second Ronan MacLeod became the besieged.

By all the saints, she was sweet and achingly soft. Her mouth moved against his, driving his pulse to madness, and he groaned when he felt her breasts harden, small and firm, thrusting against his chest. He ached to explore the taut red tips, to pull them against his teeth and make her whimper with the same damnable need he was feeling.

MacLeod felt his blood stir. He swore to let her go in a few more seconds. Maybe then he wouldn't smell her, wouldn't want her so much that he couldn't draw a normal breath.

He stared down. She was all flushed cheeks and gleaming eyes. She looked…

Dazed. Overwhelmed.

He heard her small moan, but the sheen of desire in her eyes told MacLeod the whimper came from pleasure, not fear.

It was her hands that caught his face and drew him back to her. And it was she who made a broken sound of need when his lips opened over hers again.

She tasted like the cider his mother had prepared when he was a boy, a blend of fruit, heather and a dozen subtle herbs. The result was just as smooth, just as flawless.

MacLeod didn't move, lost in the sliding textures of the kiss. She moved beneath him, their breaths mingling as his fingers sifted through her smooth hair. Desire left him dizzy as her mouth trembled, opening to his tongue.

He nearly took her then, there beside the icy loch with her odd clothes in shreds beneath them. God knew he wanted to.

Except for the first time in his adult life, Ronan MacLeod had tasted tenderness from a woman, and it shocked him. This woman did not fear him or goad him to violence. She baited him, confused him, intrigued him—but as a complete equal.

The realization stunned him.

Time staggered. All the world seemed to halt while the air thickened, heavy with the need that rose between them.

MacLeod had never *needed* a woman before. A warrior needed a battle horse, a sword and armor, but not a woman. Conquests had been simple, uncomplicated bouts of heat and skin, meant only to dim the fire of physical urges. No woman had ever asked for more from him. No woman had ever dared.

But this one would. Already she leaned into his touch and smoothed the old marks on his back with her soft fingers. Yes, this woman would want answers and honor and a lifetime of touching. She would ask for nothing less than his very soul.

And MacLeod sensed he would blindly give it to her.

He lowered his head and took her mouth again, this time

with exquisite skill. He used all the knowledge learned with the wrong women, praying that he pleased her well. Somehow, pleasing Hope O'Hara had become infinitely more important than satisfying his own desires.

With a sigh, she moved against him, pliant and strong. Her response left MacLeod dizzy and utterly disarmed. Blindly he traced the arch of her lower lip and the velvet of her mouth, storing away every detail.

Caught in the intensity of the kiss, he forgot the need to balance his weight on his good knee. Suddenly pain burned up his thigh and his muscles locked.

He bit off a curse, loath to break the contact when the feel of her was still so new. But pain flared anew, jolting up his leg. MacLeod knew what came next would be far worse.

"You're sheet-white, MacLeod." Hope laughed unsteadily. "I've never known my kiss to do *that* before."

How wrong she was. Her kiss could sway kings and topple empires, he thought. She could strike fire and work the grandest miracles.

Maybe she already had. He was not a man who had expected to find tenderness in a woman's touch, yet here he had found tenderness and more.

Miracles and more.

He lifted her chin slowly, surprised at his own gentleness. The King's Wolf was *not* a gentle man. In truth, he was a killer on three continents.

And yet he touched this one woman as if she were as fragile as the Venetian glass globe on her desk. He found he could do nothing else.

A stab of pain pulled him back to his senses. He gritted his teeth, swaying slightly.

"Are you sure you're okay?" The concern in her eyes was unmistakable.

Struck by fresh waves of pain, he tried to pull away, but Hope slid a hand around his waist.

MacLeod muttered an oath and stepped back, but she was right behind him, her fingers digging into his waist. "What are you doing, woman?"

"I'm helping you."

"I need no help," he said through gritted teeth while claws of fire tore up his leg. But MacLeod refused to heed them. Stiffly he pushed at her hands. "I am simply cold."

"Stop being so damned macho, will you? Anyone can see that you're in real pain. You can barely stand up."

"I can stand. I can also walk unaided."

"Yeah, right. If you ask me, that medieval-knight routine is getting old."

Through his pain, her words struck him dumb.

Was this all his honor amounted to, words tossed casually from her lips and dismissed? Could she not see it was all he knew—his very life?

"I will manage alone, as I have always managed before," he said darkly.

"This time you have someone to help you." She slid her arm farther around his waist. "Anyone who wasn't so busy being an idiot could see that."

"Are you naming me an idiot, madam?"

She smiled faintly. "I expect I am."

In spite of his pain, his mouth took on an answering grin. No other woman would dare say such a thing to the King's Wolf. Hope O'Hara had no idea of her danger.

It pleased MacLeod intensely that she did not.

He eased more of his weight onto her shoulder, expecting a protest, but he heard none. Her hands were warm and surprisingly strong and the warm brush of her hip at his thigh was almost enough to make him forget his pain.

"You don't have to hold back, you know. I can take more of your weight."

"Then we would both be on the ground."

"Are you calling me a weakling?"

"Nothing of the sort. You have an exceptional strength. For a woman, that is."

She rolled her eyes. "Gloria Steinem would have you for breakfast."

He studied her curiously. "What is a Gloriasteinem?"

She shook her head. "Forget it. Just forget it."

"Then tell me what manner of sport you pursue. Hawking? Hunting?"

She strained to hold him upright. "Try jogging. Four miles every day."

"Jogging? What manner of sport is that?"

"Running. You slam one foot ahead of the other and make loud, panting noises."

His brow furrowed. "Running from whom?"

"Oh, you're good, MacLeod. You're *very* good." She pressed closer, taking more of his weight.

The touch of her made his head spin. "I do not understand you." By honor, he was forgetting everything but the feel of her body sliding against his. How did she rob him of his wits like this?

"I don't understand either," she muttered. "But we have to get back into the house before we're both soaked. Only a complete idiot would go swimming in late November."

His brow rose. "I was wrong before."

They tottered up the bank, shoulder to shoulder. "Wrong about what?"

"You do not argue like a Bedouin with his camel. You are far worse. You would frighten even a Saracen with your tongue."

As she struggled beneath his weight, Hope hid a smile. She realized she enjoyed arguing with Ronan MacLeod. There had been no one to argue with since her uncle had died three years before.

Dermot O'Hara had opened a whole new world to her when she was thirteen. Desperately trying to come to grips with the trauma of losing her parents and the roller-coaster onset of teenage years, she had swung between tears and withdrawal. When all of his other efforts had failed, her uncle had teased her to wrath. They had traded insults and ingenious threats nonstop for nearly an hour and then Hope had collapsed into wild laughter.

Everything had changed between them after that. Before they were strangers. Afterward they were family.

Her uncle had taught her the value of a good argument and its two unshakable rules: no hitting below the belt and no harboring grudges later.

Too few people knew how to argue properly. It wasn't a matter of temper, after all. Good arguing required wit, patience. Panache.

Hope was starting to think MacLeod just might make a decent sparring partner once he got over this little delusion that he had been shot out of the thirteenth century.

Assuming *she* could keep her eyes off that gorgeous body of his.

"So, MacLeod, how long have you had this problem?"

"What problem?"

"The problem with your leg, of course."

He shrugged. "Long enough."

"Was it some kind of accident?"

"No."

"Then what did this to you?"

His jaw hardened. "Men did."

"Men. That's all you're going to say?"

He gave another shrug.

"Is getting answers out of you always like pulling teeth? I have news for you, there's nothing shameful about having an old injury."

MacLeod could not agree. Weakness shamed any knight. To discuss such weaknesses was unthinkable, even with a woman.

Especially with a woman.

He drew an irritated breath, looking at the dense woods just below the cliffs. "It happened up there." Memories flashed in his head: shouting and the glint of metal. Cries of fury that turned to screams. Dark and heavy, the images churned up inside him.

He did not want to remember. Not any of it.

The wind had risen, sending whitecaps across the water, and thanks to their contact, the woman was nearly as damp as he was. He felt her shiver. They would have to find a way out of the wind soon, assuming he could still walk.

"Talk to me, MacLeod."

He gritted his teeth and forced his legs over the rocky slope. He didn't want to talk. He certainly didn't want to remember. He had been an angry, confused boy when he'd left this glen, and the memories still hurt.

"I'm waiting."

He didn't mean to answer her, but somehow the words slid out. "They came before dawn, and there was no chance for us. Not even time for running, though my father would never have considered such a course."

"You were attacked?" she repeated uncertainly.

"I was twelve that summer." His jaw clenched and he felt the old bleak waves of fury. "Only a few of the MacLeod men were here. The rest had gone north for a wedding, something the cursed Sassenachs seemed to know full well." Suddenly his eyes hardened. "You are English?"

"Not me. I'm American. Yankee born and bred."

"What does this mean?"

"America. You know, that big country across the ocean. New York, Los Angeles, Chicago."

He frowned, waiting for her to say words that made sense.

"The Boston tea party and no taxation without representation?" She sighed. "Let's just say that we're the ones who fought England and won."

"You did?" MacLeod was genuinely impressed. "How?"

"Stop trying to change the subject. What happened to you next?"

He struggled up the rocky slope, each step a torment. "More of the same," he said stonily.

"More of the same *what?*"

"Fighting. Bleeding. Dying." He took a hard breath. "After their killing was done, they took my sisters." He stared at the mist drifting in a chill plume above the hills. "An English crossbow slit my knee that day."

She gasped. "So English soldiers…did this to you?"

"They enjoyed seeing me hobbled, but not dead. Killing me would have taken away their pleasure."

"But what good were you to them wounded?"

"I was sport. Young prey, better than any stag." He laughed once, a short, flat sound. "Besides, there was no time for healing. We were on the march before dusk, while the village still burned behind us."

"Why didn't you call someone to help?"

Call? No one would have heard. No one was left to hear. Clearly she understood nothing. Perhaps there was no more war in her time. "You are certain you are not English?"

"Absolutely. Now tell me what you did next."

"I could do nothing. It was war, and I was taken for Edward's army."

She came to a dead halt, frowning. "Edward?" she repeated softly. "As in King Edward? But that was…centuries ago."

"So you have told me."

MacLeod's eyes narrowed on the dense trees above the stone fence. Light flickered for a moment, then winked out. A moment later he saw two shapes moving dimly in the shadows.

Not cattle.

Not deer.

For the past five minutes they had moved as he moved, keeping equal distance but never revealing themselves.

Only men did that. And such men were no friends.

"Are you expecting travelers at Glenbrae?"

"Maybe some German students due tomorrow later in the day. And there is a club meeting scheduled at the house. No one else." She frowned. "Why?"

"No matter." He could not tell her they were being watched, stalked like deer from the forest. She would only think it more of his mad imaginings. At the moment, his greatest concern was seeing her safely back to the house.

Maybe it was English soldiers who stalked them, he thought grimly. Were he alone, he would have enjoyed the hunt. But not when protecting her was his first duty.

He cursed himself for staying so long in the loch. Her safety was his only duty now. As a knight, he had sworn to protect all women.

Hope stared at him. Maybe it was her theta waves run amok. Maybe it was just her hormones. For whatever reason, she was actually starting to *believe* the man. And that was dangerous when she had too many problems of her own.

They were crossing a mound of boulders when she felt him falter. She looked down and saw that his leg was rigid. With every step the muscles above his knee knotted, straining beneath the skin. He had to be in agony.

She stopped short. "Why didn't you tell me?"

"I will endure."

"Endure? You can't keep going on that leg. We'll just stop here until you—"

"Not here."

"And why not?"

MacLeod scanned the rocky bank and the small stone house up the slope. "What is that place?" He pointed awkwardly.

"A shed for local fisherman. They store their gear inside when the salmon are running. But—"

"It will do." He hobbled forward.

"Do for *what?*"

"A place to rest."

Her eyes narrowed. "What aren't you telling me, MacLeod?"

Up the hills the shadows moved again, slinking within the greater darkness of the forest, and MacLeod felt another cold stab of warning.

They were exposed, undefended. There was no time for argument or negotiation. "We will go up there."

"I'm staying right here," Hope said firmly. "We'll wait until you feel better."

"Not *here.*" He pulled her the last steps up the hill toward the rough building, then shoved open the door and sank down on an uneven pine bench. His face was rigid with pain as he turned away to rub his knee.

His thigh was an agony of rebelling muscles in need of rest and blessed heat. But there was no time for rest. Every instinct warned that the woman was in danger.

Was this why he had been brought to her time?

He worked one hand down his knee in stony silence. Even then he kept an eye on the open doorway, watching for any unexpected movement.

"Did anyone ever tell you that your ego is roughly the size of Siberia?"

"No." He had no idea what she was talking about.

"Consider yourself told." She sat beside him and brushed away his fingers. "Now, stop fighting."

He could never stop fighting, MacLeod thought. It was nearly all he knew. He flinched at her touch, though her hands were light. Each movement was a dangerous distraction that made him soft, and life had taught him that any softness was dangerous.

"Relax," she ordered as her hands slid over his leg.

He shifted slightly so that he had a clear view of the open

doorway and the slope beyond. From here he could see any movement in the trees.

He forced back a groan of pleasure at the slide of her hands. Too warm. Too soft. A man could drown in such softness. "Arguing with you is like arguing with a Vatican prelate."

"A pretty compliment, Mr. MacLeod."

"It was no compliment, I assure you." Against all his efforts, a sigh hissed between his teeth. She was skilled in her touch. Already some of his pain had left him. Much more and he would be a boneless mass of no use for anything. "You have worked as a healer?"

"My uncle was ill at the end of his life." Hope frowned. "It was a slow and painful way to die. Massages were the only thing that gave him any relief."

"He was fortunate that your hands are gentle."

"I only wish I could have done more." Her voice wavered. "All I could do was watch him fade away. Every day I lost a little more of him, but he never complained, not once." She blinked hard. "I don't know how we got onto this topic."

"You loved him greatly."

"Everyone did. I'd lost my parents years before, and I was so sure Uncle Dermot would live forever." She smiled sadly. "He was always so busy, so noisy. He could fill a room all by himself. And he taught me everything I know about books."

"Books? He was a monkish man, your uncle?"

"Hardly. He liked nothing more than a fine cognac and a big cigar. Endless arguments, we had over that, especially when his heart began to show the strain. And how he loved his collections. Fine leather, smoothed by centuries of hands, was worth more than diamonds, he said. Fragile pages were treasures beyond all price." Her eyes rose, gazing at something seen only in her memory. "He could tell you everything about inks and papers. He could talk for hours about stitching and binding, folios and first editions. He was a genius at details. And yet at the end, after his last stroke, he couldn't see anything," she said bitterly.

"Death is seldom at a time of our choosing. At least he died in the company of someone he loved. A man could do worse." MacLeod thought of fellow soldiers fallen far from home, with no one to mourn or mark their graves.

Yes, a man could do far worse.

He sank back against the wall, watching the open doorway.

"Have you had a doctor look at your leg?"

"A leech?" He grimaced. "All they know is how to spill blood and mutter learned phrases into their beards. In Jerusalem, Damascus and Venice, they said the same thing. Nothing could be done." He groaned with pleasure as her fingers worked the knotted muscles.

"Rubbish. What you *need* is a good orthopedist. Maybe laser surgery would help."

The strange words drifted over MacLeod, sounds with no meaning. Weakness was for others, not for him. He understood neither her fussing nor her concern. But he admitted that both were becoming highly pleasurable.

He stiffened as a twig snapped somewhere outside up the slope.

"Did I hurt you?"

"No."

"Then why did you just jump?"

MacLeod felt a prickle at his neck. Without doubt they were being watched. An attack could come at any moment.

He turned, searching for a weapon.

"I asked you why—"

MacLeod cut her off. "Be quiet, woman." He checked the lower slope of the hill, surprised she felt no awareness of danger. Outside, the wind whispered around the half-open door and a new uneasiness drove him to his feet. He found a wooden stick and tested its weight in his hands.

"Sit down, MacLeod. You're in no condition to—"

Behind Hope the door clanged shut.

She stood up angrily, hands on her hips. "Hey, who's out there?"

MacLeod lurched toward the door, but even as his fingers met wood, he realized he was too late.

Outside, the metal bolt slid home with an angry crack.

CHAPTER TEN

"PROBABLY JUST THE WIND," Hope muttered. "You sit down, and I'll take care of it."

MacLeod ignored her. Gritting his teeth against the pain at his knee, he seized the metal door handle and shoved upward.

Nothing moved.

"Why doesn't it open?" Hope asked.

"The bolt is cast from the outside," he said grimly. Someone had locked them in.

"It *can't* be locked." Hope pushed away his hands, wrenching at the handle. "I don't understand," she whispered.

Nor did MacLeod. He studied the high stone walls stretching unbroken to the timber roof. There were no windows, only a tiny slit for smoke high overhead. He cursed softly, furious that he had let himself be caught like a gangling whelp of ten. A few minutes of soft conversation had turned him into a witless clod.

But no one and nothing would get past him to harm Hope. They would try at their peril.

"It's *got* to open." Hope was still struggling with the door handle. "There's fishing tackle and a few supplies but nothing else in here. Why should someone come to lock the door?"

MacLeod limped across the room and gently pulled her around to face him. "The bolt will not open, not from inside. We must wait for someone to look for us."

"I'm not waiting. Not in here." She made a low, angry sound and pulled away to pace the floor, her shoulders stiff.

MacLeod saw that she was shivering. He tugged a length of heavy canvas down from a row of pegs on the wall. "Put this around you."

"Don't you dare snap at me," she said tightly.

"It is not a...snap. It is a polite suggestion that you cover yourself before you grow any colder."

"Polite, my eye." Even when he pushed aside her hands and draped the heavy cloth over her shoulders, she continued to shiver. "I *don't* like this."

MacLeod didn't like it either, but the only thing to do was settle back and await discovery by one of her friends. The bolt was too heavy to break, and he had no hope of climbing to the roof hole.

His companion stood stiffly, glaring at the door as if she could open it by sheer force of will.

"There is no reason to stare at the door."

"You don't understand. I can't— I don't—" Her hands clenched at her waist. "I'm not good with this. Not with small spaces and locked doors."

MacLeod saw her hands twisting. His brow rose. "There is nothing to fear. You are safe with me. I give my word."

She laughed wildly. "Safe in this tiny room? The walls could collapse any minute and we would both be crushed." Sweat stood out on her brow as she braced an arm against the door and shoved. "This thing has got to open." She leaned her whole weight forward and shoved fiercely, again and again.

MacLeod added his own weight, though he knew it was useless. With each push the door shivered, but held firm. Solid oak.

Hope still did not stop.

He took her hands and held them tightly. They were tense, shivering, and he slid the canvas down over her shoulders.

"Not ten men could break such a bolt. You must accept that you will be safe with me. I will do you no harm."

"It's n-not you I'm worried about." She drew a jerky breath.

"There is space enough for both of us."

"No, you don't understand," Hope whispered. "No one knows. I was ashamed to tell anyone."

"To tell what?"

Her eyes were dark with panic. "I...I can't say it."

MacLeod stroked back a curve of her hair and felt tears on her face. By heaven, she was crying. "I will guard your secret. I have held many."

"Royal secrets and state intrigue?" Her voice shook. "I don't believe it."

"Believe as you like. But you will sit beside me until you are warm."

"I won't *be* warm. I won't be able to rest. Not here." She stared at the narrow stone walls, then across at the locked door. "Oh, God, it's locked. I'm trapped in here...." Her breath came fast and harsh.

"Hope." He turned her face toward him. "Breathe slowly."

After a moment, she did as he ordered. Then he pulled her down beside him on the rough bench. She was still too tense, too cold.

"I can't bear being in a tiny room." She closed her eyes, shuddering. "I...I go to pieces."

"To pieces?"

"Fall apart," she said shakily. "Lose my head."

He traced her forehead. "And it is such a nice head."

"I'm being serious here, M-MacLeod."

Too serious for his understanding. It was only a locked door. The danger lay outside it. But he waited, patient, giving her time to explain. Maybe then he could understand.

She sniffed, brushed at her cheek as another tear slid from her eye. "I don't want anyone else to know."

He bent his head. "I will tell no one."

She relaxed slightly, leaning against his shoulder. "It's not the locked door or even the room that bothers me. Some part of me knows that. The doctors…the experts say it's transferred trauma from something that happened to me when I was thirteen…"

Silently MacLeod slid one arm around her rigid shoulders. What secret could hold such pain? Had she been harmed, violated? If so, he would find the jackal and cut out his black heart.

He steeled himself to hear the worst, hating how her hands shook and her breath came fast and sharp. "First breathe deeply. Then tell me all of it."

She drew a slow breath. "I was visiting my uncle when the news came. It was early afternoon and I still remember it was raining, big, heavy drops that hammered at the glass. I was looking for an old book in his upstairs closet." Her eyes closed and she pressed closer, as if seeking his heat, one animal to another. "It was so quiet that day, so still. At first…" Her hands twisted, twisted.

She was seeing a dark place, MacLeod realized. A place with images too painful to bear.

He didn't touch her, didn't soothe her, though he yearned to do both. It was better for her to finish the tale first. "Breathe," he ordered.

She swallowed, then drew a jerky breath.

"Now tell the rest."

"It was my parents…they were gone. There was a boating accident in the Mediterranean." She swallowed hard. "It was the day before my birthday."

There was more, he sensed. Something that hurt even more cruelly. He wanted to hold her, to warm her and make her forget the darkness of her past.

But it was not his right.

"I wasn't supposed to hear, of course. The lawyer came

to notify my uncle, but I was just up the stairs. I heard everything…." Tears slicked her cheeks. She stared at the walls, making no move to push the tears away.

MacLeod said nothing, feeling helpless at her pain. "What did you hear?"

"How they died." Her eyes shimmered, haunted. "They had been drinking. Fighting…" She made a flat, angry sound, brushing at her cheeks. "The door was open, and I heard everything. All I could think of was that I was alone. Really alone this time. It wasn't just another long vacation to Greece or shopping cruise to Hong Kong." She stared blindly at her locked hands. "Sometimes I even forget what they looked like. My own parents." Again her breath went ragged.

"Breathe, *mo cridhe*," he whispered.

She shook her head. "I have to tell it all, now that I've started. For hours I sat against the wall, certain if I moved, something even more terrible would happen. I waited for someone to come. I waited and waited and I couldn't speak, not one sound. It seemed like hours—a lifetime. Now I'm locked in again. I'm waiting, just like then. Waiting…"

"Not like then," MacLeod said fiercely, cradling her cold, wet face. "There is no terrible news to come. You are warm here. Safe." He pulled her into the curve of his chest and stroked her shining hair, sickened that he had not understood sooner.

No wonder the locked door had fed her fears.

"Your friends will come. Think of that instead of the past. And also breathe."

She drew in air with shaky gulps. "I have to be told to breathe. How p-pathetic."

His hands tightened on her face. He fought the image of how her mouth would feel against him now and was dishonored by the thought.

She pulled the canvas cloth tighter around her shoulders. "What do we do now?"

"Talk, since you have begun." He was finding it amazingly pleasant to hold a woman this way. There had never been time for talking before. Or for listening. No time for anything except surviving.

His fingers toyed with a curl at her ear. "Tell me what happened when they found you."

"You truly want to know?"

"If not, I would not ask."

Hope sighed and rested her cheek on his shoulder. "My uncle came. He didn't try to make me move. He just… talked. And talked, while the rain hammered on."

MacLeod had to smile at the image of the two of them. Her uncle must have been a wise man. "What did he say?"

"He told me about carrots. About books and ducks in the rain. About boats and cars and…dying." She swallowed. "Then he told me they were never coming back, but that I would stay with him now. All the time. Just the two of us." She gave a soft whimper. "Oh, God, how I miss him."

A very wise man. A very lucky man, too, MacLeod thought. He let his fingers slide through her hair. Her breath was steadier now and he was warm with the touch of her, warm with the press of her body.

And as her hair stirred against his cheek, the Scotsman discovered a new kind of pain that had nothing to do with old sword wounds.

Suddenly her scent tested his sanity. Heat snapped, racing wherever their bodies met. Each contact tightened muscles he had always prided himself on being able to control.

But with this woman Ronan MacLeod found that control was a thing of memory.

He did not move. She needed the comfort of another body, and he could not refuse her—even when his own needs grew overpowering.

"What's wrong?"

He tried to appear calm and brotherly. "Why do you ask?"

"You look pale, the same way you did outside. Is it your knee again?" She bent forward, running her hand over the rigid muscles.

Other muscles answered, hard with rising demand. "No," he grated. "I am not in pain." Not the pain she spoke of.

"You don't look fine. You look like a truck just ran over you."

MacLeod had no idea what the word *truck* meant. He felt only as if something big and noisy had struck him down. The brush of her fingers, so close to his groin, was consuming the last shreds of his control.

"Hope."

"You can tell me what's wrong," she whispered, her eyes huge in the half-light. "Did I say something, do something?"

MacLeod sighed. There could be no secrets from her. She was recklessly honest, and perhaps that was part of why she fascinated him. Honesty was not a quality he had often met, and she had enough for ten men. "The pain is not at my knee," he muttered.

Her hands moved, each stroke killing him with pleasure. An inch higher and he would die.

"Not at your knee? But you said before that—" A wave of color raced across her cheeks. "Oh." She swallowed, her eyes flickering midway down his kilt. "That."

"That," he said gravely.

She sat back, staring intently at her hands. "I…I'm sorry. I didn't think."

"There is no reason for apology."

"I'll stop. I don't want to make things any…harder for you." She started to stand up, her face bleak. "When will someone open that door? Why don't they come *now*, before I make a bigger fool of myself?"

He caught her hand, surprising himself as much as her. "Do not stop."

"But you just said— I mean, you look as if—"

"I am no callow youth, Hope. I will not be driven witless by a man's need."

Hope stared at him.

A man's need. Did she truly stir this man so deeply, she who had never shown any great aptitude with body parts and uncomplicated attachments?

She searched for the answer in his face, in his tense jaw, in the heat that shimmered in those extraordinary, changeable eyes of his.

Maybe it was the knowledge of his need that sent heat uncurling through her. Beneath her hand, his skin felt hot and tight, and she wondered what the rest of him would feel like. She coughed sharply, shocked by the hot image of his body spread beneath hers in the grip of passion.

Need burned, sent blood racing through her face. It was his turn to touch her face questioningly. "Something frets you?"

Fret wasn't the word for it, Hope thought bleakly. She was locked in a shed, struggling with cruel memories she had never been able to put behind her. And to top it off, she...

Wanted.

That was the only word for this hot, helpless yearning. She had never...*wanted* like this before.

She closed her eyes, trying to think straight. The gentle rhythm of his palm at her neck was making her dizzy. There was no excuse for making a *thing* out of this. It wasn't as if there hadn't been other men in her life.

But she'd never let any of them get half so close, Hope admitted. She'd never wanted to. And not a single one had ever sent her common sense flying out the window like this man did.

"You are afraid?"

She shook her head.

"Cold?" His hand slid up and down her arm, reviving circulation that needed no such assistance. Now she was burning up, getting hotter each time his hand moved.

"Come closer," he ordered.

If she moved closer, she would die, Hope thought. She tried not to look at his mouth, tried not to think how his body would feel against hers. "I—I have something to tell you," she blurted.

"Then tell me. I will keep your secrets."

He was grave. Too grave, she thought. Too *gentle*.

"I'm not good at this, not good with men." She looked away, anywhere but his eyes. Awkward or not, she had to tell him. He had to understand that getting involved with her would be a colossal mistake.

"Not good with what men?"

"Any men," she said breathlessly. She watched her hands open and close. "What I told you before was a lie. I can't seem to keep things light. I talk too much, ask too many questions, and I never know where to put my hands." She gnawed at her lip. "And afterward, when it's over, I never can pretend that…"

He brought her palm slowly to his mouth. "Pretend what?"

She blinked, trying to remember. "That it meant nothing. That it was just heat, just two bodies, four hands, and… heat." Her eyes shimmered. "I mean, it's supposed to *mean* something, isn't it? It's supposed to make you feel different, changed. Linked. Flesh of my flesh."

He planted a gentle row of kisses down her neck, melting acres of nerve ends beneath her hair.

"What…are you doing?"

He nipped her skin, then slid his teeth across the sensitive mound at the base of her palm. "Pleasing you."

"Don't," she whispered. "I can't think when you do that, and I'm being serious here."

"I can see that."

She shivered as his mouth did slow, carnal things that made her pulse spike. "Don't *do* that. I'm trying to make you see why men want nothing to do with me, MacLeod."

No answer.

"It won't work." Oh, God, it felt so good. So right. "It's got to stop." She wished her voice weren't so throaty, so breathless. "This is about honor, after all." She closed her eyes as he kissed the inside of her wrist. "It's a disclosure thing. You need to know the facts...." She whimpered as he found the tender hollow on the inside of her elbow and kissed it slowly.

As if they had all the time in the world. As if he had been waiting for her forever.

"Then tell me the...facts."

Vulnerable, cherished, she came apart inside, muscle by muscle. Felt her heart spin. "I'm...talking too much."

He laughed against her skin. "I like to hear you talk."

"I'm a grown woman, a responsible adult with a business to run. I don't know you, and you know nothing about me." She frowned, staring into those keen eyes, now silver, now gray. "So why...*why* can I think of nothing else but kissing you until neither of us can think straight?"

"The answer to that is easy." MacLeod's eyes narrowed. "By honor, I am thinking of exactly the same thing."

CHAPTER ELEVEN

"YOU...ARE?"

He nodded and the world tilted.

"So," she whispered, "we're talking about a kiss here? Just a kiss?"

A muscle flashed at his jaw. "We're talking about whatever you wish to give."

Clever man. "Why do I suspect you're a killer negotiator, MacLeod?"

"I have negotiated on several occasions." Heat flickered in his eyes.

His half smile set warning bells clanging. Hope was positive that this man's diplomatic skills were top-notch. He had certainly managed to disarm her in a matter of hours.

So he was throwing down the gauntlet, in this case almost literally. But it was cold out in the wretched shed, and some body heat would be useful.

The knowledge did nothing to quell her uneasiness.

Hope frowned. It had been several years since she'd had any real interest in a man. She had been too caught up in her uncle's illness. Then had come the challenge of getting Glenbrae House on its feet.

Now it appeared she was making up for lost time.

MacLeod pulled her between his legs, which were warm and hard, indecently bare beneath the scrap of wool he wore belted in some sort of primitive kilt. Every movement sent little eddies of heat swirling up toward her heart.

Her heart.

This had *nothing* to do with her heart, Hope told herself. It was sheer tactile response. Simple hormonal overdrive.

But her heart gave a small lurch when she looked down at MacLeod's dark hair, glistening and damp against his shoulders. And when her gaze drifted to his eyes, she was trapped in their shifting silver depths. Then Hope made the greatest mistake of all.

She looked at Ronan MacLeod's mouth.

And wished she hadn't. Now she needed to know what he would do if she closed her eyes and skimmed her lips slowly over his.

Just once. Just as a sort of test. It would be pleasant— even if the whole business *was* doomed to failure. Her dismal track record with men left little question of that.

"Tell me what you're thinking," he whispered. The words shivered like cool wind moving through a field of heather. They teased her skin, making her forget to breathe. "That you are not…good with men?"

After a heartbeat she nodded.

"I can show you this is wrong."

"Don't bother." She laughed shakily. "It would be a waste of time." She shivered as he slid one finger along the curve of her lips. "Are you listening to me?"

"Every word," he said solemnly. Then his hand skimmed down her back.

Her pulse jumped. "You've, uh, got a nice mouth, MacLeod," she blurted. *And a truly amazing body…*

"Not half so nice as yours. But I want to know something."

"What?"

His eyes darkened. "How you taste."

Something twisted in Hope's chest. Probably the effect of the cold and her recent bout of panic. Or maybe it was her lack of food this morning. All things considered, this had to be a perfectly natural physical response to a cluster of un-related stimuli.

MacLeod's hand moved along the back of her jeans, and instantly all thoughts of unrelated stimuli soared out of her head.

"This is not a good idea."

He made a low, ragged sound and pulled her closer. "But it is." He frowned. "Do you dislike my touch?"

"Not...exactly." A colossal lie.

"How long, Hope? How long since a man touched you this way?"

She closed her eyes. *Longer than I can remember. No, forever.* Never with such gentle confidence.

His lips closed on her finger and he drew her into the heat of his mouth, making Hope envision a joining that would bring nothing short of devastating pleasure.

She felt a stab of panic. She wasn't *ready* for devastating pleasure. She wasn't even ready for moderate pleasure. She had never been good at relationships; couldn't he see that? Life had entirely eroded that particular corner of her optimism. She had lost too many of the people she held dear to trust in relationships ever again.

Now she was locked in a shed, fighting an old, ingrained panic. He should be appalled, repelled. Instead his eyes were glinting with barely hidden desire.

"I think," she said shakily, "that we need to talk. Something very strange is happening here."

"Is it?" His lips nibbled her fingers, closed hard, then moved in erotic ways.

Hope swallowed. Why did this all feel so incredible? Touching a man had never turned her brain into oatmeal before.

Until now. Until *MacLeod*.

"What would move you to trust me?" he murmured.

Hope couldn't answer. A hard ridge of male muscle lay outlined against her hip, and she realized exactly what it was.

Heat shimmered. Hope was too honest to pretend she didn't feel his effect on her keenly. But her bad track record loomed like a shadow. Cold, hard experience had taught her that she wasn't cut out for casual intimacies. She didn't know where to start, what to expect. Today's man expected high performance and fast turnover: Hope was bad at both. The last man she had touched like this had pointed out her awkwardness very clearly, in words that continued to haunt her in bad moments.

She had sworn off men after that. Swearing off had been easier than pretending. Somehow she had never missed the touch of flesh on flesh or the slow, hot brush of lips. Until now…

But with MacLeod, the last thing she wanted was to be awkward or uncertain. Better to cut to the hard ending right now, she decided. It would save them both a great deal of unpleasantness.

"I—I can't, MacLeod."

"Can't what?"

"Do this. Touch you. *Want* you."

"But you do." His lips curved. "Want me."

She didn't even consider lying. "What woman wouldn't? But this won't work. I'm not…"

Special. Beautiful. The stuff dreams are made of.

"Not what?" he growled, his eyes narrowed with anger.

"Anything special."

He cursed softly. "They told you this?"

"Loud and clear." Hope shrugged. "But I'd rather not go into details. It's not an entirely pleasant subject, if you know what I mean." She tried for a smile. Failed.

"No, I do not know."

"I guess you wouldn't. Women must stick to you like glue. And you hardly seem like the type to worry about… technical details. Performance statistics." She swallowed as he kissed one eyelid, then the other. "I knew you weren't listening."

"These men." He frowned. "You believed them when they said you gave them no pleasure?"

"At the time it was fairly obvious."

"How? They hit you? If so, I will—"

She sighed and shook her head. "Not that. It was a look, a laugh. Simple but damning things." Something twisted in Hope's chest and she realized all the old wounds were still there, hidden but hurting. The depth of that hurt surprised her.

"Explain this."

Hope sighed. "I wasn't the high-performance ride they were looking for."

"I do not understand."

"They wanted speed and drama, MacLeod. They wanted flash and danger. Instead they got…me."

He muttered a rough phrase in Gaelic. "Whoever taught you that the lack was yours?"

"Do you want a list?" she said, laughing unsteadily.

"Fools," he said harshly. "Few Scotsmen would be so witless. *No* MacLeod," he added savagely.

She had to laugh at that automatic Highland pride of his. "So MacLeod men make good lovers, do they?"

His eyes glinted. "We could find out now."

Hope hid a smile. "What about MacLeod women?"

"Their men are plagued with blissful smiles and far too little sleep. Sometimes they even die young."

"But what a way to go." Hope's smile faded as he pulled her onto his thighs. "Just a minute. What are you…"

His lips brushed her hair. His thighs were warm, rigid beneath her.

At that moment Hope discovered a sensual intensity that she had never suspected in herself, and the discovery was unsettling. Why only with this man did the textures of skin against skin leave her throat dry and her heart racing?

He traced her cheek, moved his fingers through her hair.

"For me to touch you is wrong, you say. Are you given to the Church?"

"No."

His eyes narrowed. "You are wed?"

"No ring." Hope held out her bare finger. "No husband."

"You are not pockmarked or missing your front teeth. Why has no man offered for you?" He sounded angry, angry for her.

"I guess the right man never came along. A few of the wrong ones, but never the right one."

"Not of the Church, not diseased. Not a depraved female, are you?" His lips curved as he read her instant protest. "No, I thought not. I see no barriers."

"But there are. Dozens." Hope closed her eyes as his fingers feathered over her cheek, reducing her neural matter to jelly. "Hundreds, probably."

He chuckled. "None that are important. You bewitch me. You confound me."

Hope was feeling altogether too bewitched and confounded herself. "We don't trust each other. We certainly don't understand each other. Sometimes I doubt we're even speaking the same language." She blew out a puff of air. "And there's that other small problem. I'm from the twentieth century and you say you're from the thirteenth."

"So I am."

"You see? You say something like that and expect me to *believe* you? You may as well tell me pigs can fly and men have never walked on the moon."

"The moon?" A muscle moved at his jaw. "Men have walked *there?*"

Hope closed her eyes. He was doing it again—confusing her, tempting her, making her think he might actually be telling the truth. "You are *not* from the thirteenth century, MacLeod. You *can't* be."

He stiffened. "But I am."

"And you did not get flung down into this glen by some mysterious action of magic or fate."

A frown cut down his forehead. "I did."

So they were right back where they started from, Hope thought bleakly. "So much for trust."

"Look at me." His hand moved over her shoulder and tightened. "Look at me and really see me. Do you think I want to be here in this time? Do you think I like to be thought a fool or a liar?" His shoulder sank back against the rough wall.

Hope shivered. She didn't believe him. *Couldn't* believe him. But she couldn't bear to see him so lost and angry either.

She laid one hand on his rigid shoulder, feeling the muscles stretched taut beneath. "Maybe...we should meet halfway."

"And where would that be?" he said bitterly. "Somewhere in the seventeenth century?"

"Ronan, listen—"

"No, *you* listen. I did not choose to come here, Hope O'Hara. I did not choose to find you. But I have. And now I will not pretend that you do not stir me, goad me." His eyes darkened. "Of all the women, all the places, that I should find you here...in my own glen, seven centuries into my future..." His muscles clenched. "Do not tell me it would be bad between us. Joining our bodies would be heaven itself." His eyes hardened. "I would make most certain of that."

Hope shivered at the rough desire in his voice. She had a sudden image of his body sliding deep and hard into hers. He would be demanding, thorough, ruthlessly patient.

God help her, Hope wanted all that.

He stared at the locked door, his eyes grim. "And I would show you so, were the choice mine. Here and now, I would take you as mine, while the touch was hot and sweet for us both."

Hot and sweet.

His.

Hope swallowed, swept with need, wanting to trust him. It had been too long since she had trusted another person.

Finally she had found a hero, a man of real honor. And who expected she would find him right here in distant, sleepy Glenbrae?

He stared at her, his eyes masked. "But there are things you must know. I am hated, feared. I have done things that shame me sorely."

"There must have been a reason."

He laughed bitterly. "Out of obedience to a man who values nothing and no one. And because power, once tasted, is a hard thing to forgo."

She looked at him in confusion, uncertain what he was trying to explain.

He made a harsh sound. "It matters not," he said. "*War* and *betrayal* are simply words to you. We share nothing save our love for this house. So why do I think only of this?" His fingers opened over her breasts. Her response was instant, as aroused skin tightened beneath his searching touch. Time seemed to burn.

To crawl.

Dimly, through the sudden hammering of her heart, Hope heard a sound above her. She blinked, fighting off the pull of his eyes, trapped in shifting waves of need.

A handful of pebbles rained down from the ceiling. One struck her head and a dozen more hit the flagstone floor like distant gunshots.

MacLeod turned and cursed as he saw a dark shadow plunge through the roof hole and hurtle down toward them.

CHAPTER TWELVE

DOWN FROM THE CEILING, Banquo shot through the air, a blur of noise and gray feathers. "Come, thick night!" he cried. "Come, thick night!"

Hope blinked, feeling reality crash down. What was she thinking of? What had come over her usual logic and calm practicality?

Looking down, she saw her sweater hitched below the curve of her breasts. With a strangled oath she wrenched it down, while MacLeod watched, his eyes glinting.

She gnawed at her lip. "About what just happened. It's— done. Finished." She crossed her arms at her waist. "It…can't happen again. Ever."

He made no answer, but the look in his eyes could have scored granite.

Banquo circled the room twice, then alighted on Hope's shoulder, looking very pleased with himself. Hope took a deep breath, delighted to have a distraction. "Banquo, you dear thing, how did you find us?"

"Fair is foul," the bird rasped. "Fair is foul."

"The creature truly talks?"

"And talks and talks." Hope managed a laugh. "Morning, noon and most of the night. A regular orator, aren't you?" She stroked the bird's long feathers. "How did you find us? Did Jeffrey send you?"

The parrot fluffed his plumage. "Foul is fair," he called. "Foul is fair."

MacLeod snorted. "He speaks without sense."

"That's Banquo, all poetry and no substance. Just like several politicians I could name." Hope pushed to her feet and jiggled the door handle. "Jeffrey, you can open the door now."

No response.

She frowned at Banquo. "Where are they?"

The bird preened on her shoulder. "The greatest is behind."

"Don't tell me you escaped again." Hope's frown deepened. "Do they even know you're gone?"

"Nothing but what is not," came the shrill answer.

With a sigh, Hope turned to MacLeod. "This is no rescue after all, I'm afraid. The crazy bird disappears for a day or two, then comes soaring back as if nothing had happened. We've never found out where he goes. Just my luck that he'd do it now."

She made a tight, angry sound and moved back her hair impatiently. Her hands were shaking. She felt cold and hollow inside again. Why didn't anyone *come?*

"Hope." It was a single word, a simple breath of sound, but the rough tenderness in the word made her head turn.

"I *know* I'm safe, and I know the walls probably won't cave in. But knowing doesn't seem to help." She locked her arms across her chest, watching his face. "You…you don't have to look at me that way," she whispered.

"What way?"

"As if I was fire and you were frozen."

"Perhaps it is so."

Hope swallowed, trapped by the heat in his eyes. "You weren't listening to me."

"I heard each word you said." His slow, patient look told her that the explanations made no difference to him. He would accept only what he wished to accept.

Outside, the metal bolt shook. The door rattled noisily. "Is anyone in there?"

Hope started to answer, but MacLeod pressed a hand over her mouth. "Wait," he said softly.

The door shook again. "Hello in there?"

"Is it your friend Jeffrey?"

Hope nodded, her response muffled by MacLeod's fingers.

It was MacLeod who answered. "Aye, it is us, Jeffrey. We are locked within."

"Thank God we found you." The door latch vibrated. "But this damned bolt is shoved tight. It's going to take me a minute or two...."

MacLeod let his fingers fall from Hope's mouth.

"What kind of trick was that?" Her face was white with anger.

"No trick," he said coolly. "It was best to determine who was outside before answering."

"Best for *whom?* Are you hiding from someone? If I have a criminal staying on my property, I damned well want to know it."

"Do you always curse in this way?"

Hope snorted. "Only around *you.*"

"You need feel no alarm. I have committed no crimes."

Hope glared at him, her fury unabated. She was still glaring when the bolt slid free and sunlight poured into the room.

Jeffrey bounded inside. "Thank heaven. We've been looking for you everywhere." He looked sharply from one to the other. "What are you doing out here, Hope?" He stared at MacLeod. "With *him?*"

"We were locked in." Hope took a jerky breath and started toward the door.

Sunlight spilled over the weathered slope. *Freedom. Open spaces.*

"Locked in? How?"

Outside she dragged a shaky hand through her hair. "The door slammed shut and somehow the bolt fell. Probably from the wind."

"The wind?" Jeffrey looked unconvinced. "That's an oak door and a solid steel bolt. It would take more than the wind to—"

MacLeod cut in curtly. "We will answer questions later. Let her go to the fire. Can you not see she is stiff with cold?"

"You do look a bit odd, Hope." Jeffrey followed her outside, frowning. "Are you all right?"

"Fine. Just fine." She closed her eyes and drew in fresh air, spinning in a dizzy little circle. "It was cold in there. Too…narrow for comfort."

"But your face is bright red. You both look like you were just…" Jeffrey's voice fell away as he saw MacLeod surreptitiously straighten his makeshift kilt.

"We're fine, Jeffrey. We just need to warm up." Hope indulged in another steadying breath. "And then MacLeod needs some decent clothes before he freezes to death."

MacLeod's brow rose. "What is amiss with my attire?"

"Nothing, assuming you're an extra in a big-budget Hollywood epic set in thirteenth-century Scotland. In fact, Mel Gibson would hire you on the spot."

"What is a—"

Hope rolled her eyes. "Not again." As they followed the winding path along the glen, she slanted a cocky glance at her visitor. "Make my day, MacLeod. Tell me how you just happen to know how to thatch a roof."

TWENTY MINUTES LATER MacLeod stood scowling at his image.

He had never seen a silvered mirror crafted so large, nor had he ever seen such a misbegotten pair of leggings. Both left him feeling damnably uncomfortable.

Warily he inspected the strange metal teeth riding up over his manhood. "It is safe, this thing you call zipper?"

Jeffrey cleared his throat. "It's safe, MacLeod. Trust me.

I wear jeans every day and I've never suffered any damage. Nothing permanent, that is."

MacLeod's brow rose sharply.

"Hey, just a joke." Grinning, Jeffrey tossed a bundle across the room. "Here's a pair of socks."

MacLeod studied the knitted tubes of wool, then worked them awkwardly over his feet, feeling more and more like a performer in a grotesque traveling circus. When he walked stiffly across the room, the things Jeffrey called jeans chafed at his thighs. They were tight and coarse. He would have preferred chain mail and an iron helmet any day.

"I'm afraid I don't have anything big enough to fit your feet."

"Nothing is needed. I will wear my own boots." MacLeod shoved the sleeves of the black knitted tunic higher on his arms. "This thing, this…"

"Sweater?"

MacLeod nodded in no good humor. "The accursed garment binds too tight, choking me." He jerked ruthlessly at the heavy wool turtleneck. "I will find my hauberk to wear. I need no hair shirts to strangle me."

Jeffrey blocked his path, looking uneasy. "Hope said to give you something warm. It's going to be cold up there on the roof, and she's…she's worried about you."

"Then why does she attempt to bedevil me with these cursed leggings, metal teeth and a tube that clutches at my neck? I will freeze before I wear such malevolent devices!"

"Keep them on for now, MacLeod. She's got enough to worry about without adding you to her list," Jeffrey said grimly.

"What things has she to worry about?"

"Business, for one." Jeffrey shrugged. "If things don't pick up around here, she's going to lose Glenbrae House. From what I've heard, she's sunk every penny piece into this place."

"But she is a wealthy woman. Only one of great status could purchase this demesne."

"I doubt Hope would call herself wealthy. Even the queen would have trouble keeping up with all the repairs this wreck demands. Hope had some money from her uncle when he died, but I don't think it was as much as she'd expected. Taking care of Glenbrae House has drained her."

How was it possible? To purchase such a dwelling required a sizable competence. No, the man must be mistaken. Or perhaps it suited Hope to feign poverty.

MacLeod frowned, rubbing the tight wool at his neck. "And she is not wed?"

"Never married. Gabrielle says she's not terribly…calm around men. She gets nervous, drops things, talks too much. Something hidden there, mark my words."

"Hidden?" MacLeod demanded. If some braying ass had hurt her, MacLeod would track him down and eviscerate him slowly.

"Just a feeling I have. Being in the theater, you get a sense about people. Bloody have to, with all the raging egos around you. Oh, I could tell you stories.…" He frowned, adjusting the mirror. "Those jeans don't look half bad on you, MacLeod. A bit tight." His frown deepened. "More than a bit, actually."

The Scotsman strode to the window, feeling the cloth chafe at his thighs. Cursed garments. Jeffrey wore the same kind of attire. Even the Frenchwoman wore a pair.

Did the people of this blighted era have a dearth of tailors that they all dressed in such comfortless garb?

"Tell me what you know of Hope."

Jeffrey's brow rose. "Why should I? Are you interested for personal reasons?"

MacLeod evaded the question. "Would someone wish to harm her?"

"Hope?" Jeffrey looked shocked. "From what I've seen,

the residents of Glenbrae consider her as some sort of sur-
rogate daughter. If anything happened to her, they'd be dev-
astated." His eyes narrowed. "Why do you ask?"

"For no reason." MacLeod shoved back the fragile
curtain, and stared up the glen. The cliffs were hard, shrouded
by ragged clouds about their gray heights. Standing in the
quiet glen with sunlight on his face, MacLeod felt betrayed—
betrayed by fate, by time.

Perhaps even by his own heart.

There was nothing for him here. He would never belong
or adjust in this time. Meanwhile, his restless bond with
Hope would grow, chipping away at his logic and honor
until one day or one quiet, silver night he would take her
against him in relentless need. And she would be willing
beneath him, MacLeod knew. It would be heat and storm,
a dark heaven of the senses when their bodies joined.

But nothing more. What had he to offer a woman of her
time? He could not even be certain he would exist in this
time on the morrow.

He had lost all reason in the stone shed. He had wanted
her badly, so badly that the differences between them had
faded.

MacLeod felt a pressure at his chest, remembering her
vulnerability when he had touched her. The magic between
them passed his logic and understanding. But her fears were
not for him to resolve, nor was her heart for him to claim.
He had duties back in his own time. He had to find a way to
go *home.*

Meanwhile, his instincts were too honed from years of
war to doubt that danger surrounded her. There had been
someone watching in the woods. Almost certainly they had
thrown the iron bolt in the shed.

Had they meant to drive her from Glenbrae? Or was their
intent to do her physical harm?

The possibility made him curse.

Twenty-four hours, he decided grimly. One day from rise of sun to rise of sun, he would give her. If there was real danger here, he was certain he would find it within that time.

He watched the clouds shredded to wisps by the dark, serried cliffs. Twenty-four hours, then he would be gone, tracing his path back up to the windy heights the same way he had come. Whatever power had brought him might still be there, waiting for his return.

If so, he would find it. Then he would make his way home, back to the age where he belonged.

And he would not look back, MacLeod swore.

"Ready to rock and roll?" Jeffrey dug out heavy wool gloves for both of them. "The roof awaits. But first the boss wants to see you."

More words that MacLeod did not understand. He shrugged, telling himself that the words did not matter. He would repair her roof and give her the passage of one day. Guarding the rest of her life was not his duty.

MacLeod was *almost* successful in believing it.

"HERE WE ARE, boss." Jeffrey pushed open the door to Hope's study with a grin.

Hope waved her hand as she finished a phone conversation with Winston Wyndgate, an art dealer she'd contacted right after discovering the silver brooch. It was a toss-up which was more important—trying to sell the brooch she'd found or getting her roof patched.

She glanced up as she rang off, only to find all words dying on her lips as MacLeod strode through the sunlight and into the room.

He was spare, all muscle, and taller than she had remembered. His soft black sweater was bunched up at his powerful forearms. And below...

Hope took a sharp breath. Below, every amazing inch was visible, framed in the snug, well-worn jeans that Jeffrey had loaned him. It was fortunate that the fabric was soft with age and wear; otherwise they would have split down every seam.

Hope tried to keep her gaze above his waist, and failed. It was apparent that Jeffrey was a size or two smaller than MacLeod—especially in the most significant areas.

Hope turned away, struggling for composure. She refused to think about how MacLeod looked. What had happened in the fishing shed was finished, a temporary bout of insanity caused by her overstressed brain. It was not going to happen again.

Not *ever,* Hope swore.

"It's the best I could do on short notice," Jeffrey explained. "What do you think?"

She made her voice cool and professional. "Thank you for loaning Mr. MacLeod a pair of jeans, Jeffrey. They appear to fit…adequately."

MacLeod muttered darkly, tried to shove his hand into a pocket, and failed. Hope tried not to notice how the movement strained the already taut fabric over his remarkable anatomy. Cursing silently, she forced her expression to remain absolutely calm.

He was going to have to see that she was unreachable, untouchable. A perfectly calm and collected twentieth-century female. "Are you two going out to work on the roof now?"

"Right after we find some work boots for MacLeod. He'll need them on the roof. I remembered I might have a pair of boots out in the Mini. With luck, they won't be too tight."

MacLeod turned toward the door, and Hope couldn't avoid the snug, tight outline of his backside, hugged lovingly by the faded denim.

She made a low, strangled sound as need sang through her blood in the most appalling way.

"You okay, Hope?" Jeffrey stared at her.

"Sure. Fine." She smiled airily as she picked up her accounting ledger. "What could be more fun than paying bills? I was just about to go through some receipts and—" Her voice caught as her leg struck her sixteenth-century mahogany writing table.

She nearly toppled onto her face.

So much for being cool, sane and levelheaded. Summoning her dignity, she struggled to her feet. So what if there was no prettiness to his hard frame and she knew from personal experience that there was no fat anywhere on his body? And if the scars on his back were a further testament to hard living and fighting in dangerous trouble spots of the world, what did it matter to *her?*

Yes, a man like MacLeod might make a lesser woman swoon.

But not Hope O'Hara. She had her own inn, her own business and her own life. And if luck was with her, she'd soon have a little extra money from the sale of the historic brooch she'd discovered beside the stairs. She was going to snap out of this mental haze right now.

"Hope?"

She could handle these strange feelings, Hope told herself firmly. She wasn't a silly girl.

"Hope?" Jeffrey waved one hand up and down. "Earth to Mars?"

"Er, fine. Of course. Whatever you want, Jeffrey. Just bring back two bottles of wine and three cartons of eggs, okay?"

Jeffrey slanted a measuring look at MacLeod. "Eggs?"

"That's right."

"And wine?"

Hope frowned. "Is something wrong with that?"

"Nothing at all. Provided I can find wine and eggs in the boot of my car," Jeffrey muttered.

Hope rubbed her hands briskly, barely hearing Jeffrey.

She was feeling better by the minute. She would manage just fine. Lust was no more than a memory now.

She could handle one hunk in a kilt named Ronan MacLeod.

ONE HOUR LATER, Hope wasn't so sure she could manage breathing unassisted.

Nothing had gone right after the men went out to work on the damaged roof. First the oven had begun to smoke, sending oily clouds billowing through the manor house. Terrified, Banquo had dive-bombed the kitchen table, toppling two racks of Gabrielle's favorite copper pots and shattering a shelf of china. When that domestic crisis was finally quelled and Banquo was safely ensconced on a pedestal in the sunny front study, Hope fled to the haven of an old chintz armchair in her office to prepare herself for her meeting with Mr. Wyndgate.

Propping her feet on an unmatched ottoman, she considered her ticklish financial situation.

With luck she would get enough for the brooch to pay her most pressing debts. But there was still an outstanding tax bill from her uncle's estate, and without a significant upturn in business, the future was far from rosy.

With a sigh, she massaged a knot at her neck as Banquo flew into the room. "It could be worse, right, Banquo?"

The bird stared back at her with keen, predatory intensity. "Thunder and lightning," he rasped.

"Not today, I hope. The radio says we're due for clear weather."

"The greatest is behind," the parrot wheezed, busy preening his gray feathers.

Hope gave up trying to understand the bird and moved back to the antique writing table, which doubled as her desk. Right now its elegant polished top was half covered with letters and bills. She picked up the telephone and dialed the first number on her notepad, absently noting the papers by her hand.

Then she frowned. There should have been a ledger of winter tax records beneath her glass paperweight. And what had happened to her two last telephone statements? She hated to think she had become careless with all the financial stress in the past two weeks.

A cool voice cut onto the line. "Elizabethan Tours."

Frowning, Hope focused on her sales pitch. Glenbrae House had history, magic and an impeccable period restoration, all of which should make it attractive to travelers. She reminded herself of those facts as she launched into her presentation, outlining the uniqueness of the inn. When she was done, she held her breath, trying to be optimistic.

The manager of the tour company sounded bored. "Glenbrae House, you say? I don't recognize the name. I presume you have all the standard amenities? Tennis courts, both clay and tournament quality. Championship golf and in-room television. Room service, valet, same-day laundry." She rattled off the conditions like pistol fire. "Our guests expect the very highest accommodations."

"The tennis courts are not completed," Hope lied, "but we have some lovely hiking countryside, a pristine loch and a very historic view of—"

"Hiking?" The woman gave a tight little laugh. "My dear Ms. O'Hara, you'll have to come up with something better than hiking. Our travelers expect the very best."

Hope gripped the phone and tried desperately to stay calm. Glenbrae House's future depended on it. "I'm afraid that we can't offer golfing or tennis here at Glenbrae, but we do have salmon fishing in season. We're also planning some period festivities for Christmas. Possibly a medieval costumed event."

"What about spa facilities and circuit-training equipment? Yoga? Meditation therapy? Nutritional counseling?"

"Well, our chef can—"

"Do you have them or *don't* you, Ms. O'Hara?"

"No, but—"

"Then I'm afraid that your establishment is not up to our standards," the woman said curtly. "In fact, now I remember a recent report we received that mentioned your property. There were some major problems indicated." Papers rustled. "Yes, it appears there was inadequate plumbing and a complaint about the cooking. You may be certain *we* will not be booking anything at Glenbrae House."

Hope stared at the phone in disbelief as the line clicked dead in her hands.

Plumbing problems? Cooking complaints? Was this some sort of sick joke? The headache she had been nursing suddenly raged into a full-blown migraine.

Despite her discomfort, she gritted her teeth and forced herself to make three more calls to other tour agencies. In each case, the answer was the same. Glenbrae House, though it might have some quaint scrap of historical interest, was just not up to luxury standards. Those agencies, too, recalled recent information about the unreliable quality of its accommodations.

It had to be a mistake, Hope thought. There must be another hotel with a similar name. Glenbarra? Glenblair?

But her agitated call to the Scottish Tourist Board revealed the unthinkable. Glenbrae House had been removed from their listings. They could not recommend an establishment with improper plumbing and questionable cuisine, as indicated by several recent complaints.

Finished.

Ruined.

Hope sank back against the back of the chair and put down the telephone. Brooch or not, there would be no guests through established referrals. If she wanted to survive, she was going to have to attract visitors some other way.

Maybe she could hold a press conference and gallop naked down Glenbrae's High Street.

Maybe not.

Suddenly Jeffrey's scheme to summon up a ghostly apparition began to look more and more attractive.

CHAPTER THIRTEEN

"HOPE?"

Hope opened her eyes to find Gabrielle studying her anxiously from the doorway.

"You look pale."

Hope sighed. "I *feel* pale, believe me."

"I am sorry, but that man Wyndgate is downstairs waiting for you. I do not like to bother you, but he insists. Something about a brooch."

Hope shoved a curve of hair from her forehead, suddenly uneasy. Would he want the brooch? Was it valuable or just a trinket? And could it possibly fetch a good enough price to save her from ruin?

"I can tell him you are gone," Gabrielle said helpfully.

Hope shook her head. At the moment Winston Wyndgate was the only hope of rescue for Glenbrae House. Hope only wished his temperament were halfway pleasant and his manner less arrogant.

Gabrielle set a steaming mug down in front of her. "Drink this. It will improve your outlook."

Hope took an experimental sip, coughing as heat raced down her throat. "Lethal."

"Café au lait, my own special recipe." A dimple appeared at Gabrielle's cheek. "With a healthy dose of single-malt whisky added." Her tone became grave. "It will all work out. Just you wait and see."

After her chef left, Hope rubbed her forehead, searching for equal optimism.

Winston Wyndgate III was pacing impatiently through the sunny front salon. Sunlight glinted off his steel-gray hair, playing up the suit that had been custom tailored for his tall frame. At somewhere between fifty and sixty, he had a shrewd eye and an encyclopedic memory, a combination that made him respected but not greatly liked in his profession.

Soon after her purchase of Glenbrae, he had phoned Hope to see if there were any authentic period objects that he might consider worth his interest. But Hope had found no furniture or ceramics of any great age in the house. She refused to part with the attic full of books—not that they would fetch much at auction since they were of no great age or rarity.

When she offered tea, the professor impatiently declined. "I am interested in art, not nourishment, Ms. O'Hara. I presume you had a reason to drag me up here." Wyndgate glanced through the room, clearly unimpressed.

To Hope's irritation, her hands trembled slightly as she opened the leather box holding her discovery. "Right here."

Sunlight played over the heavy, etched silver, gleaming in the wolf's cabochon aquamarine eyes.

Wyndgate's expression was unreadable. "You found this hidden in a wall, you said?"

Hope nodded, wishing her heart would not race. Wishing that Wyndgate's decision would not affect her entire future.

"How old is the house?" he asked abruptly.

"Thirteenth century, with a restoration in brick sometime in the sixteenth century. The thatched roof was probably added to replace an earlier slate roof that had fallen from siege or age."

"Was the wainscoting present in the restored section?"

"In most rooms. But there was a second panel behind that, and the brooch was wedged there near the floor."

The dealer sat forward, his eyes narrowed. "May I examine the piece?" At Hope's nod, he spread out a black velvet cloth and slid a jeweler's loupe from his pocket. He worked in silence for nearly ten minutes, examining the deeply grooved silver from every angle while Hope watched with growing anxiety. Maybe the brooch was worthless, a modern trinket that had somehow fallen and worked its way behind the wall.

"What do you think?"

"An attractive little thing. Rather nice sculptural detail in the body." He replaced the brooch on the layer of velvet. "How much do you want for it?"

Sunlight cast sparks of light onto the hammered silver. Hope was struck as she had been before by the power that clung to the crouching wolf. "How much is it worth?" she countered.

"That rather depends, Ms. O'Hara."

On what? Hope wanted to scream.

But the academic was not to be hurried. He shifted the brooch from side to side, frowning. "I believe there may be a good deal of legend connected to this brooch."

Hope watched sunlight play over the silver like cold fire. The wolf's aquamarine eyes seemed to shift, following her.

Forget about its beauty, she thought. *Forget about history.* Things at Glenbrae House had reached the desperate stage. If there was value to the brooch, then it would have to go. "What kind of legends?"

"I believe there are only two known items of any similarity to this one. Both are in private collections." Wyndgate put down the brooch, steepling his fingers. "Works like this were usually presented by the sovereign in appreciation of services rendered."

"What kind of services?"

"Bloody services, Ms. O'Hara. I would venture to say they included tracking down malcontents, ferreting out spies and dispensing with the king's enemies. The man who wore this brooch carried heavy memories, I can assure you. Today we would call him a hired gun. He was a man of unquestioned loyalty, a seasoned warrior who would be expected to lay down his life for his king or kill any enemy that threatened the security of the realm. He was a man to be feared by man and woman alike."

Hope stared at the crouching wolf. "And he lived here?"

"The records are not entirely clear. A warrior is known to have held lands in Glenbrae sometime in the late thirteenth century. It was a troubled time, with peasant unrest, border raids and frequent famines. There can be gaps in the historical documents, you understand."

But dry history didn't interest Hope. It was the flesh and blood of the past that made her pulse race. Glenbrae House represented all those things to her.

She swallowed. Ronan MacLeod had claimed to come from the thirteenth century. The King's Wolf, he had called himself.

She stared at the brooch with growing uneasiness. "Do you know his name?"

Wyndgate shrugged. "That's one of the gaps, I'm afraid. No one records the warrior's clan or his place of birth. He was a solitary man, hardened by war and the sort of jobs that fell to his hand."

"Does the phrase 'the King's Wolf' mean anything to you?"

Wyndgate toyed with a heavy gold cuff link. "Should it?"

"It might have some connection with the brooch." Hope couldn't believe that she was actually considering the possibility that MacLeod had told her the truth. But like it or not, the coincidences were piling up fast.

"I could check further." His lips pursed. "For my usual fee, of course."

Hope brushed her palm slowly over the brooch. "How much is it worth?"

"How much do you want?" Wyndgate parried.

"It's very unusual, you said. In that case, let's say... twenty-five." Hope held her breath, waiting for a flat rejection. She had no idea what the brooch might be worth, but with twenty-five hundred pounds in her pocket, she could begin to pay off some of her most pressing debts.

Wyndgate turned slowly. "Twenty-five," he repeated softly. "You're a sharper negotiator than I thought, Ms. O'Hara. I suppose this old house is very expensive to maintain." His eyes narrowed, hawklike. "Very well, I'll pay your price, though some might consider twenty-five thousand pounds a bit steep."

Hope swallowed hard. Twenty-five thousand?

Twenty-five *thousand?*

She stared at the crouching figure. At that price, she couldn't afford to keep the heirloom. Not even if the eyes of the wolf seemed to follow her reproachfully. And she refused to consider MacLeod's outrageous story any longer.

She held out her hand. "Sold."

"Excellent. I'll make you a bank draft right now, if that would be convenient."

"That would be fine." Hope struggled to keep her voice steady as she watched Wyndgate scratch out a satisfying string of zeroes with a heavy gold fountain pen.

Now she had a chance. With luck she could keep Glenbrae House going until its reputation was restored. If so, it would be thanks to a silver wolf, the gift of a warrior from an age she would never know.

As Wyndgate slid the beautiful ornament into a thick velvet pouch, Hope felt a pang of regret. "You'll send me a picture, won't you? I'd like to see the brooch when it is completely documented."

"Nostalgia, Ms. O'Hara?" The dealer's brow rose.

Hope looked out the window over the slope to the roof, where Jeffrey and Ronan were hard at work. "Maybe I feel I owe it to the brooch's owner. *Whoever* he was."

Wyndgate shrugged. "As you wish."

Halfway to the door, he turned back to her. "Perhaps you should check the records here. You might find some documents left with the house."

"There's nothing. The books that were here at the time of purchase date entirely from the past seventy years, I'm afraid."

A shaft of sunlight touched his steely hair. "There might be something you've missed. Perhaps I should have a look before I go." He seemed to hesitate.

"Is something wrong?"

"I now recall there was some unpleasantness about the brooch, Ms. O'Hara. This warrior had many enemies who would have been happy to seize it—along with the royal power it conferred."

"You mean it might have been stolen and then left here?"

"Possibly. Or perhaps the owner hid it himself, hoping to keep it safe. I'll have a look at the Ashmoleon. Now, if you don't mind, I want to examine the stairwell where you found this. Then I'd like to see the library. If you have rather an extensive collection, there might be some useful documents mixed in." He studied her with growing impatience.

Hope folded the bank draft and told herself to stop feeling guilty. The brooch would ensure Glenbrae House's survival. As the house's owner, it was her decision and no one else's.

"What will you do with it now?" she asked. "Sell it or keep it for your own collection?"

"That depends what I'm offered for the piece." He rubbed his hands briskly. "Of course, with the proper documentation, the price could rise quite significantly. You'll understand why I'm anxious to make a systematic search before I go."

"Of course." Hope pointed the way to the shadowed stairwell and the picture above. Winston Wyndgate paid no attention to the image of the medieval knight, too intent on exploring the loose wedge of wainscoting.

Hope left him at his search.

Hope had barely reached her office when Jeffrey charged in with a plank of wood caught beneath his arm.

"Look at this beam," he crowed, barely missing Hope's desk lamp with his plank. "Rotted through, but not to worry. When MacLeod says he's good, he's *good*. In two days you're going to have a seriously excellent thatched roof."

Hope touched the stained wood. So the two men actually could repair a roof. It was clear she had underestimated them.

"There isn't much MacLeod doesn't know about thatched roofs." Jeffrey frowned, drumming three fingers on the plank. "Although he seems confused about a fair number of other things." He rubbed his jaw. "But you should see him work. He's coated the reeds with a layer of clay to reduce the fire hazard, though how he thought of that is beyond me. Then he managed to brace two of your beams that were ready to split." Jeffrey stretched contentedly. "I haven't had so much fun in ages."

Hope was about to question him further when she heard an explosive crack from the kitchen, followed by a torrent of Gabrielle's angry French.

CHAPTER FOURTEEN

HOPE RACED DOWN TO the kitchen to find a pot boiling over and the curtains flying madly. Gabrielle was huddled against one wall, a spatula clasped to her chest.

MacLeod stood in the center of the room, staring in horror at the television set above Gabrielle's worktable. At his feet were the shattered remains of an old but very ugly Sèvres platter.

"*Diable.*" He made the sign of the cross, then pulled his sword from the floor. "Stand away. This is the devil's dark work."

Hope felt a hysterical laugh build in her throat. "A television set?"

"They move, these demons."

Hope took a cautious step forward. "It's all right, MacLeod. Put down the sword. It's only reruns of *Gilligan's Island.*"

"You know their names?"

"Of course I do. Boring, but hardly the work of the devil."

He traced the mark of the cross again, this time with his sword. "Evil can be most cunning," he said harshly. "In the Holy Lands I had many visions. Around the campfire mirages came often to torment our souls in the desert light, but none were so clear as this one."

Hope saw him tense, his hand rising. "What are you doing?" She managed to catch his sword arm seconds before he would have decimated the glass screen. The man was consistent, at least. Every piece of his story meshed, right down to the part about the Holy Lands and the campfires.

But there was one small problem.

Time could not bend. Space and matter did not transmute, swallowing up unsuspecting victims.

Get a grip, she told herself.

"I own demesne lands in the fens of Norfolk and forty acres in Normandy." MacLeod's jaw clenched. "I have ridden with kings and supped with the mightiest of Outremer. Such tricks cannot deceive me."

Gabrielle was looking at him as if he were crazy. And Hope feared that any moment Winston Wyndgate might appear.

Explanations would have to wait, she decided. "It's all right, MacLeod. Trust me." She reached for the television controls, but he seized her hand.

On the screen Gilligan launched into one of his incessant arguments with the captain. It appeared to have something to do with a monkey and a very large coconut.

MacLeod stood stiffly, his whole being locked on the square glass screen. His concentration was almost frightening, Hope thought.

"How do the men fit inside the box?"

"They're not real, MacLeod. They're just images."

"So they *are* spirits."

When MacLeod raised his sword again, Hope moved in front of him. "That's enough culture for one day." She tried to turn off the power, but missed, and a moment later the screen filled with a glorious panorama of the Cartwright family galloping over the high plains of the Ponderosa Ranch.

MacLeod muttered harshly. "What manner of knights are these?"

"Not knights, cowboys."

"I know what a cow is," he said with angry dignity. "I also

know what a boy is." He gestured fiercely at the television screen. "These are neither cows nor boys. And their horses are strange."

Gabrielle and Jeffrey had crept closer behind her and were staring at MacLeod in shock.

"You've never seen a cowboy?" Jeffrey asked. *"The Magnificent Seven? Lonesome Dove?"*

MacLeod's frown deepened. "Tricks and more tricks." He kept one eye on the television while he leveled his sword protectively in front of Hope. "What kind of magic have you conjured?"

"Not magic, technology. Science, MacLeod."

His face held no sign of understanding.

Jeffrey gave a low whistle. "He's serious. The man has never seen a cowboy before."

The tiny hairs stirred at the back of Hope's neck.

Frowning, she hit the power button and the screen went dark. She had enough problems for one morning without questioning her own sanity or the arcane laws of physics. Besides, MacLeod was favoring his good knee again. Crawling up the steep roof must have been agony for him.

"You should have told me your knee was bothering you again."

"It does not pain me." Even as he spoke, he slid more weight onto his other foot, grimacing slightly.

"Yeah, right," she muttered, tugging him toward the stairs.

"No. I want to know about tel-e-vision. In my time—"

"Later, MacLeod. Since you've worked so hard, I want you to have a nice hot soak. The heat will help your knee."

"Heating water will be too much trouble," he said gruffly.

Hope tugged at his arm, anxious to get him out of the kitchen before Wyndgate appeared. "No problem. I expect I can manage to turn a few handles for you."

The cozy bathroom had high ceilings, and the walls were lined with blue-and-white wallpaper crowded with scenes of cats. Sun shone through fine lace curtains as Hope opened the tall armoire by the door. "Here are clean towels. Don't feel you have to rush." She turned when she heard no answer. "MacLeod?"

He stood frozen in the doorway, one hand clenched to a fist. "This is the place?" He traced the porcelain sink warily. "You bathe in *this*?"

"No, over here." Hope pointed to a luxurious oversize tub nestled on intricate wooden feet. "There's sandalwood or jasmine soap. Take your pick."

"Soap is for women," MacLeod said flatly. "Have you no sand?"

Sighing, Hope flicked on the faucets and watched hot water stream into the tub. "Sorry, no sand."

Hesitantly he stuck a finger into the water. "It *burns*."

"It had better burn. I paid a fortune to have the plumbing redone."

MacLeod stood mesmerized by the water, as intent as a child with a new toy. Hope decided it was time to spring her next question. "Now you can tell me what was really going on out there by the loch."

His head rose slowly. "Going on?"

"That's right. Don't think I didn't notice how you were watching the woods before we were locked in the shed."

He frowned. "I do not know what you mean."

Hope sighed. Talking to him was like trying to discuss emotions with Mr. Spock. "Don't try to distract me. I want to know why you were so uneasy. I especially want to know what happened with that door."

MacLeod stirred the water. Hope was fairly certain he was stalling for time. "Well?"

He turned, moving closer. One finger rose to her cheek. "You have water here." Very gently he lifted the fragile, glistening bead onto his finger.

The movement made Hope's entire body tighten. She

took a step backward, more angry at herself than him. "Forget about the water. I want answers."

"Answers were na what you wished of me before." The Gaelic cadences were rough in his voice. "Outside by the loch, you were open to me, *mo rùn*. Open to all that you were feeling."

Hope swallowed. He wasn't going to let her forget, was he? "That was then, and this is now."

"Is forgetting so easy for you?"

Hope had not forgotten anything, but she wasn't about to cave in to lust again. She couldn't afford to. "I'll survive."

Motionless, Ronan MacLeod watched the currents hiss and ripple. He marveled at hot water that ran from a metal hole with no fire, and lights that glowed from glass globes set on the walls. Miracles of her time, he thought, and she counted them for naught.

By honor, in this age even *bathing* taxed his reason. He could never be comfortable here.

And what of his suspicions? Once they were freed, he had immediately surveyed the area, but the two men in the shadows were gone. He could confide his suspicions, but he had no doubt they would be greeted with the same disbelief as the rest of his story.

No, she would have no more explanations from him now. "It was a trick of the shadows. I imagined I saw a horse and rider among the trees."

"A horse and rider." Hope drummed her fingers on the windowsill. "How come I saw nothing of this supposed horse and rider?"

"Perhaps you are not so observant as I am."

But Hope was certain that MacLeod had been watching the cliffs, and it infuriated her that he would keep secrets affecting her inn. She glanced up, only to find him pulling his borrowed sweater over his head.

The sweater hit the floor.

"What are you d-doing?" she sputtered.

His chest gleamed, dusted with dark hair. Every muscle was sculpted and hard. "Surely it is not customary to wear clothes while bathing? You wish to stay and observe me?" His dark brow arched. "That would be the second time."

Hope's face flamed. "In your dreams, brother."

"I am not your brother, *mo cridhe*. We both know that full well." His hands fell to the waist of his jeans.

Outmaneuvered. Outclassed. Outwitted.

Hope turned and slammed the door so hard that the wall rattled behind her. If a few of Gabrielle's copper pots tumbled to the floor, it would still be worth it, she thought grimly.

Her face was still fiery when she settled down in her study. For twenty minutes she sat grimly at her desk, misadding column after column of expenses. To her irritation, she found another file was missing, and when she tried to finish the text for an advertisement to appear in a regional travel magazine, all she came up with was a floor full of crumpled paper.

She decided to give up on the ad and attacked a pile of bills. She would transfer Wyndgate's funds the following day, but meanwhile she would have the pleasure of seeing a few creditors paid in full.

When she was finally done, she glanced at her watch, shocked to see that almost two hours had passed. Was Wyndgate still busy with his inspection?

She was about to go in search of him when her office door jerked open.

MacLeod glared at her from the threshold, his hair slicked back, damp from his bath.

His chest was bare and his face was a mask of anger.

"Enough tricks, woman. You will come here *now*," he rasped.

CHAPTER FIFTEEN

HOPE CROSSED HER ARMS and glared back at him. "Didn't your mother ever teach you to say 'please' and 'thank you'?"

"My mother died when I was four," he said flatly. "And now you will come upstairs." His voice was strained, every movement wooden.

Hope didn't care. "What if I don't want to?"

"Then you will regret it."

Her voice shook. "I guess you're out of luck, buster. I've got work to do here, calls to make. And after that, I—"

He hauled her to her feet and pushed her into the hall. "We will talk later."

Hope jerked free of his hand. "*Right now.* Why are you walking funny?"

Color swept his hard, angled cheeks. "Upstairs. We will talk there."

Hope studied him suspiciously. Something was definitely wrong, but she saw that he wouldn't say anything here. In stiff silence she followed him up the stairs to the bathroom, where steam still drifted through the air. She sat stiffly on the windowsill, trying not to notice the beads of moisture glistening on his broad chest. "Will this be suitable for our discussion, Your Royal Highness?"

"Do you jest, woman? I am a knight, not a king."

"Funny, but you *act* like a king often enough."

"And what word describes your own comportment?" He

kicked the door shut behind him with his foot, and Hope could have sworn she saw him wince.

"Self-protection," she said grimly. "All right, what's so important it couldn't wait?"

"This foul infidel's device. Why do you attempt to emasculate me?"

Hope blinked. "I beg your pardon?"

He gripped the waist of his jeans and glared in disgust at the zipper. *"This,"* he hissed.

It appeared to be caught.

Caught over a very significant portion of his anatomy.

"As you see, it does not move. You will fix it now, witch."

Hope looked down, her cheeks reddening. His zipper. It was caught. That was a man thing. Surely he couldn't expect *her* to help him.

"Just pull on the zipper," she said unsteadily.

"Do you think I have not tried, woman?" He tugged the tight jeans upward, and his face stiffened with pain. "No wonder the men of your time are unnatural in their courtship. They are all unmanned by this execrable device with metal teeth."

Hope tottered between hysterical laughter and raw embarrassment. After all, MacLeod did appear to be in genuine pain. She had no choice but to help him.

Inspiration struck. "I'll get Jeffrey." She started for the door, only to feel her wrist seized tightly.

"You will show me yourself. I will have no man pawing over my nether parts."

"But you'll let *me?*" Hope said breathlessly.

Heat shimmered in his eyes, a mix of racing anger and darker desire. "Only because you will treat them more cordially. Someday they will have use to you."

"Dream on," she snapped.

"Were the choice mine, we would be lovers, Hope O'Hara."

Her pulse skittered at the image. "I take back what I said before, MacLeod. Your ego is even *bigger* than Siberia."

"I know not what a Siberia is, or an ego is, but I know how you felt when I touched you. You trembled. Small sounds tumbled from your lips."

"*That* was a mistake."

"There is no dishonesty at such a time. Your body spoke clearly even if you cannot."

Hope refused to continue the conversation. Desperate to change the subject, she looked down, seized his waistband and pulled at the zipper.

He bit back a sound of pain. "Be gentle, woman."

"I can't just reach in and—"

"You will have to," he said raggedly. "The accursed thing will not move for me. It is an enigma beyond the most learned theologian. *Do* something," he said in a strangled voice.

Carefully Hope eased the zipper up and down. Nothing happened.

Stuck tight, just as he had said. Meanwhile, MacLeod's face was turning pale.

She bit her lip, thinking frantically. She didn't have a great deal of experience in the zipper department. She had never helped a man undress before. She had never even *watched* a man undress before.

This reminder of her inexperience only added to her uneasiness.

"Why do you not do something?"

"I'm thinking, okay?" Hope glared at the soft denim. The zipper was caught midway, with the opening stretched in a tight V. If his jeans hadn't been so tight in the first place, none of this would have happened.

Unfortunately, she couldn't blame him for that.

She pushed the zipper together, trying to work the metal handle upward. The only result was his muttered curse.

"Sorry."

"Finish it," he thundered.

"I'm trying. If you'd stop moving, it might help."

"I would stop moving," he said grimly, "if you would stop trying to sever me into pieces."

"Don't look at me," Hope hissed. "It's the zipper. You're too…big."

"Soon I will *not* be."

Hope's hands shook on the taut denim, distended with the shape of his body. She thought about cutting the legs up the side, but doubted that Jeffrey had any others.

No, she would have to find a way that didn't sacrifice the jeans. That meant covert operations. Deep, covert operations.

She clutched stiffly at his waist. "Don't move."

His muscles tightened, but he said nothing. His body was absolutely motionless as she eased one finger beneath the zipper. She made a strangled sound as she felt warm skin.

Hard, warm skin.

In the tight place, the suggestion of erect muscle left her breathless and largely incompetent. "Stop moving."

"I have not moved."

"Then stop breathing," she snapped. Inching lower, she felt pressure against her fingers. She looked up, startled. "You're not wearing anything underneath these." It was an accusation, not a question.

"I donned them just as your friend Jeffrey gave them to me," MacLeod said in a stony voice. "Braies and chausses would not accord beneath."

"You're not wearing anything else? There's only—" A second later the question became immaterial as Hope made full contact with the area in question. Flushing crimson, she shoved at the zipper tab, desperate to be finished. "Stand *still.*"

Her pulse was hammering, and her hands trembled as they explored the forbidden terrain beneath the locked zipper. She tried not to think about what she was touching.

"I would stand still if you were more careful with your hands," MacLeod said grimly.

"There's not exactly a lot of room to maneuver in, Einstein."

"If you do much more of what you are doing, I shall be dead like your Einstein anyway, so nothing will matter."

Hope's cheeks were flaming. The wretched zipper still didn't budge. Throwing caution to the winds, she sank to one knee before him.

MacLeod went very still. "What are you doing?"

"Major surgery. Keep quiet and don't move." Carefully she slid her hand lower. Something prevented her progress. Something warm and hard.

Her gaze shot upward and locked on MacLeod's face. "You are—"

"Of course I am," he said tightly. "What do you imagine when I can feel your hands against me?"

Hope closed her eyes and offered a desperate prayer for divine intervention. Then she pulled the denim fabric away from MacLeod's body and gave one sharp, swift jerk.

To her shock, the zipper came free with a muffled hiss. Instantly she took a step backward, resolutely ignoring the gaping jeans.

MacLeod stood unmoving. His eyes were closed, his hands locked in fists at his sides.

"Are you…all right?"

No answer.

"Oh, God, I hope I didn't—"

"No, you did not, but only by God's mercy. Now go away, woman. I would choose to be alone when I commence my imprecations. By all the saints, if you do not kill me one way, you will certainly kill me another."

"Curse away to your heart's content. I've got, er, work to finish, calls to make. I'll be gone for hours, probably."

His eyes opened and fixed on her face. "It will take far more than hours for me to forget the feel of your hands."

Hope turned and fled, unable to bear the hard challenge in his eyes and the way her heart lurched in response.

At the bottom of the stairs, Banquo flew past her head, then settled on her arm. Hope sank down on the bottom step, stroking the soft gray feathers. "What's happening to me, Banquo? When am I going to get some control around him?"

"When the battle's lost and won," the parrot crooned.

"I can't wait that long." Hope gave a weary sigh. "First the brooch, now this impossible man." She closed her eyes, feeling her hands shake. "I don't have time for him, for what he makes me feel. I know there's the roof to finish, but…" She frowned. "Yes, maybe it would be better if he left."

The bird's gray feathers ruffled and then stilled. "That will be ere the set of sun."

"Banquo, what are you talking about? Where is Winston Wyndgate, by the way?"

The bird soared. "Upon the heath. Anon!" With a low cackle, he flew down the corridor toward the kitchen, leaving Hope to stare after him with narrowed eyes.

Another mystery.

Just what she didn't need.

"BUT SHE *NEEDS* HIM, Perpetua."

Morwenna stood at the window of the tidy cottage. Sunlight crowned her snow-white head and a bright red shawl covered her frail shoulders. "She doesn't realize it yet, but she will."

Her sister sighed. "I hope they don't murder each other before they decide things."

"We knew they were both strong-willed. Without that, where would the challenge be?"

"I wonder if I'm getting too old for these challenges," Perpetua muttered, sinking into the handmade rocker before the fire.

Without being stirred, the flames kindled. Heat grew, filling the room.

"Ah, that's better." Perpetua closed her eyes on a sigh.

"But something is worrying me, Pet. There's something we didn't count on," Morwenna mused.

"She has no husband and he has no wife. What other problem could there be?"

The fire blazed, hissing and popping in the grate. "I don't know. It's—gone blank since MacLeod came, and I can't see the way I should. Maybe his coming took more out of me than I knew." Morwenna traced the mist her breath left against the window, drew a line of graceful symbols, and smiled as snowflakes appeared out of nowhere to drift over the green glen. "Almost Christmas. I love Christmas."

"Will you please stop making it snow, Morwenna? We'll have enough of the white stuff soon enough. And it's not Christmas yet."

"But I love snow," the woman at the window said softly. "I love how it smells on the air and how the tiny flakes cling to my skin. It makes me remember when I was young." She touched the shawl about her shoulders gently. "When I was beautiful and so much in love…"

Behind her, Perpetua rose. Silently she crossed the room and laid her hand on her sister's shoulder. They stood at the window, staring out into the first, dancing flakes of snow that veiled the glen. For a moment there might have been the skirl of pipes in the air. There might have been a flash of color, bright, bonny tartan on braw young men riding down toward the loch.

Riding down to war.

For a long time the two women stood at the window, neither speaking.…

Both lost in memories soft as new-fallen snow.

On the far side of the loch an eagle shot from the trees. Dead leaves spun up in a gray vortex, driven by the wind.

There was a flicker of movement beyond the shore, as if

from some hidden form caught beneath the heavy woods. Another bird took startled fright.

But when the clouds sailed free and the sun returned, there was no more motion, no more trace of frightened animals.

Only the loch moved, capped with smooth crests. Undisturbed, it rippled on, as old as the dark Highland hills.

CHAPTER SIXTEEN

GLENBRAE HOUSE WAS silent, shadowed in the Highlands' early twilight. Clouds of gold and trailing lavender banked the cliffs, but inside, all was still, from weathered eaves to the old tower stairs.

And it was there at the base of the stairs that MacLeod saw the painting. A mere wisp of color, ghostlike in the dusk.

A man in trailing hauberk, chain mail and long gauntlets. A man with regret in his eyes and too much fighting in his face.

Himself.

Who had captured his likeness here by the first turning of the stair? Who had seen beyond his habitual mask to the darkness of his wary heart?

But it was his image; of that, he had no doubt. The gauntlets were his own, crafted at the hand of a singularly skilled armorer of fine Bordeaux steel. Each rivet was clear, down to the leather straps at the cuff and fingers.

Him.

In that moment MacLeod realized he was part of this house, part of this remote glen. Perhaps his contribution had been greater than he knew.

History, he reminded himself. The ancient past.

It was his future he contemplated now. How could he leave the way he'd planned? Honor dictated that he stay as long as Hope O'Hara was in danger.

But duty demanded that he go, returning to his time and

the people who also needed him. If he stayed longer and his invisible bonds with this twentieth-century female grew stronger...

He bit back a curse. Once again he felt betrayed, a man lost, turned out of his own time. He wondered if the face in the fresco showed the same angry marks of betrayal that lay upon his soul.

The final beams of daylight filtered through the hall, touching the image on the wall. MacLeod saw the sadness in the eyes, the stiff arrogance in the shoulders.

Did he look so? Had he worn his past so clearly about him?

He lifted his hand, half expecting to feel his own flesh and blood caught there upon the wall.

But the half-light played strange tricks, and MacLeod could have sworn his fingers met no obstacle, passing senseless deep into stone.

Into the cold depths of his own heart.

He pulled his fingers back with a muffled curse. There were too many tricks in this place, too many devices to make a man question his logic.

Intent on his own image, he did not hear the light step behind him or the soft chuckle.

"Most impressive, is he not?" Gabrielle stood beside him, studying the ghostly fresco. "A man who knows too much of war and far too little of things that truly matter."

His brow rose. "And what things would that be?"

"Laughter. Fine wine. A dozen noisy children in a sunny house."

"Hmm."

She did not turn to look at him, and MacLeod was glad for that.

"And what do you know of these things that truly matter?"

She gave a shrug that could have meant any of several things—acceptance, regret or anger. "I know because they are things that I've never had. Never hoped to have." Her voice fell. "Before I came here, it went badly for me. No work. No money. No hint of any future. There were nights on rainy streets when I was hungry and cold...." Her shoulders stiffened. "Times when I thought of selling my body, since it seemed I had no other skills."

"But you did not?"

She turned then, a glint in her dark eyes. In the half-light he saw pride and angry pragmatism.

"We shall pretend, Scotsman, that you did not ask that question."

He gave a tiny smile and nodded.

"This man," she said presently, pointing at the shadowy knight, "has also known cold nights on rainy roads. He has known the power of shifting dreams and he thinks his heart is whole, but he is wrong."

MacLeod looked at his own face, dominated by dark, wary eyes. "He is?"

"But of course. The heart can only be whole when given. Then the dreams take shape, truly real. In that moment all the things that truly matter begin." Silence fell and then Gabrielle sighed. "What do you mean to do about Hope?"

He tried to resent the question but failed. "Leave, most likely. It is her wish as well as mine."

"Is that so?"

MacLeod's face hardened. "She has no need for me here. She can hire another man to fix her roof. She can hire twenty."

Gabrielle gave an exasperated snort. "With what, may I ask? With kind words and promises of hot meals? No, Scotsman, I think not."

He made an angry gesture, driving a hand through his hair. "But she must have wealth. This house, these lands..."

Gabrielle shook her head. "Every penny went to the purchase and the repairs. It has been months of dust and sawing and work. And just when the future looked secure, the letter came. Taxes," she hissed, making the word a curse. "Enough to break her."

MacLeod didn't speak. Couldn't, when her words had such a ring of truth about them.

"She needs a strong pair of arms and an honest heart. She needs…someone like him." Gabrielle traced the harsh features on the wall.

MacLeod didn't speak. He was too busy thinking about Hope, wondering if any of this could be true.

"Not," Gabrielle murmured, "that anyone asked me."

As he strode outside without a backward glance, she was pleased to see that she had finally penetrated that prickly shell of his. And though it was impossible, she could have sworn she heard him curse.

In perfect medieval French.

"HAVE YOU SEEN HIM?" Hope's face was pale, her shoulders stiff.

Gabrielle frowned and put down her knife. "Seen who? Jeffrey?"

"Him. MacLeod."

"I saw him go outside. Ten, perhaps fifteen minutes ago." Hope's fingers twisted, restless. "Which way?"

"Over the lawn. To the stable, perhaps." She pointed out the window, where dusk gathered over the glen.

"I see." Hope drew a rough breath. "Very good."

"What is very good? What are you going to do?"

"Exactly what I should have done yesterday. Something I've put off too long." She ran one hand across her waist, as if to smooth away a wave of uneasiness. "I'm going to make him leave."

HE HAD TO GO. Definitely had to go.

She couldn't have him wandering about, overturning her life with that harrowed look in his eyes. A list of the man's problems could have filled a book. Meanwhile, he disturbed her, distracted her, making her forget she had a hundred problems of her own.

That was why he had to go tonight.

Hope kept the words running through her head as she walked toward the stables. Her feet hissed softly on the damp moss and the wind played through her hair. There was just enough light from the rising moon to pick her way over the uneven slope.

Beyond the stable wall she stopped, aware of a muffled stamping and the murmur of a low voice. She crept to the wall's edge, blinking as she stared into sudden light.

A candle flickered on a rough stone bench, touching a rider and horse as they moved in a controlled dance. At a slight urging from MacLeod's leg, the great horse danced sideways, light as air. Another movement sent him prancing in place. Then, to Hope's awe, the great animal lifted a foreleg smooth as silk and kicked laterally.

There were names for paces like that, she thought. There had to be a whole science to that sort of movement and control that seemed effortless but had to be anything but, especially with an animal so large. Horses like that could only be seen in exhibitions and beer commercials. People didn't actually ride them anymore, not as MacLeod was doing. Not as he had done the night he'd jumped the cliff. A knight in full armor would need a mount large enough to bear the weight of man and armor, she thought. A horse with enough endurance to carry his master through battle upon battle…

What was she thinking? Hope shook off her rambling thoughts and eased back, feeling as if she had intruded on a dream of great beauty, a dialogue of movement and grace captured in silence by candlelight.

Then the horse's head rose. He sniffed and reared.

MacLeod turned, seeing her for the first time. Smiling

slightly, he whispered to the horse. The gray mane fluttered as man and beast bent in a low bow.

Hope stepped into the light, struggling for words. "That was…beautiful. He's good, so good. How did he learn those things?"

"Work. Many nights we've spent at this, haven't we, Pegasus?" The horse tossed his head, snorting.

"It shows. He's amazing. So are you." Hope swallowed, remembering why she'd come. "But I need to talk to you."

MacLeod's hands clenched on the gray mane and he slid to the ground in a smooth movement that marked a man who had spent a great part of his life in the saddle.

But not now, Hope saw. The horse carried neither saddle nor bridle. "How…?"

MacLeod strode past her, the horse following at a sedate pace, head erect and entirely conscious of his regal grace.

As Hope followed them into Glenbrae's old stable, she had her second surprise. All was clean, the dirt floor raked and the rough wooden benches now free of litter and leaves. "You did this?"

MacLeod shrugged. "It was a small matter."

But Hope had seen the sorry state of the stables, littered with ten years of leaves and miscellaneous debris. Cleaning it had been beyond her, yet he had done it all in a day.

She trailed her hands over the gleaming saddle, leather straps and bridles hung neatly on the walls. His armor shone behind him, freshly cleaned. Hope saw a barrel of sand on the floor and realized this was his method. Simple or not, it had worked.

He was a man to take care of things. In his quiet way he would move into a room, carve out his own order and transform everything in a matter of hours. She didn't know whether to be grateful or irritated.

She touched the chain mail and the shining gauntlets, and

then a movement in his helmet caught her eye. He shifted quickly for a man so tall, blocking her way. "Did you wish to say something?"

Hope could have sworn he sounded guilty.

If so, she was going to find out why. Maybe *he* had moved those papers on her desk. Maybe he had done things more destructive than that.

She pushed past him. "What have you got in that helmet?" Expecting the worst, she reached over the rim, seeing nothing but shadows.

Something stirred against her fingers. She heard a muffled meow as a wriggling ball of warm fur pressed against her palm.

Two fluffy heads peered over the helmet's rim, blinking sleepily. A pair of kittens slipped over each other in their eagerness to stand.

"Kittens? Is this what you were trying to hide?"

She could have sworn his face flushed as he reached for the nearest one. Black and white paws skittered over his shoulders, then settled in the wool cradle MacLeod made of his long tartan. "They were alone, hungry. I heated milk in the kitchen and fed them with a cloth."

The kitten purred softly, shoving its velvet nose and face against MacLeod's neck in a haze of happiness. Absently MacLeod settled its wriggling white body beside his friend. "They're hungry again." He opened a jar on the edge of the table, poured milk into a clean rag, and offered it to the greedy newborns.

Hope stared in amazement. Kittens. The man was hiding *kittens* from her.

She took a ragged breath and forced her splintered thoughts back under control. It didn't matter if he was good with animals, she told herself grimly. She couldn't afford to trust him. He had to *go*.

"I need to talk to you, MacLeod."

He looked up, one brow arched.

"I am listening."

"It's like this. I've been thinking, quite a lot actually." She tried not to watch the kittens swaying happily against his gentle hands.

"And?"

"And I've decided. There's no discussion, no arguing. My mind is made up." She locked her arms at her chest, hoping it would still the fluttering there.

It didn't.

"What should I not discuss or argue about?"

"You." She raised a hand as if to forestall anger or protests. "There's no other way. You've got to go, MacLeod."

"I see." He dripped more milk on the rag for his tiny charges.

"Aren't you going to ask why?"

He shrugged. "It makes no difference. You said your mind was set."

"Well, I'll tell you—since you haven't asked. You're entitled to some sort of explanation."

"I am neither kin nor mate. You owe me no duty or honesty."

Hope chewed her lip, watching the kittens meow contentedly. "You saved my life, and I appreciate it. If there were some other way, I'd let you stay." Her fingers tightened over her waist, digging restlessly. "I've spoken to the church in Glenbrae. They have a temporary residence until…"

"Until what?"

Hope took a shaky breath. "Until you sort things out, get your life back in control." She tried to smile, tried to ignore waves of abject, raw guilt for what she was doing. But self-preservation had to come first.

"Very well. I shall leave when I finish here." He set the kittens back in his helmet and calmly began gathering his equipment.

Hope's fists opened and closed. Candlelight spilled over his broad shoulders, sculpting his high cheekbones and proud chin. But there was no flicker of emotion in his eyes as he lifted harnesses and saddle.

"Damn it, stop being so *calm,* will you?"

"One of us needs to be calm."

"Are you saying I'm upset? Are you saying I care? Because if you are, you're wrong. I don't c-care. And I don't trust you, not for a second. I don't trust *anyone.*"

"I see."

"Just what do you see?"

He turned slowly. "You." There was something rough and almost dangerous in his voice. "Maybe I even see things you do not wish me to see."

His long legs crossed the room in three paces. Hope took a step back, only to feel the table behind her. His hand rose toward her, then past, jerking down a bridle from the wall. In the process he grazed her hip with the edge of his hand.

MacLeod tossed the leather strip into a basket on the floor, then reached behind Hope for his gauntlet.

His thigh slid between her legs and his gaze never wavered from her face.

"What are you doing?"

"Satisfying myself." His eyes darkened. "Satisfying both of us." He reached back for his hauberk, and their bodies met shoulder to thigh.

"Stop," Hope whispered. "I need for you to go."

"And I will. Tonight." He watched her face as his hand slid into her hair. "Be hard, Hope. Never apologize for this. It is the way you will survive—now and after I have gone."

Hope didn't feel hard when their bodies touched. She felt angry and confused.

And dangerously vulnerable.

She blurted out the words that had bothered her since that

morning. "Tell me why you went with those soldiers after they killed your family."

His hands stilled. "So you can laugh?"

"So I can understand."

With a harsh sound of despair, he locked one hand to her head. His fingers were rigid, as if they wanted to push away—and couldn't. "There were broken bodies beneath my feet and blood that shone in pools. All that matters is, I failed them. I turned away. I lived and they did not."

"There must have been a reason that you went."

"They had one of my sisters. She was their bond against me."

"Oh, God," Hope breathed. She tried to dismiss this as yet another fantasy, but the hurt in his eyes was too real. "What happened to her?"

"She went to London. At the court, I was told. She died long after, when I was already in the East. When it was too late to matter or to grieve for what she had become."

"But why was one boy so important to them?"

He took a sharp breath. "Because I could fight. Because I took five men at once, with no help. I would have died but for his order. I *should* have died...."

"Whose order?"

"Edward. The king you say is centuries dead. He could not win against us," MacLeod said flatly. "Though he quartered Wallace, he could not kill what Wallace and the Highlands had begun. When he looked at me, his eyes twisted, and instead of one angry, frightened boy, he saw a country, young and proud. Because it frightened him and he was king, he attacked. Perhaps that arrogance made him a great ruler." MacLeod shrugged. "All I know is that I remained his prisoner, caught in his grip for ten long years and more." He lifted Hope's head, staring deep into her eyes. "I have done things to haunt my sleep. You are right to send me away."

Those hard, broken words took away any fear Hope

might have been able to muster. Honor suited him like the weathered, ancient kilt across his thighs.

"If you did these things, it was at another's order, not by your choice." She heard her words and swept aside the warnings of logic. It didn't matter whether she believed him. He believed, and his anguish was almost enough to convince her. All she cared about was that he was lost and alone and riddled with anguish.

He made an angry gesture with one hand. "Do not try to forgive me. Wherever I go, I bring danger. Even here. So I will leave." He pulled away, only to feel her palm against his shoulder.

"Fear me," he said roughly. "It is the only way you will be safe."

Slowly she touched the scar beside his mouth.

"It is dangerous for you," he said. "This time it would not stop between us with one kiss."

"Why?" Hope whispered.

"Because you make me blind. You make me want to claim you as I once claimed all this land."

His hands dipped. The tiny buttons at the front of her sweater shifted, straining beneath his callused fingers. "Tell me to stop."

All her words fled. The only thing left in the silent half-light was the angry glint in his eyes. Even then, Hope felt the hurt in him.

Somehow it matched her own.

A button tore free and hit the table. She still didn't pull her gaze from his.

"What do you want from me, Hope O'Hara?"

"I…I'm not sure. Nothing, I thought."

Another button pulled free. "And now?"

She made a low sound of confusion.

The wool drifted open. When MacLeod saw she wore nothing underneath, his breath jammed in his chest. "Snow against roses," he whispered. "A sight to stir a man's blood to madness. Tell me now to leave," he ordered hoarsely.

He palmed her breasts, then slowly traced the tight crimson nipples. Hope's pulse raced like autumn thunder in her ears. Then she said different words. "Show me, MacLeod. Show me what it can be like. Just once," she whispered.

He pulled her against him with a curse, creamy skin and heated crests meeting the hot friction of his broad palm. "Do you feel it now, *mo rùn?*" She was cradled in his thighs, every hard outline of his growing desire clearly felt. "Do you understand, Hope? They lied, those men. You would not disappoint a lover. By all honor, you would only drive him to heated madness."

His mouth covered the aching skin caressed seconds before. His dark hair fell over her shoulder, warmth against the greater heat of his mouth.

Hope made a small, choked sound. She had expected awkwardness, but he gave her grace. She had expected stiffness and distaste, but heat shifted into raw pleasure and something odd began to happen near her ankles, building in hot, racing spirals.

She had never known this kind of electric need. She had never felt so naked, no open.

So precious.

His teeth rimmed her breast, then closed around her. His name was a ragged plea whispered in the still, calm air as desire sank tiny teeth into her core. She moaned, caught beneath the silken probing of his tongue.

Wind sighed around the stone walls. Like a sleepwalker, Hope heard the distant murmur of the loch and the soft crunching noise of the horse at his straw.

Time seemed to crawl, endless and sweet in the stable's gloom. She tried to speak and could not. She tried to argue or protest and she could not. Wanting was too close, need too furious. His fingers turned her fluid, pliant, restless.

She took a racing breath and touched his face. "You can... We could..." She swallowed, trying to say things she'd never said before. "You don't have to worry about complications. Entanglements. I wouldn't try to hold you."

How could a woman look so vulnerable? MacLeod wondered grimly. And how could he be such a fool to consider her breathless offer?

Her face was flushed and her hair a tumble of chestnut curls. Desire painted a glorious blush over her creamy skin and tightened her breath.

Honest, she was.

Too honest for the safety of either of them.

In MacLeod's world, women manipulated and schemed, using their bodies as coin in a complex game for power or status. Never were they honest. Never were they claimed by true desire, as she was now.

Maybe he had known the wrong women, MacLeod thought bleakly. If so, they had taught him well.

With expert eyes he measured her response. She was trembling, open. In a moment he could be sheathed in her heat. She would gasp and rock against him, lost in passion deep enough to blind them both.

And he wanted that fiercely. But there were complications. There always were, despite her obscure promise.

Gently he ran his hand through the silken cap of her hair. In his time, no woman would dream of having her hair shorn like this.

Like the rest of her, it delighted him.

Somehow he managed to keep his hands from shaking. Storming Damascus had been easier than this, he thought ruefully as needs long unassuaged raced to fiery life.

In a moment he could bare the rest of her and draw another husky moan from her lips. He could make her laugh, then topple her headlong into darkest pleasure while he watched her, skin to skin.

Heart to heart.

MacLeod stilled, realizing he had never wanted a woman so badly.

Why now? Why only with her?

Hope's eyes opened, the sun-washed green of a summer glen, and he tried to remember he was a knight. He reminded himself of honor and chivalry and oaths of pure, courtly love. But it was difficult when she shifted against him, all heat and yearning.

In a moment they would be on the oak bench. And a moment later he would be buried inside her, teaching them both about dark worlds of shifting pleasure.

He arched her back, coaxing her nipple to a greedy point. She filled his hands, filled his senses, filled his heart.

Bodies met and need bolted. As he drank in her taste with hard, searching lips, she made a lost sound. Her fingers tugged at the soft hair on his chest, then angled lower, where the folds of wool gathered at his waist.

His body tensed. "Dangerous, *mo cridhe*."

"No. Not dangerous enough."

MacLeod forgot the stable, forgot the date, forgot the horse eating contentedly a few feet away.

Her sweater slid off her shoulders.

But he would not have her, not the way his body demanded. The kittens meowed softly as he pulled her close and swept her onto the table, chest to chest, then stilled her protest with his lips.

Heat grew. She made a restless sound and her head tilted back.

For MacLeod there was nothing but her mouth, nothing but the heat they made together so perfectly.

He fought for control even as he found her heat beneath her garment of soft wool. With expert hands, he slid aside lace and silk and moved within her, showing her about grace and aching beauty. "Feel this, Hope. Feel me wanting you. Wanting us."

His legs braced her, showing his desire. But his control did not waver.

"Oh, God, I—can't." Her voice shook.

"You can. You will." Time, explanations, nothing mattered but *this*.

He felt her stiffen, liquid against his hand. Her eyes closed as he eased farther, sheathed perfectly by her deepest heat.

"Beautiful," he whispered. And then he moved again, finding her hidden softness, showing her just how beautiful she was to him. How loved.

Her back arched. Her hands dug into his back and she cried out his name. MacLeod closed his eyes as he felt her tense, then close around him in swift, hot tremors that left him cursing inside. Wanting inside.

So close. So flawless.

But all this could never be his.

Somewhere above the loch a night bird cried in lonely protest, racing beneath the moon, and darkness enfolded the glen.

CHAPTER SEVENTEEN

HER EYES OPENED TO HIS, hazed with desire. "What am I supposed to say?"

"Nothing." He traced the line of her cheek, smiling slightly.

"That's…it?"

He nodded.

She took a short, unsteady breath. Candlelight gilded her face and her expressive mouth. "So what happens now, Macleod?"

"You tell me how beautiful you are. Because you are."

She swallowed. "But the rest. I mean, just now. You didn't—"

"No, I did not." He touched her face, wishing he could hold her forever. "And I will not." Though the movement was a sword cut at his heart, he eased away from her and smoothed her clothing.

"You're…going?"

He nodded, turning away to gather his armor and leather.

"You're going now?"

He did not answer.

"Just like that?"

"So you can remain hard. So we both can remain hard," he added grimly.

Hope felt something slide into her hands.

"Keep them safe for me. They need…someone."

Hope looked down at the balls of fur wriggling against

her skirt. She lifted the kittens to her face, fighting back a hundred questions.

Because it was too late for questions. Now more than ever. He had to go. And she had to watch him.

He led the horse to the door and blew out the single candle, now long guttered. Moonlight traced his cheeks with rough beauty as he turned. "Remember how it felt, *mo cridhe*. Remember when another man touches you and makes you taste paradise, as one surely will." Moonlight touched his gauntlets, shoved beneath his arm, and Pegasus gave a hugging snort.

"But…"

Then he was gone.

Hope watched without moving until she could see no more of him.

Then, like a sleepwalker, she stumbled back to the house, past Gabrielle and up the hall. She did not bother to shove away her tears as she skirted the brooding portrait hidden in the night's gloom, where it stood firm guard over Glenbrae's ancient secrets.

CHAPTER EIGHTEEN

SOMETHING WAS WRONG.

The floor creaked and a door moved. Was it Ronan?

Hope lay in bed and listened to the wind and the dozen sounds of a settling old house. But there was no echo of a man's footsteps or his booming laugh.

Beside her the telephone pealed shrilly. After wrestling with the cord and knocking off all her pillows, she managed to find the receiver. "H'llo?"

"Where is it?"

Hope gazed blearily at the luminous face of the clock beside her bed. It was 1:32 in the morning. Wind tapped at the window, and outside the sky was black. "Mr. Wyndgate?"

"That's right. I want to know where the bloody thing *is*."

Hope stifled a yawn and sat up groggily. "Where what is?"

"The brooch, of course." The collector's voice was very close to a shout. "Don't pretend you don't know what I mean. I placed the brooch in a box and drove directly back here to my country house. I dined and had a short walk, then settled down to work. But then I found that both the brooch and box were gone."

"I don't understand."

"I should think it's quite clear, Ms. O'Hara. No one else but *you* knew about that piece."

Hope watched lightning crackle against gray banks of clouds. "Why would someone steal the brooch?"

"I would hardly steal from myself, Ms. O'Hara. I have a

shattered exterior window and a door that did not damage itself. Did you find a better offer and decide to send someone to steal the brooch back?" he hissed.

Hope straightened slowly, fighting waves of sleep and confusion. "I haven't seen the wolf since you left here this afternoon."

"Can you explain why nothing else was removed? Why did they know exactly what to look for?"

Hope didn't feel up to explaining anything. The man must be crazy. It was the middle of the night. She was still caught in a dream of cutting gray eyes and a haunting, angular face. She already felt guilty for the sale she had made, though it had been necessary in order to keep Glenbrae House solvent. "This is pure nonsense," she said firmly. "I don't have your brooch, and I certainly didn't pay anyone to steal it from you."

"Be very careful about what you say, Ms. O'Hara, because you're going to have to prove every word in court. You've pocketed a great deal of my money, paid to you in good faith, and I have your signature on a bill of sale. Police do not look kindly on this sort of arranged theft."

Lightning streaked through the sky. Something cracked and skittered down the roof.

Arranged theft? Now he had crossed the line.

Hope's fingers clenched on the receiver. "And if you say much more, you're going to be facing a slander suit."

Cold laughter filled the line. "Indeed? I think that you're lying. I also think that you're going to be very, very sorry that you tangled with me, Ms. O'Hara."

The line went dead.

Hope's hands trembled as she hung up the phone. The accusations were preposterous, she told herself. No police investigation would turn up any evidence that she had been involved in stealing the brooch. In spite of that, the collector's accusations left her distinctly uneasy. If someone

CHRISTINA SKYE 193

had wanted the silver wolf enough to steal it, no one was safe until the thief was found.

"WINSTON WYNDGATE paid you *how much?*" Gabrielle dropped the whisk she was using to make breakfast.

"Twenty-five thousand pounds," Hope repeated, toying with a piece of toast. "He said it was a very fine piece."

Gabrielle looked stunned. "It must be solid platinum to be worth that kind of money."

"Not platinum. Some kind of hammered silver, I think. But the piece has historical significance and it's very old."

"It must be as old as Methuselah to be worth that much to a cheapskate like Wyndgate."

"Winston Wyndgate, the antiques collector?" Jeffrey ambled into the kitchen and fished a piece of featherlight crepe from Gabrielle's pan, then sighed. "You outdo yourself again, Gabrielle."

"Enough flattery. Sit down and eat before my crepes are ruined."

Jeffrey seemed fascinated by the color that filled Gabrielle's face, but he said nothing as he slid behind the oak table. "I've heard of Wyndgate. He's a regular hawk when it comes to fine antiques. You can be sure that if he offered that much, your piece was worth even more." He tugged at his hair, leaving it more untidy than ever. "I know a silversmith in Rye, an old friend of the family. Would you like me to get his opinion?"

"It's too late," Hope said tiredly. "The King's Wolf is gone, and I, for one, am glad of it." She tried not to remember that MacLeod was also gone.

She had slept badly, worse than badly, her dreams haunted by images of border raiders, shouting Highlanders, and a warrior in a black cloak who had died centuries before. The bang of loose shutters had done nothing to help settle her rest.

Nor did the knowledge that her enigmatic visitor was gone.

Money or not, Hope cursed the instant that she had found the old brooch. It had brought her nothing but uneasiness and bleak dreams. And of Ronan MacLeod, she refused to think anything at all.

THAT EVENING at half past five the Glenbrae Investment Club came to order.

Within twelve minutes, eight stocks had been sold, four new stocks had been purchased, and over ten thousand pounds had changed hands. The air was tense, the room was noisy, and every one of the white-haired club members was in seventh heaven.

Morwenna Wishwell pounded the polished wooden desk with her gavel, but no one in the disorderly group seemed to pay the slightest attention. Tables rang with the pounding of fists, and white heads shook as elderly ladies and gentlemen threw themselves into the debate over the next stock predicted to skyrocket.

A slender woman in exquisite pearls and paisley sniffed loudly. "I don't care what you say. Fidelity Fund is the one to watch."

"Ach, rubbish." Archibald Brown, the Wishwells' nearest neighbor, waved his half-filled teacup, managing to spill a very fine Keemun brew over his muted tweed jacket. "'Tis RK Telephone for me."

"What about that new biotech company?" A woman with shining white hair sat forward enthusiastically. "I hear they are injecting growth genes in clogged arteries and making new blood vessels for heart patients."

"Biotech?" Archibald Brown sniffed. "All fine talk, ye know it as well as I, Samantha. It takes years for human trials."

Morwenna wielded her gavel again. "Has anyone checked the Toronto Stock Exchange Index today?" Somehow she managed to be heard among the clamor.

A frail old gentleman with wire-rim glasses and glowing cheeks raised a file in unsteady fingers. "I've got the papers here. Primary reports are over there by the coffee cake. I say we should go for oil and gas and forget the Koreans."

"You'll na put money of mine into the energy sector, man," Archibald thundered. "Bound to fail. Rising costs, that's all you'll see there."

"Bound to fail, is it?" the man with the glasses demanded, pushing from his seat.

As the two gentlemen prepared to square off, Morwenna intervened once more. "Stop that, you two. Fighting solves nothing, which I've told both of you since you were in short pants. Now, settle down and behave so we can analyze the profit margins according to our agenda."

From the doorway, Hope watched. She kept listening foolishly for a sound on the stair or a low, rough laugh from the courtyard. But Ronan MacLeod was gone, his horse and armor with him.

She told herself she didn't care.

And she knew it was a lie.

With a sigh, she forced her thoughts back to her guests. Every meeting of the Glenbrae Investment Club was a theatrical event that tottered on the edge of chaos. The members took fiercely personal interest in every stock or mutual fund bought and sold, and they were quick to express their scorn for weak choices. The group's varied backgrounds in politics, international trade and military duty gave them broad expertise, which they built upon at every meeting.

She turned to see Gabrielle carrying in a platter with blue corn bread and her special three-alarm black bean soup spiced with Tabasco sauce.

"Just in time." Hope managed a smile. "They're fighting again."

"This will stop them. It is hard to fight on a full stomach, so my mother always said."

"Especially when your mouth is on fire," Jeffrey added, carrying in two huge pitchers of steaming spiced cider.

"You've outdone yourself yet again, Gabrielle." Hope closed her eyes, inhaling the fragrance of cinnamon, nutmeg and cloves.

"It is nothing. A bit of this, a pinch of that. Of course, the green chiles and fresh cilantro were not so easy to find, but I have my ways." She raised her shoulders in an expressive Gallic shrug.

"Where do those people get their energy?" Jeffrey said. "They've been arguing for nearly two hours without a break. Even the lady with the gavel knows more about mutual funds than my father, and that's supposed to be his specialty."

"Oh? Does he work in London?" Hope asked casually.

"He used to."

"But, Jeffrey, you never told me your father was an important man of finances!" Gabrielle put a hand on his arm. "You must go in and join them. They are always thrilled to have new members."

His face reddened. "I don't care a whit about bonds and markets. I had enough of that from my father, morning to night." He charged past Gabrielle, pitchers clinking and cider sloshing.

"They don't seem to be on the best of terms." Hope frowned. "I wonder if his father knows where Jeffrey is."

"Or if he *cares*. What father would not want to know where his son is? Me, I think I will find him and tell him." Gabrielle stared after Jeffrey, a look of fierce protectiveness in her eyes.

"I don't know, Gabrielle. Jeffrey was very adamant that he wanted nothing to do with his father. He might not thank you for interfering."

"*Pfft.* As if I care for any thanks. His father should know," she said firmly. "On the day that I met him, Jeffrey had not eaten for three days. *Three days*," she repeated. "In fact, I would like to tell this so important man of finances a thing or two about his duty as a father."

"But how will you find him?"

Gabrielle smiled darkly. "Me, I have many sources."

Hope didn't doubt it for a second. She only prayed that Gabrielle's interference would not make things worse.

Jeffrey charged out of the sitting room, his hands empty, his face blazing red.

Gavel in hand, Morwenna Wishwell stared after him. "I'm afraid it's something Archibald said. It seemed innocent enough at the time. He merely remarked that the boy looked the spitting image of an old friend of his in London, someone he knew in his World War Two days. Your friend looked extremely upset and then he just charged off. Shall I go and have a talk with him?"

"Better let him cool down," Hope said. "Apparently he and his father are not on the best of terms."

"Poor unhappy soul." Morwenna moved closer. "But tell me, Miss O'Hara, have you had any unexpected visitors here?" Her bright eyes glinted with curiosity.

"One." Hope frowned. "A man arrived here two nights ago. He saved my life, actually." She looked away, trying not to remember.

The lady's sharp eyes widened. "Did he indeed?"

"If he hadn't come by when he did, I'd have broken my neck."

The old woman clapped her hands in excitement. "So it worked. Our calculations were correct."

"Calculations?"

"Oh, nothing, my dear." Morwenna gripped Hope's arm. "Tell me what he's like."

"It doesn't matter. He's gone." Hope swallowed. "He left yesterday."

Morwenna's two sisters emerged from the noisy room to join them. Morwenna grasped Perpetua's hand. "We did it,

Pet," she said excitedly. "He's come. But now he's left us, Hope says. Why would he—"

"Hush," her sister said softly.

"But—"

Perpetua gently but firmly patted her palm. "We don't want to bore Miss O'Hara. It appears she has other things to worry about. As usual, the gentlemen have gone through all the food and they're back to fighting again."

Hope gave a slow, distracted nod. "I'll get the chocolate mocha pound cake."

"But what was his name?" Morwenna demanded.

"MacLeod. Ronan MacLeod."

A little sigh emerged from the three sisters in unison. "MacLeod," Perpetua said slowly. "The name sounds familiar. I wonder if he was related to the Portree Mac-Leods by any chance."

"But why did he go?" Morwenna persisted.

"Because it was best. For both of us," Hope whispered.

"Oh dear, they're fighting again." Honoria tugged at Hope's hands, pointing to the meeting room. "Talk to them, Miss O'Hara. Tell them you'll send them home without any cake if they don't behave."

Hope sighed as Archibald Brown delivered a resounding left hook to his opponent, who looked perfectly delighted to answer in kind. Two chairs toppled and a tweed jacket went flying.

Was there something in the water?

She was about to intervene in the altercation when Gabrielle touched her shoulder. "It is the telephone for you. It is your friend Jamee McCall. Now you will talk and I will see to these men who act like little boys."

Hope sent a last anxious glance at Morwenna as she left the room to take her call. "Jamee, is that you?"

"I'm surprised you remember my name. An odd sort of friend you are. You never return any of my calls."

"It's been a little…complicated here."

"Hope, is something wrong?"

Hope sighed. She had never been able to keep secrets from her oldest friend. "So, Lady McCall, how does the noble life of ease suit you?"

"Noble life?" Hope's American friend, married for less than a year to the twelfth laird of Glenlyle, gave an audible snort. "I've married into chaos. It was bad growing up with four brothers, but nothing prepared me for Glenlyle at Christmas. We've got half-stitched teddy bears stacked on every table, scraps of tartan jammed in every corner, and as usual, Ian is working himself to pieces."

Hope chuckled. "I suspect that both of you are loving every second."

"Actually, I do believe we are. But what about you? How is business? Have you had any more visitors?"

Hope stared out at the front salon. Archibald Brown was struggling to his feet, and Morwenna and her two sisters were brushing off his jacket and tie. He had been toppled by a left hook from his adversary, who disagreed with his stock assessments.

Life was never dull in Glenbrae.

"We'll manage."

"That's not what I asked, my wonderful, infuriating friend."

"I know it wasn't."

"If you have room, Ian and I would love to come visit. We've been planning to come down for a long stay. We could leave just as soon as we finish the last shipment of bears for Windsor. My brothers are dying to see the place, too. I'm sure they would be delighted to join us."

She waited. An unspoken question hung in the air.

Hope's fingers tightened on the telephone. She wasn't ready for Jamee to see Glenbrae House until it was full of paying guests. She wanted desperately to succeed here. "I'd love to see you and Ian. Your brothers, too, of course. But right now…things are a little hectic."

"You're full?"

Hope bit her lip, trying not to lie. "Actually, we have some German visitors due any minute."

"That's wonderful, Hope. Are they business travelers? People who will be impressed by the detailed restoration work and the fine antiques you've gathered?"

"Not exactly."

The last of the investment club members were filing down the path at the front of the house, and Jeffrey waved to Hope from the stairwell. He was carrying a microphone, a black light and Hope's voluminous costume. He pointed at his watch.

Showtime, Hope thought. "I've got to go, Jamee. Give my love to Ian, will you? And to all those cute little bears."

"But, Hope, I…"

"Talk to you soon, Jamee." Feeling guilty, Hope hung up before her friend could ask any more pointed questions.

She watched her friends vanish up the glen and suddenly felt empty inside.

"Hope, we don't have much time." Jeffrey held out her costume, grinning. "We need one last run-through with all the modifications and this version should be quite something to remember." He paused. "Are you listening? Hope?"

"Ready to go, Jeffrey."

"Grand. Just break a leg, all right?"

"I certainly hope not."

"I'M SO GLAD we saw you there by the loch. Your name is MacLeod, you said?" Morwenna Wishwell smiled up at the tall man in a well-worn tartan.

"So it is. Do you need my help getting back home?"

Morwenna took his arm. "That would be lovely. It isn't far, but in the dark it's easy to stumble." Morwenna Wishwell hadn't missed a step yet, and her feet looked entirely steady. In fact, all three sisters looked hearty beyond their years.

But MacLeod was happy to stay far from Hope's sight. He had found random footprints by the rear gardens and a broken lock on a lower window, but nothing that should have left him so convinced of her danger.

He should have been putting his mind to finding a way home. There were people back in his own time who needed him. He hadn't the leisure to flounder about here in a world of talking boxes, bath bubbles and a woman who turned his soul upside down.

It was time to go home, just as he had promised her.

He stared at the black hills, ignoring a black, racing regret.

"Mr. MacLeod? Is something bothering you, dear boy?"

Dear boy. No one had ever called him that. He tried to be angry at the delicate white-haired lady, but couldn't. He suspected a very keen mind beneath that fragile manner, and there was something oddly compelling in her tone.

"Perhaps."

"We can help." Morwenna patted his arm. "My sisters and I are very skilled in managing things."

"What kind of things?"

"Oh, whatever you like, my dear boy. Trees, weather. Even people on occasion, though they are much harder."

MacLeod felt an uneasy pricking at his shoulders. "And how do you…manage these things?"

They walked past the stone fence into the greater darkness of the forest. Somewhere an owl called, once and then again, the sound echoed by the sharp bark of a fox.

MacLeod had never heard any owls here in the glen. Nor had he seen any foxes.

His uneasiness grew as he heard another shrill bark from a blur of white along the cliffs. MacLeod watched the sleek form race up the glen, then vanish. "What was that?"

"A white fox, I believe. He lives up there in the mist."

"I never saw such a creature."

"Not many people have. Now, what were we discussing?"

"How you manage things."

"Oh, yes. There are always variables, influences, external factors."

"I do not understand," he said.

"No, of course you wouldn't. They didn't speak of such things in your time, did they?"

He spun about, then froze. "What did you say?"

The woman's laugh was gentle as the moonlight just peeking above the cliffs. "In your time, young man. *Your* time, which is not this time."

Foreboding gathered, pressing against his chest. "You know?"

"All of it, I'm afraid. How you came in the storm and how you saved Hope O'Hara from falling. You performed even better than we had—" She stopped, cleared her throat. "It must be a terrible shock to you, coming to this world."

The wind crept across his neck. "You did this. *You* brought me here," he said hoarsely. "You worked the magic and cast the black spells."

She smoothed his arm companionably. "Nothing black, I assure you. Never that. And 'spell' doesn't really describe our methods. There is hard science, careful calculation and the balanced focus of the mind. Yes, the mind is the most important tool of all." Her eyes widened, and MacLeod thought he saw a tiny crescent moon held captive there.

"I do not care about why or how. I want to go back. Now." He felt rooted to the damp earth, claimed by the glen that stretched dark and strange around him. He could not be part of it.

Not his glen. Not now, as the moon rose chill through the trees.

"Go back? After all you've seen?"

He laughed bitterly. "*Because* of all I've seen."

"Logical, I suppose. And what about Hope?"

MacLeod watched clouds trail over the moon. Memories of her touch, her laugh, her soft, broken sounds of passion, assailed him. "What about her?"

The woman sighed and shook her head. "So hard. Always so impatient, but most of all with yourself. You will have to change that." She murmured a phrase, lilting and archaic words that made him turn in shock.

"You speak the old tongue?"

"Oh, yes. An older tongue than even you know, dear boy." She added another phrase.

"You are *sidhe*." It was both praise and accusation.

"We are…many things. Leave it at that." The moon deepened in her eyes, a silver lantern that soothed him, compelled him, offering memory or forgetfulness.

He blinked, trying to clear his head. Trying to remember what he had asked. "I cannot stay. I am no part of this place." He heard the pain in his voice.

"You are what you choose to be, Highlander."

"Easy for you to say."

"Not easy. Never easy." Suddenly there was steel in her words. Steel and anger. "Not for those who remember. Not for those charged to hold the legends against time."

Something made MacLeod look down and touch her frail shoulder. "None can do it so well as you, I ween."

A smile tugged at her lips, and mischief hung all around her. "In that you're right, MacLeod of Glenbrae." The scrutiny sharpened. "So you will leave her? Walk away as if you'd never met, never touched, never dreamed?"

"What do you know of that?" he demanded angrily.

"Enough," she said calmly. "Now answer."

He turned. "I must." Again the wind touched his hair, and this time he could have sworn it held the first flakes of snow. "I *must*."

"You will break her heart if you go."

He glared ahead into the night. "She will be better without me."

The trees shivered. "Just as well. Hope O'Hara is weak, after all. Not a match for one like you."

"She is not weak," he whispered. "She is fire and steel, more beauty than a man deserves to hold."

"But a temper, nevertheless. She would curse your days and plague your nights."

But what nights, he thought. *What passion to share and sweetness to give.* "Her temper is no worse than mine," he said gruffly.

"And she is busy. Always fussing about her inn, always interfering in the lives of her friends. There would be no rest for you."

Snowflakes whispered across his face. No rest. Nor would he want it any other way with Hope O'Hara.

But his will was cold and unflinching. "I cannot stay. I have duties of my own, given by a king. Hate him, I must, but an oath cannot be broken or all honor is lost."

A low cottage was before them now, the long, overhanging eaves dusted with snow. A lamp burned in one window, drawing him as if in a dream.

"Honor." She said the word in the old tongue in a way that made his skin tighten. "Now, there's a word few men speak of today." She stood at the end of the path, studying him. "And you wonder how they fare, back in your time. You worry that there will be harm or loss by your actions."

"Do you see everything, mistress?"

"Much, dear boy. Very much." With a sigh, she moved to the window. With one finger she drew a circle in the frost veiling the pane. Then she blew faintly. "Look, then. Stare within and see how they fare without you."

"But I can't..." MacLeod stopped as the circle began to glow with dim images.

He saw his groom, surrounded by villagers. The boy

pointed to the fields, speaking with excitement and new maturity. Those around him listened, nodding.

"They will be fine, you see." The woman's voice was a rich hum of sound. "You are not needed there for a while."

MacLeod shoved a hand through his hair. "And I am needed here?"

"There are factors we did not consider. Variables. Danger..."

He turned tensely. "Danger to her?"

"Yes—no." She made an angry sound. "We cannot see, no matter how we look."

"You must keep her safe," he said fiercely. "Give me your word on it."

The circle on the window faded into melting tracks of water. "We cannot. That is why we called you, MacLeod of the Isles, MacLeod of Outremar and the Crusade. She needs a warrior, a hero." She stepped back into the shadows and pulled a long canvas sack from the bushes. "Here. You may require this."

After a moment's reluctance, MacLeod raised his hands. The sack was smooth and heavy beneath his fingers. "What is it?"

"You'll find out soon enough. Now you'd better go. Tonight she will have need of the King's Wolf."

He made a flat, bleak sound. "But who will protect her from *me*?"

"Give her one month, MacLeod of the Isles. Keep her safe until the moon waxes and wanes one cycle."

MacLeod raised his head, watching the moon caught in the dark arms of a tree. Again the high cry of an owl filtered through the glen.

There was no answer behind him.

"Hello?"

He turned to find the windows dark, the lantern gone. Silence gripped the little clearing, and no living thing moved save himself.

He shivered, touched by something beyond his knowing. It was not fear but comprehension that made him step back and turn away without speaking.

Give her one month, MacLeod of the Isles. Keep her safe. The trees dipped. *One month, we ask of you.*

The silent urging brushed his face like snow, though he fought its charmed, faerie pull.

Follow your heart, Highlander. Now, before your time runs out, as ours did.

He felt a sudden premonition of danger somewhere in the darkness.

Hope…

He turned and ran while a fox cried shrilly in the night.

CHAPTER NINETEEN

SKY AND LOCH HAD BLURRED into black as Hope took her place at the top of the stairwell, clad head to toe in her luminous costume.

Outside, snow drifted down and wind played through the glen. Then an engine backfired and Gabrielle poked her head excitedly from the kitchen.

"They're coming! *Dieu,* there must be twenty of them. Young and old. Big and small. In a bus, they come." Gabrielle seized Hope's hand and dragged her toward the back stairway. "Come, you must hurry. *Vite, vite.*"

Hope rolled her eyes, feeling more dishonest by the second. "How do you say 'boo' in German?"

"Forget this boo. You will keep to the plan that Jeffrey has given," Gabrielle said sternly.

"Fine, fine, let's just get it over with." Hope suddenly frowned. "Where is Banquo, by the way? If he charges through the room and knocks down all the wiring, we're sunk."

"Already taken care of," Gabrielle said smugly. "I put him in his cage for the night."

"Has everyone else gone?"

"Every last graying head. Though I wish one younger man were not gone," Gabrielle murmured.

Hope pretended she had not heard.

The lights flickered, then went out, as prearranged. Hope slid her hood into place as ghostly light rippled off her full-length skirt. Thunder boomed down the staircase, her signal to appear.

She prayed that she wouldn't catch her foot again, topple down the stairs and break her neck.

Cold wind rushed past her face. Hope turned, sensing a presence nearby. "Banquo?" she whispered. "Is that you?"

When the silence held, she shrugged. Nerves, she told herself.

Another peal of thunder cascaded through the hall.

The German tourists stood in a huddle by the door, staring upward. Suddenly Hope felt the drama of the moment. If they wanted a ghost, then she would give them one.

MACLEOD RAN, ignoring the branches that slapped at his arms and chest. A warning beat in his heart as he shot across the field, passed the loch's stony edge and plunged through the black orchard.

No owl cried to greet him.

No fox barked from the cliffs.

The earth itself seemed to mock him, hindering his progress and catching at his feet. And as MacLeod ran, his fear grew apace.

Give her one month, MacLeod of the Isles. Keep her safe until the moon waxes and wanes one cycle.

No time to make sense of their odd speech. No time to understand what magic they had worked to bring him here.

Only Hope mattered.

Glenbrae House was before him when he made out the prints of running feet. From the woods they came, flying along the stone fence toward the south wall of the house. MacLeod tossed the canvas sack over his back and fell to one knee.

The prints stopped abruptly in the middle of a dark tangle of holly vines, as if the runner had vanished into air.

Frowning, he scanned the lawn and the stable beyond.

When he looked up, fear roiled into fury.

High above, a window lay open, its long lace curtains flapping in the wind. MacLeod drew back, just able to make out a black shape vanishing over the sill.

Follow your heart, Highlander.

Now, before your time runs out, as ours did.

With a ragged curse he peeled open the sack and ran his hands over the smooth, curved wood inside.

SHOWTIME.

Hope's heart pounded as she gripped the stair rail.

A bloodcurdling scream erupted through Jeffrey's carefully prepared audio system, and dim light played over the walls, outlining plumes of drifting smoke.

"Glide," Hope whispered, remembering Jeffrey's instructions. She was supposed to be terrifying, unworldly, and all she felt like was an idiot. At the top of the landing, she raised her hand as another scream tore free from the audio system.

Down below her, the tourists huddled closer.

Praying she didn't look as idiotic as she felt, Hope took four more steps along the stairs, then swept her arm and trailing sleeve over the banister. The lights dimmed, and she felt the fan kick in, fluttering the folds of her gown and lacy sleeves. At the same moment, a ghostly "head" separated from the back of her body and flew off through the air directly toward the German visitors.

The tragic, beheaded ghost of Glenbrae House made its first official appearance, greeted by screams and gestures and a torrent of excited German.

Hope was starting to believe the scheme might actually work when a cold draft played over the top of the stairs. She prayed that Banquo hadn't found a new route of escape. If so, pandemonium would be unleashed any second.

The lights flickered twice, and she realized Jeffrey was

signaling her to continue to the bottom of the stairs, where she would regain her "head" as they had rehearsed.

Hope looked back, but nothing moved in the gloom. No doubt Banquo was safe in his cage after all.

Touching the banister, she found the piece of twine that Jeffrey had left, marking the spot where she was to stop. Exactly as planned, the ghostly head sailed back to her. She caught the mound of stuffed canvas, released it from its string, and tucked it under one arm while more otherworldly laughter echoed through the house.

The Germans moved back toward the front door, then stampeded into the night.

Jeffrey crowed in triumph. Gabrielle emerged from behind a sofa, clapping wildly. Both froze at the sight of Ronan MacLeod bent on one knee beside the window.

"Make no move," he said, reaching to the floor beside him. The bow shifted in his hands, its nocked arrow pointing upward. "Stay, you in the shadows."

He was *here?* He had stayed?

Something snagged Hope's skirt, throwing her sideways. As cold air gusted over her shoulders, she struck the banister and felt her gown rip cleanly in two.

And then she was thrown forward into the shadows, where the steps rushed up in an angry blur to meet her.

"HOPE."

A word. A voice that tried to reach her.

The word came again, tense and angry. No, frightened now.

She frowned, trying to open her eyes. Tried to sit up and failed.

Hope.

Her name, possibly. And someone moving, brushing her face.

Wet. The taste of salt on her cheeks. Why was someone crying?

Why was *she* crying?

"Can you hear, *mo cridhe?*"

She knew *that* voice. Knew its timbre and its swell, its velvet lilt and burr. "MacLeod?"

"Aye." The deep voice shook. *"Gloria dei."*

Was he speaking Latin or some other ancient tongue? Hope could not understand him. "Why…are you here?"

"To annoy you."

She tried to laugh but couldn't. All she knew was that he was close, his arms clenched tight around her. "I…fell," she rasped.

"So you did. A terrible ghost, you make."

The first, sweet sight of him stole her breath. His face was set in harsh lines of worry and there were scratches on his neck. His eyes burned like those in the ancient portrait.

"My arm hurts and I think my head's going to explode."

He laughed for the first time. "You would be far worse if we hadn't pushed the pillows beneath to catch you. You've slept for a quarter of an hour already."

"You came back." She touched the hard jaw, the sculpted cheekbone, loving each in turn. "Why?"

"Because you needed me."

"But how did you know—"

"Hush," he whispered, his lips pressed to her face.

Jeffrey cleared his throat and poked his head over MacLeod's shoulder. "You okay, Hope? Great performance, but we could have done without that last bit of gymnastics on the stairs."

"So could I." She tried to move, winced at the pain in her shoulder, and stayed exactly where she was. "What did our visitors think before they ran away?"

"They were delighted, so I gathered from my limited German. Wanted to know when the next show was. *Son et lumière* and all that." Jeffrey shook his head. "We'll be omitting that last part from the next performance, however."

He slanted a look at MacLeod. "But we could use your razzle-dazzle with the bow and arrow. Pretty amazing, MacLeod. Did you learn to handle that thing in the army or in the circus?"

"Army," came the flat answer. "A bow has its uses."

"Me, I'd take a rifle. But why did you shoot up the stairs?"

MacLeod cradled Hope's face. "I thought I saw something."

Hope remembered the wind that had gusted along the stairs and the blur of movement at her back. "You saw something, too?"

MacLeod hushed her with one finger. "No more talk. You need to rest. And this time do not argue. I do not converse with ghosts or headless apparitions." His lips curved. "Even one of such great beauty as you."

Snow hissed against the window as he settled Hope into her bed. The window was closed now, its metal latch locked, and MacLeod had made a quick search of the house. But he had found no sign of the intruder, and any further searches would have to wait until Hope slept.

He smoothed the blue covers over her. "You must be wealthy to own silk for your bed."

"Not silk. An imitation."

His brow rose, but he did not question her. Already the room seemed less foreign, and the light that burned in its small dome was welcome. "Your head?"

"Fine. Almost." She smiled, still too pale.

The bruise on her forehead made him scowl. "It hurts?"

"Not much."

"Your shoulder?"

"Only when I think about it." She gave a laugh. "Which is every second. Stop scowling at me, MacLeod."

He sat beside her on the bed, easing one hand beneath her head, his relief shifting into something darker. "I thought I'd lost you."

"I'm still here. So are you, though I told you to go. How did you know I needed you?"

A perfect question. One she had every right to ask.

But MacLeod wasn't certain he could answer it himself.

He thought about the scuff marks outside the back window and the lock that had pulled free, useless in his fingers. He thought about the shallow depressions in the snow beside the loch, marks that could have been left by a boat hastily beached. Whoever had broken into Glenbrae House could have come by water and left the same way, back into the night.

Were those reasons for him to stay?

Or were they simply excuses?

MacLeod's hands tightened, fisted against her soft sheets. "I want you, *mo cridhe*. About this, I will never lie. I want you now, here in this bed while the snow speaks against the window. I want your hands on me while you cry out in passion." His mouth took hers with a slow hunger that left her panting. "I want your laughter, Hope. And then I want the feel of your skin while I make you forget any other man and any other passion," he whispered hoarsely, nipping her chin, her throat and then her soft, full mouth.

She traced his jaw. "You don't ask for much, do you?"

"Everything." He stood up slowly. "But I can't have everything, can I? So I will have nothing." He stared at the light. "How does it darken?"

"Push the button."

After a moment he did, plunging the room into shadow.

She turned to follow him with her gaze. "What am I going to do with you, Ronan MacLeod?"

"Believe me," he said. "Just—believe me. And maybe the trust will come after that."

Then he opened the door and left the room, though it was the hardest thing he had ever done, as man or as warrior. Outside he held the wood frame, his head bent.

Trying to forget his honor and how much he wanted her.

Follow your heart, Highlander.

Now, before your time runs out, as ours did.

Silently, he took his position beside the door. His body was tense, alert to any danger, and the bow not far from his feet.

The King's Wolf had returned to Glenbrae.

PART THREE

The Quest

The ghost of Banquo
No more to fear...

CHAPTER TWENTY

Glenbrae House
December

IT WAS ALMOST CHRISTMAS, and Christmas was Hope's favorite time of year.

So what was wrong with her?

She stared blindly at the clutter on her long pine worktable. Bright raffia bows decorated wreaths of fresh berries. Pinecones and cinnamon twigs were twined with velvet onto a circle of cypress sprigs, and the fragrance was heavenly. Behind her the fire hissed and popped, its glow touching the walls of her workroom overlooking the loch.

With only two weeks until Christmas, she had her hands full. Stockings of antique lace were ready to hang beneath the ornate mantel in the front salon. Silver foil birds decorated homespun baskets heaped high with dried lavender, rose petals and orange-clove pomander balls. Light, color and fragrance filled every room.

Glenbrae was starting to feel like Christmas. Hope only wished she felt more in the mood for celebrating.

It wasn't because of any lack of business. For the past three weeks she had had a small but steady stream of visitors, beginning the night that the headless ghost made its first appearance. After that, word of Gabrielle's cooking and the ghostly visitations had spread fast. Two German student groups stopped for brief stays, followed by a medieval choral society from the United States. A chance referral had brought honeymooning couples. For an added air of romance, Hope added scented pinecones to the fire burning in the largest suite, bubble bath in the sunny south-facing bathroom and tiers of votive candles. Chilled champagne in etched crystal goblets conferred the final touch of luxury.

Right now Hope saw her most recent honeymooners holding hands on the rear terrace. Snow dusted the air and the wind held a chill, but neither seemed to notice, shoulder to shoulder in a lingering kiss.

It was a storybook scene of beauty and romance.

Somehow the sight only left her feeling lonely.

Frowning, she twisted a length of gold ribbon through a pine wreath, then tacked on a fragile lace angel with foil wings. The wreath would sit on the mantel beside an arrangement of cut flowers. All she needed was the holly for the front door.

She glanced outside, wondering why Jeffrey hadn't returned from his mission to bring an armful of green sprigs. A man was striding along the old stone fence, the wind combing his long, dark hair.

MacLeod.

The collar of his leather jacket was turned up against the wind, and a huge fir tree was angled over one shoulder.

Hope felt the hot little lurch that struck her whenever she saw him. To her absolute disgust, she was no more able to control her physical response to him than she had been four weeks earlier. He was still the most incredible man she had ever seen—and also the most irritating.

She scowled, watching the tree sway on his shoulder. She had told him not to bother about a tree. She had made it clear that she and Jeffrey would choose one later that afternoon. As usual, he had paid no attention.

Though the concept of cutting a tree and bringing it

inside to decorate had at first seemed foreign to him, he had questioned Jeffrey, then vanished shortly after breakfast. Now Hope realized why.

He had chosen a tree, then cut and hauled it back over steep, stony ground to the house. Hope could see him grinning like an idiot, with fir needles dusting his hair and shoulders.

She wanted to hate the man. She wanted to close her heart to him.

Ronan MacLeod made either thing impossible.

Frowning, she concentrated on arranging pine boughs and fresh fruit around scented candles for the salon, appalled to see that her hands were trembling.

Her vision blurred with tears. It was Christmas, blast it. She ought to be full of joy, looking forward to the peace of the season and the companionship of her new friends.

But Hope was too honest to pretend. She knew the source of the tears that blocked her vision. She knew exactly what—or rather who—made her hands tremble.

It was the tall man striding up the glen with the tree over his back. It was the sight of his cocky grin when they argued, which was too often. It was the sadness that crept into his eyes whenever he thought she wasn't looking.

Over the past weeks he had examined, questioned and explored everything he had come in contact with. He had poked into every corner of Glenbrae House with a focused intelligence that was almost frightening. He had borrowed books from Hope, studied maps and old prints and had even gone into the village library to scan their volumes. He didn't seem to have a particular question to be answered: instead, every detail of his life here at Glenbrae seemed to baffle and intrigue him.

He might almost have been a man coming awake from a long sleep, or a child dizzy with exploring new toys. Whether Hope liked it or not, his excitement was contagious. One day he grilled Gabrielle from dawn to dusk about current French culture. The next day he interrogated Jeffrey about England's political structure.

When a guest produced a portable CD player with an album by Enya, MacLeod was transfixed. The pounding bass of contemporary Celtic fusion bands made his eyes twinkle and his toes tap. Hope actually caught him gyrating beneath borrowed headphones while he added a section of new mortar to the kitchen wall.

She had already decided on her Christmas gift to him: a handheld video game with the noisiest games available. She could hardly wait to see his face.

Assuming he was still here when Christmas dawned.

Judging by his behavior, there was nothing to hold him. To Hope's chagrin, everything had changed since that night in the stables almost four weeks before. Oh, he had been friendly and helpful. He had tackled the tiniest repairs and the grittiest problem.

But he hadn't touched her once. He hadn't even looked at her measuringly or given a sign that he found her remotely attractive. They might as well have been siblings.

Or strangers.

That was exactly what she wanted, wasn't it? There was nothing between the two of them. He said no more about himself than was absolutely necessary, keeping his past life and his future plans a mystery. He absorbed everything and confided nothing.

Stubborn, impossible man.

"Merry Christmas," Hope whispered to the air, tying damask bows around the first of four silk-covered hatboxes to be arranged beneath the Christmas tree. Blindly she reached for another box, thankful for the work that had kept her sane and preoccupied.

But work didn't occupy the nights. In the darkness she remembered things that were better forgotten. It didn't help that MacLeod slept in the room next to her. She heard every mutter and every creak of the bed, all too close—but a thousand miles away.

Did she trust him?

Absolutely, Hope admitted. He was unfailingly patient, disgustingly gentle. His kittens liked nothing more than to tumble all over him and lick his face in abject adoration.

They were females, Hope had discovered. No doubt that explained it.

But her second question was far harder. Did she *believe* him?

She stared through the French doors, remembering how he had raced out of the storm. She replayed the sight of his great horse as it performed impossibly fine movements to Ronan's slightest command. A crusading knight would have such a horse as that. A traveler from the thirteenth century would have shown Ronan's initial shock and fear, followed by the same enthusiastic curiosity about every detail of modern life.

The pine wreath snapped beneath Hope's fingers. If she had allowed herself to confront the question, the answer would have been yes, she did believe his story, outrageous and impossible as it was. There was a rock-hard vein of honor to the man and an old-fashioned streak of chivalry that could not be denied.

Yes, he could well be exactly what he said, a knight torn out of the late thirteenth century.

As always, Hope felt a lurch of panic at the thought. Probably it was she who was narrow-minded and confused. Perhaps her twentieth-century mentality simply could not accept the magical possibilities that his presence here implied.

Because Hope was neither a philosopher nor a physicist, her answer was simply to avoid the question. She accepted Ronan for what he was: a man of strength and honor, a sturdy right arm and a source of desperately needed help.

So what if he occasionally stumbled over contemporary

slang or missed every movie reference? So what if he stared at a telephone as if it were an instrument of the devil? She had concerns that were far more painful.

It was no use trying to pretend Ronan MacLeod hadn't touched her heart. She was aware of him every second of every day, whether he was helping Gabrielle nurse the old wood-burning stove or showing Jeffrey how to whittle a bird out of fine-grained elm wood. Hope even knew how he slept, disdaining the soft bed to curl on a mound of blankets in the middle of the floor.

She enjoyed his company. She loved the sound of his low, musical accent and the boom of his laughter through the hallways. He was forthright and intent, his smile open and friendly.

And that was exactly the problem.

Hope realized she wanted far more than friendship, and it was painfully clear that she had misunderstood his initial interest. Dazed and disoriented after the storm, he must have reached out to the nearest person, namely her. Now that he was adjusting to life at Glenbrae, his guard was restored, and all their earlier intimacy was forgotten.

With an angry sound, Hope kicked a log that had tumbled from the wicker basket near the fireplace. In the process she struck an iron poker and pain shot up her leg.

Bloody log.

Bloody *man*.

She was clutching her toe tenderly when Gabrielle opened the door behind her. "You are exercising, Hope?"

"Exercising my right of free speech," Hope said hoarsely. "You might want to cover your ears."

"Sit down by the fire and stop working," Gabrielle ordered. "All day you run from room to room, starting one project and stopping in the middle to begin another. You make me exhausted just to watch." Her eyes narrowed. "It is because of MacLeod, I think."

Hope turned back to her worktable. Pride made her cover her hurt. "I don't know what you're talking about."

"I'm talking about the way you look at him. The way you manage to be in the kitchen whenever he's fixing the stove or helping Jeffrey. I am talking about how you feel."

"I find him very pleasant. He's been helpful around the inn."

Gabrielle muttered an angry phrase in French. "Like children, both of you. Always so polite, always so distant. Just good friends?" She glared at Hope, her dark eyes burning. "And me, I am Charles de Gaulle."

Hope's throat burned. Any moment her humiliating secret would tumble out. It was bad enough that she'd fallen for a man with no explainable past; now his rejection had opened old, unhealed wounds.

But she refused to fall apart. Summoning her pride, she glared back at Gabrielle. "Just because you and Jeffrey are head over heels doesn't mean that everyone has to be in love." Hope regretted the words as soon as she had said them, but by then it was too late.

Color swept through Gabrielle's cheeks. "At least we admit the way we feel."

"Gabrielle, I didn't mean—"

The chef raised one hand. "It is your choice to act as you will. I speak only because I see how you frown, how you worry. No, do not answer. You must decide your life as you choose. No one else can give advice or make your decisions for you." She frowned, putting a package on the loaded worktable. "And this comes to the kitchen. It must be for you. Perhaps a secret admirer."

Hope hesitated.

"Open it," Gabrielle urged.

The plain brown paper shredded away beneath Hope's fingers. Inside a simple box she found layers of fine tissue paper. Beneath the paper a slender column of silk tumbled free, butter-soft, the exact color of spring violets. Lace edged the tiny silk straps, and rosebuds dotted the hand-rolled hem. The low neckline would hint at shadowed skin, as exquisitely sensual as the long slit at one side.

It would make a woman feel like a fairy princess; it would make a man think of nothing but taking it off.

"Women would kill to receive such a gift," Gabrielle whispered. "But who sent it? There is no card or name on the paper."

"Maybe it's a mistake."

Gabrielle's lips pursed. "For a mistake, it fits you perfectly."

Hope lifted the shimmering silk against her body, watching light play over the surface. A woman would wear such a gown to meet her lover. A bride would cherish such a gown for her honeymoon.

"Me, I go back to work," Gabrielle murmured. "Otherwise I will begin to be jealous."

As she closed the door behind her, Hope let the garment slide through her fingers. The package must have been delivered by mistake. It was probably meant for one of the visitors at the inn.

Mistake or not, Hope couldn't resist another touch. She let the shimmering purple folds fall against her body and closed her eyes, imagining the scent of roses and night-blooming jasmine.

And a man. A man who had eyes for no one but her.

A cool wind skimmed her shoulders as the door jerked open behind her.

"I've found a tree. I have holly, too, so that you can—" The holly slid forgotten to the worktable as MacLeod took in the sight of Hope and her luminous purple gown. "I'm sorry if I'm interrupting," he said tightly.

Hope's first instinct was to drop the gown, but something held her back. She saw that MacLeod's cool, impassive mask had finally slipped. Friendly curiosity had vanished beneath something darker and much more personal.

"What are you staring at?"

He didn't speak, circling slowly as he took his time looking at her. With any other man, Hope would have found such intense scrutiny intolerable.

"MacLeod?" Hope's fingers tightened on the fragile silk.

"It is beautiful." His voice was husky. "As are you."

"Do you think so?" Some demon made Hope smile beneath lowered lashes. "It's for sleeping in." She stroked the silk along her body.

Heat filled his eyes. "So you were planning to sleep?"

"Oh, I thought I'd get around to it sometime." The husky tone of Hope's voice suggested she might get around to more important things first. "It's an early Christmas gift."

MacLeod's hand tightened on the corner of the table. "A gift?"

"From a very close…friend." Let him chew on that.

"How close?" He wasn't friendly and impersonal now. He wasn't cool and confident. His shoulders were stiff and a pulse was beating visibly at his jaw.

Hope liked the sight. She strolled closer, letting the gown ripple, letting him imagine how it would fit with nothing beneath. "Maybe that's none of your business." Her lips curved as she reached up to tug a sprig of holly from his hair.

Oh, he was angry. She could see the storm in his silver-gray eyes. Maybe they were finally getting somewhere. Hope suddenly remembered their conversation when they were locked in the shed.

You don't have to look at me that way…as if I was fire and you were frozen.

Perhaps it is so.

She wanted to see that same look in his eyes now. "Jealous?"

Heat snapped white-hot between them. His hands locked over her wrists. "Should I be?"

"No fair. I asked first."

"Life is often unfair. So answer. Do you wear this for another man?"

Hope tilted her head back, studying his face. "That's confidential information."

His hands slipped up her arms. "Maybe I could find out."

"Maybe you could." This time the challenge was hers.

She saw it register in his eyes. Anger and something else shimmered for a moment, and then both were carefully banked.

When he stepped back, his expression was unreadable. "It is the wrong time." His callused hands were surprisingly gentle as he pulled a piece of lace from her hair.

Hope's heart jackknifed at his touch. She swung away from him and jammed the gown angrily back into its box.

He didn't matter a bit in her life. If he left tomorrow, it would make no difference to her.

But when Hope looked down, she saw that she had wired a pair of scissors into the middle of her wreath.

Just perfect.

MacLeod picked up the evergreen by the door and slid it over his shoulder, laughing softly.

"What's so funny?" she demanded.

"I'm not quite sure. Perhaps it is you. Perhaps it is this beautiful house you've made here." He ran a hand through his hair. "Perhaps it is simply the idea of Christmas." He looked down at the gown in its plain box. "I'll remember."

"You'll remember what?"

"Everything."

Hope glared at him, wondering what he would remember but too proud to ask. "I don't have anything to remember."

For a moment darkness filled his eyes. "For some people that would be a blessing. Now I will go to arrange your tree." His broad muscles flexed as he turned.

"Oh, MacLeod."

"Yes?"

"Don't expect any Christmas gifts from me," Hope said sweetly.

"None were expected." He glanced at the box that held the gown, and grinned lazily. "By all honor, the sight of you and that gown were gift enough."

THIRTY MINUTES LATER, Hope stared down at a second brown paper package lying on her bed. Jeffrey had brought up this one from the back terrace. Like the first, this one was also unaddressed, but for Hope's name scrawled on the front.

She spent the next fifteen minutes straightening the linen closet and trying to convince herself she had no interest in seeing what was inside the brown paper, but finally curiosity won out.

Carefully she shook the package and listened for a telltale rattle, but heard only a whisper of fabric.

Common sense sailed out the window. She tore into the brown wrapping, shredding it away in one stroke. Tissue paper emerged, bright with gilded angels. Then Hope went very still as the tissue paper parted.

It was lace, what there was of it. It was white and frothy, every woman's secret fantasy. A low, square neck fell to a tight, pleated bodice crowned with fluttering sleeves. The skirt was knee-length, elegant and full, layers and layers of it.

Hope held one hand behind the fragile fabric. It would lure and seduce, all magic, hinting at what was—or wasn't—worn beneath.

It would delight any woman who wore it and torment any man who saw it.

Hope played with the delicate coral ribbon threaded through the fitted bodice and felt her heart melt. It was perfect, absolutely perfect. She touched the delicate patterns,

aching to put the gown on, but her clock told her there was
no time.

Like it or not, Winston Wyndgate was expected any
moment. She'd let him search her house twice, which had
revealed neither the brooch nor any documents of historical value. He had grudgingly dropped his harassment about
the missing brooch.

But Hope still sensed his suspicion centered on her. Only
when the brooch was found would she be entirely cleared.

As the clock struck three, a sleek black BMW raced up
the drive at fever pitch. Trust Wyndgate not to be late.

She lowered the gown back into its simple package,
letting the lace slide through her fingers. After Wyndgate
left, there would be carols and a tree-decorating ceremony.

Hope sighed.

The gown—and its mysterious donor—would have to
wait.

CHAPTER TWENTY-ONE

WINSTON WYNDGATE'S waistcoat of paisley silk gleamed beneath finely tailored tweeds. His cuff links were of antique silver and his shirt was of Irish linen. But it was the happy smile on his face that made Hope truly uneasy.

Gabrielle had shown him to a sunny room that overlooked the back lawns. Hope did not offer her hand when she entered.

"My dear girl, how healthy you look. Your Christmas decorations are superb." He raised his arms in a dramatic gesture like a seasoned lawyer working on a jury.

Hope was not about to be manipulated by a man who harassed and threatened her. "I'm glad you enjoy them." She took a seat by the back window. "But I doubt you came all this way to discuss Glenbrae's decorations."

Wyndgate rested his arm comfortably on the mantel, every inch at ease. "No, of course not. And I will come to the point, for you must be very busy this time of year." His eyes narrowed. "With your inn finally full, you're no doubt beginning to make a nice return on your investment." The sunlight glinted on his silver hair. "And I'm sure, like myself, you wish to see this unpleasant situation with the brooch resolved."

Hope frowned, waiting for him to get to the point.

"To that end I've hired a private investigator to find the brooch. He's a good man, CID background and awards commendations. I've worked with him on several cases of art theft, which is why I particularly wanted him for the job."

Hope stiffened. What was Wyndgate getting at?

He toyed with an herb basket on the mantel. "Charming, quite charming. Now, where was I? Oh yes, Beresford. Just last week he came up with an interesting discovery. Quiet as this area of the Highlands would appear, it has not always been so. According to his report, twenty-five years ago there was a string of robberies here in Glenbrae and the surrounding villages. This area was a haven for blue bloods then— salmon fishing, grouse hunting and sport of all kinds. Problem was, they refused to leave their valuables at home. Jewelry, period rifles and whatever baubles were at hand— nothing was safe. Not even the books in their libraries."

Hope frowned. "I still don't see what this has to do with me."

The collector drummed his fingers lightly on the mantelpiece. "Beresford has reason to believe that the robberies have begun again."

"But that's *ridiculous*. We've had no problems here. No one in Glenbrae has."

"None that have been made public," Wyndgate murmured. "Usually these things are hushed up by the insurance companies. Theft is bad for corporate morale, you know. Shareholders worry about their investments."

"You think that the same person stole the brooch? If so, why would he wait twenty-five years to start stealing again?"

Wyndgate steepled his fingers. "Haven't got a clue, I'm afraid. I've taken the information to the authorities, of course. Someone should be coming up to speak with you within the next week. They've assigned a man by the name of Kipworth, Detective Sergeant James A."

Hope pushed to her feet. "I'll be delighted to speak with Detective Sergeant Kipworth, of course. And now if there's nothing else…"

"No, nothing." Wyndgate's eyes narrowed. "I thought I would stay over for a day or two in the village. Poke about myself, if you see what I mean. Thought I'd take some pictures of the stairwell for my records. You don't mind, do you?"

Hope shrugged. *It's a free country.*

But his presence unsettled her. She couldn't be comfortable until the brooch was found, and both of them knew it. "I wish you good luck, but I doubt you'll find much. If any village is the picture of order and tranquility, Glenbrae is it."

"You remember what they say about judging books by their covers, Miss O'Hara." Wyndgate turned at the doorway. "Meanwhile, I suggest that you be careful. Glenbrae is not the haven of tranquility you believe it to be. I suggest you consider locking your doors. And of course, don't trust any strangers.

DON'T TRUST ANY STRANGERS.

Hope tried to shrug off Wyndgate's warning as she dressed for the night's festivities. There was nothing suspicious going on in Glenbrae. If so, she would have known it.

In spite of that, Wyndgate's last words left her uneasy.

She looked in the mirror and straightened the silk ribbon in her hair, a perfect match to her long tartan skirt. Her red satin blouse added the color she needed. Something bright. Something happy.

Something that would distract her from the depression that seemed to be growing all day.

She had invited Archibald Brown and the Wishwell sisters tonight, along with the quieter members of the Investment Club. Having the whole group would have been too dangerous to her breakable ornaments. After the guests finished trimming the Christmas tree, they would sing carols before the blazing fire. Then Gabrielle would usher in an assortment of traditional desserts, from mincemeat pies to lemon curd cake and syllabubs. Even now the exact menu was a closely guarded secret.

Hope tried to summon up a proper sense of gaiety for her first Christmas at Glenbrae. Outside, snow feathered down and the glen lay blue-gray in the grip of twilight. All was quiet, mountains and loch caught in a veil of unbroken peace.

Only *she* seemed to be restless and uneasy.

She squared her shoulders, refusing to dwell on the things she had lost. She had made wonderful friends, and tonight was her way of thanking them for their inspiration and encouragement. They expected her to be happy, and so she would.

In fact, she was going to smile her way through the evening if it *killed* her.

"BUT IT STILL makes no sense. Why do you cut down a tree and carry the whole thing inside rather than just one log?" MacLeod frowned at Jeffrey, who was struggling to lift a bulky oak log onto his shoulder in response to Hope's request for firewood to last the evening.

"Because it takes the whole tree to hold the ornaments."

"Ornaments?"

"Decorations. Shiny bells and glittery stars." Jeffrey grunted as he dropped the log. "Things to make you happy and remind you this is the season for giving. Don't tell me you've never had a Christmas tree before."

MacLeod shrugged. Over the past weeks he had learned to guard his answers carefully, for fear of giving away the truth of his past. As a result, each day he tottered between excitement and savage frustration. There were too many things to learn, too many mistakes that could expose him.

He had no reason to believe anyone would accept his story as the truth. From the books he had skimmed and the television he had seen, MacLeod had discovered the twentieth century to be a time as wary as his own. People were easily frightened by anything that could not be explained by the normal rules of their science.

And *he* certainly could not be explained.

If he wasn't careful, he would be declared mad and be strapped into one of those tight canvas jackets he had seen on a late-night movie.

"A Christmas tree? Not that I can remember," he said cautiously.

"Foul luck," Jeffrey said sympathetically. "My parents were never big on sentiment, but at least they saw to a tree for us every year." He frowned at the pile of logs. "You'll enjoy tonight. Hope's been planning this for days now." He grunted, trying vainly to lift another log.

MacLeod pulled it free and dropped it effortlessly on the pile already cradled in his arms.

"Show-off." Jeffrey sniffed, studying him intently. "So, MacLeod, is there something going on between the two of you?"

"Going…on?"

"Don't give me that icy look. I've seen the two of you together. Hope used to shimmer whenever you were around. Her eyes positively caught fire. But now she never smiles. Come to think of it, neither do you."

MacLeod shouldered the last pieces of wood, shoved the shed door shut with his foot, and started up the path toward the inn. "I hadn't noticed," he said tensely.

"And I'm the Pope," Jeffrey muttered.

MacLeod's brow rose. "You do not look like any pope that I have ever seen."

"Forget the Pope. Tell me about Hope and why she never smiles anymore. Something's wrong. You must have noticed."

MacLeod stared at the lights up the hill. He had noticed the changes, of course. Lately she seemed to take every opportunity to avoid him. But it was the safest choice for them both. When they were together, they either argued or lost their wits in a haze of pure lust.

Since the lust could lead only to further frustration and pain, it was better that they spent no more time together than was absolutely necessary. Once he left and went back to his own time, Hope would understand why he had tried to spare her.

"It is only normal," MacLeod muttered. "She has been busy preparing for this holiday of hers."

"Christmas doesn't belong to just Hope. And it's more than that," Jeffrey said firmly. "You've both been marching around like storm troopers."

MacLeod's brow rose. "Storm what?"

"You know, wookies. The force is with you."

"It is?"

Jeffrey sighed. "*Star Wars,* MacLeod. Darth Vader and Han Solo. Luke and Leia."

"Oh, that." In truth, MacLeod had no clue what Jeffrey was talking about. In the weeks since being catapulted into this chaotic time in English history, he had confronted a thousand mysteries of arcane speech and baffling behavior. He had gleaned what he could from television, books and the things they called magazines. The rest he simply lied about. The important thing, MacLeod had learned, was to appear casual and confident no matter the subject or question.

In a way, behaving like a twentieth-century male reminded him of the cutthroat behavior of King Edward's nobles at court.

MacLeod scowled. Sometimes he felt as if he had become too comfortable with glib smiles and cool laughter. Soon he would simper with the best, agreeing with everything and saying nothing.

The thought made him curse.

"Don't glare at me, MacLeod. If you ask me, the problem is that Hope's in love," Jeffrey said flatly.

"Love?" MacLeod's scowl grew. "Is she claimed by a

local Glenbrae man?" The thought was a knife stroke deep into his chest.

"*Claimed?* Lord, man, where do you come up with this antiquated jargon? If you mean is Hope *seeing* anyone, the answer is no. According to Gabrielle, she hasn't been involved with anyone."

MacLeod was disgusted at the wave of relief he felt at Jeffrey's answer. Irritably he hitched the logs higher against his chest. "I believe that destroys your speculation."

"Not quite." Jeffrey cleared his throat. "There is one other possibility. Someone else."

"Who?" MacLeod demanded.

Jeffrey rolled his eyes. "You really must think I'm an utter fool."

"*Who?*"

"Don't growl at me. *You,* that's who."

MacLeod cursed fluently, secure in the knowledge that Jeffrey would not understand medieval French. "You are dangerously wrong about these—delusions of yours. There is nothing *between* Hope and myself. There can *be* nothing."

"Why, are you married?"

MacLeod nearly stumbled.

"I thought not. You're not exactly perfect husband material. Oh, you've got that dark, brooding look women seem to like, but you're as slippery as a snake on ice. No past and no details. No woman could ever pin you down."

One could, MacLeod thought. A woman with a sharp tongue and a vulnerability that made him ache. A woman he knew had been far too long without a man's touch.

But he wouldn't take things one step further. Honor forbade it, when he might be yanked away from Hope at any moment. Meanwhile, things had gotten far beyond the Wishwell sisters' control. Whenever he demanded answers from them, he got gentle evasions. Whenever he demanded dates and predictions, they stammered apologies.

MacLeod knew that there would be no help from the old ones, and bedamned if he would leave a bastard child behind him. He had seen too many in his lifetime.

He looked up at the house and saw Gabrielle and Hope silhouetted in the window. "I don't want Hope hurt. That is the reason things are...as they are."

"Does she know how you feel?"

"It makes no difference," MacLeod said grimly.

"Maybe it does to her. If there are risks, she should know about them. It's her life, too. It's only fair that she should know."

Everyone spoke about fairness in this age, MacLeod thought. It was a source of intense concern with them that all things be *fair*. But life had taught MacLeod that there was never any fairness—only that the strong survived and the weak were crushed.

"There are reasons—things she doesn't know."

"Then *tell* her."

MacLeod's face hardened. "No."

"Damn it, she's special, MacLeod. She cares about the people around her. They're all the family she has now. So don't give me any more of your lame explanations. If you two want to go on pretending that there's nothing between you when even a blind man could see the truth, then go ahead and pretend. Just don't think you're fooling anyone but yourselves. Now, let's go inside and pretend to be having fun. Deck the bloody halls and all that," he muttered.

CHAPTER TWENTY-TWO

LAUGHTER SPILLED INTO the corridors of Glenbrae House. The air was thick with the scent of pine needles and spiced cider. Gabrielle and Jeffrey stood by the fire that blazed in the library, arguing companionably, while Archibald Brown and the Wishwell sisters strung the last angels on the tree.

Merry Christmas.

Hope stood watching the neighbors and friends she had come to know so well in the past months. These people had welcomed, cajoled and inspired her as the fledgling inn took shape. Even their conspiracies had been endearing, Hope admitted to herself. They had all been her greatest supporters, and it was fitting they should be here at Christmas to enjoy the final result.

Tonight was her small token of thanks to them for all their months of generosity and kindness. She was only too aware of how much she owed these friends. And if something was missing, some small corner of her heart that remained wounded and incomplete since the loss of her parents and her beloved uncle, Hope refused to show it. Not tonight.

She forced a smile into place as she entered the room.

"There she is now," Archibald Brown called, holding up a glass of sherry. "Dear lass, come and put an end to our wee argument."

"Not about stocks and bonds, I hope." Hope crossed to the fire, smiling at the elderly gentleman, who had already managed to dust confectioner's sugar all over his tweed lapels. "I'm afraid you'll have to argue that subject all by yourselves."

"Nay, nay, 'tis not stocks we're arguing over. Tonight there is a moratorium on all financial matters. It seemed safer that way," Archibald said with a twinkle in his eye. "We're disagreeing about the prior owner of Glenbrae House. I recall he was an elderly diplomat from London, but Morwenna swears he was a retired military man from Edinburgh."

"I can't help you there. I was told only that the last owner died twenty years ago and left the manor in total disrepair. We found a few mementos during the renovations. Old rail tickets, receipt books and a few random pieces of correspondence. Nothing with any substance, I'm afraid."

"A pity." Archibald brushed absently at his lapels. "Of course, any man who let a braw place like this fall to rack and ruin would be marched out and shot, were the choice mine." He sighed contentedly, his face glowing in the firelight. "Rare good luck that ye decided to buy the old place, lass. 'Tis life and heart ye've put here again."

Perpetua held up her glass of spiced cider. "A toast," she said gravely. "To Hope O'Hara and the magic she has created here. May this house always remain a place of beauty and joy."

Hope felt a lump in her throat as she stared around the room. Goodwill glowed in each face, warm as the embers of the fire. "Glenbrae House is finished only because of your encouragement, inspiration and help. I hope that you will always think of this as your second home, because in the very truest sense, I will always think of you as my second family."

Her eyes blurred as applause rippled. She brushed at her eyes, thankful when Jeffrey and Gabrielle moved to the ancient piano and launched into a loud chorus of "Deck the Halls."

Somewhere between the first verse and the second, Hope

turned away, tugged a shawl around her shoulders, and slipped out to the long porch running along the back of the house.

Over orchard and glen, snow drifted, silent and sublime. The moon was a sliver above the trees, casting silver enchantment over Glenbrae.

Hope felt the beauty and peace, but as if from a distance. She should have been excited, dizzy with happiness on this night. The inn was finally complete, and despite all the setbacks, her clientele was growing, just as she had hoped. She was surrounded by a dear, eccentric circle of friends in a place of rare natural beauty.

So why did emptiness still gnaw at her heart? Why did her happiness carry shadows of regret? Now of all times, why did the memories of her lost parents and uncle intrude, like an unraveling hole that could never be filled?

Hope brushed a tear from her cheek. The sounds of enthusiastically off-key carols drifted through the windows, a gentle contrast to the soft sigh of the Highland wind.

Merry Christmas.

She did not hear him until he was close behind her, but she knew who it was even before she turned. Her body recognized him, and her heart greeted him with a swift, excited lurch.

"A beautiful night, is it not?"

"Very."

"I hope I do not disturb you."

Hope's hands tightened on the weathered oak rail. "No."

She turned as the silence stretched out. He wore a black sweater shoved up over his forearms and a pair of wool flannel trousers that she had bought for him in the village. His worn leather jacket was the gift of Archibald Brown, a hand-me-down from his son, a broad-shouldered rugby star. Right now the leather was dusted with snow, as were MacLeod's hair and eyelashes.

He looked delicious enough to eat, Hope thought, but the

sight of him broke her heart in two. She didn't *need* this, didn't want this when she was just learning to stand on her own two feet. No awareness this deep and painful could be healthy. "Actually, you are disturbing me a little," she sighed. "A *lot*."

He leaned on the rail, looking out into the field that was fast filling up with snow.

"You're not going to ask why?"

"If you want, you will tell me."

There it was again, the steadiness and calm confidence that Hope had seen in so few other men. In another man it would have been arrogance, but not in him. MacLeod would not ask or press her. It was his way, quiet, tough and irresistible.

Maybe he *was* a knight.

And maybe she was *nuts*.

"Before you arrived here, I found something in the stairwell," Hope said slowly. "A silver wolf with aquamarine eyes. It looked very old."

He said nothing, but Hope was certain that his shoulders stiffened.

"I don't suppose you ever saw it."

He shrugged. "Why would I see such a thing? It is your house, after all."

"And what if I sold this silver wolf for a great deal of money to a man who seems to think it has great historical significance?"

"It is your right." He did not look at her, his eyes on the distant cliffs.

"Twenty-five thousand pounds, MacLeod."

"It is money, no more." He looked at her then, his brow rising. "What answer do you expect of me?"

"I'm not sure. You seem to know everything else about this beautiful house...."

"The silver wolf has nothing to do with me," he said harshly. "I am glad if it has brought you good."

"As a matter of fact, I considered it a miracle." She

sighed. "So now I've got everything I've worked for—my inn, a growing business and wonderful friends. Why am I standing out in the snow like an idiot, watching the moon and fighting back tears? Tell me that, MacLeod."

His hands tightened on the smooth railing, but he said nothing.

Hope took a deep breath. "Why is it we wish and want and wait, but when we finally find the thing we want, it's never what we thought it would be? *Never.*" Hope blinked as snow dusted her cheeks and tickled her eyelashes. "Go on and laugh, MacLeod. At least this time you would be justified."

"I'm not laughing." His voice was husky. "This place, this glen, this house—I can understand exactly how you feel. There is magic here."

"Do you feel it, too?"

His eyes darkened. "More than you know."

"But I love Glenbrae. I love these people, and this house is everything I've ever wanted. So why am I crying?"

"Because life is like the river we can never step in twice. The water flows, always moving, always different, just as we are always different. There's no way to stop the change, Hope. That is why we feel pain."

She frowned. "Are you saying we shouldn't try to hold on to the past?"

"I'm saying that pain might be good. On your television, everyone runs away at the first mention of pain. Everyone talks about happiness, always happiness." His gaze scoured the faint line of the distant cliffs. "But I've watched weak men become heroes when pressed. I've seen evil men do generous, unselfish deeds when the need was great enough. Without pain and change, we would never grow." He raised his hand and a snowflake settled gently on his palm. It hugged the callused skin for long heartbeats, then melted. "Like that," he said softly. "Beautiful and then gone. It lasted but a moment. Yet would you take it back or deny the beauty of that moment?"

"But why—" Hope made a low, angry sound. "Oh, Lord, why am I asking you, of all people? I still don't know where you came from or why you're here. And I—"

His kiss was gentle as a snowflake settling over her mouth. And like a snowflake, she melted in his heat.

This, Hope thought. *This is what I want. This is what I'll always want, even when I'm worn and stooped with age and my hair has gone snow-white.*

Suddenly none of her questions mattered. She tried to speak and tell him, but his palms closed over her cheeks and his mouth opened, drawing a slow moan.

He murmured a rough phrase Hope didn't understand.

No matter. The hoarse edge in his voice told her all she needed to know. He hadn't forgotten. And now his indifference was gone.

His palms slid around her shoulders. Her hands found his jacket. She shoved, pushing beneath the soft leather and finding the man beneath.

Warm skin met and Hope felt MacLeod shudder. Not indifferent. Not at all.

The ribbon fell from her hair, dragged free by his trembling hands. And then his body was against her, hard with need.

"Ronan, I—"

"No. No words. I want nothing to come between us, Hope."

She wanted to tell him how he left her ragged inside. She wanted to tell him she could feel his heart race. She wanted to share the thousand swirling discoveries as their bodies met.

The snow drifted down around them and suddenly there were no more words. Her world shifted, all touch and scent, while the night wrapped around them, offering its dark protection.

"What are we doing?" Her hands threaded deep into his hair and she sighed as he pulled her against him. "No, forget I asked." She ran the pad of her thumb across his chin, over one high cheekbone, and along the small crescent scar above his eye. "When? I'll murder whoever did it."

He drew a ragged breath, and snowflakes danced around his face. "You'd have to travel far to find him. To places where there was fighting, always fighting."

"Was it Vietnam? The Gulf?" Hope frowned when he didn't answer. "Ronan?"

He didn't recognize the words she said, but he knew that they were places of war. It had not ended, not even in her time.

He sighed. "No to both. It was another place, a place you would only know from books. It's so far away that sometimes even I forget it. But leave off this talk of war." He eased beneath the soft silk of her blouse. "You smell like morning, like sunlight on heather." Silk and lace pulled free. "When I saw you in the doorway, wrapped in light and wearing that piece of cloth in your hair—"

"A bow, MacLeod." Hope laughed unsteadily. "That's what it's called."

"Bow," he said hoarsely.

"Forget about the bow," she whispered. "Say my name instead."

He did as she asked, whispering the word against her mouth. Then said it again, pressed against her neck amid swift, searching kisses.

"I tried to forget." His hands clenched on her waist. "I tried to stay away. By all the saints, I tried and failed." He caught a strand of her hair and brought it to his lips. "But I saw you in the light with snow falling around you, and all I could think of was—" He drew a slow breath.

"Was what?"

"How fast I could tug that cloth from your hair and the silk from your shoulders." His eyes darkened. "I can guide an arrow to its target at two hundred paces. I can fell a grown man with one blow, but against you I am powerless." His hands tightened. "Turn from me, *mo rùn*. Turn from me now."

For answer, Hope slid close and leaned into his warmth. It wasn't fear that made her knees go weak and her pulse zing. It wasn't fear that demolished every scrap of her careful logic.

"Kiss me again and I'll think about it." She let her body flow against him, her long skirts whispering in the night. "Or are you afraid you'll give away all your dark secrets?"

His hands rose, tangled in her hair. He tilted her face back, staring at the pale skin dusted by snowflakes.

MacLeod felt something break inside him. "Aye, I know the feel of fear. My hands are trembling and I can barely see," he said harshly. "My fear is for you, for the things that could happen to you if…"

He made a sharp, angry sound and then his mouth burned over her face.

When she could think again, when she could remember how to frame words, Hope pushed him away with shaky fingers. "Say the rest. Finish the sentence," she ordered. "*What* could happen?"

He shrugged. "It isn't important."

"You're lying, MacLeod. You know more than you're saying. First there was the incident in the fishing shed, then that night on the stairs when I fell." Her hands fisted. "What's going on?"

"So stubborn," he said huskily.

"No more than you. At least I'm not keeping secrets."

"We all keep secrets." His hands closed over the snow-covered railing and he gripped as if for his very life, an anchor while his world swept away around him. A half smile touched his face. "But you have friends waiting inside and I'll leave you to them. No doubt they are missing you this night. Merry Christmas, Hope." He eased up the collar on his jacket and turned away.

"Merry C-Christmas? Damn you, Ronan. I'm not letting you walk away. I want the truth."

His jaw clenched. "Maybe I've forgotten the truth. Maybe I never knew what the truth was until now."

"That's no answer."

"It's the only one I can give."

Hope searched his face. "What are you so afraid of?"

That I'll start what I can't finish. That we'll topple into this sweet madness together, but you'll awake one day alone, hating me, and I'll be seven centuries away, useless to you when you need me most.

His shoulders tensed. One hand rose. Then he frowned, tugging something from beneath his jacket. "For you." Lightly he leaped over the railing, dropped to the ground and disappeared into the night.

Hope blinked as the snow veiled his broad shoulders. There were tears in her eyes as she whispered his name. Something terrified him, and he was not a man to be easily frightened. The problem was that sometimes Hope actually found herself believing the story he had told her the night of his arrival. By physical appearance alone, he could certainly be the knight in the stairwell. But tonight of all nights she would not think about it. Christmas was a time for *possibilities,* not impossibilities.

With trembling hands she tore the red paper from his gift. Snow dusted a pair of chocolate eyes and soft, curly fur the color of old champagne.

A bear? This powerful man with shadows in his eyes had given her a *bear?*

Exuberant voices drifted through the window as Hope raised the soft body to her chest. Her hands tightened and she blinked back tears. What had he seen outside the shed, and what silent fear drove him away from her now?

Maybe I've forgotten the truth. Maybe I never knew what the truth was until now.

She sighed, wanting his touch. Wanting answers. Some part of her even wanted to *hate* Ronan MacLeod.

So why did the aggravating man keep making it impossible?

CHAPTER TWENTY-THREE

"WHAT'S WRONG WITH HOPE?" Morwenna asked. "She's crying."

Perpetua looked up from a mound of popcorn and holly waiting to be strung onto ropes for the front door. "Crying?" Her eyes narrowed. "Nonsense, she's simply smoothing her hair. Really, Morwenna, you must control this raging imagination of yours."

"She's *crying*, I tell you," Morwenna hissed. "I saw her come in from the porch. MacLeod was out there with her." Behind Morwenna the fire popped noisily, casting a glow over the faces of the three sisters. Each was dressed in a different color of velvet, set off by brooches of antique silver and uncut agate.

"MacLeod?" Honoria surveyed the room with near-sighted concentration. "But he's not here."

"I *know* that. He didn't come inside."

"And you think…"

"I *know* it," Morwenna hissed. "The man has got her twisted up in knots. Oh, she puts on a good act, one that would fool most people. But we're not *most* people, are we?" Morwenna twisted a strand of holly between her fingers. "If that man's hurt her, I'll turn him into a toad," she muttered. "An ugly, *one-legged* toad."

A log hissed on the fire, twitched, then collapsed in a storm of orange sparks.

"Morwenna, do get hold of yourself," Perpetua said curtly. "In a moment you'll have the whole house on fire."

"Fire? Oh, sorry." One surreptitious wave was enough to settle the angry orange flames back to normal.

"She's probably missing her family. All gone, you know." Perpetua drummed silently on the mahogany tabletop. "This noise and laughter must make her remember her uncle. He was a man who knew how to throw a grand party, I understand."

"Forget about her uncle," Morwenna said with unusual irritation. "What she's *missing* is one hard-as-nails, handsome-as-sin medieval Scotsman who doesn't have enough politeness to come inside and say hello."

"The man is hardly the sort for chitchat, my dear." Perpetua sighed. "You knew that when you voted to bring him here."

"I *thought* he was a man of honor."

"No," Perpetua corrected gently, "you thought he would *change,* become docile as a tabby cat and just as easily managed. But Ronan MacLeod will never be a sensitive twentieth-century male in touch with his nurturing female side. He'll try, but he won't succeed. He is doomed to be forever politically incorrect, I fear. After all is said and done, how could he not?"

"Nurture, shmurture," Morwenna snapped. "Hope's unhappy, Pet. We're to blame, and it's got to stop."

"What would you do, my love? Wave your hand and make all their differences go away? You can't, not with people."

Morwenna took a slow breath and sank onto the couch. "But the man will break her heart, Pet. You mark my words. Then I'll have to give him terrible nightmares."

"He already has those," Perpetua said gently.

"In that case I'll take away all his friends."

"Already done," her sister murmured.

"Whose side are you *on?*"

Perpetua smoothed a length of ribbon between her strong, gnarled fingers. "No one's. Or maybe everyone's. It's our job, remember? We've tampered all we may, and even beyond, I fear. Like it or not, any more interference will be at grave cost to all of us, Hope included."

"Is that so?" Morwenna's eyes glinted with defiance. "Just you listen to *me*. I'm not going to see Hope hurt. He's the one she's *meant* to have, if only he'd forget that blind honor of his."

"We cannot change him." Honoria sat forward suddenly, her eyes gold in the firelight. "Honor *is* the man." Suddenly her voice fell. "'Come what may, time and the hour run through the roughest day.'" Her eyes widened. "*Him. The ghost.* I feel him clearly. He's coming to Glenbrae." She pushed to her feet, her brooch awry and her hands trembling. "Storms and lightning when he finds out what we've done."

Morwenna stared after her sister's retreating back. "What does she mean, Pet?"

Snow hissed against the windowpanes, building white wedges between the wooden casements.

"I'm not sure." Perpetua reached out into the night to explore what Honoria had touched, but the darkness mocked her, formless and silent. She heard the wind sigh over the roof and grumble through the tall pine trees by the loch. She heard the question of an owl near the stables.

Hope seemed to hear, too, where she stood by the window, watching the snow.

"I wish I knew," Perpetua whispered. "But I can see nothing save shadows. Nothing beyond broken dreams. For them both, I fear."

The strains of "Silent Night" echoed from the back of the crowded room, and Perpetua rose to her feet. As she turned toward the piano, her face bore the hard lines of care and great age.

ALL THE GUESTS HAD LEFT.

All the songs had been sung.

MacLeod stood in the silence of midnight, feeling snow

brush his face and cheeks. In his hands he gripped a rough wooden box with a bark roof.

Inside lay three figures carved of fragrant cedar. The manger was light and the figures even lighter, but the weight in his heart made his feet slow as he crossed the dark yard before the inn. A shopkeeper in Glenbrae had gasped in shock at the sight of his ancient French currency, but he had been only too happy to give MacLeod a few supplies and several articles of clothing in exchange for the old coins.

No room in the inn. Not for one such as he, MacLeod thought as he settled the rough manger in the snow before a fir tree decorated with red tartan ribbons. This gift, like the bear he had given Hope, was small.

Gently he laid down a circle of smooth stones from the loch, and within the ring he placed the manger. Next came the carved Mary, Joseph and finally the baby Jesus in a wooden cradle filled with pine needles.

When he was done, he sat back, listening to the sigh of the wind across the glen. Behind him the house was quiet, all its leaded windows dark. As the stars glistened through the falling snow, MacLeod mused upon the peace of the night and the faith that had carried three travelers on a faraway search for a child newborn.

In comparison, his own journey seemed insignificant.

And what of his secrets? In the past week, their weight had grown until he thought he would choke. But it would be useless to tell Hope his fears for her safety, or that every instinct warned him her inn was being watched. To his fury, there was nothing he could do but wait. Any attempt to warn her would only add to the mistrust between them. The three canny sisters were no help at all now, for their powers seemed to have failed completely.

Nor could he tell her of the visions that came in the night as he lay trapped between two worlds and two times. In painful clarity he moved down streets where he was invisible, spoke greetings to people who looked right through him. Past and present blurred together in a numbing dreamscape split by the cries of his fallen comrades, and he awoke sweating and shaken, while pale light seemed to drain from his body. At first he had tried to ignore the shaking and the weakness that followed. Then the dreams became worse.

In his heart, MacLeod knew the signs were a warning. He was a man caught out of nature's order, his very existence here an affront to divine design. He could not stay, not alive.

The only question was when he would disappear, wrenched back to his own time.

He touched the carved figures in the manger, searching for answers, but no answers came. Meanwhile, the longer he stayed, the deeper his feelings grew for Hope. He would *not* call it love. MacLeod wasn't sure what that often misused word meant, in truth. But he was deeply aware of her, keenly connected to her emotions, his day turned upside down by a single smile.

Love?

Who was to say? All he knew was that in spite of his knightly vows, whenever he was near her, he forgot all reason and honor. Touching her only brought keener pain, for it showed MacLeod all he yearned for but could never have.

Better to hold her away until she hardened her soul to him. Better to close her heart now, before the line was crossed.

Yet her heart would not harden. In spite of his distance and indifference, the desire leaped between them, fresh and sharp, whenever they touched.

MacLeod glanced at the dark sky. A star burned overhead, winking red and gold like a jewel against the night.

He stared up into its distant light and asked for strength. He prayed for answers, and an honor that seemed to slip away with every second he remained in this contentious age.

But he had neither answers nor honor in return. The star

winked on, remote and unreadable. Even the wind seemed to mock him like low laughter.

And then an icy mound of snow struck him dead between the shoulders as he knelt before the decorated tree.

He turned—and felt his heart twist. She was dressed in black wool from neck to toe, and a silly red cap slanted over her head, its white tassel bobbing from a long tail. She smiled as she packed a second mound of snow into a careful, lethal ball.

MacLeod didn't speak. Maybe he had forgotten how. The sight of Hope taking careful aim, smiling with wicked glee, was too painful. He watched the wet missile and did not twist away, his thoughts full of foolish wishes and futile regrets, like a child forgotten at Christmas.

Maybe being hit in the face would make him forget the things he could not have.

Powder sprayed over his face, but he barely noticed, entranced by the moonlight glinting on her pale cheeks.

"*Fight,* MacLeod." The long hat bounced as she shoved her hands to her hips. "You know how to fight, don't you?"

Far too well, he thought. *Better than any man should.* But fighting was the easy way out. Staying and sinking roots was far harder.

"Not with you. Not tonight." His voice tightened. "Better that you go away."

She frowned, moving closer. "What's that by your foot?"

"Nothing."

"Blast it, Ronan—" With a quick sidestep she darted past and swept up the house of wood and bark. "A manger," she whispered. "You made a manger for me?"

"It is only a simple thing," he said gruffly.

"It's…beautiful." Her voice caught. "I can see each face and strand of hair. You've carved Joseph in the round, with an olive tree growing beside him."

MacLeod shrugged. "To symbolize life."

"And Mary has a twining rose."

"It seemed…right for her inward beauty."

"You're very good."

"There was time whenever we camped. The long nights left too much time for thinking. I made things instead."

"I see." She frowned. "It was therapy. Treatment, you might say."

"We all had ways of…coping. Is that your word?"

She nodded gravely, then rose to her toes and kissed him. Gently. Quickly. As if afraid to linger or explore for fear of what might happen next.

"It doesn't matter what you call it." She set the manger carefully back in the snow and moved an old star of beaten tin onto the branch directly overhead. "First my bear and now this. I—I don't know how to thank you."

"There is no need for thanks. They are my gifts to you. I have none other, and it is your custom to give gifts among friends, I have learned."

Again something flashed in her face. "So now I have to give you something in return. Something unexpected. Something…useful." A smile touched her lips. "Turn around while I find it."

"There is no need to—"

"Just turn *around*, MacLeod."

"Very well." He shoved his hands into his pockets and stared at the tree. The tin star seemed to gleam with fragile light, spinning and twisting while snow drifted gently over the manger, dusting the figures inside. The night seemed to draw close and the hills to hold their breath.

Maybe there is room at the inn.

Just for this one night.

Behind him Hope's feet crunched over the lawn. "You're leaving?" MacLeod turned slowly. "I don't understand."

"It's simple, really. You had one kind of therapy in that

camp you spoke about, wherever it was. You're not going to tell me where, are you?"

He shrugged.

"I didn't think so. Let's just say this is another kind of therapy." She dug her hands into the snow. "A good snowball fight is better than any psychotherapy, if you ask me."

"You think I need...this psychotherapy?" he asked grimly.

"You said it yourself. We all have secrets." She molded the snow, her eyes glittering. "What are you waiting for?"

His lips twitched, and he felt the beginning of a smile. "So you wish to fight with me?"

"That's the general idea, champ. Usual rules—no holding, no going for the face. No shoving snow down the collar." Hope danced from side to side, grinning wickedly. "Well, maybe once or twice down the collar." Her third missile sailed off without warning and caught MacLeod square on the shoulder, powdering his neck thoroughly.

"This is cheating," he said. "You attacked without notice."

"Where I come from, that's not cheating, that's superior tactics!" Hope danced behind the decorated tree, already shaping another snowball. "So stop meditating and get to work."

Snow drifted down, painting the night with enchantment, and MacLeod was lost before he knew it, given over to the magic of a woman and a night and a beautiful old house that looked on with silent indulgence while the little tin star twinkled above the manger.

He accepted the stark realization then. He loved Hope O'Hara. He wanted to stay with her, fight with her, laugh with her. The dream could no longer be denied.

Desire twisted deep in his chest. In all certainty he had loved this woman from the first moment he had seen her in the rain, dangling crazily from the edge of the roof. Her smile was a rare gift, a candle that lit the way for all who knew her. Her loyalty was absolute, and her concern for her friends was unshakable.

But even if he couldn't stay to enjoy that smile of hers, MacLeod vowed they would have this one perfect night to remember.

He scooped up a handful of snow and shaped it carefully, ducking as she shot another white clump past the tree.

"Come on, MacLeod, you're not even putting up a fight here." More snow hurtled toward him, slapping home soundly against his chest. "Sheesh, this is like taking candy from a baby."

"It is always dangerous to underestimate the enemy. Good tactics depend on good preparation."

"Lame, MacLeod."

His eyes narrowed as he stalked her, packing snow between his hands. She popped out from behind the tree, feinted left, then leaped out of reach just before his snowball hissed past.

"You can do better than *that*. Come on, they must have taught you all about tactical assessment and terrain strategies in that army you served with."

No, they had taught him nothing, MacLeod thought. Not about the things that truly mattered. Not about the sound of snow hitting a little tin star or the way a woman's laugh could echo in the night and fill a man's heart until it could hold no more joy.

"Of course they did," he said, tracking her over the snow. "But they taught me to know the enemy first." He shot around the tree and spun left, chuckling when she threw a snowball just as he had expected. Then he lunged forward and scooped her up in his arms.

"Hey, that's cheating. No holding and no lifting," she protested.

He laughed as she stuck snow down the front of his shirt and smeared it over his chest. Another snowball, pulled from inside the tail of her cap, was ground over his face.

"Come on, MacLeod. You're losing here and you don't even know it." She sputtered as he scooped up snow in one hand and dangled it with silent menace over her head. "I don't think you're going to use that."

His smile grew. "No?" Snow sprinkled over her cheeks, sparkling on her eyelashes. "Do you still think so?"

She glared, all warrior. "So you surprised me. Now I go to strategy two."

"Strategy two?"

Her fingers burrowed beneath his jacket and sweater, aimed unerringly for his chest. "MacLeod, you're soaked."

"It feels good." His grin grew. "So do you."

"Don't change the subject. A snowball fight is serious business." A dimple flashed at her cheek. "Give up yet?"

"Never." His voice was grave, full of rough challenge.

"And you still refuse to put me down?"

His brow rose. "Is that a threat, Ms. O'Hara?"

"Too bloody right it is." She attacked in earnest, tickling every bare inch she could reach, uncovering ribs and chest and sides until MacLeod shook from the effort to hold back his laughter. He tried to catch her hands, but couldn't without putting her down. His eyes promised retribution even as he twisted beneath her lethal fingers.

"You'll never win, MacLeod. Cry uncle."

"Why would I want to complain to a relative?"

"Surrender, I mean." She traced his sensitive ribs, besieging him with yet another attack.

When his sides ached and her touch threatened to reduce him to lunacy, MacLeod launched a defense of his own. "One unfair tactic deserves another," he muttered, then locked his mouth to hers and let the heat shoot through both of them.

Over the hammer of his heart, he heard Hope's little gasp settle into a sigh. He grinned as she wrapped her hands around his snow-covered neck. "Cheat. *That* was unfair tactics," she protested. "And I was so sure you were a man of honor."

"I seem to forget all my honor around you," he said gravely.

"Good." Her mouth softened and she skimmed his lips with her own, merciless and slow. He responded with dark urgency, trapping her for the touch he must have or die. He felt the thunder of her heart as he sank to his knees in the snow, keeping her locked in his arms.

When had the night grown so still and his need so great? Why did the little star seem to wink and gleam at them from the tree?

Then MacLeod simply didn't care. He shoved off her hat, cursing. "Hope, sweet Hope." His hands twisted in her hair as he scattered kisses over her face and neck. "I tried to stay away. By St. Julian, I tried to forget your scent and the feel of your mouth."

She wriggled closer. "Why?"

"Because it was the right thing to do. I have nothing to offer, no worth and no future. All I have is a past too immense to share. In every way that counts I am a failure."

She trapped his cheeks, her eyes furious. "Now you're getting me *really* angry. You can save a kitten, train a horse and repair the most wretched stove. Those figures you carved look like perfect historical replicas. You could probably be a millionaire inside of a year if you put your mind to it." Her hands tightened. "So *don't* tell me you're a failure, with nothing to offer."

His jaw hardened. "I don't have anything to offer. Not one shred of what you deserve. And any minute, time might shift and I might have to go—"

"Go?" Her voice broke. "Go where? What do you mean?"

He saw the loss in her eyes and realized it was too late for them. The line was crossed, whether he wanted it so or not. By some deep mystery, her heart was given, just as his was. Now they would have to bear the consequences, whether in joy or sorrow.

"MacLeod, talk to me. What did you mean?"

"Nothing, my heart. Not a thing that matters." A lopsided smile twisted his mouth. "Can't you do any better than that for a kiss, woman?"

He winced as powder bombarded his head. Then they were tumbling over the new-fallen snow, giggling like noisy children. Neither could find bare skin fast enough. Her hands raced over his waist; his palm nudged her breast. And they froze.

Snow drifted into their eyes and longing drummed in their veins. "This counts, Hope," MacLeod whispered. "This will change things. So tell me what we're doing."

"The right thing," Hope answered, pulling him down for a searching kiss that left them both gasping.

His jacket hit the snow with a hiss. Her scarf caught on his shoulders, then sailed through the air and dangled crazily from the fir tree. The night was breathless with need and dreams when he rolled to his back, cushioning her from the cold as he drew her down on top of him.

"I've never wanted like this before, Hope. No woman ever." He ran a line of soft kisses up her neck, delighting in her shuddered response as she arched against him.

And I will never feel this way again, MacLeod knew with absolute certainty. There would be no pleasure in any other woman, no joy in any other's kiss. Not after touching her.

"Merry Christmas," he whispered, loving the feel of her body against him. Loving how she shifted restlessly, thighs to his thighs, wanting in her eyes.

He covered her heart, feeling her pulse race, just as wild as his. She shuddered as he palmed her breast, sighed as he grazed the hardening nipple.

MacLeod had never been a reckless man, but now he was. He wanted to look at her and then bring his mouth slowly everywhere his eyes had savored. He wanted to find her pulse points and leave her panting when he drove her over the edge of pleasure.

Honor or not, he would have all those things from her *now*.

Lights filtered through the dense snow. Blinking, he raised his head and gradually made out two fiery circles of light like torches. A car?

He scowled at the noisy modern conveyance, an entirely unsatisfactory substitute for a horse. The lights drew closer. Whoever it was wasn't stopping.

"A car," he rasped, shoving down Hope's sweater, trying to straighten her clothes and order his ragged thoughts. "Someone—coming."

"Car?" She sat up, frowning. "But who—why—"

Tires crunched over the snow, then skidded to a halt. A metal door creaked.

"Good Lord, I almost didn't see you there in the snow." A man's voice boomed out, hard with anxiety. "I'm bloody sorry to intrude, considering that you two were—" He cleared his voice. "We were supposed to arrive earlier, but I'm afraid we were lost in the snow. It was a hard drive through those last mountains. Bad timing, I'm afraid."

Terrible timing, MacLeod thought. He pushed to his feet, blocking Hope from view. "What town are you searching for?"

The man in the parka brushed snow off his face, frowning. "The town of Glenbrae. We must have taken a wrong turn over the last ridge, because the place we want is supposed to be very near."

"What place is that?"

"A historic inn, Glenbrae House. I don't suppose you know it, do you?"

CHAPTER TWENTY-FOUR

HOPE STRUGGLED TO HER feet, brushing snow from her hair. "In that case you're right where you're supposed to be. I'm Hope O'Hara, the owner of Glenbrae House. This is my friend, Ronan MacLeod. But do you have reservations?"

The man in the parka nodded. "We faxed them last week."

The snow was growing heavier, and Hope shivered. "I'm afraid we didn't receive any faxes, but we *do* have rooms available."

"I'm delighted and relieved to hear it. My wife and daughter are still in the car. I think they'd given up hope of ever reaching Glenbrae." The man smiled with devastating charm as he shook Hope's hand. "I'm Nicholas Draycott. I did wonder when we didn't have a return confirmation from you. We tried to phone several times en route, but there seemed to be an electrical problem."

"The storm might have toppled the lines." Hope shivered as snow swirled through the courtyard, eddying around the tree and manger. "I expect you'll want to get inside and warm up." She smiled awkwardly at Ronan as he draped her scarf around her shoulders. "Maybe we all should."

The car door burst open again and a small, muffled figure exploded over the snow. "Daddy," she called anxiously, "is this the place at last? We've been driving forever over those mountains." She held out a worn stuffed bear. "I can't keep Mr. Gibbs awake any longer." She stifled a yawn. "I'm feeling tired, too."

Nicholas Draycott swung his daughter up into his arms, making her squeal with delight. "Yes, it's the right place, imp. Soon you and Mr. Gibbs will be tucked into a nice, warm bed before a roaring fire."

"With some cookies and a cocoa," Hope suggested, after a questioning look at the child's father.

"I'm sure Mr. Gibbs would like that." Nicholas Draycott tousled the blond hair spilling beneath his daughter's cap. "I expect Miss Vee would enjoy it, too. Genevieve, meet Ms. O'Hara. She owns Glenbrae House."

Genevieve Draycott shook hands, gurgling with laughter, cut short by another yawn.

"Are we at the right place, Nicholas?" A tall woman with shining blond hair and high, etched cheekbones stepped out into the snow. Her smile was genuine and her accent was distinctly American, Hope noticed.

"It looks so, Kacey. This is Hope O'Hara. She has just promised Vee and Mr. Gibbs some cookies and hot cocoa inside."

"It sounds divine. Maybe they'll share." Lady Draycott's laugh was engaging as she offered her hand to Hope. "I'm so pleased to meet you, Ms. O'Hara. We've heard such wonderful things about this house and how you've restored it. Nicholas's estate is very old, so we have a fair notion of all the headaches of owning a historic house. Draycott Abbey has been in his family for generations, and though we both love it, at times it seems the house is conspiring to overwhelm us."

Draycott Abbey. The name was vaguely familiar to Hope, but she couldn't say why. "You live in the Southeast, I take it?"

"On the border of Kent," Nicholas said. "But we had our hearts set on Scotland for Christmas, and we weren't to be deterred."

Genevieve leaned forward in her father's arms, her eyes

wide. "We have a moat and swans. But best of all, we have a real live *ghost*."

"Now, *that* must keep you and Mr. Gibbs busy," Hope said.

"Adrian is a perfect friend. He tells us grand stories about kings and popes and armies. He talks about bad ladies, too." She frowned. "He seems to know a lot of them."

Nicholas brushed her cheek. "Vee, I thought we talked about that subject already."

"No, you talked and I listened, Daddy. That's not a talk, that's a lecture. Besides, Adrian is real. I see him every day, so I don't think I should lie and say I don't."

"I believe it's time for bed," Nicholas said firmly.

"Come on, love, let's go sort out the bags." Kacey lifted her wriggling daughter to the ground.

"In a minute." The girl looked out at the snow, frowning. "I saw something over there by the fence."

Nicholas glanced worriedly at his wife, who shook her head.

Seeing their uneasiness, Hope gently intervened. "I'll take Genevieve up to the house, if you like, and see to your rooms. Ronan, would you help them with their bags?"

On their way back to the car, Kacey and Genevieve stopped to admire the manger. "These pieces are very unusual. You can see the faces in perfect detail. Are they heirlooms?" Lady Draycott asked.

"Actually, Mr. MacLeod made them."

"Really?" Kacey studied the figures intently. "I've never seen anything like this outside a museum." She started to say more, but her daughter clutched at her hand.

"I *saw* him, Mama. Over there by the fence. He had gray fur and black paws. It was Gideon, just like I told you before."

"He couldn't be here, darling. Not all this way from the abbey. You probably saw a rabbit."

Her daughter's lip quivered and she lowered her head. "It was Gideon," she said tremulously.

Kacey pulled her close, straightening her cap. "Maybe we should discuss Gideon later, my love. It would be rude to keep Ms. O'Hara and Mr. MacLeod waiting, don't you think?"

After a last, longing glance out into the snow, Genevieve nodded, but her eyes were sad. When her mother and father moved around to sort through the suitcases in the car, she went to stand beside Ronan, who was staring north toward the cliffs. "Do you see something, too?"

He looked down at the small figure with a worn bear clutched to her chest. His smile was swift. "Not really. I just...felt something."

"I did, too." She pointed gravely. "Over there past the fence. Mother says it was a rabbit, but she's wrong. It was a cat. A great gray cat with black paws, just like the one I see back home." She frowned. "He follows us sometimes."

"Now, I wonder why a cat would do that."

Mr. Gibbs wavered and nearly fell before Genevieve caught him. "I'm not sure. Sometimes I think he's protecting us. At least, that's how he makes me *feel*. He's got very special eyes."

"Then you must be lucky." He brushed snow gently off her cap. "I never had a cat to protect me when I was your age."

She stared up at him, her eyes unnaturally grave. "I don't think you would ever need to be protected."

"Now, there you might be wrong." MacLeod stared off to the north, where snow now veiled the high cliffs. "We all need protecting sometime or another."

She tucked her hand confidingly into his. "Then I'll ask Gideon to protect you, too. He won't mind."

MacLeod's eyes crinkled as he grinned down at her. "Gideon? Is he a friend of Mr. Gibbs?"

"No, Mr. Gibbs is my favorite toy, but Gideon is *real*," she said firmly. "He can do anything." She moved closer to MacLeod. "Is something wrong?"

MacLeod had turned back to the cliffs. "For a moment, I thought I saw…" He shrugged. "Never mind. You had better bring Mr. Gibbs inside before you're covered with snow. I'll take in your bags."

After a quick smile, she ran to her parents, who were helping Hope close the lid of a wicker basket stuffed full of crayons, toys and coloring books. MacLeod waved once, watching them disappear into the house.

After they had gone inside, his smile faded.

He bent down, studying the snow. He'd been looking for human tracks, but instead he found a set of small, fresh paw prints moving delicately along the fence and across the courtyard, not three yards from the car. Then they circled the decorated tree, and strangest of all, they stopped in front of the manger.

There they simply vanished.

"DO YOU THINK she guessed?"

Kacey Draycott paced anxiously, looking at her husband. Genevieve was sound asleep in her camp bed with Mr. Gibbs clutched in her fingers while the fire sent golden patterns playing over her cheeks. "Jamee will kill me if Hope guesses."

"You're safe for now." Nicholas Draycott, the twelfth Viscount Draycott, sank onto the bed and tugged off his boots. "But she soon will. The woman is no fool, nor is that friend of hers. MacLeod, wasn't that his name?"

His wife nodded sleepily. "Very odd, those wooden sculptures of his. I've seen similar pieces in museums, but nowhere else." She slid beneath the lavender-scented sheets with a sigh of contentment.

Nicholas grinned down at her, the faint silver flecks in his hair shining in the firelight. They made him look exceedingly handsome, his wife thought.

"There you go, imagining another mystery. Just because he's good at reproductions doesn't exactly make him a thief, my love."

"I didn't say he was a thief, Nicholas, but there's something strange there, all the same." Kacey stared at the fire. "I think Jamee was right to be worried about Hope."

"She seemed happy enough to me. Rolling around in the snow certainly put a nice bit of color in her cheeks."

Kacey sniffed. "Spoken like a man. As if sex explains everything."

"It explains a lot, between the right people."

"Hmm."

Nicholas pulled off his heavy sweater. "What's that supposed to mean?"

"It means—hmm." Kacey rubbed her forehead, frowning. "Genevieve is talking about Gideon again. She's convinced that cat is real, Nicholas."

"Maybe he is."

"Then why haven't *we* seen him?"

"The abbey is a strange place, my love. The lighting plays tricks in those old stone halls, and things flit around the corner of your vision. You tell yourself they're shadows, but one day you might discover they're not."

Kacey sighed. "And does that explain the ghost?"

"Nothing can explain the ghost," Nicholas said tightly. "The less Vee says about him the better, believe me. I was hoping the trip up here might give her something new to talk about. Actually, that's one of the reasons I agreed to come when Ian and Jamee phoned and asked for our help."

"Remember, we can't mention Jamee's name, no matter what."

The earl's silver-gray eyes gleamed. "You might be able to buy my silence. For a price, of course."

Kacey glanced at Genevieve, then at her husband. "Is that so? And what would that be?"

"One kiss. One *long* kiss. It will have to last me, I suppose. This whole trip is turning out to be a huge sacrifice."

"Liar. You were even more intrigued by this house than I was when Ian and Jamee called last week. You love nothing more than interfering in other people's lives, and you know it, Nicky. It must be all those centuries of lordly privilege bred into your blue Draycott blood."

Nicholas raised one dark brow. "I think I've just been insulted."

"Soundly."

"For that, the price just doubled, Lady Draycott."

He looked handsome but tired. She almost regretted acceding to his friend's request to look in on Hope O'Hara to be sure she was safe. Ian was one of Nicholas's oldest friends, and he very seldom asked favors, so Nicholas had agreed immediately. Unfortunately, it had meant leaving their beautiful abbey at their favorite time of year.

Somehow the season wouldn't seem right until they got home, Kacey thought. At Christmas the abbey always seemed at its most beautiful. She missed the murmur of the moat and the church bells ringing over the gentle downs. She missed their own bed with the casement windows overlooking the moat.

She slid her hands around Nicholas's neck and pulled him closer. "Maybe we'll have to negotiate terms, my lord," she whispered.

"Maybe," he said huskily. With unerring skill he found his target on her left rib and left her gasping on the verge of noisy laughter.

"*Stop* that," she hissed, vainly trying to wiggle free. "You'll wake Genevieve any second. And I still say there's something *funny* about that man."

"Forget about Ronan MacLeod. You're under direct attack, my dear, and a real Englishman never stops when he's ahead." Nicholas pulled the quilt over their heads and tugged her against his chest. "But I might consider it. With the right inducement, of course."

The quilt stirred and then settled. Then there was only the soft echo of laughter, the rustle of fabric and the low hiss of the fire.

CHAPTER TWENTY-FIVE

MACLEOD FINISHED HIS nightly inspection with his usual silent concentration. At first the locking mechanisms of the inn had been completely foreign to him, but with time he had come to understand the inner workings of spring latches and dead-bolt locks. Now snow swirled around him as he checked each door and window in turn, part of a nightly ritual he had never mentioned to Hope.

Satisfied that there were no signs of intruders and all entrances were secure, he stood staring at Glenbrae House. It still felt like his home. He knew each scar and imperfection and had spent hours repairing those that he could manage. He felt a wave of possessive pride as he watched the high thatched roof grow white beneath falling snow. The tiny mullioned windows were dark now, and smoke rose in a thin plume from the highest chimney.

All was silent. In the dead of night, his worries and dramas suddenly seemed of little importance.

At the sound of low drumming, he tensed. Horses at the run, he thought, or an army on the move. He turned, already in search of his bow and quiver.

Then he saw the lights flashing high above.

Neither horses nor an army, MacLeod realized. Only these outlandish ships that skimmed the air with the help of metal wings. Airplanes, Hope called them.

Infernal pests, MacLeod called them.

Frowning, he forced his body to relax. The plane lights

winked out and silence returned, broken only by the hiss of the wind.

As he stared at the darkened house, MacLeod wondered how the villagers fared back in his own time. Did they set out torches and fine wax candles to welcome in the holiday? Were gifts of fruits and sweet almond paste offered among friends while the muddy streets rang to the tunes of traveling minstrels?

And did they miss their grave lord, so newly returned from the sands of the East? Or were they relieved to be rid of the King's Wolf?

By honor, they would have found him unrecognizable in jeans and black leather jacket. MacLeod both looked and felt entirely different from the man who had ridden out of the storm. He laughed more. He took the time to listen, to ask questions, and found endless excitement in the gadgets and mechanical ingenuity of this age.

Even his language had changed. He was no longer the king's man, no longer Glenbrae's dour seigneur, so he was free to speak and act as he chose. He had even grown comfortable with jeans and their accursed zippers.

MacLeod would have enjoyed the changes more if he knew how much time remained for him to share with Hope. He had actually ridden back to the cliffs two weeks earlier, searching for whatever force had swept him here into this time. But he found only stones and dirt, no glistening portals or magic ring of stones.

Meanwhile, the written sources he had found in the house had offered no answers. By their accounts, the King's Wolf had come and gone at will. Despite his restlessness, Glenbrae Village had prospered and an abbey had been built, along with a small school. But of his death, there was no mention.

MacLeod stared into the darkness, cut off from his own time as surely as the cliffs, lost behind a curtain of snow. Beneath the fir tree his manger was rapidly filling up with snow. He raised each figure, shook off the snow, then restored each one to its rough home. There was an ache in his chest when he stood up, remembering Hope's happiness at his gift.

She called his carving therapy, treatment for some deep mental trauma. He had seen enough television to know there was even more war here than in his own time. Any soldier would be expected to have scars.

MacLeod chose to let her believe what she liked about his past. He couldn't change her mind. He didn't want to change a single thing about her. He remembered her laughter and how the snow dusted her lashes. She was magnificent and impossible and he loved her beyond all limits or permission. If the Draycotts hadn't arrived when they did, he would have had her, there in the snow, and honor be damned.

Cursing himself for a blind fool, he shoved his hands deep into his pockets. His knee ached slightly, but he welcomed the pain. It reminded him who he was and where he truly belonged. His past could not be erased with the sweep of a hand. He must never allow himself to become comfortable in this world, since he could be pulled away from it at any instant with no warning and no chance to explain.

Though it was selfish, he made a wish in that gentle night while the wind hissed through the fir needles. He asked that Hope remember him when he was gone. It would have to suffice, for he himself would have nothing else but memories of her when he returned to his own time.

MacLeod heard a sound from the darkness where a white shape hurtled over the trees. A snowy owl soared over the glen, on the hunt for its dinner.

As he started for the house, a shadow moved against the snow. Gray and calm, a cat padded over the white drifts, leaving the same prints that MacLeod had seen earlier.

"Where do you come from, my friend?" the Scotsman

asked, bending to smooth the gray fur. Purring, the great cat brushed against MacLeod's knee.

"Lost, are you?"

The purring grew.

"Good Lord, the man thinks you're *lost*, Gideon." The words rumbled out of empty space.

MacLeod spun around, staring into solid darkness. "Who walks there?"

Low laughter played around his head. Diamonds glinted against cuffs of white lace and sleeves of blackest velvet.

How came a stranger to saunter out of the night amid the first hard snow of the season? And why was the cut of his jacket so strange?

MacLeod scowled at the new arrival. "How have you come here?"

The visitor blinked. "Is he addressing *us*, Gideon?"

"Of course I am. *You*, at any rate. I don't make a habit of conversing with animals."

The lace cuffs danced as the traveler strode over the snow. "You can *see* me?"

"Well enough. Do you take me to be blind?"

"As blind as most mortals. You *truly* see me?"

MacLeod glared. "I begin to wish I did not."

"A joke. He jokes with us, Gideon. Describe my garments, man."

"Lace of white and black above it. A very odd sort of dress."

"How is it possible?" The man in black rubbed his jaw. "Not drunk, are you?"

MacLeod answered with his stoniest glare.

"Ah, I begin to understand." The man's eyes hardened. "Dead, are you? Still not comfortable with the idea?"

"Nay, but *you* soon may be."

The visitor broke into delighted laughter. "He *threatens* me, Gideon. A rare jest and no mistake. Behold me, the ghost of Draycott Abbey two hundred years dead, and the man threatens me with death."

The cat stared up through the snow, his keen eyes unblinking.

"What manner of lie is this?" MacLeod hissed. "You are no more a ghost than I am. Did you come for Hope? Are you the foul toad who locked us in that shed?"

"I haven't the slightest idea what you're talking about."

"Give me answers or I will sweep that accursed smile from your lips."

The visitor stroked his lace, smiling lazily. "Do try it, my dear boy."

MacLeod's eyes glinted as he lunged. His hands opened, aiming for the elegant jabot at the man's throat. But nothing impeded his movement. There was no resistance of any sort beyond the chill sweep of the wind.

"What joke is this?" MacLeod hissed as his fingers closed on dead air.

"No joke. As you see, I am entirely beyond the threats of you or any other mortal."

MacLeod made a tentative pass with one hand, only to watch his fist slide through the perfectly cut velvet. "You must be a trick of the television devices of this accursed century."

"I am no hoax cast by a television camera. I am a *ghost*. A famous ghost." Adrian Draycott drew himself up to his full, imposing height. "The guardian ghost of Draycott Abbey, to be precise."

"I've heard of Draycott Abbey. In his time, its seigneur was a clever man and his lands were well run. I rode beside him once on the Crusade." MacLeod laughed darkly. "But *you* are naught but a weak image."

"An image, am I?" Around Adrian's head, snow whirled in angry eddies. Shadows gathered, clinging to his body as he wavered, then abruptly disappeared. "What do you think now, Highlander?" His voice boomed from the whirling snow.

MacLeod was unimpressed. He had seen too many astonishing sights to be convinced by the image of a single disappearing male body. "I think that I've seen better illusions on the evening news." A sense of strangeness gripped him that he could speak of such things with ease and acceptance after four short weeks. Clearly he had changed more than he'd realized.

The visitor winked back into solid shape. "I'm no trick," Adrian thundered. "Furthermore, you are *not* supposed to be able to see me! No one can."

"For a television figure, you are remarkably repetitive. You must be an infomercial." MacLeod shook his head and turned away. "I am going inside to get warm."

"You cannot go. I refuse to have it."

MacLeod kept walking.

"Gideon, *you* try something."

Tail twitching, the cat cut off MacLeod's progress. Pressing against his boot, he uttered a low, liquid call.

MacLeod's skin prickled. Who was this incomprehensible figure with his feline companion? Suddenly he recalled how Lord Draycott's daughter had stared anxiously into the snow. "Gideon? Is that your name? Do you know Miss Vee?"

The cat went very still, his great eyes ablaze.

"What do you know of the Draycott child?" Adrian demanded.

"Be quiet or you will wake the whole house," MacLeod muttered.

"Bah! No one can hear me except Gideon, much to my regret." Adrian's dark eyes sharpened. "And now *you*, of course. But you spoke with the child when she arrived?"

"I did. She sleeps inside, with her toy bear next to her." He glanced down at the cat. "She believes that Gideon protects her."

The figure in black smiled gravely. "She might well be

right. But he does not work alone." The guardian ghost of Draycott Abbey rubbed his hard jaw. "You are *certain* you are not dead? A lost soul caught between life and death here on earth?"

MacLeod watched the cat pad delicately through the snow and curl up beside the rough manger. "Perhaps I am. If being tossed seven centuries from my own time makes me dead, then so I am."

"Now you truly begin to interest me." Adrian smoothed his elegant cuffs, frowning. "And your name would be...MacLeod. Ronan MacLeod," he pronounced triumphantly. "I knew a MacLeod once. He could sing a tune to squeeze a man's heart in two. Even better with a sword. I remember a noisy inn near Edinburgh where we found two women who—"

The cat meowed loudly.

"You are correct, Gideon. Pray forgive my digression." The abbey ghost tapped his jaw thoughtfully. "But what holds you in this quiet glen, Highlander?"

At MacLeod's feet the cat stirred.

"*Them?* I forbid you to say their name, Gideon. They are the bane of my existence."

The cat's tail twitched.

"You say the Wishwell sisters have done this thing?" He strode to MacLeod, glaring. "Well, man, is what Gideon says true? Have those three crones been at their magicking again, despite all my warnings?"

"I'm not certain I like your tone," MacLeod said. "And it is only a fool who speaks ill of the *sidhe*."

"Folderol," Adrian snapped. "They are meddlers whose spells invariably go awry. Why did they capture *you* in their net?"

"To protect someone they hold dear."

"Ah. A woman." Adrian nodded as if the whole mystery had suddenly become clear. "*Cherchez la femme.* But there is no problem in that, my boy. My enchantments do *not* go awry, so I will simply send you back." He steepled his fingers in concentration. "What place, what time?"

"Same place, but the year is 1298."

"That old, are you?" Adrian clicked his tongue. "I'll soon see your misery put at an end. All it requires is a bit of focus and an act of will for you to—"

MacLeod raised his hand sharply. "Nay."

"I don't understand."

"You'll speak no words and make no enchantments. Not tonight."

Adrian's brow rose. "You wish to stay in this time? There may be penalties, you know."

"I am not ready to return." MacLeod's eyes locked on the darkened window near the snow-covered roof. "Even if you could manage it."

"You want revenge, do you?"

MacLeod shook his head. "No, not revenge."

"Then you wish the woman to return with you?" Adrian touched his fingers to his chin. "It *might* be possible, with the right calculations. It would require Gideon's help. I confess, I've never sent two back in time."

MacLeod made a short, impatient sound. "No, she cannot go back with me."

"I see," Adrian said slowly. "Because you do not want her."

"Because I *do* want her. But I want her as she is now, and Hope O'Hara would never survive in my age. Her light, her joy, all would be squeezed dry."

"Perhaps you do your woman an injustice, Scotsman. She may be tougher than you know."

Your woman. Were it his choice, it would be so. But seven centuries—and MacLeod's violent past—stood between them, along with several dozen broken laws of nature. "The only injustice I do is to wish for things that cannot be," MacLeod said grimly. "History and written books cannot be changed so easily. Meanwhile, the danger to her remains."

"Danger? The three crones told you of this?"

MacLeod nodded.

White lace fluttered as Adrian paced back and forth before the trees. "If there's danger to her, there is danger to the others, even to the child. This, I cannot tolerate."

"What can you do?"

"More than you might guess." Adrian's eyes glittered. "But I can take no action until I sense clear intent, and there is none yet. Did the crones tell you more?"

"They said their vision was blocked. They could do no more."

"Typical of them. No doubt they botched their preparations and turned some innocent rodent into a sack of potatoes."

"You'll not speak of them so," MacLeod muttered, reaching for Adrian's lapels. As before, his fingers slid right through the perfectly cut velvet. "By all the saints, what am I doing out here in the snow arguing with some fragmented part of my imagination?"

"Imagination? I'm beyond *your* imagination, mortal. In my day I was the confidant of kings."

"So was I," MacLeod countered flatly.

"Men quaked before me and women vied to warm my bed."

"Did it please you?"

"What has pleasure got to do with it?" Adrian thundered. "It was my due."

"Answer my question, ghost."

Adrian muttered angrily, his lace all awry. "Of course I enjoyed it. What mortal wouldn't? There was power, endless days of it. I had gold and laughter and endless praise. Women of blinding beauty." He stopped abruptly. "Yes, it was enough. For a while. Then I saw through the hollow laughter and the angry eyes. By then it was too late for changing." He laughed bitterly. "No, I did not enjoy it. But if you tell anyone I said that, I will haunt you for five centuries, Ronan MacLeod. I have a reputation to consider, after all."

"A dark one?"

"The very blackest. My legend is evil itself." He stared deep into MacLeod's eyes. "This is something that the King's Wolf would understand well."

MacLeod stiffened. "What do you know of that name?"

"Enough. Does she know of your black past?"

"She believes none of my stories." MacLeod bent down to the little tin star, twisted sideways on a clump of fir needles. Gently he pulled it free. "Hope thinks I'm a wounded soldier."

Adrian's keen eyes narrowed. "Aren't you?"

"Not the way she thinks. I'm from seven centuries in her past, wounded in battles she can only read about in books."

"And you enjoyed it?"

MacLeod spun around, a vein hammering at his forehead. "You want to know if I enjoyed the killing? If I liked the screams and the dust?"

"Did you?"

One of MacLeod's hands fisted around a fir bough. "It was…my duty."

"Did you?"

"The King's Wolf would enjoy such things. His legend was built on fear and revenge. They were his finest weapons."

"And what of the man behind the legend? The man who wore the silver wolf at his shoulder and bled when it pricked him?"

MacLeod kicked at the snow. "I cannot change what I am or what I have done. But there was no joy for me, if that is your question."

The fir bough snapped beneath his fingers. Green needles rained down on the drifting snow like fallen blood.

"Honesty at last. An excellent start." Adrian rubbed his hands briskly. "Now to work."

"Go away, ghost. I am tired." *And I am afraid of believing in your dreams.*

Adrian's brow rose. "Leave just when you're beginning to be interesting? Out of the question, man." He stared off to the north, where the dark outline of a cottage lay faint against falling snow. "We have work to do."

MacLeod's brows snapped together in an angry line. "I am *not* staying. It is impossible. Do not torment me with impossible hopes."

"Nothing is impossible to an open heart. Oh, the things I could tell you, Scotsman, the places I have been. Miracles, some would call them." Adrian's lips curved. "But you're not impressed, are you? The Kings' Wolf must have seen sights of his own."

MacLeod shrugged, hating the lurch of excitement he had felt at the possibility of staying in this place, this time.

With Hope. Because without her, all would be dust and noise and empty laughter.

"Tell me about…possibilities, ghost." He touched the tin star gently. "Tell me about things that are possible with an open heart."

"Rather be in a kilt, would you?" Adrian's eyes glinted. "That can be arranged, too." He murmured softly to himself, sketched a figure in the air.

MacLeod flinched in shock to find himself stripped of his jeans and wrapped in a heavy wool tartan with a leather tunic covering his chest. "*Pie Jesu,* how did you—"

With a clang, a pair of metal gauntlets slammed down on the snow before him.

"Sold them, didn't you? Had to buy things for Christmas. Oh, she'll be in a rare fury at that, my boy. Especially when she sees what's in that silver box of yours. Never try to understand a woman at Christmas, I warn you."

"She won't find out," MacLeod said grimly. He took a step, enjoying the freedom of the heavy wool, but half expecting the kilt to disappear.

"Oh, it's real enough, snatched off the display dummy in a darkened museum. Suits you, true enough. Women would swoon." Adrian steepled his fingers. "Now I need to think, so leave me."

His lace fluttered and grew pale.

"What are you planning, Draycott?"

"So now you say my name. Interested in spite of yourself, I think. And afraid to hope that there could be miracles at work tonight."

MacLeod frowned. Life had taught him that hopes were useless deceptions meant to punish fools. Maybe he was afraid to believe anything else. "Nothing real can come of dreams."

"You believe this?" Light glimmered around Adrian's slowly fading head. "Learn to hope, MacLeod. Learn to dream. What you find may surprise even you." His lace fluttered, exquisite as the drifting snow and as quickly fading. "Come, Gideon."

The cat stood, meowed low.

Somewhere far over the lonely glens, church bells chimed twelve times, then once more, a pure, faint peal that hung long in the chilly air.

Then the sounds faded. White lace winked out abruptly, and black velvet was swallowed up by the night. The Scotsman was left alone in the snow, alone in the darkness.

He looked down, fingered the heavy wool, studied the paw prints that had vanished at the edge of a snowdrift. Most of all he stared at a little tin star, wondering about lost dreams and open hearts.

"SOMETHING'S WRONG." Morwenna Wishwell paced anxiously, her eyes on the window. "There's more snow than we usually have, and the wind is too strong."

"Do stop worrying, Morwenna." Perpetua tasted the stew steaming over the fire, added a pinch of bay and thyme, then nodded in satisfaction. "Perfect."

Behind her the wind howled around the eaves. The door shook twice, then banged open, revealing a tall figure in velvet as dark as the night that seemed to enfold him.

Morwenna froze, one hand clutching her chest. "Pet, look. He...he's found us."

"Of course, my dear. Are you shocked that your meddling did not go undetected?" Adrian Draycott strode inside, with his black cape flapping about his shoulders.

"Stop hounding my sister." Perpetua blocked his way. "A bully, that's all you ever were, Adrian Draycott. You don't scare me a whit."

"No, I don't, do I? Always had the spine of ten men, my dear." His eyes darkened. "But this time you have gone too far. You're dealing with a man, not some shivering rodent out of your garden."

"He knows," Morwenna whispered, white-faced.

"Of course I know," Adrian thundered. "You've dragged a poor mortal across the centuries to do your bidding. Don't try to deny it." He crossed his arms, glaring at Morwenna.

Perpetua stood her ground. "I don't know what you're talking about."

"I'm talking about Ronan MacLeod."

Perpetua hid her dismay with a sniff. "What was done was done by all of us, three as one. And you'll cool that sharp tone of yours or you'll leave this instant, Adrian Draycott. I'll see to that."

Adrian glared.

Perpetua glared back.

The fire hissed in the grate. Orange flames shot up the chimney.

Adrian began to laugh, a low rumble that climbed up his

chest and filled the whole room. "As I live and breathe, you three have made a rare mess this time."

"You neither live *nor* breathe," Perpetua corrected irritably. "And we need none of your interference."

"No?" Adrian slid off his cape and held his hands out before the fire. "Cold as death out there. Shouldn't wonder if this glen was haunted. Now, start at the beginning and leave out nothing. Some of that stew would be nice, too, for I'll need my wits clear about me tonight. No one ever made a stew as fine as you, Perpetua, my dear."

The woman in the shawl glared at him. "And no man ever knew his way around a compliment half so smoothly as you did."

Adrian raised one hand. "Enough bickering. Our battle's gone on long enough. Maybe together we can find a way through this muddle. You're certain of the danger?"

Perpetua nodded reluctantly.

"That settles it. I won't have my mortal wards put in danger. I am with you in this, like it or not." He stared into the fire, his face a play of light and shadows, irritation and regret. "It's time we put the past to rest. Lives were lost and good men died."

Morwenna made a soft, broken sound and shoved one hand to her mouth.

"I've said I'm sorry, blast it. The choice wasn't mine, nor was the execution of it. It's what men do, how they live their life. War is in the blood."

"And they died for a few dreams, hunted down like animals," Perpetua said.

Adrian ran a hand across his brow. "It was…wrong. But they wouldn't have listened, no matter what I said. Glory can be a heady wine, especially to a Scotsman." He straightened his shoulders. "We're wasting time. There is work before us." He took a chair before the fire and raised one brow. "Well, what are you waiting for? Do you have any care for those you've meddled with?"

With an irritated sigh, Perpetua sat opposite him, followed by Honoria. Finally Morwenna followed, her face very pale.

Adrian settled back in his chair, hands held to the fire. "Now, tell me how you began. Leave out no word or detail. And then you had best pray that we are *all* very canny." His silver eyes gleamed as an owl called from the high woods. "For something is most definitely afoot in the night."

CHAPTER TWENTY-SIX

GLENBRAE'S HIGH CLIFFS, usually angry and flat, were draped in silver. Winter stretched rich and silent, painting the glen an unbroken sweep of white.

Hope rubbed a haze of mist from the window, telling herself she wasn't waiting for MacLeod's quick step in the hall or the click of his hand at the doorknob. She wasn't waiting for his crooked smile and heart-stopping laugh.

Angrily she shoved back her hair. She was *not* going to lose her head over a handsome-as-sin soldier with gaping holes in his past.

With a sigh she rested her forehead against the cold window. Who was she trying to fool? She was losing her head—had already lost it. She was already his, caught by bonds deeper than words or logic. And tonight by the snow-covered fir tree she had been well on the way to showing him just how much he meant to her.

She paced restlessly, remembering his laughter.

Ah, God, his wonderful, callused hands.

If not for the arrival of their late guests, he would have taken her there in the snow, and Hope would not have denied him. There in the night, only skin and pulse and heat had mattered. There was rare gentleness in the man, no matter what dark warnings he repeated. She knew he would not have hurt her.

But loving him might. Touching him tonight had made that clear.

Hope had survived many things in her life, an awkward adolescence, losing her family members one by one, and near bankruptcy. But she wasn't certain that she could survive Ronan MacLeod. He could be gone tomorrow in the morning mist, just as he had warned.

She lowered her head, arms locked at her knees while angry tears pricked behind her eyelids. Blast him for coming just when she was getting her life in order. Damn him for making her want more, for seeing dreams that only he could make real.

Hope rubbed her head, thinking of his manger and the figures carved with such exquisite skill. The project must have taken him weeks. What kind of man carved a *manger* in this day and age?

A man with a granite code of honor.

A man who would always choose his own road.

She thought of her desk, crowded with bills and menus. Only yesterday a fax had confirmed the upcoming visit of Detective Sergeant James Kipworth. If the snow continued, there would be calls to make, plans to change, extra food to lay in. At their present rate, they would run out of eggs and milk in four days, and fresh produce in five. That left her with—

Nothing.

Her brain simply shut down, numbers and plans forgotten. Outside, snow whispered against the window like the voices of those she had lost in her life. Everyone Hope had loved most had died, first her parents and then her great, noisy uncle, a man she had been certain would outlive her by decades.

All she had were a few letters and a trunk full of faded photographs. Greece in autumn, Paris in spring, Minnesota in July. But memories didn't keep you warm. Hope had discovered that after one too many haunted dawns. Even Gabrielle, Jeffrey, the Wishwells and Archibald Brown, dear friends one and all, couldn't fill the void in her wounded heart.

It just wasn't the same.

Hope had always prided herself on her pragmatism and her ability to take care of herself. Now Ronan MacLeod slammed into her life and left her wanting a hard shoulder to lean on. The knowledge of her slowly unraveling independence left Hope terrified.

She didn't *want* to need him.

She certainly didn't want to love him.

Her shoulders bowed as strain and exhaustion took their toll. With firelight dancing around her, she closed her eyes, slipping into the dark wells where dreams began.

Why doesn't he come…?

THE SNOW FELL ON, silent and pure, waves of white against the dark sky. MacLeod circled the house, waiting for the sharp prick of danger between his shoulder blades, an instinct that had saved him on a dozen bloody battlefields.

But nothing moved in the night. No warning tightened his chest. Tonight the greatest danger lay inside Glenbrae, where one high, dark window mocked him. He thought of Hope. Pacing, asleep, waiting. Dressed in lace or sheerest silk.

The woman he loved.

The man MacLeod had been, hardened soldier and inveterate wanderer, urged him to find her there in the darkness and take her as he would have in the snow, fast and desperate. In the darkness there would be no time for questions or honor.

No time…

And time was the question, wasn't it? The person MacLeod had become was all too aware that taking would be only the beginning. With the heat of their bodies they would forge new dreams and a future that MacLeod barely dared to imagine.

He slid a hand across his brow, struck by a wave of exhaustion. His leg ached and the cold bit into his bones, but he did not move toward the silent house and the high, dark window beneath the roof.

Honor held him still. Honor made his hands fist as snow hissed over the heavy thatch. Hope had needed a miracle on the night he'd been brought here. She needed someone still to share the burdens of this beautiful, demanding house.

What she had was MacLeod, although he wasn't sure if his appearance in this time was a miracle or a curse for her.

Only time would tell.

Meanwhile, flawed or not, he was the only warrior she had.

HOPE HEARD THE WATER running next door and jerked upright. She hadn't been sound asleep, merely drowsing before the fire with her legs tucked beneath her and a tartan thrown across her shoulders for warmth.

She'd been waiting for MacLeod, waiting for what had seemed like hours. Maybe even lifetimes. That would explain the instant familiarity she had felt with him.

But she wasn't going to get caught up in philosophical dilemmas. Tonight was a night for being practical.

And for being desperate.

Because tonight she was going to put them both out of their misery.

She took a long look in the antique cheval glass by the door. Her hair glowed, sleek and glossy, a smooth cap around her pale face. The gown from her anonymous donor spilled around her slender body, all lace and satin rosebuds. It clung, it hinted, it teased, as seductive as she'd imagined.

Time to go.

The tartan hit the floor. Her heart was hammering and there was a wild streak of color in her cheeks.

Fear, she told herself. Raw fear.

Head high, she pushed open the door to MacLeod's adjoining room. All was in darkness except for the gilt patterns cast by a dying fire. The air held a hint of steam from the open bathroom door.

Hope's bare feet made no sound as she crossed the room. Though her hands were trembling, she wouldn't turn back. She had found her dream tonight by the little manger and the tin star. Now she was going to reach out and make the dream come true.

The door opened without a sound. She could see Ronan behind the shower door, forearms to the wall, head lowered beneath a biting stream of spray. The exhaustion in his broad shoulders almost made Hope turn away.

Almost.

She took a deep breath and raised her chin. Quickly, before she could change her mind, she swept back the heavy glass door. "Three things, MacLeod. And *don't* interrupt me."

"What are you *doing* in here?" He lunged for a towel, but Hope blocked his hand, terrified if she didn't finish, the words would never come.

"Don't interrupt, just listen." She shoved back her hair, and there was no way she could know how vulnerable the gesture made her look. The single light frosted her skin, all hollows and curves, though she could not know that either. "First, this." She pointed to the froth of lace draping her body. "Is this from you? Did you send it here?"

His surprise was genuine. "It was not my gift."

"I thought not. Two, did you mean what you said tonight by the manger? Did you really…want me?"

His head bowed. Hope began to suspect the exhaustion she had seen was regret and the tension of some internal battle he was fighting.

He took a harsh breath. "Go away, Hope."

"After you answer me."

His eyes clouded with anger. "I wanted you. I still do," he said grimly. "In my present state, that's all too obvious.

Contrary to what your experts say, cold water is of no help in this situation."

Hope looked down and felt her legs melt. That tall, lean body glistened, slick with water, all ridged muscles and angry control. Even as he stood with his side to her, Hope saw the hard inches arrowing from a nest of dark hair, testimony to the battle he was waging—and losing.

"You see now?"

"What am I supposed to see? That you're a man and not a machine? That some things even you can't control?" Hope reached past and shut off the water. She wasn't going to back down now—and she wouldn't let him back down either.

She held out her hand, relieved that it shook only a little. "Here."

He stared down at the small packet resting on her palm. "A Christmas gift? There was no need."

Hope stared at him. "Take it, MacLeod. And don't pretend you don't know what it is or why I'm offering it." Color filled her cheeks as he lifted the small foiled square. "I haven't had a lot of experience with these things, but I know what's right."

She waited for recognition, for the rebuff that would crush her. Her uneasiness grew, racing into panic. "Well, *say* something."

He stared at the packet. Frowning, he turned it back and forth in his fingers.

With every passing second, Hope's willpower fled. She was making a fine mess of this. What had made her think she could carry it off? Where men were concerned, her life had always been a complete disaster.

"What kind of experience do you lack?"

Surely he didn't expect details. She wasn't about to make a litany of her bungled relationships, not when she had worked so hard to forget them.

"Give that to me." She lunged for his hand, but MacLeod

pulled away, frowning. She spun nervously, bolting for the door.

Her cheeks flamed as MacLeod trapped her against the wall. His body was rigid with demand, but his hands were surprisingly gentle. "Talk to me, Hope."

"I don't walk to talk. I *wanted* to s-seduce you, damn it, but I've changed my mind. L-let me go," she blurted, awash in embarrassment. Why was it things like this never happened in the movies? There was simply a knowing glance, a soulful smile, then a swift cut to beautiful bodies moving in perfect symmetry.

But life never worked out like the movies, Hope thought bleakly. She had proved that just now.

She twisted wildly, all too aware of his thighs pressed against her fragile lace gown. "I s-said forget it, MacLeod," she hissed. "I've changed my mind."

"I don't want to forget it." He whispered a kiss against the curve of her neck.

Hope's heart pounded. "I don't want your pity."

He eased closer. "Does that feel like pity pressing against your hips?"

Hope swallowed. "N-no."

MacLeod still held the packet in his locked fingers, the foil unbroken. "Why did you run from me just now?"

Hope made a strangled sound of embarrassment. "I told you I wasn't good at this. But right is right, MacLeod. This is 1998, and there are…ramifications." Hope realized he still didn't understand.

"Explain what you've given me."

"It's…just what it appears to be," Hope said, rigid with embarrassment. "You *must* know."

MacLeod drew a sudden breath. As he stared, his mouth twisted. "This is meant for a lover. It is to protect both of you."

Hope shrugged. She wouldn't answer what had to be completely obvious.

"I said nothing because I did not understand you, Hope. Such things were managed differently in my time."

"Come on, MacLeod. You don't actually expect me to believe—"

"In *my* time," he continued flatly. "Back before television or municipal bonds. Back before plastic or cardboard or latex. When there was no queen on the throne, only a king who harrowed the Highlands. That is what I've been trying to tell you, Hope. This is *not* my time. This…protection you offered me was nothing I had ever seen." He slanted his lips over her cheek and cursed softly. "I've never had a woman offer me protection before. You take my breath away."

Hope closed her eyes, feeling the heat of his body stealing into her. She was suddenly aware of her hammering heart and his utter nakedness. "You…don't need to use it for me," she blurted. "I'm not—I can't—" She drew a ragged breath. "I can't make a child inside me, MacLeod. Something went wrong a while back. A minor glitch, but irreversible, I'm afraid." She stared at the center of his chest, unable to look up. "There's no need to worry about the possibility that we could—that I would—"

"Make a child," he finished gently. "Dearly would I love to watch a child grow within that sweet body of yours, my heart." He drew her hands around his waist until she was holding him tightly. Only then did he release her, slanting her face up to his. "I wish you would stop studying my chest."

"This isn't exactly *easy* for me," Hope said unsteadily. "I've never owned one of these things before. I've certainly never offered one to a man whom I've just propositioned."

"But you did now. With courage and wit that were singular." He traced her bottom lip with his tongue. "I've wanted you like this. I've wanted you against my mouth, trembling while I made you forget every reason this is a bad idea."

"You don't have to make me forget. You don't even have

to convince me. I want you," Hope said gravely. "I want what we'll have together, even if it's only for a week, a month." Her voice shook. "A night. Even that, I don't mind."

"But I do," MacLeod said savagely, resting his forehead against hers. "I want you tonight and all other nights. I want to stay and watch you work miracles with the house I never had time to make into a home. But I cannot," he said bitterly.

"Why?"

Something dark filled his face. And still he hesitated.

"*Tell* me."

"Better than that, I'll show you." Barefoot, wearing only his tartan at his hips, he strode to the door, tugging Hope behind him.

CHAPTER TWENTY-SEVEN

"WHERE ARE YOU *TAKING* ME?"

Hope frowned as MacLeod crossed the hall, then plunged down the steep stairway in the old north tower. She shivered as he drew her to an abrupt halt before the portrait.

"Look at him, Hope. He seems familiar, doesn't he?"

As always before, Hope was struck by the similarity of the high cheekbones and proud brow. "What are you trying to say, MacLeod?"

"The same thing that I said before. This house, that portrait…both are mine. Not now, but seven centuries in your past. This man whose features scowl in dark arrogance. See the faint trace of gray in his hair and the lines at his brow?"

"I see them, but I still don't understand—"

"Maybe this will help you understand." MacLeod's eyes were hard as he moved to the wall where the portrait was lit by a single sconce. "Touch it," he ordered, never taking his eyes from the figure.

"But I don't—"

"*Touch* him." Desperation edged his voice as he stared at the man who could have been his twin.

Gently Hope traced the shadowed cheeks, the mail-covered shoulders and the narrowed mouth, waiting to feel anything unusual. "I don't understand. Nothing happened. The painting is whole and I'm still alive."

"Exactly," MacLeod said tensely. "But when I do the same…"

He braced one shoulder against the wall, closed his eyes, and reached out for the gauntleted fingers of Glenbrae's ancient laird. Hand and shadow slanted together, touching the old fresco, and where they met the weathered image, they disappeared.

"Do you begin to see now?" he whispered. His shoulders were rigid, his body stiff. "I've only just discovered that this is my way home, Hope, the answer I have searched for since the night of the storm. I do not belong here in your time. My being, my molecules as you call them, are an affront to your reality. Somewhere at the edge of the portrait, that imbalance is corrected and whatever part of me touches it is sent home. To *my* time, Hope, not here but seven centuries back, in a Glenbrae without electricity or cars." His voice fell. "In a Glenbrae without *you*."

"No," Hope breathed, torn between shock and raw denial.

"Yes, all of it is true. You still do not believe?"

"How can I?"

MacLeod nodded as if he had expected nothing else. His eyes burned into her face, almost as if to lock the image in his mind. "I'll show you the rest now. Then you'll have no choice but to believe. And if it fails—if I fail—" His hand tightened on hers, held, then slid free as he leaned toward the shadowed image on the wall.

Eyes closed, he moved forward. His shadow fell over the cold plaster until wall, man and shadow met, merged.

Then Ronan MacLeod vanished without a trace, swallowed remorselessly back into the past just as his hand had been.

Hope gave a ragged cry and dug at the wall, but met only stone and cold plaster. The man was gone. Only his image remained behind to mock her.

She swayed, dizzy with shock and fear. "MacLeod," she whispered, palms pressed to the figure who studied her with icy arrogance.

Ronan's face.

Ronan's eyes.

Or the Ronan he would become, in a century Hope would never know. "Come back to me," she said raggedly. "I believe you."

Light touched the cold face. The wall lay rigid, insensate, without movement or understanding.

She closed her eyes, forehead to the cold stone. She prayed then, with raw, silent intensity. She sank to the floor, feeling the night close around her, flinging back her prayers. She shoved at the floor, the stairs, desperate to find any hole or fragment of an entrance.

There was none.

MacLeod had vanished beyond any contact, pulled back to his own time in a world where he was the King's Wolf, hated and feared.

"Don't go," Hope whispered.

Shadows covered the icy face. The proud, sensual mouth did not move.

She turned away, a hand thrown before her eyes, unable to bear the sight of this picture that was such a pale imitation of the man she had come to love, a warrior of honor and generosity who had found her across time.

Why had she doubted him? Why hadn't she just *believed* him? His story had never wavered. He was a man who did not know how to lie.

The realization came too late.

Hope shivered, shoulders bowed. He had told her the truth, for all the good it had done him. His tales of Edward and the Crusades were fact, not the ravings of a scarred mind. And the scars on his back had been earned in war on horseback, on a steed who well deserved the name of Pegasus.

Hope could no longer hide from the shattering truth.

Nothing moved in the shadows. No warm laugh echoed through the curving tower stairs.

She pushed to her feet, one hand on the cold plaster. So the pattern stayed true. Once again she had lost the one she loved most deeply.

Blindly she started up the stairs, unable to bear the silence MacLeod had left behind him. She brushed the cheeks slick with tears, cold with regret.

Why hadn't she *believed* him?

The sound came like a memory, soft and rustling.

Hope didn't move, afraid to turn. Above her head something glinted on the wall, light that scattered in the pattern of a cross.

She waited, afraid to look, afraid to hope. "If you're there, tell me. Don't break my heart again…"

Something struck the floor.

First a foot, then a muscled leg and arms, shimmered into solid form and MacLeod toppled forward, white as death. "Hope," he said hoarsely.

No illusion. A hard, beloved voice.

She flew over the cold steps, caught his swaying shoulders and helped him stand against the wall.

But away from the portrait. Far from where the icy image could do him more harm.

He coughed, his arm rigid at her shoulders. "Almost— couldn't find you. Like two doors back to back." He swayed forward, his face grim. "This time something—wrong. There was darkness, cold. Couldn't find the way." He bent double, broke into a wracking cough. When the coughing passed, he gave an unsteady laugh. "Maybe I do need your protection." His hand found hers, linked, tightened. "Do you see now? Where I've come from, and why there are a thousand reasons that I should not be here wanting you. *Loving* you."

Hope cradled his face and traced the scar just above his brow. "No reasons that count, MacLeod. None that I'll let count." She felt his muscles tighten beneath her fingers. "And I'll do everything I can to prove that to you."

"Is that—" he coughed once "—a threat, my heart?"

"A promise," she whispered, lips to his jaw. "Another proposition. See what a wicked woman I've become under your influence."

He made a low, lost sound, then straightened. A heart-beat later, she was in his arms, caught to his chest as he climbed out of the shadows and the cold.

"Ronan, stop," Hope ordered, caught between joy and shock. "I can walk, you idiot. There's no need to be so dramatic."

"I want to be dramatic. As a knight, I've been trained well in all the rituals, and I would give you nothing less. For a long time I thought ritual was all there was, but you laid that particular lie to rest the first time I touched you." His hands tightened and energy seemed to flood back into him. "You believe me now?" His eyes darkened. "The truth this time."

Hope nodded. "I only wish I had believed you sooner. But, Ronan, how were you brought here? *Why?*"

He stilled her with a low, hungry kiss that made her heart tilt.

"Don't ask me, for I have no other answers. I am a warrior, not a scientist. I know only that it happened and somewhere a door opened for us. This was the miracle I have prayed for in the cold, hard hours of the night." He touched the curve of her cheek. "I saw you there sometimes, an image in my dreams. I thought it was a curse, my penance to see a woman I could never have or hold in my hands."

He set her down slowly. "Do I go beyond this door, my heart? Do I take you as I've wanted to take you, without regrets or reservations?" His hands tightened. "Even if you wake tomorrow and find me gone, pulled back to that other place, and I can never find you again?"

She didn't hesitate, didn't need to. "Yes," she breathed. "Yes to both and all. But I won't let you go away again, I warn you."

Ronan stared at her face, wishing it could be so easy and that her will alone could hold him here. But he wouldn't think of loss, not tonight. The memory of that dead space beyond the portrait was still too fresh.

He slid a chain of beaten silver around her neck and straightened the etched cross that bore a single diamond at its heart. "For you. That's what kept me—and nearly made me lose you forever. In my time it came from the hands of a very clever silversmith in Venice. I wonder if his canal is still banked by white roses."

"It must be priceless," Hope breathed. "Especially *now.* But you shouldn't have taken such risks for me," she said fiercely.

"Love is always a risk, the greatest risk of all perhaps." He opened her door and lifted her across the threshold. "I might make mistakes tonight, Hope. In my time men and women were different about these things. There was less talk, less planning. What happened, happened." His eyes burned over her face. "If I hurt you, tell me."

"As if you could hurt me. As if I wouldn't want anything you chose to give me, knight."

MacLeod closed his eyes, need a fire that healed even as it burned. He carried her through her bedroom to an adjoining room where a long, glassed balcony overlooked the whole glen.

A single wood beam ran the bottom of the windows, and he pressed her hands around it. The firs moved below them, their dark needles tossed in the wind as Ronan slid the lace slowly from her shoulders and began a lesson without words, a lesson made of touch and tongue and hard, drawn breath. He bared her skin, inch by inch, with swift kisses that left her skin burning.

The lace slipped, trailed down, finally pooling at her feet. She was soft. God, she was silver and innocence in the moonlight. He honored her strength with his mouth pressed to that supple spine and then to the sensitive hollow at the curve of her back. She was trembling when he slid his palms to the sensitive skin that crested in peaks, hard with desire.

"Ronan, I'm not—"

"Yes, you are. Beautiful. I'll prove it to you now, *mo rùn*."

Her voice broke as he turned her in his hands and nearly swayed at the sight of her.

"Don't…look at me like that," she whispered.

"I have to. Any man would. But especially a man who loved you." He stroked his way down the curve of her breast, circled her slowly with his tongue, then drew her into his mouth inch by teasing inch until she swayed against him.

Almost as lost as he was.

"A man would have to be blind or dead not to want this," he whispered, following the line of her chest, tracing her ribs and her stomach, then lower still.

Her soft curls were a mystery that he explored slowly, finding her taste and opening her gently. She trembled and would have fallen but for her hands locked on the heavy beam.

"Want me, Hope," he whispered. "Want me inside you, while I show you how love can feel." He slid into her velvet folds, teased a ragged moan from her throat, and knew she was close to the edge, just where he wanted her.

His fingers moved, parted, eased deeper. MacLeod felt her stiffen, then gasp his name while her hands rose to clutch at his rigid shoulders.

And then she raced over the crest, trembling against him, shaking like a leaf.

MacLeod knew the moment of her pleasure with the unerring instincts of a man who had known many women. He had liked most of them, pleased all of them, but loved none of them.

Not like this. Not with the blind, all-encompassing hunger Hope made him feel.

He waited until the tremors faded, then sent her up again, with tongue and stroking teeth, liquid against her sleek folds when she throbbed against him.

She swayed and began to sink, her fingers tangled in his long hair. "Ronan," she breathed. "I think I'm dead."

"Not yet." He drew her against him and let her feel the desire bladed against her thighs.

Her eyes darkened. "If that's supposed to impress me, it's…succeeding." She found the edge of his tartan and worked the folds free. With a hiss the heavy wool struck the floor.

Hope's lips curved in a crooked grin. "Dear me, MacLeod, now I'm *really* impressed. And I have just one thing to say to you."

He waited, frowning, his logic broken into tiny pieces as it always was around her. "And what would that be?"

"I think I'll show you instead." She eased to one knee, tracing his rigid length slowly. Then her lips closed around him on a sigh.

MacLeod shuddered, lost in the sensation of her hands and mouth, his body locked in a fierce struggle for control. "Hope, no. *No.*" He pulled himself back from the edge, then tugged her up against his chest. "By God, you will be the death of us both, woman."

"Is that good or bad?"

His jaw clenched. "Good. Extraordinary. Assuming that I live through it."

"But I wanted to take your breath away—"

"You do."

She gnawed at her lip. "I wanted it to be perfect."

"Even if it isn't perfect, it still is," he said hoarsely. "So it is when love is given. The details do not matter. It is the look in your eyes that makes this perfect to me. That crooked smile and the husky, broken sound you make when I touch you."

Her eyes were huge, luminous. "I don't…"

"You do. You did it twice and once more just now."

"So you're keeping score now, MacLeod?"

"Keeping...track," he corrected gently. "Of everything. I do not want to forget a single second."

Her hands tightened. "In case something happens?"

"The chance is great. I will not lie, Hope. History says the King's Wolf returned to Glenbrae." He shook his head. "If history can change, I swear I'll find a way to do it. Until then..." He eased her thigh across his, groaning while she cradled his heat. "Until then, we must write our own legends, my heart."

Moonlight spilled through the high windows, dappling her body in shadows.

Beautiful, Ronan thought. Honest and brave. Her face and smile all that he had glimpsed in dreams. And he had loved her even then.

She traced the frown lines at his brow. "You think too much, MacLeod. You keep score too well."

"Keep track," he whispered as he lifted her against him, parted her, made her breath catch when she sheathed him. She opened to him like a flower, clung on sleek petals until he shook with the need to drive deep and impale her. He closed his eyes, trying not to feel her hands dig at his shoulders, trying not to feel how perfectly their bodies fit.

The scent of cloves and roses clung to her skin. In the darkness, hunger had a thousand names, a thousand reasons. He meant to savor every one.

But she caught him unawares, twisting to drive him back and pin his rigid body beneath hers. "I'm not very good at this, MacLeod."

"Any better and I'll be dead," he muttered.

She shifted. Softness ached, then spread to cradle him. "I'll keep that in mind," she whispered. "But meanwhile..."

Meanwhile he died. Meanwhile his heart tilted and his

very reason fled. She was too soft, too tight, too giving, the sum of all his dark imaginings.

"Is this…the general idea?"

His hands locked over her hips, sliding her lower. "Do I have the look of a man dissatisfied?"

"Not quite." Hope gave a breathless laugh. "I can't believe I'm touching you, doing this. Talking as if this was the most normal thing in the world." She sighed, sinking down, taking more of him. "As if it wasn't like finding a little corner of heaven." She touched his scarred chest gently. "Hope O'Hara and a man who probably has his sculpture on a church wall somewhere. You could even be considered a national legend."

"Only the bad sort, I'm afraid. The kind that mothers use to frighten willful daughters." A tremor shook her as he rocked against her, slow and hard. "But tonight I am no more than a man, Hope. A lover you are driving to a fine madness."

"Madness. I like the sound of that." She sank, gloved him exquisitely. "You're a hard man to proposition, MacLeod. Not that I've had much practice." Her lips curved, sinful. "With hard men, that is."

"I like how you make your propositions," he breathed. The fit was perfect and his control was nearly gone when he linked their fingers and pulled her close to trace the tip of her breast with his teeth. His hand slid between their joined bodies. "I don't think you need any more practice," he muttered hoarsely. "I am the one in danger of death at any second."

His fingers moved. He felt her instant, shuddering gasp.

"Not fair, MacLeod. That's—cheating."

His smile was a slash of silver in the moonlight. "I never said I'd be fair, Hope. Only that I'd love you as no other man ever has. And I will." One slow thrust, one brush of his hands, and she was lost again, her eyes blind as she arched against him.

Dear God, how much I love her, MacLeod thought, watching the passion catch her. If only he could see the future. If only there were more time for them.

If only...

Her eyes opened. "I can see how you became a legend, Ronan MacLeod. And I think I've forgotten how to speak." She planted a dazed kiss against his mouth, her cheeks aflame. "I can't move. I can't even remember my name. Any suggestions?"

MacLeod groaned as she closed around him, all heat and silk. He didn't feel like a legend. He felt like a man in extremis as her muscles tightened, drawing him in, draining him of sanity. "Then forget your name. Forget all else but how we fit together, *mo rùn.*"

His heart hammered with an intensity that was almost painful as he gripped her hips and impaled her until he could drive no higher. Thigh to thigh they moved. The only sound was his groan, her broken cry.

Beneath them snow swept through the glen, and the black arms of the oaks tossed in the wind. Darkness raced, pounding at MacLeod's mind as he found the small, shining door that love and Glenbrae's miracles had opened between the centuries.

There, matter and time twisted, losing all meaning.

Hope stiffened. Her body closed around him and she cried out his name, clutching blindly at his shoulders.

This time MacLeod followed her.

No more keeping score. No more guarding his wary heart.

Honor be damned, duties be damned; he threw back his head and rocked against her high and hard, spilling his hot seed deep. He knew a grim satisfaction as her legs locked around him and she twisted, shot through with pleasure yet again, then collapsed blindly against his chest.

CHAPTER TWENTY-EIGHT

SOMEWHERE BEYOND MIDNIGHT, Hope stirred. MacLeod had managed to tug a pillow beneath her head and find a blanket for them to share.

Snow danced against the window and he smiled sleepily when he felt her fingers tug at the soft hair at his chest.

"So," she said huskily, "how does it feel to be a legend?"

"Maybe I should ask *you*." He drew her head onto his shoulder and smoothed the warm curve of her hip. "Books have been written about less, woman."

She chuckled unsteadily. "Don't make me laugh, MacLeod. It takes energy that I need to breathe."

A grin worked over his lips. "And I was so busy feeling sorry for myself. A sculpture on a church wall, I believe you called me."

She snuggled closer. "Go ahead and deny it."

He shrugged. "Guilty, I'm afraid. There were three at last count."

Hope traced his jaw with her fingertip. "You really are a legend. You're making me feel panicky again, MacLeod. How is a normal woman supposed to measure up to that kind of reputation?"

"Like this." His thigh moved. Slow and sweet, he entered her on a glide of pure magic.

No fury this time. No blind desperation. Only a slow, shuddering pleasure where his body rode hers. Only his hands, locked around hers as he watched her eyes darken, watched her pleasure begin again.

And he kissed the soft, broken moan from her lips when the glide took her higher and stole her breath.

In truth, Hope O'Hara made him feel like a legend, MacLeod thought. She made him feel like a man who could claim kingdoms and start dynasties. Here in this beautiful glen he was changed, tamed, freed of his dark past.

The wolf no longer paced inside him.

Purest magic, all of it. MacLeod prayed he would have the rest of his life to thank her. If not, he would simply hoard whatever precious moments they were given.

The silver cross glinted. In the pale moonlight it lay cold between their heat, reminding MacLeod of old vows and fallen friends.

He closed his eyes and felt Hope's arms around him, her hair like a curtain at his cheek. *This,* he thought. All he wanted or could ever need. One heart and one breath.

The silver cross shifted, warm with their heat when he groaned and found the sweet, dark mystery, then rode it down into forever.

And Hope was there, waiting for him.

HOPE STRETCHED SLOWLY, eyes closed while the first hint of dawn filtered through the window. There was a strange weight in her body, a warm tugging in muscles she'd never even imagined. The man was *amazing.*

A smile played over her lips as she draped herself across the lean, rugged body that had driven her to delirious pleasure throughout the night.

The silver cross slid over her skin, brushing MacLeod's chest. *I love you,* she thought. *Now and tomorrow and forever. I'll love you no matter how long it lasts or where it takes us.*

She touched his face, flushed from the stubble on his jaw.

A dozen other places carried the same flush. She felt thoroughly manhandled, sweetly depraved.

Entirely cherished.

She eased one hand under the blanket and nuzzled his warm chest. "Did I forget to say good morning, MacLeod?"

His smile was a dark curve of pure satiety. "Not that I recall. But possibly I don't recall too much after the last hour, when you toppled me onto the bed—"

"I didn't."

"—and proceeded to make havoc with my body."

"Havoc?" She laughed huskily. "I wouldn't quite call it that." Her hand slid lower. "Such an amazing body. A legendary body. A man who is a rock among men."

He gave a low groan as she swept down the rapidly hardening length of him. "Not always a rock."

"Feels that way to me." She planted swift, hot kisses over his jaw. "The body of a man who knows exactly how to keep score."

"Keep track," he muttered hoarsely as she goaded him with sweet, searching fingers that closed like a glove. He caught her hand and twisted, sweeping her beneath him on the bed. "I have a new opinion of beds, by the way. They have their particular uses." She was soft against his hand, soft against his mouth when he nuzzled her tight, warm curls.

His name was a moan when she arched against him, seeking blindly. He entered her when the dazed pleasure faded from her eyes, delighting them both.

Hope suddenly stiffened, staring over his shoulder. "What's that...*thing?*"

He moved deeper, smiling. "Which...thing are you referring to, my heart?"

Hope rasped, "Rogue. I mean the piece of stone that's grinning at me from the side table."

MacLeod studied the weathered piece of stone he'd brought inside several days earlier. Something about its eyes had intrigued him. "I found it by the stables. An old carving, the sort you'd expect to find on a church wall. I thought you should have it before someone else found it."

"It's cute," Hope murmured, moving beneath him in warm, silken rhythm. "In an ugly sort of way."

"Like me."

"Nay," she whispered. "You're all beauty, MacLeod. Nothing cute about you."

The eyes of the stone gargoyle seemed to follow her, holding some grave secret as Hope felt the silver coils tighten and shimmer through her. "Kiss me," she said, suddenly frightened. Suddenly all too aware of the fragile nature of the miracle that held them together.

His body moved over her, into her, fierce and hungry. Hope opened to him, flesh, mind and spirit, offering him her joy and all the time they could steal.

Skin against skin, desire became a dark rhythm.

"Is this—the general idea?" he rasped.

"If that's supposed to impress me—" she closed her eyes, gasped, letting the silver ride through her "—you're definitely succeeding, MacLeod."

There in the blue silence of dawn they forgot their names, forgot how time could harm them, forgot everything but how they fit together, a legend and his love.

One breath and one dream.

CHAPTER TWENTY-NINE

ALL NIGHT THE SNOW FELL, and at ten o'clock the next morning it was still coming down.

Hope was in her office surveying unanswered mail and unfinished paperwork when she jumped at the sudden sound of knocking.

Gabrielle tottered in, shivering beneath a double layer of athletic fleece. "Bad news. The stove, it breaks."

"Not again."

"Yes, again. Also bad, we have enough milk for two days. Eggs for only one."

Hope shoved back her hair, wishing she had slept more than an hour the night before. Her eyes were gritty and she just managed to hide a yawn. But she had to smile at the memory of MacLeod's very distinctive manner of saying hello in the morning. "I thought we had enough basics on hand for three or four days."

Gabrielle swept a hand through the air. "The chocolate soufflés yesterday used a great part of it. I did not know there would be so much snow." The chef glanced out the window at the unbroken world of white. "And snow and snow and snow…"

"We'll have to manage, Gabrielle. Stretch everything out. You have beans and sausage for a cassoulet?"

Gabrielle tapped her jaw, considering the possibilities of the savory, simmered casserole crusty with sausage, cheese and beans. Her face brightened. "A very good idea. Perhaps cooked long with just this much cheese, and then a hot bread and some wine to go with it. Yes, it will do." Suddenly her eyes narrowed. "Your face is burned?"

Hope cleared her throat, trying not to remember exactly how her face had gotten burned. "Must be a trick of the light."

Jeffrey appeared at Gabrielle's shoulder, his hair dusted with snow. "Bad news. The roads are officially closed. All deliveries to Glenbrae are canceled until the weather clears."

"Grand." Hope sighed. "Now we've got no way to restock supplies."

"At least one meal is covered. The Wishwells have invited everyone up for lunch. They have plenty of supplies and stew enough for an army, they said."

Hope frowned. "I wonder why they prepared so much."

"Beats me." Jeffrey grinned. "And they really do have enough. When I brought them some firewood, they insisted I stay to eat." He whistled appreciatively. "I haven't had stew like that since our old cook retired." He brushed Gabrielle's cheek. "Except for yours, of course."

"Hmmph. Wait until you taste my cassoulet," Gabrielle charged.

"That will take care of lunch, and cassoulet for dinner. Meanwhile let's pray for sunny weather and lots of melting snow," Hope muttered.

"Speaking of snow, there was a man walking up from the village when I came back. He said he'd wait in the library," Jeffrey said.

"Not another unexpected guest, I hope."

Jeffrey scratched his head. "He said he was just up from Edinburgh. Some kind of policeman, I think."

"*Detective Sergeant Kipworth?*" Hope leaped to her feet. "He's here? Oh, Lord, I forgot all about him."

"He seemed quite keen on that manger of MacLeod's. Said he hadn't seen anything like it in his life."

Hope started down the stairs.

"Wait. There's one more thing." Jeffrey glanced at Gabrielle, who nodded, color in her cheeks.

"It is for you to tell, Jeffrey."

He shifted from foot to foot. "We, uh, we didn't expect it, not a bit. We hope you'll be happy."

"Happy about what?"

Gabrielle took Jeffrey's hand. "That we will be married. Jeffrey asks me last night and I finally agree. With this snow, it is very quiet, very romantic. But I would marry him in any weather or any place."

Jeffrey flushed beet-red, but managed to look entirely delighted. "I still can't believe she said yes."

"You two." Hope drew a shaky breath, feeling a pang of sadness. Ah, well, nothing ever stayed the same, she told herself. "I'm so happy for you. Gabrielle can find a wonderful spot in a swank restaurant in London, and you'll soon be a star set designer, Jeffrey."

"No," Gabrielle and Jeffrey said in the same breath. "At least not right away," Jeffrey explained. "We rather thought we would stay here and help you. I've got some ideas about a local theater. Nothing too adventurous at first. A few small productions with visiting troupes from Edinburgh or Manchester."

Hope sat down shakily. "Stay *here?* I can't let you. There's nothing here in Glenbrae to compare with London or Oxford or…"

"So now you tell us how to run our lives?" Gabrielle took Hope's hands. "We stay because it is our choice. Not for work or money, but because of friends like you. Because of the beautiful mist that covers the loch at dawn and because Glenbrae will be a wonderful place to make a family." Again she colored.

"You're sure?" Hope felt her eyes blur with sudden tears. "Really sure, you two? There is so much more you could have."

"Nothing so important that it can't wait," Gabrielle answered for both. "So you do not get rid of us so soon, Hope O'Hara."

"I don't *want* to get rid of you. But think what you're giving up."

Hope's protests were cut short by a raucous shriek. "A drum. A drum! MacBeth doth come."

"Ho, Banquo, what speech is this?" Jeffrey called, ducking as the parrot streaked past in a blur of gray wings.

"Eye of newt and toe of frog." Banquo settled down on the edge of Hope's desk and fluttered his feathers. "Wool of bat, tongue of dog."

"Good Lord," Jeffrey muttered, "the crazy bird is actually quoting *Macbeth*. Where did he learn that?"

"I don't know. He was living in the stables when I bought the house. Rather a local mascot, I was told." Hope frowned. "He must have learned the lines in a theater or with a traveling troupe. He looks fairly old, come to think of it, but with parrots, who knows? I remember reading that they can live for decades." She stroked the bird gently. "What do you have to say, Banquo? Where do you come from?"

"Fair is foul. Fair is foul."

Hope sighed. "No help there. I suppose I'd better find Officer Kipworth before we're all clapped in irons."

Jeffrey was still staring at Banquo. "All the same, it's odd. Bloody odd."

"That he can speak?" Gabrielle took his arm. "Many birds can do this."

"No, it's what he says that bothers me. I happen to know *Macbeth* exceptionally well, and I've never heard some of those lines."

Gabrielle shrugged. "Maybe he's confused."

"Maybe. All the same, I'm going to do some checking. One or two calls should be enough." His eyes narrowed. "Assuming the phone lines are still working."

Hope raised the receiver, then muttered an oath. "Out cold. Damn and blast."

"I'd better check on Archibald and some of the others." Jeffrey tugged on his coat and scarf. "If anything happened to them, there would be no way we'd know."

"Bless you, Jeffrey. I didn't even think of that. Maybe I should come along." Hope looked out at the snow, which showed no signs of slowing.

"I won't hear of it. Besides, your detective sergeant wouldn't look kindly on his chief witness skipping out the back door."

Hope felt a pang of uneasiness. "I think Wyndgate still considers me a suspect."

"Only because he is a fool. Do not worry." Gabrielle held open the door. "Shall I go along for moral support?"

"I'll manage. All I have to do is tell the truth, after all." Hope hesitated. "I don't suppose you saw MacLeod when you were out?"

"He was down at the stables feeding that great beast of his." Jeffrey pulled on his heavy knit cap and looked questioningly at Hope. "I'll fetch him if you like."

"There's no need to bother him." Hope lowered her head to hide the color that filled her cheeks. She remembered how she had awakened in his arms. Her hands had been fisted in his hair, the sheets shoved on the floor, and she had been draped over him like wrapping paper on a gift box.

And he had been wide-awake, enjoying every sinful second of it.

The rest didn't bear remembering.

Not in mixed company.

"I should be able to handle Detective Sergeant Kipworth just fine. After all, it's just a few questions," she said firmly.

James Kipworth was fit and ruddy, with long arms and pale green eyes that missed nothing. After showing Hope his ID, he declined a cup of tea and got swiftly to business. "You are not currently a suspect, Ms. O'Hara, but until I finish my inspection, I can say nothing more."

"Inspection?"

He surveyed the sunny room. "A crime has been committed, and it is my job to follow every lead, Ms. O'Hara. You must understand the importance of that."

Hope hesitated. "But I still don't understand why someone's been sent all the way from Edinburgh."

"We have reason to believe the stolen brooch was resold there. That brings the case under our jurisdiction." He fingered a row of books, frowning. "I suppose you've noticed that the phone lines are out."

"We just found out. I'm praying the weather clears by tomorrow."

The sergeant stared northward and shook his head. "Not much chance of that, I'd say. More snow is my guess. Two, even three days of it."

"I hope you're wrong. Meanwhile, I expect you'll need a place to stay. You won't be getting through the mountains in this weather."

"A room would be most appreciated." His eyes narrowed as he picked up some of the figures from MacLeod's manger, now ensconced on Hope's desk. "Do you collect old mangers, Ms. O'Hara?"

"That one is only a replica, actually."

"Someone local, I understand."

Hope nodded but hesitated to say more, suddenly aware of a world of questions that threatened. What if he asked for MacLeod's papers or proof of some identity? There would be nothing to show, and that would lead to even more questions.

"Is something wrong, Ms. O'Hara?"

"Er…no. I was just worrying about the weather." She knew she was pale and turned away to conceal it.

The officer set the figure carefully back in its place.

"Whoever your carver is, he's got a light hand." Without pausing, he slid a small, dog-eared notebook from his front pocket and smiled broadly. "Now, perhaps you will show me where you first found the brooch."

There was no change in his voice, no break in his matter-of-fact manner.

The man would be one killer interrogator, Hope realized. A person would be answering questions before he even heard them, blurting out secrets and confessing to crimes he never knew he'd committed. "It's just down the hall."

"Fine, fine. After that, I'd like to have a look through the rooms."

"Rooms? I don't understand."

"I'll need to search everything, both public and private areas. Standard procedure, you know." Beneath his calm tone, Hope detected a will of iron.

She thought of the explanations to the guests, who would be rightfully upset at the intrusion. A current police investigation would hardly help her business. Hope frowned. "You don't really think the thief is *here,* do you?"

Beyond the leaded windows, more snow fell, heavy and silent, swept up in eddies by the wind.

The detective sergeant opened his notebook and chuckled softly. "I believe that I am supposed to ask the questions, Ms. O'Hara. The sooner I do that, the sooner I can be on my way, which is what we both want."

Pages riffled and Kipworth cleared his throat. Hope hated the uneasiness uncoiling through the pit of her stomach.

"I would like to start my examination after you answer a few questions."

"Of course."

The pale green eyes were deceptively keen as they flickered over the desk and bookshelves. "You were the one who found the brooch?"

Hope swallowed, remembering that night on the stairs.

It seemed like a century ago. Everything had changed since MacLeod had come to Glenbrae.

Or maybe it was simply that *she* had changed. Suddenly she had someone to laugh with, someone to plan and share with.

"Ms. O'Hara?"

"Sorry. What did you say?

"I was asking about the brooch." He closed his notebook with a snap. "Why don't you show me exactly where you found it."

GABRIELLE PEEKED INTO Hope's office an hour later, her expression wary. "Should I swing my heaviest pan and knock him senseless?"

Hope rubbed the knot of muscles throbbing at her neck. "No need. He was nice enough. He'll be looking through the inn, starting with the public rooms. After that he'll be checking the guest rooms and living quarters."

"He suspects *us?*"

Hope tried to bank her own angry sense of violation. "He's simply being thorough, Gabrielle. The brooch was very valuable for historical reasons, Wyndgate is an important man, and he paid me a lot of money for it. I expect he's put more than a little pressure on the police to produce the thief." She smiled bitterly. "If there are any clues here, Detective Sergeant Kipworth means to find them. He reminds me of a hungry dog with a very big bone."

"The kitchen, too?"

"The kitchen, too."

"If that man lays a finger on my cassoulet, I will give him a word or two. I won't have my dinner ruined, investigation or no investigation."

"It's his job." Hope winced as her muscles tightened painfully. "We all need to cooperate as much as possible."

"Police." Gabrielle blew out a hard stream of air. "I knew

one in Paris. He arranged for expensive cars to be stolen so that he could find them."

Hope massaged her forehead and watched snow swirl over the leaded window. "What happened to him?"

"Promoted in three months, he was. The evening papers called him a hero." Gabrielle sniffed and flipped one hand. "Police."

"ARE YOU SURE you won't come with us?" Jeffrey stamped his snowy feet on the edge of the carpet. "Perpetua particularly wanted to see you."

"I can't leave now, Jeffrey. There are a thousand things to do here."

Jeffrey frowned. "Is something bothering you, Hope? I mean, besides the fact that you're running out of food and in the middle of a police investigation." He gave a dry laugh. "As if that isn't enough."

"I'm fine, Jeffrey."

"If MacLeod has done something or bothered you, I'll call him out. Even if he can tear me into little pieces."

Hope's lips curved at the image of hand-to-hand combat at Glenbrae House's front courtyard. Very medieval, she decided, and that was entirely appropriate. But there was nothing wrong that a week's sleep, a delivery of food and a closed police investigation wouldn't cure.

The officer's questions had just left her feeling edgy and all too aware of MacLeod's peculiar situation. His silent presence was starting to grate on Hope's nerves, and the threat of more bad weather only added to her uneasiness.

It was just as well that MacLeod was busying himself in the stable. He had hinted about a secret to be completed before Christmas, and no amount of wheedling would dig any more details out of him.

Hope touched her cheeks, sensitive from being thoroughly manhandled during their long hours of lovemaking.

She wished he would come back. She wanted the man, not his gifts. She wanted to hear his cocky laugh and feel his callused hands.

Laughter trailed through the hall as Lady Draycott and her daughter raced around the corner. Miss Vee was bundled into a bright parka, her eyes full of excitement.

"Off to the Wishwells for lunch, are you?"

Genevieve nodded, wriggling with barely contained energy. "Mr. Gibbs is coming, too. He loves the snow." She pulled the bear from beneath her parka, revealing a brilliant fuchsia sweater and matching knit beret. "See?"

"Very dashing," Hope agreed.

"I hope the snow won't stop until we get there. Miss Morwenna said I could eat stew and pet the cats. They have three, did you know?"

Hope smiled. "I don't think you need to worry about the snow melting away anytime soon."

Kacey Draycott helped her daughter tuck Mr. Gibbs into a safe pocket. "By the way, I've been meaning to ask you about those figures in the manger. They are remarkably like a set of rare chess pieces I saw in Paris several years ago. Mid-thirteenth century or thereabouts. I remember them because that style of carving in the round is unique. You are certain yours are only reproductions?" Kacey Draycott frowned. "If those are authentic, they would be worth a great deal of money. I could suggest a reputable dealer. Several museums would probably be interested in bidding, too."

Thirteenth century.

Hope watched wet snow slip down the window. Sounds filled her head. Of course, the *style* was thirteenth century. That was exactly when MacLeod had learned it. "You're certain of the date?" Hope said softly.

"Near enough. I'd put it around the Fourth Crusade. Medieval weapons are my real specialty, but I've built up a collection of folk sculpture over the years. I rather covet those pieces myself, but I doubt I could afford them." Her eyes narrowed. "Come to think of it, they would be about the same period as that lovely cross you're wearing."

The cross he had given her. The cross she had promised to wear always.

Hope had a sudden image of Ronan MacLeod, angry and disoriented the night of his arrival in the storm. He had insisted that Glenbrae House was wrong, the rooms were wrong, the furniture was wrong. That the date she gave him was impossible.

Thirteenth century.

Hope's scalp prickled as the enormity of their miracle struck her. By all laws of nature, they never should have met.

She thought of a man swept through a fold in time, forever lost to his own world. He had come seven hundred years to find her, against all logic and all odds. Hope swore she would make him happy. Most of all she would love him, driving away the hell of a thousand battles that still shadowed his gray eyes.

"Look, Mama, someone's coming." Genevieve Draycott ran to the window. "He's all covered with snow and he's wearing a kilt. Aren't his legs cold?"

"I expect he's used to it, my love."

"It's Mr. MacLeod, isn't it?"

"I think you're right, Miss Vee."

Hope swallowed, feeling her pulse kick sharply. Desire was one thing in the sultry darkness while hormones ran amok. But in the daylight, reason prevailed.

Maybe he'd changed his mind.

Maybe he already regretted everything.

Parkas rustled. "Can we go say hello, Mama? I want to see his kilt."

"Most women would," Kacey murmured.

Hope heard laughter and the stamp of boots, then the

sound of a door closing. Greetings flashed back and forth, pleasantries exchanged as if from a great distance.

And then she was swept up against Ronan's chest, locked in a kiss that could have sizzled graphite.

CHAPTER THIRTY

"LOOK, MAMA, THEY'RE kissing again."

"So I see, my love."

Genevieve considered for a moment. "Is that how grown-ups make babies?"

Kacey Draycott cleared her throat. "Not exactly, Vee."

"Sarah's nanny told her that babies come on milk day and the delivery man leaves them off, but I don't believe it."

"That's very wise of you."

"So where *do* they come from?"

Silence spun out.

"Mama, why do you look so funny?"

"I think, my love, that we should leave them alone while you and I…go discuss some things."

Dimly Hope heard a door shut. Over the hammering in her head she felt a cold draft slice through the room.

Reason returned. "Ronan, that was awful."

His brow arched. "Then I'll try again."

"No, not how you kissed. I mean the timing. It was terribly rude of us. Now you've chased them away."

"Nonsense. Lady Draycott appears to be a woman who can handle anything. And her daughter could probably charm the growl from a tiger."

Hope frowned down at his neck. There were two faint red lines running from his ear to his shoulder. "Did I do that?"

"Among other things." MacLeod laughed. "I'll be glad to reveal the extent of the damage upstairs."

"Upstairs? We can't. Ronan, where are you *taking* me?"

"Upstairs." His hands locked around her. "For a survey of your amenities, Ms. O'Hara. As a prospective guest, I'll need to check your inn thoroughly." His eyes darkened. "We'll inspect the private rooms. Test the beds."

"We can't. It's the middle of the morning." Hope took a shaky breath. Dear Lord, there was a detective roaming around already. "When you didn't come back, I thought you might already be regretting this...."

He stopped, studying her face. "Regret loving you? No man could be so foolish, my heart. Is that what all this protesting is about?"

Hope shrugged. "Maybe." She felt the lurch of her heart and the rising heat of him at her hip. "Ronan, you're—"

He gave her a slow, dark smile. "So I am. It appears to happen whenever I'm around you."

He carried her into his room and set her down by the window. Sunlight filtered over her flushed cheeks. "You're wearing my gift." He touched the silver cross gently, then turned to close the door. As he did, his foot struck something beside the window.

Hope heard the crack of shattering porcelain. She winced at the sight of her oldest blue and white vase in pieces on the floor. Beside it lay the ugly weathered gargoyle that MacLeod had brought in from the stable. Now a crack ran through the stone from end to end.

"Forgive me for the vase," MacLeod muttered. "Someone must have moved it since last night. Now I've ruined your statue."

"Wait," Hope said, frowning. "There's something inside it, Ronan." She brushed away chips of stone and broken pottery, tugging at a layer of heavy plastic folded inside the carving.

A flat rectangular form emerged, dusted with dirt and stone powder. Ronan peered over her shoulder, rubbing his heel. "What is it?"

"Some kind of book, I think." Hope eased yellowed pages out from beneath an oilskin covering. "Very old, by the look of it." Then her fingers stilled. "It—it can't be."

"Can't be what?" MacLeod sank down beside her.

"Look at those handwritten letters." Hope drew a low breath. "Look at the script and those margin notes. It's *Macbeth*," she whispered reverently.

"I have heard of this lord who killed his king. He was a villain. Why write about such a man and such an unnatural crime?"

Hope ran a finger gently over the old pages, feeling excitement race through her. "Because evil was to be a warning to others. Look at this." She pointed to the next page. "'Newly corrected by W. Shakespeare.'" Her hands shook as she laid the pages on her lap. "Shakespeare himself," she repeated. "The date says 1616."

"It is valuable, then?"

"Valuable beyond price," Hope breathed. "My uncle always believed that *Macbeth* was the most disputed of Shakespeare's plays. He was convinced that Shakespeare abbreviated the play himself, and then his version was corrupted by others. If this is real and a genuine work, corrected by the playwright himself..." She looked up. "We'll have to find Jeffrey. Drama is his specialty. He'll know if it's real." She started to rise, but MacLeod held her still.

"Are you certain you should do that?" His eyes were hard. "If this is so precious, maybe it would be better not to mention it to anyone else."

"You think Jeffrey..."

MacLeod rubbed his neck. "I don't know. I only think it would be better to wait."

"I don't like this. Not any of it," Hope said angrily. "You make me suspect everyone."

"Even me?" MacLeod slid the book back into its hiding place, frowning. "My own arrival has been anything but a normal one. This all may be a great and cunning plan by me to confound you, seduce you and steal this precious manuscript."

"Are you quite finished?" Hope said dryly.

"Mmm."

She drew him around to face her and ran a finger along his jaw. "Idiot. As if I suspected you. Any criminal with half a brain could concoct a better story than the one you told me, MacLeod. Being flung through time? Then swept back again by the force of touching his own portrait?"

He caught her hand, his eyes hard. "You believe me?"

"Always and absolutely. I'm only sorry it took me so long."

The tension seemed to slide out of his shoulders. He murmured something in Gaelic, lifting her to her feet. "I want you, Hope. Past controlling. If you don't want that, then tell me now and I'll go swim in an icy loch." He sniffed. "For all the good it will do."

"Stop giving me orders," Hope whispered, her fingers busy tugging at his shirt.

Sunlight glinted over the floor as MacLeod shoved the door shut with his foot, not breaking the searing kiss even then. The lock clicked shut behind them.

Hope blinked, caught between his hard thighs with a fine rosewood desk behind her. His heat was unmistakable. "Here?" she said shakily.

"I'm not at all certain we would make it to the bed." His mouth traced hot spirals along her neck as her sweater slid free and hit the floor. "The knowledge that you trust me..."

"I always *trusted* you, my love. *Believing* you was the problem." She closed her eyes, arching as he savored the curve of her breast. "Oh, God, Ronan, when you do that, I forget everything."

She shoved at his belt, tugged at his shirt, beyond waiting or logic.

Suddenly the door rattled behind them.

"Is that you, Ms. O'Hara?"

Hope stiffened. "Kipworth," she whispered. "The police officer from Edinburgh."

"Shall I send him away?" MacLeod growled.

"We can't. It's business." Hope stared down helplessly. She was slanted over the desk, her sweater dangling from one shoulder.

"Ms. O'Hara, are you *in* there?"

"Tell him to go away," MacLeod whispered.

Hope cleared her throat. "Er—yes?"

"So you are in there. I heard a loud noise up here, almost like something breaking. I was afraid something might have happened to you."

"I—I'm fine."

"Excellent. I have a few more questions to ask about the brooch."

"But I was just about to—"

"Make love with a wild Scotsman," MacLeod murmured, his lips savoring her taut breast.

"*Stop*," Hope said wildly.

"Stop what?" the police officer called, outside in the hall.

"Uh, I was about to stop—work. I was going to clean up. Take a bath."

"When will you be finished?"

"An hour. No, two," MacLeod said darkly as he stripped away her skirt and found a risqué lace triangle with delicate embroidered roses. "Dear sweet God," he muttered. "Maybe never." His hands were slow, masterful. By the time the lace slid free, Hope felt her brain beginning to dissolve.

"Ms. O'Hara?" The doorknob rattled.

"In…a while," she managed to answer. "I'll be down as soon as I can."

"But I'm afraid this is urgent, Ms. O'Hara. My questions cannot wait."

"Neither can I," MacLeod whispered hoarsely.

"I'll call you. Find you," Hope said. "After a bit. Until then—"

"Go jump into the loch," MacLeod finished grimly.

"Meanwhile, you should go downstairs. Talk to Gabrielle." She sighed as MacLeod's shirt slid free and her hands savored warm, muscled skin. "I love you," she whispered. "Adore you. Trust you." Her lips curved. "And I want you madly, MacLeod. Did I make that plain enough?"

MacLeod closed his eyes, his fingers digging into her shoulders.

They barely noticed the footsteps moving back down the hall.

Breathless and greedy, they stripped away the remaining clothes between them. His hands tightened. "Look at me, Hope. Watch me loving you."

"With greatest pleasure."

Against the desk, he set her, thigh to naked thigh. His breath was harsh, labored, as skin ground close and softness shifted.

Desire flared, keener now that they knew each other's pleasures. MacLeod shuddered, fighting for control. This time he wanted to see her, watch her pleasure flood through her eyes, hear her wild gasp of climax.

"So, MacLeod," Hope whispered. "How are my…amenities?"

"Extraordinary," he rasped. "Beyond description." He cupped her hips, filling her with slow, maddening power that left them both giddy.

"Is that good?"

His hands tightened as he drew her back, his lips to her neck. "Definitely…five stars."

"Show me," she whispered. "Now before I die."

He trapped her, possessed her. She arched blindly, closing around him, greedy for his heat. Hot and fast, he took her up, then up again, while her nails dug into his back and she gasped out his name.

He filled his lungs with the scent of her, stored away the sound of her soft, breathless moans. He prayed the memories wouldn't have to last him.

Then MacLeod forgot everything else as he took her up one last time, then dragged her against him while he followed her down where nothing remained but love shimmering around them.

CHAPTER THIRTY-ONE

SOMETHING DRIFTED OVER the floor. Idly Hope watched gray shadows spin across the rug.

No doubt she was dreaming. After the things that Ronan had done to her in the past three hours, she expected that serious hallucinations were only to be expected. Lust did that to a person.

No, *love* did that to a person, she thought.

Her lips curved as the movement of the shadows over the rug made her think of Ronan's eyes, shadowed with passion when he finally pulled her down onto the bed. And his mouth, that cocky, clever mouth that made her forget her own name.

Hope drew a deep breath. Acrid air burned her throat.

Smoke. No illusion this time, and no dramatic creation by Jeffrey. Glenbrae House was on *fire*.

She threw back the covers just as the door slammed open.

Grimly Ronan tossed her a heavy robe. "There's smoke all along the stairs. You've got to go."

Shivering, Hope tugged on the robe and boots. "What about the others?"

"Jeffrey and I are searching for them." He pulled her against his chest, his mouth savage. Then with a curse he released her. "No time. It's getting worse by the second."

Outside, the air was crisscrossed by dank ribbons of smoke, and the reality of their danger hit Hope like a blow.

"We can't let Glenbrae House burn. There's so much history here, so much love."

"It won't burn. I won't let it," he said grimly. "But first you must leave." MacLeod guided her down the stairs through drifting smoke that made her eyes water.

Smoke danced madly as they ran back toward the kitchen. "Where are w-we going?"

"Outside through the back entrance. The roof will go if those flames catch hold. The clay I put in is no protection against this kind of fire."

Hope shuddered as MacLeod pushed her through the kitchen, shoved open the inner glass door, then closed it securely before opening the heavy outer barrier of wood.

Gabrielle and Jeffrey were huddled in the center of the courtyard, arm in arm. Nicholas Draycott carried Genevieve on his broad shoulders. The girl was pale, trying not to show her fear as she clutched at her mother's hand.

Suddenly Genevieve stiffened. "Mr. G-Gibbs. He's inside in the fire." She struggled to slide down from her father's back. "His fur will catch on fire. I've got to find him."

MacLeod turned, frowning. "Which room?"

"The B-Blue Bedroom. On top of the dr-dresser, I think."

Dear God, he's going back in for a stuffed animal. Hope caught MacLeod's hand as Nicholas Draycott strode forward and said, "MacLeod, I can't let you do this."

"You stay here and take care of your wife and daughter."

"It's out of the question."

Genevieve's voice cracked. "But, Daddy—"

"*No.* I'll buy you another Mr. Gibbs. A dozen of them, Vee. We can't risk a man's life for that."

The girl bit back a watery sob. "I guess…you're right."

MacLeod clasped her hand hard, then turned. "Not just for the child. I saw something at the upper window just now." His eyes hardened. "Someone could still be inside."

Hope turned. Dark clouds feathered through an open window near the roof. "But you can't go back in." She reached out for MacLeod, a thousand protests on her lips.

All of them were too late. He was already gone.

SMOKE COILED over the roof.

Hope paced back and forth over the snow, watching for a single angry spark to leap to the thatch.

One would be enough.

One speck of flame and everything she owned would be lost.

She barely heard the crunch of snow beside her. Detective Sergeant Kipworth cleared his throat, as if he was out of breath. "I just checked the rear window. The fire appears to be coming from the library."

Hope bit down a ragged wave of panic. MacLeod had broken every rule of nature to cross time to find her, and she wasn't going to lose him now. Even the precious book they had found inside the gargoyle meant nothing compared to losing MacLeod.

"I can't bear waiting. I'm going back in."

The officer clamped a restraining hand on her shoulder, studying her face. "You love that house, don't you?"

Hope nodded, feeling tears slide down her cheeks.

"There's nothing else that comes close, is there?"

"Only one. Right up there." Her eyes sought the upstairs window, watching for a hint of movement. *Let him come. Please, God, let him come now.*

"There's something you left inside?" The sergeant sounded worried.

"Someone. A man who's too honorable for his own blasted good."

Kipworth turned, following her gaze. For an instant a man's tall body was outlined against the upper window. "I thought everyone was out." Kipworth made an angry, impatient sound and turned his collar up around his face. "Bloody stupid fool."

He was still cursing as he strode back into the smoke-covered house.

SECONDS CRAWLED BY, each marked by an eternity of agony. Where was he? Why didn't he come?

Something wet slid over Hope's fingers. She realized she had scooped up a handful of snow, which was melting between her clenched fists. Her nails bit into her skin, but she barely felt the pain.

Beside her, Genevieve stirred restlessly. "Where's Mr. MacLeod, Mama?"

"Inside, my love." Kacey Draycott's voice was strained. "He'll be out as soon as he can."

"I want him to come."

"We all want him to come, Vee."

"I...I don't need Mr. Gibbs and I'm sorry I sent Mr. MacLeod in. If he's hurt, it will be all my fault." Her voice broke. "I'll make the policeman arrest me and put me in jail if anything happens to Mr. MacLeod. But then I'll never see you and Daddy again..."

"Hush, love. Mr. MacLeod went back in because it was right. He thought someone was still inside."

Smoke twisted out the upper window. Hope began to pace again, arms locked to her chest.

Genevieve stiffened. "Did you see it, Mama?"

"See what, love?"

"The cat. It was Gideon, I'm sure of it. He was there by the window just before it closed. And I saw someone with him."

Hope peered through the trailing smoke. Sure enough, the window was closed now.

Ronan. He had made it that far. God, why didn't he hurry?

Fear clamped hard over Hope's chest. She could bear the agony no longer. She turned and started toward the door.

Nicholas Draycott was there before her, his eyes harrowed but determined. "I can't let you go in."

"I'm *going*. It's my house and my life."

"And you can't throw it away. You have family, friends—people who care about you."

Without Ronan, they would mean nothing. Hope pushed past the Englishman, gasping as he caught her wrist. She struggled fiercely, her eyes blurred by tears. "Let me go. I'm going back inside. If you try to hold me here, so help me, I'll—"

A door squeaked. Snow crunched. "You'll do what, my shrew?" His laugh, shaky but alive, was broken by a cough.

Hope reached him in a heartbeat. She ran her hands over his face, his neck, his shoulders, balanced between joy and tears. "You big, crazy fool." She wrapped her arms around him and pulled his face down to hers.

He tasted of salt and smoke—and blood. Hope gasped. "Your lip—Ronan, what happened?"

"Couldn't see in the smoke. I ran into a bookcase. You should see the books." He cradled her wet cheeks, pulled her trembling hand to his mouth and kissed it fiercely. Abruptly he pulled away with a hard oath. "You're bleeding. My God, your nails—"

Hope closed her fingers, hiding her palm. "It doesn't matter. All that matters is you're alive. We'll start over if the roof burns, Ronan. We'll find another house, another glen." Though the thought wrung at her heart, Hope managed a shaky smile. "One where it never snows."

"That would be a grave loss, my love." He traced the line of the last tear sliding down her cheek.

"Excuse me." They glanced down to see Genevieve tugging at MacLeod's kilt. "I'm sorry I asked you to go in," she said in a watery voice. "It was wrong. And I don't even care that you didn't get Mr. Gibbs." She hiccupped, part of a sob that she couldn't hold back. "Well, only a little."

MacLeod caught her small hand in his big one. "Only a little? I suppose he'll understand. But you'd better explain to him yourself." He patted his sleeve, then eased a lumpy shape from beneath one cuff.

The furry head and body were instantly enveloped against Genevieve's chest. "You found him!" She danced up and down, the worn bear clutched to her heart. "Mama, Daddy, he brought me back Mr. Gibbs!"

Hope looked away, remembering when life had been simpler and a worn bear was the only thing in the world.

She swallowed, hiding a watery sound of her own.

Ronan MacLeod just couldn't stop being a hero.

THE AFTERNOON SUN peered thinly through gray clouds. Detective Sergeant Kipworth searched Hope's library, examined the burned and smoky section of floor near the fireplace, and pronounced his belief that the cause was a defective flue. It had taken two unpleasant hours to brush, sweep and scrub away the soot, but the process revealed little serious damage. The flames had spread only to the surrounding columns near the fireplace. Except for a small section of singed rug and the acrid smell of smoke, the house was starting to return to order.

Hope realized just how lucky she was. In a period building like Glenbrae House, fire could have raced through every room. She would have to clean the linens and air out all the rooms, but the damage could have been far greater.

Maybe she had a guardian angel or two after all.

With a sigh, Hope looked at her watch. Two o'clock. She sniffed the air, wondering why she didn't smell the rich fragrance of Gabrielle's cassoulet.

A moment later her cook wobbled into the room, her face ashen. "I am very sorry. I try, truly I do. But I just can't—" She gasped. Her body went rigid and she raced from the room.

"Gabrielle, what's wrong?"

"She's sick. So am I." Jeffrey tottered over to a chair. "Stomach, if you know what I mean. It's hit both of us bloody hard. She keeps moaning that she has to cook, but she can barely stand up."

"Gabrielle's never sick." Hope stared anxiously down the hall. "Oh, heaven, the doctor won't be able to get through the snow."

"It's nothing mortal." Jeffrey gave a weak grin and eased his chin carefully onto his hands as if it might break. "The headache is the worst part. Feels like bits of glass shifting around behind your eyes." His voice was soft but firm. "We'll be fine. It's probably one of those twenty-four-hour things." When he wavered to his feet, the dark circles beneath his eyes were unmistakable. "Now, if you'll excuse me, I'll go back upstairs and check on Gabrielle. Then I plan to sleep for about four decades." He rubbed his forehead with shaky fingers. "That is, if you can spare me."

Hope couldn't, of course, but she wouldn't tell him that. "We'll be just fine. Go up and rest. But shouldn't *I* go check on Gabrielle?"

"I advise against it. She hates being sick, hates being waited on. Very nasty temper." Jeffrey wandered out with one hand to his head, his skin the color of old oatmeal. "Better leave her to me."

Nicholas Draycott stood outside the door, watching Jeffrey lumber upstairs. "Something wrong?" He shifted an armful of logs against his chest, smearing his immaculate tweed jacket with wood shavings.

"Oh, Lord, I forgot about the logs. I'd better go—"

He blocked her way. "You'll do no such thing. I can manage a few logs quite nicely. MacLeod already took the rest up." He gave Hope a quick, measuring look. "I rather like the man. He doesn't say much, but he doesn't miss much either. He seems quite keen on you, too, not that it's any of my business."

Hope colored slightly, noticing the glint of humor in Lord Draycott's eyes. "I expect you don't miss much either, Lord Draycott."

"Nicholas, please. One can't be formal with a pile of logs in hand."

Hope chuckled. "I see why Genevieve is smart as a whip. Not that your wife isn't just as sharp."

"Sharp at what?" Kacey Draycott clumped to the door with a smile and a pile of logs. Her cheeks were brilliant red, snow dusted her hair, and she looked, Hope decided, absolutely lovely.

"Just about everything, my love." Nicholas frowned. "And I told you not to carry those logs inside. Ronan and I will take care of it."

"Men." Kacey blew a strand of snowy hair off her forehead. "They always have to be heroes. As if a woman can't balance a few logs."

"Where shall we take them, Mama?" Genevieve appeared, red-cheeked like her mother and equally delighted to be carrying three tiny logs of her own. "Upstairs or into the kitchen?"

Nicholas sighed. "Outgunned and outnumbered, as usual. I think I'd better slink off to the kitchen myself. It appears that you are in need of a cook, Ms. O'Hara."

"Cook?" Hope stared, speechless. The earl's usually tidy hair was all awry and his tweed jacket was getting dirtier by the second. "Oh, no, I couldn't possibly let you."

"You can if you want to eat," he said reasonably.

Kacey smiled at her husband. "He's a wonderful chef, Ms. O'Hara. You won't be sorry. Nicholas gets far too few chances to cook these days since his lion of a butler considers it beneath the dignity of a viscount to sully his hands in the kitchen. Now, you just stay there and rest. We'll take charge of everything."

"But—"

"No buts."

Hope stared, speechless, as her three guests filed out. She had a moment of sympathy for Nicholas Draycott, feeling very much outgunned and outnumbered herself.

"YOU'RE GOING TO COOK? Really, Daddy?" Genevieve stared with great round eyes at her father as he rolled up his sleeves and tested a cleaver.

"Of course, I am, Duchess." He bent down to tug her golden pigtail. "After all, everyone should know how to do a few tricks in a kitchen." He caught up an apple from a basket, minced it into paper-thin slices, then handed one to his daughter, who was too amazed to speak.

"I think I'll try my hand at lion's head soup."

"You going to catch a lion? Oh, I don't think it would be nice to eat *his* head."

"Not a real lion's head, Duchess. Something wonderful and tasty. The Chinese give everything poetic names, even their food." He smiled. "Especially their food. And they have every right, because Chinese cuisine is the highest art form on this planet, mind you."

He searched through the commercial-size refrigerator and pulled out a handful of greens. Within seconds, neat, regular rows of vegetables filled the board in front of him.

"When did you learn that, Daddy?"

"When I had a great deal of time on my hands, Duchess." He glanced at his wife. "In a faraway place called Thailand."

Kacey paled. "Oh, Nicky—"

"Hush, love. It's all forgotten now, all but the good parts." He looked out at the snow, lost in a distant place and time. "There was an old cook there. He came from Szechwan and was a master with spices. The man could do amazing things with a knife." The viscount carved two radishes into perfect roses, then presented them to his wife and daughter with a flourish.

Genevieve's eyes grew even wider. "It's beautiful," she whispered. "So are you, Daddy."

"I quite agree," Kacey said huskily.

Nicholas swept them into a long hug. "The luckiest man in the world, that's what I am." His voice was a bit unsteady as he set Genevieve on the wooden table. "Now for the bad news, troops." He moved away and rubbed his jaw. "For Chinese food, the preparation is a killer. I'll need four good hands. I don't expect you know of any?"

Genevieve wriggled with excitement. "I do, I do. Can I use the big knife?"

Nicholas thought of the razor-sharp blade and felt his heart lurch. "Maybe the small knife. With a lot of supervision."

As he instructed his daughter, keeping one eye on the stove, something nagged at the back of his mind. There were factors at work here at Glenbrae House that Nicholas did not understand, and he could not quite accept that the fire had been an accident. There had been a striking amount of smoke for such a small area of actual damage.

A coincidence?

Nicholas didn't think so. But why would someone go to the trouble of setting a fire that went nowhere?

He frowned as he pounded a piece of ginger root to near oblivion. Jamee and Ian had been entirely right to call with their worries. His instinct told him something was not right here.

A movement pulled his eye to the window. For a moment he thought he saw a gray shape move toward the loch, low and sleek.

A cat?

He blinked, and then the dark shape was gone. Only snow stretched over the courtyard and along the rocky slope.

He must have imagined the cat.

But the odd prickle of uneasiness did not leave him. Nicholas had a keen sense for people, an ability that had been tested in dozens of dark alleys and war-torn corners of the world. He had given that up when Kacey came into his life, but the old instincts still served him well.

Within minutes he had sized up Ronan MacLeod as a man who could be trusted when the bullets began to fly. As soon as he finished cooking, he intended to track the Scotsman down for a long, detailed talk.

CHAPTER THIRTY-TWO

AS SHE WALKED PAST the kitchen toward her office, Hope heard the sound of childish laughter. She closed her eyes on a stab of pain.

Family. Belonging.

Things she had had so little of in her life, yet they were the most important of all gifts. As Lady Draycott's low laughter joined her daughter's, something burned at Hope's chest. How could she be jealous of a happy family?

She buried the thought, appalled. Just because her own relations had been lost, she had no right to resent the joy of others. The Draycotts seemed linked by a special love, so strong at times it was nearly tangible.

Maybe *magical* was a better word, Hope thought. But there would be no childish laughter for her. No sticky hands and cherub cheeks. Medical science had made vast advances, but they still couldn't work miracles. She touched her stomach, trying to imagine the feel of a child growing there.

MacLeod's child.

Her hands clenched. How much she wanted that. He deserved to have a son with his keen eyes, or a daughter with his willful mouth.

She fought down a wave of regret and walked to her desk, pouring a cup of tea with trembling fingers. She hadn't thought about having a family for months. Not since she had come to the glen, in fact. Glenbrae had worked its special magic upon her, sweeping her up with vistas of high hills and endless sky.

So why was she thinking about family now?

Because of a man in a kilt. A man with a cocky grin whose child she yearned to hold at her breast.

The cup shook in her fingers, spilling hot tea over her. *Fool,* she thought. There was no point in wondering if Ronan's child would have his father's dark curls and eyes like a Highland sky at dawn. But sweet longing poured through her, and Hope's fingers closed over her hollow stomach, aching to feel new life taking shape.

Tears blurred her vision and somewhere a phone rang shrilly. Hope frowned, wondering why the phone on her desk remained silent. When she lifted the receiver, there was no sound. Another thing to repair.

She walked to the front hall and picked up the extension there. She heard a quick click, followed by static. "Hello?"

More static, muffled this time.

"Hello, can you hear me?"

Another click, then silence. "Hello?" Hope repeated.

The phone lines had been going on and off for hours. As soon as repair crews fixed one line, another toppled, victim of the heavy snow. Not for the first time, Hope wished she had invested in a cellular phone. Now, she would have to find out what was wrong with the extension in her office.

Banquo swooped down from the rafters as she walked back to her office. "Thunder and rain. Thunder and rain."

How Hope wished. Outside snow covered glen and cliff, white drift upon white drift. "Wrong stage directions, Banquo. Turn the page."

"Turn the page," he rasped. "Turn the page."

Hope held out a piece of apple from her mostly uneaten lunch. He gobbled the treat greedily, then rippled his gray plumage. "The moon is down," he cried. "Something evil this way comes."

Suddenly her eyes narrowed. "Banquo, is that poetry you're spouting at me or is it Shakespeare?" She thought of the yellowing pages discovered sealed in oilskin. Had Banquo somehow known about that precious manuscript, perhaps even learned his poetry from someone who had delighted in reciting Shakespeare? But why would anyone seal a priceless folio inside an old gargoyle?

The black eyes glittered as the bird shredded another slice of apple.

Now that the idea had been planted, Hope couldn't forget Banquo's shrill warning. "Something evil this way comes." If Wyndgate's report was correct, a thief was once more at work and no one was safe.

She jumped at the sound of sudden footsteps. Two callused hands circled her waist and swung her high into the air.

"Ronan! You'll give me cardiac arrest."

"Nay, lass, not cardiac arrest. What I'll give you is sweet. Torturingly slow." He brought her slowly down against him, letting her feel the instant effect on him.

Hope's eyes widened. "Ronan, you're—"

"Of course I am, lass. A sorry man I would be if the touch of you didn't leave me rock-hard and in acute pain."

"But we just— It was only a few hours ago that you—" She flushed.

"Aye, so it was. But that was then," he muttered, bracing one hip against her desk and driving his hands deep into her hair. Then he whispered an erotic suggestion that stole her breath.

"We can't," Hope said. "Can we? I mean, here?"

"I was never a very patient man, lass. I'm willing to try if you are." He grinned as his knuckles brushed the curve of her breast, drawing her gasp.

"But—"

"Why not?" he said huskily. "There's a door, isn't there?"

There had to be some good reason, Hope thought as his hands shifted. She looked at her desk, imagining the scene he had suggested and feeling her cheeks burn. "I'll think of a reason why not in a minute. Just as soon as you stop manhandling my body."

His smile was pure sin. "I much enjoy manhandling your body, lass. It's so responsive. And you make such remarkable little sounds when I—"

"Sounds? I do not." Hope shivered as he brushed the inside of her thigh.

"Just like that one."

How did he reduce her brain to oatmeal within nanoseconds of contact? It was criminal.

She stood up swiftly, smoothing down her skirt. Someone had to set ground rules or they would be in bed all day.

Hope chewed on her lip. They would set times, places. They would discuss the subject in a calm, logical fashion and reach an agreement about suitable choices. Hope was all set to explain this to MacLeod when he caught her lower lip in his teeth and nipped it gently.

Her careful plans fled. She slid her palms over his chest, delighting in his instant shudder.

"Nay, wait. This is important." Slowly he pulled a package from behind his back. "Merry Christmas, lass of my heart," he said huskily.

"Ronan, you shouldn't have." Hope shredded away the fragile paper, bright with golden cherubs.

"I hope it pleases you."

The paper fell away, and her fingers melted over whiteness as soft as a dream. It was a sweater, angora and silk and clearly costly. "But how, Ronan?" Her eyes widened. "You sold your sword to buy this, didn't you?"

He looked affronted. "Nay, ne'er that, lass."

"Your horse?"

"Ach, as if I would part with Pegasus." He shook his head firmly.

"Your gauntlets."

He shrugged, giving a guilty smile. "I have no need of them."

"But they're priceless, Ronan. Historical artifacts with vast educational value. Museums would kill to—"

"Be quiet, my little shrew. It's almost Christmas, and Christmas is a time for giving to the ones you love."

"Oh, Ronan, it's beautiful," she whispered. "So soft."

"I was hoping you would try it on for me. But after that, I warn you, it's going off. Slowly." His eyes narrowed, promising pure sin. "Now look at the rest."

With an effort Hope forced her gaze away from that lovely mouth, trying not to remember how much pleasure it could give. "There's more?" She lifted the paper and three more things fell onto the desk. A hat, full and soft, to hug her dark hair. A scarf, long and fluffy, almost as warm as his hands. A third thing equally soft.

"Mittens?"

His dark brow rose. "For the snowball fight I'm going to have with you later today. It's all-out war, I warn you. No rules, no fouls, no limits. And when we're done, I'll make love to you the same way."

Hope swallowed. She couldn't afford to think about it or she would never get any work done. "Go. Gabrielle and Jeffrey are sick and I've got a thousand things to finish here."

MacLeod stiffened. "What sort of illness?"

"Some sort of flu, Jeffrey thinks."

He stared at her intently. "How do you feel?"

"I'm fine, MacLeod. It's something fast and devastating, according to Jeffrey. Just temporarily debilitating."

"Flu, you call it?"

Hope remembered she was dealing with a resident of the thirteenth century. "Fever, accompanied by rumblings in the stomach. General unpleasantness. Hell when it's going on, but over soon enough."

"Ah, that." MacLeod nodded. "Flu," he repeated. Hope knew he was storing the word for the future.

He spread his fingers over her wrist. "How is your pulse?"

Hope sighed. "Racing. And it has nothing to do with the flu."

A grin crooked his lips. "Perhaps I can find a way to make it race even harder."

"*Go,* MacLeod."

He didn't move. "Why is no one else showing the effects of this…flu?"

"Maybe they took vitamins. Maybe no one was exposed besides Jeffrey and Gabrielle. Science still can't explain who gets sick and who doesn't." Hope stared at him uneasily. "You don't think it was…"

He averted his gaze, toying with the scarf. "Did I say such a thing? Too suspicious, you are, lass." He slid the fluffy wool around her neck and knotted it jauntily over one shoulder. "And you have the habit of thinking too much when I am touching you."

Hope closed her eyes as his hands slid urgently over her breasts. She was appalled to realize how much she wanted him and how easy it was for him to distract her. "You— you're going to have to go, MacLeod. Now while I have some semblance of my mind left."

"I very much like the parts that are left, lass."

"Only because you're a hulking chauvinist."

"That would be an insult?"

Hope couldn't help but smile. "You catch on fast, don't you?"

"Not fast enough," he said gravely. "Otherwise, we would not be here talking."

Hope prayed for willpower. "Go, MacLeod. As it is, I've let guests carry in logs and take over making dinner."

"Lord Draycott seems very handy with a knife. You made a good choice."

"That's not the point."

"No? Should you choose someone who can't cook?"

"You don't understand, MacLeod. Guests don't cook. English lords *definitely* don't head to the kitchen to toss together a few courses."

"But they should. And you, sweet lass, should stop worrying if they do."

"I'm good at worrying. Which reminds me…" Hope closed her door, reached into a locked lower desk drawer, and removed the precious folio, still wrapped in its oilskin pouch. "I think you should put this someplace safe. After that fire…I know it was an accident, but I don't feel this should stay in here." Some instinct warned her that nowhere in the house was safe. A professional thief would be able to crack any code or lock, and it would be easy enough for him to find the folio then. Hope chewed thoughtfully on her lower lip. "I was thinking the fishing shed might be a good spot, until we can make better arrangements."

MacLeod watched her, grave and unmoving. "You trust me with this? Something you deem valuable beyond gold and jewels?"

"Of course. I trust you with that and with my heart as well." True, she realized. She knew no reservations. The man inspired total and complete trust. That was the thing about heroes—from the thirteenth or any other century.

"You choose your time, so you do, lass. You say such a thing and expect me to leave."

Hope managed to ignore the heat in his eyes and took a step back. "Yes, I do. Because you're a grade A, certifiable hero, MacLeod, like it or not."

He muttered harshly. As he slid the folio beneath his leather jacket, Hope expected that the Gaelic phrases were none too kind. "I'll find a sound place for your precious document, never worry." His eyes glinted, full of sensual challenge. "But I will expect an ample reward. I'll see you wearing my gift—and not a bit more."

Hope swallowed. "Go on, you great, hulking Scot. Otherwise I will get no work done here."

"Then I'll find my own sad way to the stable. At least my fine horse knows the true worth of a man's love."

He was laughing as the door closed. For some reason the sun seemed to leave the room with his going.

Hope sighed and she scrubbed her face with her hands. She took a sip of her tea, cold now and bitter from the long steeping. At least it would clear her head.

She paid three bills and made a list of linens that had to be replaced. Her next task was retrieving a very old book of Chinese recipes from the library. Nicholas Draycott had been excited when she'd mentioned the old volume, and since he was presently engaged in cooking a gourmet Chinese meal, Hope decided the least she could do was make the book a gift to him.

A sudden wave of exhaustion hit her. Rubbing her neck, she tried to think where she had put the slender volume. A current of air drifted over her neck and she watched the chintz curtains flutter.

Of course.

She remembered now.

Pale sunlight filtered through the tall windows, casting weak light over the rows of leather bindings and hand-tooled letters. To Hope, the library had been one of the best discoveries about Glenbrae House. Stepping into a room rich with good leather, old paper and printer's ink never failed to raise her spirits. No doubt books were in her blood, the legacy of her uncle, who had spent his life collecting rare works and fine first editions.

Frowning, she scanned the nearby rows. Shakespeare.

Walter de la Mare. Captain Sir Richard Francis Burton, in
all his scandalous glory.

The next case contained three shelves of maps and a
section of classic children's books, which were Hope's favor-
ites. Finally, at the back of the room, half hidden by a thick
velvet curtain, she found the trunk with old cookbooks.

*Cooking in Provence. Cooking in Venice. Cooking in the
Seven Seas.* Blast it, where was the Chinese volume?

Muttering, she knelt on the floor, examining a pile of books
that had fallen at the back of a shelf. Without warning a wave
of dizziness struck her, making her stomach lurch.

Food, she thought. Breakfast had been half a piece of toast
that morning. She had planned to take a break for lunch, but
had never found the time to eat it. As soon as she had the book,
she would snitch something from Lord Draycott. Even now
delicious scents emanated from the kitchen.

She sank onto the floor, pulling the top books onto her lap.

Cooking in the Alhambra.

Cooking in Rome.

Footsteps padded down the hall. Hope heard the soft click
of the door opening, followed by a faint, insistent ringing. It
took her a moment to recognize the sound of a cellular phone.

"Yes, of course it's me, damn it." The words were low,
muffled. Hope frowned, trying to place the voice.

"I'm at Glenbrae House, of course. Where did you
think I'd be?"

Detective Sergeant Kipworth, she realized.

She leaned forward breathlessly. Eavesdropping or not,
she wasn't going to miss any clues to the progress of his
investigation.

"I told you not to call me here. It's too dangerous."

Dangerous? Hope rubbed her forehead. The room
seemed to blur for a moment.

"What did you get on this fellow MacLeod? Any arrest
record?"

Hope stiffened. Why were they investigating MacLeod?

"I see. You're sure of that?"

Hope felt her heart pound. Surely they couldn't be suspicious of Ronan.

"No previous occupations or prior addresses at all?" Kipworth bit back an oath. "That's impossible and you know it. You're simply not trying the right places."

More silence.

"Then take your bloody computers and fix them. He had to come from somewhere and be born to someone. Start with his National Registration number. Maybe he's got a passport."

Hope pressed a hand to her lurching stomach. They would find no National Registration number and no prior domiciles for Ronan MacLeod—not for roughly seven centuries, and not many computers would be looking back that far. It would almost be funny, she thought, if the whole idea weren't so harrowing.

Kipworth scanned a row of books along the wall. He was coming closer, Hope realized.

"Of course I'm still looking. Every bloody inch of the place. The book must be here somewhere," he snarled. "Otherwise, I'd be out of this wretched little town in a second."

Hope gasped at the menace in his voice.

"Just you listen to me. I've been tied up in this business for too long already. I'll find your book, just the way we agreed. But there's been a little change. That's right, a change." He laughed softly. "The price just doubled."

Silence.

Hope rubbed her forehead as the floor bled into gray and then re-formed. Shivering, she sank back, thankful for the comforting support of the window. What was *wrong* with her?

"Yes, I know you have a buyer for your precious folio of Shakespeare and I know he's losing interest. That's why my fee just doubled."

Kipworth knew about the folio? But how could he, when she and Ronan had only discovered it that morning?

She rubbed her eyes, trying to ignore another wave of nausea.

"The others? I'm doing nothing about them for now. The cook and her boyfriend are out of the way. It was easy enough to slip something in their drinks since they're always hanging about together in the kitchen. This fellow MacLeod will bear some looking at, too. But it's Hope O'Hara I'm after. She has to know where the book is."

It's Hope O'Hara I'm after.

She blinked, trying to make sense of what Kipworth had just said. How had he learned about the precious folio and why was he arguing about money?

As she sank against the wall, a board squeaked. The sound echoed sharply in the silent room.

Kipworth swung around instantly. "Who's there?"

Hope eased back into the shadows. If he found her now, how would she explain her eavesdropping?

Footsteps paced closer and Hope had a sudden, horrible vision of being shot in her own house, convicted by posterity as a cold-blooded thief.

Then the heavy curtain rippled in a gust of air and Banquo swooped overhead with a shrill cry. "The moon is down," the great bird cried. "The moon is down."

"How did *you* get in here? I made certain that I latched the door behind me." Cursing, Kipworth strode to the door.

Banquo was faster. He soared outside, then circled back over Kipworth's head. "Enter three witches."

"I've heard quite enough *Macbeth* for one day. Come a bit closer and I'll teach you all about tragic endings."

As Banquo soared away, Hope realized he had saved her from discovery. She released the breath she'd been blocking in her throat.

"Yes, I'm still here. That was just the bloody parrot with

his infernal chatter. That's the one, always quoting Shakespeare. What do you mean, does he know where the folio is? Are you suggesting that I interrogate a bloody bird?"

Hope realized that she was shivering, sharp, tight movements that wrenched her whole body. Something slid down her nose.

Sweat. She was freezing, yet burning up at the same time.

"Hope O'Hara? Don't worry about her. She'll be out of the way soon enough. I gave her enough to put her in bed for a week." Kipworth paced beyond the curtain, laughing tightly. "And if that doesn't work, I'll have to think of another way, won't I?"

The floor swam wildly beneath Hope. He had drugged Gabrielle and Jeffrey, and then he must have drugged her tea. Dear Lord, she couldn't let him find her here.

She wobbled to her feet, remembering that Lord Draycott was in the kitchen. If only she could get through the door and down the corridor to the kitchen before Kipworth heard her. She inched toward a potted ficus tree flanking the rear door.

"Yes, I know all about your bloody lordship and his pretty wife. They'll get their precious book soon enough. Yes, I know they're obsessive about their collections. I also know that they're getting impatient."

Hope stared bleakly at the door. *Your lordship and his pretty wife.* Were the Draycotts somehow involved?

She drew a broken breath, trying to sort suspicion from truth while her stomach lurched with sickening force.

She was getting worse. Probably Kipworth's drug was just beginning to take effect. She had to make a decision quickly. As nice as he was, Lord Draycott was a stranger, a man who had appeared without notice or introduction. He could be anyone or anything.

Even a criminal.

She couldn't afford to trust anyone. Only Ronan.

She rubbed her throbbing head, trying to remember where he'd gone. The stables?

She dragged a shaking hand across her eyes. Out the back door, past the pantry. Through the mudroom. If she was very quiet, she could make it.

Holding her breath, she eased open the door behind the ficus. A faint breath of air drifted through the room, but Kipworth didn't appear to notice as he bent over the ornately carved fireplace.

His voice sounded distant and strained. "You heard about the fire, did you? Rather brilliant of me, I thought. A perfect way to clear out the house. No, of course I didn't take any chances. It was all smoke. The rags I set to burn at the edge of the grate looked terrible enough, but there was no real danger to the house, I made certain of that. But the bloody woman didn't carry anything out. The folio must still be inside, unless she's already hidden it somewhere else."

Hope saw Kipworth fumble in his pocket, then pull out a flat oval shape.

"The mantel? Yes, I noticed that. All kinds of carving. It might be some kind of puzzle. Your friend was a very clever man, and he could have hidden that folio you stole anywhere in the house."

That folio you stole…

Hope barely heard, her gaze locked on the flat, gray form in Kipworth's hands.

A snarling wolf with fangs bared.

The King's Wolf, she thought. Kipworth had the brooch? Had *he* stolen it from Wyndgate?

But she didn't stay to hear more. She crept along the hall toward the dark pantry. At the back door she bit back an oath. The heavy bolt was thrown, and she didn't dare to move it for fear of attracting Kipworth's notice.

She shook the door lightly, trying to focus. What to do next? The breakfast room would take her right past the door to the library where Kipworth was standing, but Hope realized she had no other choice. Any second she could lose consciousness. Kipworth must have poisoned the tea when she had gone out to answer the phone. Probably he had placed the call to draw her from the room. A very clever man, James Kipworth.

Although that would hardly be his real name.

Her vision blurred again. She wobbled through the mudroom, hearing no sound from Kipworth nor from the kitchen. Perhaps the Draycotts had gone out.

She dug her fingers into her temples, trying to concentrate. Five feet more, she thought. A wedge of shadow blurred the floor in front of her; beyond that lay the kitchen and its outer door to freedom and Ronan.

She inched forward, her heart pounding. She could see the edge of the door now.

Almost there…

Silence all around her. Pain and shadows.

Then she ran dead into James Kipworth's hard chest.

CHAPTER THIRTY-THREE

HE TURNED HER SLOWLY.

His hands on her shoulders were no longer comforting but tight with suspicion. Hope wondered how she had ever thought his face was pleasant.

"Ms. O'Hara, is something…wrong? You're not looking at all well."

Hope managed a weak smile. "My stomach—I'm afraid I'm coming down with whatever Gabrielle and Jeffrey have."

"You're sick, too?" His eyes were kindly now, concerned.

Or they would have seemed so if Hope hadn't overhead his recent conversation.

The man was a thief and possibly a killer, and Hope knew she would have to clear her blurring thoughts to have any chance of escape.

She put one hand over her stomach, wincing. He would expect her to be sick, and she obliged with a soft groan.

He put out a hand to steady her. "Good Lord, you really are sick. Perhaps you'd better go upstairs and rest." So concerned. So sincere.

Hope shivered. "That's where I was headed."

"Then why did you come from the back of the house?" His eyes narrowed.

"I had to make a stop—my stomach…" Hope gave an embarrassed laugh. When his expression relaxed, she realized the story had worked.

"Then there's no sense chatting when you probably feel

like death itself. We'll take up my questions after you feel better. Meanwhile, I'll keep an eye out for any problems down here."

I'll just bet you will, Hope thought grimly. Then she had a stroke of inspiration. "This blasted flu is making me forgetful. I know there was a message I was supposed to give you, but I can't remember what."

His eyes narrowed. "A message? From whom?"

"From Mr. MacLeod, one of our staff. He said there was something you ought to know about, something he had found in his bedroom."

Kipworth drew a slow, silky breath. "How interesting. I'd better go have a chat with him. Where did you say he was?"

"He went off to the upper orchard, then to the cliffs," Hope lied calmly.

Something flickered in Kipworth's eyes. "Why would he go there? Surely he knew I was here inside the house."

Hope thought wildly. She pressed a hand to her stomach, which lurched with pain that was no longer feigned. "I—I can't seem to remember," she mumbled. "There was something he wanted you to see. He carried it from the old fishing shed. Does that make any sense?"

Her face was all innocence, all trust. It was a prize-winning performance.

Kipworth patted her shoulder. "You just leave Mr. MacLeod to me, Ms. O'Hara. I'll look into the matter fully." He touched the delicate silver cross at her throat. "Such a pretty piece. Another gift?" His hand lingered.

Hope could barely stand to be so close. How could a man lie so calmly? "My favorite one. Was there anything more?" She shivered—and realized too late that Kipworth had felt it, too.

"Is something else wrong?"

Hope shrugged. "I'm feeling sick again." She lunged up the stairs with another groan of pain. "I hope you find the thief," she called. "Whoever stole that brooch should be put behind bars."

He stood looking up at her, a small, grim smile on his face. "My sentiments exactly. And you can be certain I won't stop until I complete my job."

So honest. So conscientious.

Hope suppressed another shudder as he strode down the rear hallway and disappeared.

A little time now, thank heavens. Think.

She gazed longingly at the kitchen. There were no sounds now, but the Draycotts might still be nearby. If only she could trust them.

But she couldn't trust anyone. Not after what Kipworth had said. Anyone could have been on the other end of the line.

She had to find Ronan *now.*

Warm parka, Hope thought.

MacLeod's sweater and scarf, mittens shoved in the pocket. Wool trousers and heaviest boots. All the time she fought hot, awful waves of nausea. She thought about taking something for the pain, but decided against it. An interaction might make her even worse.

Out the window she saw a dark form striding purposefully over the snow toward the orchard. "Kipworth" was wasting no time following his latest lead.

Hope plunged down the rear stairs. Fighting dizziness, she headed in exactly the opposite direction and prayed that Ronan was still out in the stables.

"DADDY?"

"What, Duchess?"

"Why is the policeman hiking in the snow near the orchard?" Genevieve Draycott braced her chin on her palms as she stared out the window. "Do you think he's going to have a snowball fight?"

Nicholas followed his daughter's gaze. "I rather doubt

it, my love. Policemen don't usually have snowball fights."

"Why not?"

"Too busy. Too serious, I suppose."

Genevieve tilted her head, frowning. "Ms. O'Hara and Mr. MacLeod were having a snowball fight the night we got here. They seemed to be having lots of fun. I like them."

Nicholas Draycott remembered very clearly the intimate scene they had witnessed in the light of the Land Rover's front beams. A snowball fight was the least of what they had interrupted.

He cleared his throat. "They did seem to be having fun, didn't they?" He stared through the window at Detective Sergeant Kipworth's retreating back, feeling a tug of uneasiness.

"Nicky, is something wrong?"

Now was not the time to discuss his uneasiness with his wife, especially with Genevieve hanging on every word. "I suspect that the man has a well-developed sense of self-preservation. No doubt he is headed outside so he can decline any taste of my cooking."

Kacey did not laugh, too quick at reading her husband's moods. "Nicholas, if there's something you're not telling me…"

Genevieve tugged at his sleeve. "Daddy, the oil is burning. And the vegetables are turning a funny dark color."

"Damn and blast." Muttering, the viscount spun back to the stove, his thoughts racing to some disturbing conclusions. First had come the fire, followed by the sudden sickness of Gabrielle and Jeffrey.

Coincidences?

Every warning instinct clamored into red alert.

"I'm afraid that dinner will have to wait," he said tightly. "I've got to make a call."

"But the power lines…"

Nicholas frowned, already reaching into his jacket pocket for his cellular phone.

THE AIR WAS STILL with a bitter, ringing cold as Hope made her way through the dark strands of Norway spruce along the loch. Beeches girded the stone fence, their few remaining leaves clinking like small, golden coins in the wind. White and green ran together before her eyes.

South of the stable, a sullen row of clouds swept over the hillside. It was less than a quarter mile to the old stone building, but in her weakened condition the distance would feel like twenty.

As pain burned through her stomach, she stumbled through the snow, careful to keep Glenbrae House between herself and the rise of the cliffs, where she prayed the counterfeit police officer was still busy searching for MacLeod.

A fir tree slapped wet powder against her face, and with every second the light changed, gray clouds racing before the afternoon sun. This time of year the weather could shift in a second. Even without the promise of more snow, it would be twilight within minutes and full darkness in less than an hour.

Soon the man who called himself Kipworth would reach the cliffs and realize he had been tricked. He would turn back and see her footprints. And then…

Hope forced away the thought. She had enough to worry about just putting one foot in front of the other in the deep, mounded snow.

She slid sideways, lost her footing, stumbled to her feet, clumsier now with growing exhaustion. She was nearly at the edge of the garden—or what would be the garden when spring melted three feet of snow. A thin, furious shout whipped down the hillside. She turned to see Kipworth raise his arm, waving furiously.

He knew. Now he would come after her.

Fear kicked hard in her chest. Only minutes now and so much ground left to cover.

She lowered her head and struggled forward, dimly realizing there was no pain or sensation at all in her feet. Her fingers, too, felt heavy and rubbery. Had she been completely rational, Hope would have been alarmed at the growing numbness.

But weariness gripped her. She closed her mind to all but the next painful step before her.

Weaker now. Slower. Every movement an agony as the drug burned through her veins and whispered seductively for her to rest.

For one last moment the sun floated golden on the horizon, then winked out. Within seconds twilight gathered in earnest, long shadows that closed into sudden darkness.

Night lay upon Glenbrae.

Hope looked south, desperately searching for the row of beech trees that marked the edge of the stable.

Nothing. No trees or bushes anywhere.

She froze, hit with a sickening realization: she had taken a wrong turn. Dizzy and disoriented, she could see nothing in the darkness.

She foundered over the snow, fighting panic. Too late she felt a sickening lurch beneath her feet and the wild sway of the ground.

Not an earthquake. Not her imagination.

Something real and far more dangerous.

Hope had never come here before, warned away by dozens of concerned Glenbrae residents since the very first week of her arrival. Now in her panic she had stumbled where no one was safe.

Fear gripped her as the peat bog whispered around her, sucking and hissing. In every direction the snow stretched unbroken, hiding all trace of terrain and any clue to escape.

She took a wary step forward, felt the moss beneath her feet shake like a flat boat on shifting waters. The ground whispered and bubbled, rocking the wet snow above the hidden bog.

And then Hope began to sink.

CHAPTER THIRTY-FOUR

"WHAT DO YOU MEAN, they've sent no one here to Glenbrae House? I told you the man's name was Detective Sergeant Kipworth." Nicholas Draycott's fingers tightened on his cellular phone as he paced through the kitchen.

"I heard you the first time." Ian McCall answered with unusual harshness as he struggled to control his own uneasiness. "I'm only telling you what I turned up this morning, Nicholas. I've been on the phone tracking this man Kipworth ever since you called yesterday. The inspector on duty in Edinburgh said that they had planned to send someone down to Glenbrae to investigate, but he didn't make it in the snow. He had to turn back."

"Damn and blast. So our inspector is a fake."

"I'm afraid so. I'm leaving shortly. I have a friend who can handle a helicopter in any kind of weather. Meanwhile—"

"Meanwhile, I'll keep track of Hope."

As Nicholas hung up, his wife blocked his way. "I want to know what's wrong, Nicky. I want the truth this time."

"There's no time. I've got to find Hope."

Kacey frowned. "I saw her go out a few minutes ago. She was headed south, probably toward the stables."

Snow was coming down in thick, wet flakes that muffled all sound. It would also fill in any existing tracks, Nicholas thought. "She's out there," he said savagely. "And he's coming after her."

"The policeman?"

"He's no policeman."

His wife paled. "Oh, God…"

"Exactly." He jerked on his parka and gloves with savage energy.

"Are you going out for a snowball fight, Daddy?" Near the window Genevieve danced from foot to foot, all eagerness. "Can I come?"

"No, Duchess. Not this time. You and Mummy are going upstairs. It will be a kind of game, all right? Just between the three of us."

His daughter nodded, clearly thrilled at the thought of a private game between the three of them.

"Good girl." Nicholas bent his head, speaking softly to his wife. "Take Genevieve upstairs and lock yourself in the bedroom. Shove a chair, a bookcase and anything else you can lay your hands on in front of the door."

His wife's eyes were wide and frightened. "But—"

"Don't let anyone in but me. Do you understand? *No one.*" He took her face fiercely between his hard fingers. After a moment Kacey nodded.

"Good. Remember, no one but me. Go now."

He watched the two most important people in his life run upstairs and waited to hear the click of the lock. Then, jacket in hand, he sprinted toward the front of the house. The glen was already blanketed in darkness when he reached the courtyard.

When he looked down, Hope's footprints were nearly covered by fresh, blowing snow.

AGAINST THE SHADOWS and the silence, Hope stood frozen. She felt the sucking mouth of the bog beneath her feet.

They would find her here when the snow melted—tomorrow, the next day, maybe in a year's time. Or they might not find her at all, her body pulled inexorably beneath the shifting black waters of the bog.

She dug her nails into her palms and welcomed the pain, a sign that she was still alive and the game was not done yet. Soon Ronan would realize she was gone, and he would come after her. Hero that he was, he would not be dissuaded by small problems like relentless darkness, three feet of blowing snow and a deadly peat bog.

Though it hurt her frozen cheeks, Hope felt the beginning of a smile.

But every movement hurt. She managed to raise her foot several inches and sway forward. Like a drunken swimmer she lurched from side to side, making a few precious inches of headway with each effort. Around her the bog hissed, unwilling to be cheated of its prey.

Hope fought her way forward, grim and determined. She moved again—and gave a gasp of relief when her foot hit solid earth.

Snow whipped at her face, and she was too tired to sweep it free, too cold to care. She sank down against the snow, at the edge of exhaustion.

Beyond fear.

Beyond planning. Beyond thought of any sort.

Her only plan was to wait, to wait in utter silence. Ronan would come. All she had to do was stay alive until he found her.

She heard the crunch of snow, sickeningly close. She froze, her heartbeat drumming in her ears.

"Hope." It was a gentle whisper, seductive as the falling snow. "I know you're there. Your footprints led me right to you."

Fear. Knuckles shoved against her mouth to keep from crying out. And always the cold, an old friend now.

"You know it's useless," Kipworth whispered. "You know you'll never get away from me."

Ronan *would* come, Hope thought. All she had to do was wait.

"Don't expect your mystery man to come riding in on his charger. I passed him on the way back from the cliffs and told him you had walked over to see the Wishwell sisters." He gave a low laugh. "Yes, I know about them, too. Just as I know you've found the folio of *Macbeth*. I want it, Hope. Very badly. And I'm going to have it."

She wouldn't believe him. Ronan would come. He couldn't be tricked so easily.

More crunching steps, closer now. Then the hollow click of metal upon metal.

"Do you know what that was? No, I don't expect you would." He laughed softly. "It's a handy device in my particular line of work. A silencer, very good at distances up to thirty feet. So you see, my dear, no one is going to hear me when I start shooting. And no one is going to hear your screams either. Not MacLeod. Not the elegant Lord Draycott."

So the Draycotts had been innocent guests after all. Too late for regrets now. Nearly too late for anything.

A scream built in her throat.

More crunching. Somewhere to her left.

"I'm coming, Hope...."

MACLEOD WAS ABOUT to leave the stables when Nicholas Draycott sprinted out of the darkness, panting hard.

"Is—Hope—" He dragged in a breath. "Is she out here?"

"No." MacLeod's eyes hardened. "What's wrong?"

"Kipworth—not from the police. She left, probably to find you. She's out there somewhere in the snow."

MacLeod muttered a hoarse stream of Gaelic, and Draycott didn't need a translator to recognize curses. "I will find her. Then Kipworth will regret that he was ever born to woman." MacLeod tore off his jacket.

"What can I do?"

"Are her footprints still clear?"

"Gone, for all practical use. The wind has kicked up and there's more snow on its way."

MacLeod stood bare-chested. "No matter. I will find her." He dug his fingers into the dirt of the stable, then tracked dark lines over his chest, a token of battle, first to right, then to left.

He did the same to his cheeks. "If I fail, let me be cut down with her. Give me no breath to draw if hers should fail first." Slowly he dropped the dirt back to the floor. "It is done. Draycott has heard, as my witness."

"My God, man, you'll freeze like that."

MacLeod pushed past him. "It is our way." He pulled his quiver from the floor and shoved it across his bare shoulder. "My heart will bring me all the heat that I need tonight."

Within seconds, he was swallowed up by the darkness.

So cold.

She faded in and out of consciousness. Cold whispering, a lover now. Rest, just for a while. Sleep...

Hope forced her eyes open. If she slept, she would never wake again.

She pulled off her parka and shoved it beneath the snow. White sweater, white hat and scarf. Ronan's gifts, all white. Wearing them would hide her, giving Kipworth no chance to see her. No hope...

Shivering again.

Somewhere a beech tree whispered. Dry, cold leaves blew onto her face. There might have been a light somewhere to her left or it might have been her imagination.

Shivering.

Wait. Wait for Ronan.

Lace fluttered, ghostly white against the snow. Silk and black velvet took form around broad shoulders. The ghost of Draycott Abbey paced the night, his feet unimpeded by the mounded snow.

"The blackguard. I should have known. Never liked the police."

He halted, stared north with eyes narrowed. "Yes, of course I know he's there." A gray shape appeared, footprints light against the snow. The cat cried, low and questioning.

"Yes, they're safe for now, locked in a bedroom just as Nicholas told them. If they weren't quite safe, I wouldn't be out here."

The cat's tail flicked once.

"Nicholas has gone after her, along with MacLeod. She is safe for the moment, but as soon as they're within Kipworth's range…"

The wind growled sullenly, snapping wet snow into the air.

"I'm glad that you agree. It will take both of us this time, my friend. I wouldn't dream of calling on the Wishwells. This is far beyond their talents."

A sound like a muffled cough drifted on the wind. Adrian's eyes grew darker. "Desperate, he's become. He knows his time is running out. But it's running out for her, too, with this infernal cold."

The cat surged forward through the snow, every muscle tensed. Then his footprints vanished.

"Well done, Gideon." Adrian sighed. "Like it or not, the Scotsman is going to need our help before the night is out." He rubbed his hands together, scowling. "I never liked Scotland. Too bloody cold."

As the wind swept fallen leaves across the snow, his lace-clad form shimmered and vanished.

MACLEOD FOUND the first hint of Hope's tracks just beyond the eastern curve of the loch. She had been moving slowly, stumbling twice within a yard.

His hands fisted. He could feel her pain and all her terror. Someone would pay for that, he swore.

He barely felt the cold on his chest now. The battle heat was upon him, savage and consuming. He stood listening for any sound, but heard nothing except the wind.

Eyes lowered, he searched in gradually widening circles so he would miss no clue of her. He found another print. Beside it lay the mark of her body where she had fallen, only to struggle back to her feet.

Brave woman. He would tell her that when he found her. And he *would* find her.

A slope rose before him, ridged with drifting snow. MacLeod took it on the run, his bow caught in one hand.

At the crest, light slashed out of the darkness, blinding him. He heard a cold laugh.

"Well, well, here's Mr. MacLeod." The barrel of a flashlight glinted down the barrel of Kipworth's gun. "Come and join our little party."

CHAPTER THIRTY-FIVE

CAUGHT, MACLEOD THOUGHT grimly.

But he had planned to be caught.

"Where is Hope?" Hands on his bow, he strode forward. He had to find her, and the best way was by allowing himself to be taken by her pursuer.

"So here's our mystery man," Kipworth hissed. "Not exactly dressed for a party, are you?"

"Where *is* she?"

"I'll ask the questions here. Now, put down that pathetic weapon and move to the top of the snowdrift, where I can see you."

Light glinted coldly along the metal barrel of a gun. "First tell me where she is."

"Stubborn bastard, aren't you? Wyndgate told me you were the one to watch out for. A regular fly in the ointment."

"Why would I be like an insect in gelatin?" All the time MacLeod spoke, he inched to the right until he could see what was beyond the banked snow. He prayed that Hope would be there.

"Very amusing." Kipworth's arm tightened. "But I'm losing my sense of humor in this bloody cold, so I suggest you move. *Now.*"

At the edge of the slope now.

Three steps would bring him to the crest, MacLeod thought. "First Hope. Then I will put down my weapon."

"You don't seem to understand, fool. You have *no* bargaining power out here. I have the gun, remember?"

Not quite close enough. "What can your small weapon do that my bow cannot?"

"Where are you from, Mars?" Kipworth sent a bullet into the snow only inches from MacLeod's foot. "Does that answer your question?"

MacLeod laughed calmly. "Should I be frightened by that weak bit of noise?"

"You want blood? I can give you that if you want." Kipworth's arm rose. "You missed me on the stairs several weeks ago. Your arrow went past my head. I couldn't even search the house without running into one of you, and that set everything back for weeks. Whoever thought the woman would be such a fool to buy that wreck of a house?" Kipworth jerked the muzzle impatiently. "Without her interference, we would have found the stolen folio long ago."

MacLeod understood only part of this, but he kept inching over the snow. "We?"

"Why so curious?"

"I like to know why someone is attempting to kill me."

Kipworth laughed tightly. "Logical enough. Wyndgate had a business associate with access to the *Macbeth.* It took three years of planning, but they finally pulled it off. The bloody theft of the century and no one could know. They planned for Wyndgate's friend to go underground and stay there while Wyndgate looked for a buyer with a large bank account and no messy moral concerns about where the folio had come from. He couldn't exactly put it out in a case in his living room, you understand. Something like that would have attracted immediate attention and a host of unpleasant questions."

MacLeod kept inching sideways. "But you found a purchaser?"

"Finally. By then Wyndgate and his friend had a falling

out. He died two years ago, and the stubborn fool kept the book's location a secret to the end."

"Bad luck."

"An understatement." Kipworth turned suddenly. "Stop *moving*, damn it."

MacLeod shrugged. "But why Glenbrae House?"

"Because the man had worked in the area in the past. He knew the glen was isolated and its residents were eccentric, to say the least. The house was empty. No one was likely to bother him in this town. He and the parrot lived very quietly."

"Parrot?"

"That bloody bird you call Banquo. I suppose you'd recite Shakespeare, too, if it was all you heard for five years." Kipworth frowned. "I should have shot the bird when I had the chance."

Low and unsteady, a voice drifted over the slope. "Ronan, do what he s-says."

Panic swept down MacLeod's chest. "Are you hurt, *mo rùn?*"

"No, cold. So cold. But the gun, you can't let him—"

"Shut up, both of you," Kipworth hissed. "You have five seconds to tell me where the folio is hidden. Otherwise, I start shooting—and this time it won't be at the snow."

MacLeod stared at the man before him. "In the stables," he said flatly.

At the same instant, Hope wobbled to her feet. "In the kitchen," she rasped.

"Very neat of you. You're both so honorable that you turn my stomach." Three bullets drilled past MacLeod's face. "Stop wasting my time, or I'll do a hell of a lot more than *this*." The next one tore through MacLeod's shoulder.

He moved only imperceptibly. The pain was nothing compared to his last wound, the searing thrust of a Persian scimitar edged with Chinese poison.

"Very impressive, MacLeod. Maybe this will change your mind." Kipworth lowered his gun. "A shattered kneecap will cripple you for life. Let's see how you like that, Braveheart."

"Stop," Hope called hoarsely. "The book isn't worth his pain. I'll tell you where it is."

"Tell him nothing," MacLeod ordered. "Trust me, my heart."

"*Trust me,*" Kipworth mimicked. "Very touching. Now, put down the bow," he snarled. "Otherwise my next bullet goes through Ms. O'Hara's pretty little cheek. All that scarring and blood loss would be such a shame."

MacLeod's eyes narrowed to slits. "I will see that you die slowly for this."

Kipworth laughed, gesturing with the gun. "One of us will. Now, put down the bow, and remember, I'm a very nervous man. If you move too fast, I might shoot something." He swung around, aiming the weapon over the slope, where Hope stood silhouetted in the flare of his flashlight. "Like *her.*"

MacLeod barely noticed the blood oozing thickly over his chest. His only thought was to stop Kipworth before he could hurt Hope. He slipped the polished curve of wood from his shoulder, then sank slowly to one knee. "Will this place be satisfactory?"

Hope gasped as light struck him. "Ronan, your shoulder. There's b-blood everywhere."

"It's nothing."

Kipworth gestured sharply. "Sorry to interrupt this tearful reunion, but I have work to finish and an appointment to keep. Drop the bow, MacLeod. Then kick it away from you."

MacLeod shrugged. "As you like." He placed his quiver carefully on the ground, waiting for the best moment to lunge at Kipworth. Death was what the traitor planned. He would never let them live after they turned over the priceless folio.

If all else failed, MacLeod would take the bullet meant for Hope.

As wind hissed over the slope, sweeping snow into a thick curtain of white, Kipworth brushed wildly at his eyes. "What the bloody hell was that?"

Within the flying snow a gray shape appeared, racing out of the night. In one powerful movement he leaped, striking Kipworth's arm.

"Damned cat." Wyndgate's accomplice twisted blindly, kicking at the snow. "Get out of my way."

The cat crouched, snarling. Rising, MacLeod moved closer.

"Tonight everyone's a hero, even the bloody *cat*," Kipworth hissed. "Don't come any closer, MacLeod. Remember, all I need is *one* of you alive."

Lace fluttered above the slope. "I'm afraid you've greatly miscalculated, my friend."

Kipworth glared into the darkness. "Who said that?"

Eyes agleam, the Draycott ghost took shape on the snowy slope. "What say you, MacLeod of Glenbrae? Shall I knock him flat or blind him?"

"Who was that?" Scowling, Kipworth scanned the snowbank. "Come out where I can see you."

"The man appears to be nervous," Adrian said thoughtfully. "It would be but a second's work for me to disarm him."

"No," MacLeod whispered. "It will put the woman in grave danger."

Hope watched MacLeod's lips move as he spoke to thin air. Was he hallucinating, disoriented from the cold and his blood loss? Or was he simply trying to distract Kipworth? Either way, she prayed his scheme would work. She knew he would go after Kipworth at his first chance. Unarmed, he would take the bullet meant for her.

The folio wasn't worth his life.

"Ronan, let him have the book."

"Well, well, she loves you above the book. Lucky man." Kipworth stumbled over the drifting snow. "Now, stop talking to yourself and put down that bow. Then get over here where I can see you."

MacLeod sank to one knee in the snow, only inches from his dropped quiver. "I will place it here."

"Of course you will. It's too late for any more heroics, MacLeod." Kipworth laughed raggedly. "I have no more need for you now that Ms. O'Hara has so kindly agreed to tell me where the folio is hidden." His pistol found a new target. "I suggest you choose your next words carefully, because they are going to be your last."

"No." Hope dug at her feet, then flung snow wildly at Kipworth, who cursed, temporarily blinded.

Three muffled shots burst the night's silence, snapping white powder over the slope. Kipworth's next bullet raked across Hope's hand, drawing blood. The ground blurred beneath her feet in a searing wave of pain.

Afterward, she would always wonder if the next moments were dream or delirium.

She heard the cry of a cat as a dark shape soared, striking Kipworth's back. At the same instant Hope could have sworn she saw a man in lace and black velvet glide before her, blocking Kipworth's next wild volley. But who *was* he?

She looked wildly for MacLeod and saw him on the ground, struggling with Kipworth for the pistol.

"He's yours then, Scotsman." Hope heard the words faintly, as if in a dream. Dear Lord, was she hallucinating from hypothermia? "I shall see to the woman's safety in your stead, though she has done a most impressive job on her own."

Another bullet hissed over the snow. As Hope watched in amazement, the metal oval rocked from side to side, then stopped cold to drift in midair.

"Excellent," came another whisper at her ear. "It appears I still have the touch." Lace seemed to ripple around a man's hand outlined before her in the darkness. Then the bullet twisted sharply, rocketing back toward the man who had just fired it.

Wyndgate's accomplice swore loudly, caught beneath MacLeod in the snow. His gun pitched up and down. "I'll hit her again, I swear it." He cursed as the bullet slammed back down the muzzle and exploded.

The gun went flying from his fingers. "My hand, it's burning—" Kipworth groaned in pain as the cat climbed over his prone shoulders, teeth bared at his face.

"Well done, Gideon. The same for you, Scotsman. Now, let's be done with this loathsome jackal, shall we?"

Hope heard the male voice clearly this time. But it appeared to be coming from the empty space beside her shoulder. "Who *are* you?" she whispered.

All along the slope, wind rose in angry spirals. White powder blanketed the night as Kipworth was dragged to his feet by a force that Hope could neither see nor feel.

"S-stop," he shouted, flailing wildly at the darkness around him. "L-let me go and I'll forget the folio. I'll forget *everything* if—"

Abruptly he was hoisted upward, his feet dangling above the ground. Then he flew headfirst into a snowdrift.

MacLeod started after him. "I wasn't done with him yet."

"No more time," the voice answered. "She's frozen through and needs to be tucked in before a roaring fire. You *both* do. Don't be bloodthirsty, Scotsman. This is no time for that excessive honor of yours."

Hope squeezed her eyes shut. The ground seemed to sway. "R-Ronan."

She felt MacLeod grip her shoulders. "Let me see your hand."

"No need. You came," she said raggedly.

"Always." He cradled her icy cheeks and kissed her fiercely. "Can you walk back? I'll carry you if you can't."

Hope gave a shaky laugh. "I can manage. Just get me away from here."

As she spoke, a motor whined in the darkness and Kipworth lumbered out of the snowbank, his eyes wearing a look of sheer terror. "You can't do this to me." His arms flailed blindly. "G-ghosts don't *exist*."

Low, diabolical laughter rang through the night, rising to a chilling crescendo as phosphorescent light played over the slope.

"You don't f-frighten me, do you hear?" Kipworth plunged off into the night, trailed by invisible hands that seemed to jerk him from side to side like a rag doll.

Or maybe Hope was simply dreaming.

She rubbed her eyes. "Did I imagine what I just saw?"

"That depends," MacLeod said slowly, "on what you just saw."

The whine of the car motor grew louder as she started to demand a straight answer. Strange, how heavy her arms were and how very cold the world had become. She peered over the hill, watching snow swirl up around her, white and silent.

Two car lights flared. "My head… I don't think I can…" Hope saw the dark outline of Nicholas Draycott's Land Rover loom over the snow, then blur before her eyes. "M-maybe you will have to carry me," she whispered.

The last thing she felt was MacLeod's arms closing hard around her.

CHAPTER THIRTY-SIX

DAWN STREAKED THE eastern cliff as Hope paced anxiously in the corridor outside Ronan's room. Even bundled in double layers of heavy woolens, she still felt cold. But her mind was sharp, entirely focused on the man beyond the closed door, the man who had insisted on carrying her through the snow to Nicholas Draycott's car.

The drive back to Glenbrae House remained a blur to Hope. She had slipped in and out of consciousness. All she remembered clearly was Ronan's hands. Ronan's warmth. Ronan's ragged Gaelic words of endearment.

The Wishwells had been waiting when the Land Rover finally reached the house, and with them was an elderly doctor who had been visiting Archibald Brown. Hope never questioned what had brought her neighbors to Glenbrae House. She had been too busy worrying about the man she loved.

"What's taking the doctor so *long?*"

Gabrielle put a hand on her shoulder. "Your Scotsman is tough, Hope. He'll be fine."

"Will he?" Hope whispered. "There was blood everywhere, Gabrielle. But he kept walking and baiting Kipworth. He was trying to draw his attention away from me." She choked at the memory of Ronan's blood staining the white snow as the two men struggled wildly for the pistol. "It's my fault," she said raggedly. "It was *me* Kipworth wanted, not Ronan." Hope slid one hand onto the door and let her head sink against the cold wood. "He wanted something I had. A very precious book. Only I didn't know I had it, not until it was too late."

"Stop this," Gabrielle said tightly. "You can't possibly blame *yourself* for what Kipworth did."

"I have to. If not for me, right now Ronan would be out in the stable feeding that great horse or stealing slices out of your fudge." Hope's voice broke. "And if he doesn't… make it—"

"Don't *talk* like that."

"I have to, Gabrielle. After all this time, after all the people I've lost, I found a hero one night during a storm. And now I might lose him." She made a broken sound and her fingers clenched white on the door frame.

"Your hero will be back stealing my fudge in a week," Gabrielle said, though her own voice was husky with tears. "And he'll be arguing with you sooner than that."

"I'd gladly let him win," Hope whispered. "I'd never disagree with him ever again, if only…" Her hands locked at her middle. "What's taking so long?"

"There are tests to be done. An examination."

"The doctor would tell me if…if Ronan weren't going to…" Hope swallowed hard, swaying.

"Sit down before you fall down," Gabrielle ordered. "Let the doctor do his work. He's very experienced, according to Archibald Brown."

"You're right," Hope said. "I have to believe. I won't *let* him die. He doesn't have the slightest chance of getting away from me ever again."

With a creak, the door opened. Instantly Hope spun around, her hands clenched. An elderly man in worn tweeds strode out, rubbing his neck.

"Doctor, how is he?"

"Strangest white blood count I've yet to see. And I

could swear the braw lad had ne'er glimpsed the sight of a needle before."

"Will he—" Hope took a breath. "Doctor, is he going to—"

He rubbed his jaw, frowning. "Ms. O'Hara?"

Hope nodded blindly, expecting the worst.

"Five minutes, and na a second more, lass. Puir man's lost a deal of blood and needs his rest."

The words seemed to echo hollowly as if from a great distance. "Rest? You mean he's not going to—"

"Die?" The doctor patted her arm. "Ach, good Lord, no. The man is as strong as an ox, provided he stays off his feet and under those blankets. He seemed intent on ripping out his IV and charging off in search of you if I didn't promise to send you in immediately."

Hope brushed at her wet cheeks and pushed open the door, then froze.

MacLeod lay in bed, framed by the glow of a table lamp. He was too pale, his features tight with pain he would be far too stubborn to admit.

His eyes opened as Hope sank into the chair beside the bed and took his hand gently in hers. "Someone told me there was a hero in here," she said. "I wanted to thank him, you see, because he saved my life."

MacLeod's fingers tightened. "Not a hero." His voice was rough. "I wasn't fast enough. You almost died tonight, *mo rùn*. I should have known. I should have felt it the first moment you were in danger from Kipworth."

Hope felt tears burn at her eyes. Maybe this was what loving someone meant. Maybe love made you want to give and give, and somehow you always wanted to give more.

"Stop it, MacLeod. You kept me from dying tonight. Kipworth—or whatever his real name is—would have made certain there were no witnesses when he was done. I'm alive *because* of you, and don't you forget it," she said fiercely. "That makes twice now, in case you've forgotten."

His eyes burned over her face. There was the faintest tug at the corner of his mouth. "Are you...keeping score now, *mo rùn?*"

Hope smiled tremulously. "Keeping track. Just like someone else I know. Someone who's arrogant and stubborn and who I—I couldn't possibly live without."

Her voice fell away as their hands locked tightly and Ronan slowly drew her down against his good shoulder. Hope felt some of her terror fade, though she knew it would be months before she could forget the sight of Kipworth's face and the sound of his wild laughter.

The door opened a crack and the doctor peered in, frowning. "I am sorry to interrupt, but I have three men out here demanding to give blood to my patient. I keep telling them that he doesn't *need* blood, but they refuse to go away."

The door opened wider, revealing Jeffrey and Nicholas Draycott. Behind them stood Kacey Draycott and Ian and Jamee McCall, all looking very anxious. "Are you satisfied now?" the doctor asked crisply, hiding a smile. "As I told you, the man will be fine. All he needs is IV liquids and some rest."

"If you're quite certain," Nicholas said slowly.

He was convinced by the sight of Hope's blinding smile just before the doctor eased the door shut. The viscount turned and saw Ian and Jamee McCall staring at him. "It's a long story," he said. "Let's go find some of Gabrielle's cappuccino and I'll start at the beginning. It all began with the book which Wyndgate stole, probably about eight years ago."

Jamee hung back, staring at the closed door and worrying about her friend. "She's happy with him? Really happy, Nicholas? She's had so much pain in her life and so many losses..."

Her husband, the twelfth laird of Glenlyle, slid an arm

around her shoulders. Together they waited for Nicholas's answer.

"I think," the viscount said slowly, "that if those two people hadn't been born in the same century, they still would have managed to find a way to be together. They were meant for each other, if you ask me. Ronan MacLeod seems to know every corner and shadow in this old house. In fact, if it weren't impossible, I'd almost say he had to have seen it built." He turned away, his eyes narrowing. "I'll tell you more after I check on Kipworth and that bastard he was working for."

"Wyndgate, you mean?"

"That's the one. I found him going through Hope's desk when I got back." Nicholas Draycott smiled coldly. "I decided they both deserved a nice long stay out in the fishing shed, where I gather Kipworth had locked Hope and Ronan in several weeks ago. No heat out there, of course. Before I threw the bolt, I confiscated their coats just to keep them in a properly penitent state of mind. Given this snow, they might have quite a wait until they're taken into official custody." Draycott's smile grew. "I'm determined to find out the rest of the story of this *Macbeth* folio and exactly how Wyndgate arranged its theft. Possibly we can…persuade him to give us all the details before the police arrive."

Ian's hands closed to fists. "Why don't we *both* go have a look at them?" He stared outside at the gleaming snow. "But there's one thing I still don't understand. I could swear I saw a cat when we drove up. There were prints leading over the snow, but they simply vanished beside the Christmas tree."

"Maybe you can explain that to me, too," Nicholas's wife said as she slid an arm around her husband's waist.

But before Nicholas could answer, they heard the sound of husky laughter beyond the door, then a muffled protest and the creak of the bed.

Nicholas cleared his throat, hiding a smile.

As he did, there was a scuffling noise in the front hallway. A short man with wild gray hair and snow dusting his jacket burst inside and glared up the stairs. "Where is that bounder Wyndgate? By God, when I get my hands on the man—"

He went very still as sunlight struck the group of people starting down the stairway. He seemed to struggle for control, his jaw working hard as he looked down the line. His gaze stopped on Jeffrey. "It was truly the *Macbeth,* wasn't it? The lost folio stolen eight years ago from the British Library?"

For a moment no one answered. All watched in embarrassed shock as he sank slowly onto the lowest step, his face in his hands. "I should have known he couldn't be trusted. I should have stopped him as soon as I suspected he was offering stolen property."

"Father?" Jeffrey's voice was high and tight as he moved forward. "*You* were Wyndgate's buyer?" He made a sharp movement with his hand. "You've done some low things before, but never *that* low."

Nicholas Draycott cleared his throat uneasily at the sight of what appeared to be a private family altercation. "You're Jeffrey Balford? Son of Lord Balford?"

"I don't choose to use that name. My father and I haven't seen eye to eye on my choice of a career, you see. Or on anything else." Jeffrey scowled. "We went our separate ways a long time ago."

Lord Balford sat up stiffly. "I only wanted what was best for you, Jeffrey. What your mother would have wanted."

"Rubbish. You wanted what was best for you. What would make *you* look powerful and important among your friends. I don't care a whit about finances and banking. You know that and have always known it."

His father passed a hand over his eyes. "Maybe I did want it for me. And I'm sorry, Jeffrey. It seems I've made a great many mistakes where you're concerned. But…I've missed you."

Jeffrey stood stiff and still, looking angry and confused, yet at the same time intensely vulnerable. "Maybe it's too late for apologies."

"I hope not. When Wyndgate came to me about this folio, I never knew what he was dabbling in. But it's brought me to you." He stood slowly, looking uncomfortable. "I'm not going away until we talk. *Really* talk, the way we should have done long ago." His voice broke. "After your mother…"

The silence drew out. Jeffrey stared hard at the corner of his shoe, then looked at his father. "I suppose we could try. But first, meet Gabrielle." He caught Gabrielle's hand and tugged her forward. "She's the woman I love and we're to be married. Don't even think of trying to argue with me about it," he added fiercely.

Lord Balford looked at the two of them and smiled ruefully. "So I'm to gain a daughter-in-law." He took Gabrielle's hand. "I always knew that Christmas was a lucky time of year. Now I have not one but two people to welcome into my life."

"You don't oppose us?" Gabrielle asked softly.

He gave an unsteady laugh. "Jeffrey has finally stood on his feet and made a commitment to a career—and to the person he loves. How can I disapprove of that?" He took their hands in his. "Besides, my friend Archibald gave me a slice of your rum mocha velvet cake, and my first taste convinced me I had died and gone to paradise. You are a true artist, young woman, and it would be my very great pleasure to see that you receive all the recognition and support that you deserve."

Jeffrey grinned.

Gabrielle blushed.

Nicholas Draycott chuckled. "All in all, a fitting finale. It seems that MacLeod is healing rapidly, and another old wound is to be healed. It's not precisely from *Macbeth,* but still, all's well that ends well." Grinning broadly, he took his wife's arm and headed for the kitchen. "Actually, I think we should let Wyndgate and his friend suffer out in the fishing shed a bit longer. Cappuccino and scones, anyone? Or perhaps you'd prefer some exceptional Chinese cuisine." He grinned at his wife. "Since Gabrielle is going to be busy getting acquainted with her new father-in-law, I might as well take over in the kitchen."

EPILOGUE

Draycott Abbey
Southeastern England
Late spring

THREE WHITE-HAIRED ladies stood in the spring sunlight, studying the high gray walls covered with climbing roses.

"It looks just the same," Morwenna whispered. "A house full of secrets. A house that will last forever."

"Not forever," Perpetua said. "But near enough."

They walked in silence over the grassy slopes. "We'll need a car. Someone's bound to ask how we got here," Honoria reminded her sisters.

Perpetua gave an absent wave and a trim Mini appeared behind them on the gravel drive.

"We should come and visit more often," Morwenna said, watching a pair of swans cut through the silver moat. "There's a rare beauty here, an old magic."

"And you are quite welcome to come," a voice said gravely from the ridge behind them. Adrian Draycott shimmered into view, looking elegant and imperious. "It was your choice to stay away, not mine."

"Perhaps we'll change our minds," Perpetua said stiffly. "After a tour, that is. Let us see what you've done with those roses we brought you from Provence."

Adrian laughed and bowed deeply. "After you, my dearest ladies. I believe we still have time before the others arrive."

A CAR GROWLED along the drive, its radio spilling forth an exuberant Celtic tune. Hope tapped her hand in time, delighting in the feel of the wind in her hair and the faint smell of roses. "There it is," she said, awe filling her voice at the sight of high granite walls and thousands of tiny leaded windows. "Draycott Abbey. It's just as beautiful as I've heard."

No sound came from the seat beside her. MacLeod was trying hard not to clutch at the door handle while his blood raced. She was a fearless driver, and riding in a fast automobile was still not an experience he took lightly.

But he swallowed, forcing his fists to uncurl and his body to relax as the car came to a stop. She was a wonderful driver, he told himself. And perhaps there were some advantages to a car over a horse after all.

"Ronan?" Hope turned, a frown in her eyes. "Did I drive too fast again? Are you—"

"I'm fine, lass. Just taken aback by the abbey. There is so much color, so much light." He slid out, then moved around to open her door. "Let's have a look. I want to see how much things are changed here."

Hope blinked at him. "You've been here before? In your...own time?"

He nodded, taking her arm. "You look very beautiful in that dress, did you know that?"

She brushed at the soft, draping silk. "You spent far too much for it in London."

"We can afford it. And you, my love, deserve it."

She flushed. "I can't believe that all the bills are paid. The Investment Club has been unbelievably lucky this year. Strange, I always seem to earn back exactly what I put my heart on."

Ronan pulled her forward, staring around him at the high oaks. "Too bad. You leave me no dragons to slay or duels to fight in your honor."

"You've saved my life twice, MacLeod. Isn't that enough?"

He touched her hair. "Keeping score, are you?"

"Keeping track. Because you steal my breath away, so you do."

Beneath the green leaves of a whispering oak he caught her hands and pulled her close. "Then marry me, lass. Stop delaying and arguing. We'll announce our news here before all your friends."

"*Our* friends," Hope corrected. But as before, a shadow haunted her eyes at his words. "And I can't give you what you need."

"And what, sweet lass, is that?" Ronan toyed with her earring, a long dangle of silver.

"A child. A family," she said tightly.

"Is that so? Perhaps you've already done that, *mo rùn*. What do you think these people are inside? Gabrielle, Jeffrey, Nicholas and Kacey. Even that great stubborn laird of Glenlyle and his wife? They are family in all the ways that count. The bonds need not be limited by blood, lass. I've learned that well. *You* taught it to me."

"Are you sure, Ronan? Because there are other women. You could—"

"Dinna fire my blood with such nonsense," he growled, his hands closing hard over her wrists.

"But—"

The green oak was at Hope's back when he kissed her savagely. His body tensed, hard with demand. He held her, overwhelmed her, only pulling away so both could draw sharp, ragged breaths. "You yield in this?" His face was stern. "No more talk of loss and all the things you canna give me."

Her fingers traced his jaw with aching tenderness. "Bully," she whispered.

"I'll not be made to change my mind. It's you I'll have and none other. You and those people within the abbey are all the family a man could wish for, and far more than the King's Wolf ever hoped to find."

"Brave wolf. But what of your time, your glen? It will be different here—you've seen just how different. Maybe there is yet a way for you to..." Hope swallowed. "For you to go back," she finished, in a rush that took every bit of her will to finish.

MacLeod caught a wayward strand of chestnut hair at her cheek. Only one secret had he kept from Hope, and that was the Wishwells' secret to give or withhold. Their skills were not the sort to be chattered about lightly. He had discovered that there was blindness in this modern age and a fear of seeing magic and miracle even when they lay clear as day before one's eyes. "You've no reason to worry about that."

"But what about the portrait?"

MacLeod thought back to the cold emptiness he had experienced between times and had to fight back a shudder. "Closed, my love. Sealed tight."

"I don't understand, Ronan. You mean..."

"I can't go back. Even if I wished it, and I do not."

She laid a trembling hand against his chest. "You're certain? You've tried?"

"Three times, and each time I failed."

"You never *told* me."

He smiled crookedly. "In case I failed. But I had to be sure, *mo rùn*."

Her head sank against his shoulder. "Such a risk you took. If you had gone, had been lost—" Her hands tightened.

"But I was not lost, lass. And now you have no hope of escaping me. I'll harry you and vex you and make you wish I'd been truly gone into that cold wall."

"Never."

Her hands dug hard at his waist, burrowing beneath his fine formal jacket and elegant white linen shirt. "And if you ever, ever say such a thing to me again, I'll—"

"You'll do what?" he whispered, breathless beneath the sweet assault of her hands and the brush of her body.

"I'll bind you with ropes and strip away all your clothes and teach you the true meaning of torment, MacLeod of Glenbrae."

His eyes closed. "It sounds to be paradise, my lass. A grave temptation." He slid his hands into the shining, wayward cap of her curls, at the same time exploring her mouth.

She gave a low, broken sound of pleasure and need, tugging the shirt from his bright, newly fashioned kilt, a gift from the laird of Glenlyle and his American wife. The colors were too bright and the wool too new and stiff, but MacLeod did not tell them so. With time the cloth would soften and fade, more to the manner he was accustomed to wearing. Until then he would endure his velvet jacket and finery because they pleased Hope.

She caught his shoulders and bit at his lip. "Your mouth, MacLeod."

He frowned. "You have some complaint against it?"

"None at all," she said breathlessly. "Except that it drives me wild."

He smiled against her lips. "Then maybe we should go somewhere quiet. Beyond the moat and the roses. This old abbey seems as if it would not resent a pair of lovers who chose a quiet spot among its shadows." MacLeod looked off at the weathered granite walls and the endless climbing roses. "It has only grown finer with age." He nodded, remembering the flattery and the endless deceit, the constant stratagems by Edward and his polished courtiers. But he had liked the seigneur of these lands. MacLeod was certain he would be pleased with all that his abbey had become.

"Of course he would," a voice boomed at his shoulder.

Lace rippled. Velvet shone in the warm spring sunlight. Adrian Draycott shimmered into view and shot an assessing glance at MacLeod. "And it's rather dashing that you're looking, too. You still see me, I suppose."

MacLeod nodded slightly.

"Not for long, Scotsman. The portal is closed. With it sealed, all contact with your own time will be lost." Already Adrian's voice seemed to fade. "You're sure in your decision to stay?"

Read my heart, MacLeod said in silence to the abbey's imposing guardian ghost. *She will be my home and my time. Her friends will be my friends, and her joys, my joys.*

A shadow moved beyond the roses. MacLeod recognized that gray shape immediately. *Gideon is well?*

"As fine as any creature may be. The best and most loyal of friends."

I owe you my thanks. MacLeod touched Hope's cheek. *We both do.*

"Save your thanks, Scotsman. I believe you are called to make a signal contribution to your country today. That folio would bring you money beyond your dreams, you know."

She is all the dream I need. If it pleases her to make a gift of this folio, then it pleases me also.

"Well said, MacLeod of Glenbrae. And God's peace and blessing follow you both." His black velvet jacket seemed to waver as the smell of his beloved roses filled the air, rich and sweet. "Then it's goodbye, my friend. Once the portal closes completely, there will be no more link for us. I only wanted to be certain of your choice."

Certain beyond all doubt, MacLeod thought. He did not choose to speak of it to Hope. She would only plague him with more choices that he did not want.

Around them the moat rippled and gurgled. Somewhere a curlew trilled from the glade.

And as he stood with his hands cupped on Hope's cheeks, a church bell rang far out over the distant downs—twelve times and then once more.

MacLeod shook his head, feeling the brush of ghostly fingers. But of course, it was only the wind, he told himself, lost in the sight of Hope's blinding smile.

And the words that seemed to echo faintly in his mind?

Imagination, he decided. This powerful old abbey was a place to make men imagine and dream, with the pulse of history beating deep within its halls.

Somewhere beyond the moat and the Witch's Pool, lace fluttered for a moment. A tall shape seemed to stand among the roses, surveying his beloved domain. Then lace and velvet fled. Only a cat lay drowsing in the sun, his amber eyes keen on the abbey.

MacLeod felt an instant of disorientation and loss—but only an instant. "So, lass," he said to the smiling woman in his arms, "do we evade them all and find a quiet glade?"

"Later, Scotsman," Hope whispered. "First you have a queen to meet." She slid his shirt into his kilt, smiling.

"Strange, that. A queen upon the throne." He shook his head.

"And not the first."

"So you tell me." He straightened his shirt and jacket, looking every bit the dashing Highland laird—and not at all the heartsick warrior that he had been.

Hope held out her hand. "You steal my very breath, MacLeod. You always have, from the first moment I saw you riding out of that storm. Will you join me at the abbey?" she asked, formal in spite of her smile. "Jeffrey and Gabrielle will be waiting, along with his father, who seems to like having a French chef in the family."

"Almost as much as he seems to like having his son back," MacLeod murmured. "And the laird and his wife will be there, along with the Draycotts and their charming daughter?"

"All of them."

MacLeod straightened his shoulders. He would ask her hand of them, these braw friends who were all the family she had now. He was a knight trained in all the proper form and ritual, after all, and he must ask her hand of those who loved her most.

"Let us go then, lass of my heart." He guided her forward into the sunlight and the drifting perfume of roses. "There will never be a better time to meet a queen, I warrant."

He did not look back at the last shimmer of lace above the moat, nor at the great cat who watched them from the hedgerow.

"HE'S GONE TO US, Gideon."

Adrian Draycott watched from the glade, a sudden sense of loss in his heart. "He was a friend of real courage."

At his feet the great cat stirred, meowing softly.

"I know well it was for the best, my friend. He's set securely in this time now, by his choice and the love of the woman at his side. In spite of that, I shall miss him. It was pleasant to have someone who could see me."

Gideon's tail flicked once and his keen gaze settled on the far slope.

Gold shimmered beyond the Witch's Pool. Low laughter drifted over the moat.

"Grey?" Adrian turned. "Is that you, my heart?"

Light gathered over a dress of cloth of gold. A woman stood in the dappled shade of an oak, her smile fierce. "And have you forgotten that I can see you, too, my love? That I can touch you?"

"Never," Adrian said. There was a new firmness in his ghostly step. "And now that you're here, we've work to do. The capstone needs to be braced and our roses must be tended." His eyes took on a wicked gleam. "But first I mean to have a closer look at that extraordinary folio." In a heartbeat space shifted and a volume appeared, floating in the afternoon sunshine.

"You mustn't," the woman in gold whispered. "The queen is about to arrive for the viewing, and all the others are already gathered in the library."

"I'll only be a few moments. It was an extraordinary skill the man had, after all. I recall he visited once and gave his finest performance here. He acted himself on occasion. Did you know that?"

The woman in gold took his arm, watching the old, fragile pages turn gently in the air. "It was a stirring play and it will be again, if young Jeffrey has his way. He means to stage a performance outside near the moat. I have every certainty that it will be a great success." Her eyes twinkled. "With our help, of course."

"Of course," Adrian agreed.

Together they paced along a row of dancing roses, arm in arm and hearts in perfect accord.

INSIDE THE ABBEY came the sound of sudden laughter. In the front hall, flanked by all Hope's friends, MacLeod sank to bended knee and took her hand.

"I would have your hand, Hope O'Hara. To cherish and protect. To encourage and support. For all my mortal days." His eyes darkened. "If you will have me."

She swallowed, wild color filling her cheeks. He was her champion and finest friend. How could she deny him anything? "I will. To cherish and protect as you do. To encourage and support for all my mortal days." Her eyes glinted with a hint of tears. "And even beyond that," she whispered, only for her Scotsman to hear.

LAUGHTER ECHOED.

Clapping exploded through the rich rooms and bright, silent halls.

The sound drifted to the portrait of the eighth viscount high above in the Long Gallery.

"He looks just the same," Morwenna Wishwell mused. "Just as handsome and as arrogant as he always was."

"But he's guarded his abbey well," Perpetua admitted reluctantly. "And he will do so again, I think."

At Morwenna's side, the curtains rippled. As the fragrance of roses filled the room, an image glinted against the leaded windows.

A woman smiled there, having been given her heart's dream and the news of a child to come.

A Scotsman paced there, then turned as the woman whispered in his ear. He nearly stumbled in his shock and joy.

"Three bairns, I think," Perpetua said softly.

"Nay, 'twill be four," Morwenna said. "Three braw sons to make their father's hair turn gray, and a lass who will make the inn ring with her laughter."

"She'll be a singer with a voice like an angel's. She'll bring all the old ballads to life."

"No, she'll be a scientist," Perpetua insisted. "Equations and theorems for her."

"She will do *just* as her heart wills," Honoria said sagely. "As we all must. And right now we'd better rejoin the others before they discover us gone."

They moved together, their hands joined. Joy filled the air, and even the abbey's shadows seemed to take on light.

Then there was only emptiness and the ring of laughter from the hall where MacLeod began a ring of toasts to his radiant future bride. Sunlight streamed over the moat, and bees droned among the roses.

Up in the Long Gallery the curtains stirred. A gray shape ghosted through the door and padded over the fine Aubusson carpet. Ears pricked, the cat studied the silent room.

Waiting.

The air seemed to stir and hum, and the gray ears pricked forward. Then in one powerful bound, Gideon sailed up, up toward the priceless oil portrait of the abbey's eighth viscount.

Canvas shifted.

Pigment glinted.

And then the gray shape vanished within, met by a ripple of welcoming laughter. As he did, a single rose petal drifted down through a sunbeam, then came to rest on the floor beneath Adrian Draycott's feet.

* * * * *

Author's Note

Dear Reader,

What fun it has been to watch Hope and Ronan's adventures at magical Glenbrae House. I have been tantalized by Ronan's story for several years now, and it was exhilarating to see this tough, principled warrior in action, fighting for the woman of his heart!

If you're interested in reading more about the kind of life Ronan might have led in his own time, be sure to find *Chronicles of the Crusades*, edited by Elizabeth Hallam (New York: Weidenfeld Nicolson, 1989), which records the rich sweep of drama, betrayal and danger of those who followed the call to take up the cross on Crusade. For more technical details about the soldiers of Ronan's time, nothing can beat the Osprey Men-at-Arms series, in particular *Armies of the Crusades* by Terence Wise (London: Reed International Books, 1978).

For those of you curious to learn what a knight wore under his hauberk and chain mail (hey, inquiring minds want to know!), you'll find it all in the Osprey series.

Interested in details of military life in the thirteenth century? Try *The Medieval Soldier* by A.V.B. Norman (New York: Barnes and Noble, 1971). For medieval life recorded in all its rich, unforgettable detail, read *Life in a Medieval*

Village by Frances and Joseph Gies (New York: HarperCollins, 1991).

Even today *Macbeth* remains one of Shakespeare's most hotly contested plays. Likely the work had already been much abbreviated by the time of its first printing in the folio of 1623; worse yet, the additions of another writer were probably already present. A significant number of passages are corrupt and others do not meet the craftsmanship of the master playwright who finished *King Lear* during that same period. Immediately struck by possibilities, I have explored the theme of "what if": What if a folio prior to the 1623 printing existed? What if that folio contained uncut and unadulterated text approved by Shakespeare himself? But what if that text was stolen and hidden by a very clever thief?

You know the rest.

Just don't ask me where the idea for Banquo came from. Maybe Gideon.

If you have enjoyed *Christmas Knight,* I hope you'll drop by my Web site at www.christinaskye.com for excerpts of my upcoming books, reader contests, historical recipes and a backstage peek at the heroes and heroines I have come to love like dear friends. While you're at the Web site, take the haunted abbey tour—if you dare. Adrian will be waiting for you! And don't forget to send me e-mail at skye1800@aol.com.

For all those of you who ask about stories for Adrian and Nicholas: yes, they have already been written. Nicholas's story appeared in the Avon anthology *Haunting Love Stores.* Adrian's magical story appeared in the anthology *Bewitching Love Stories.* These and all my other Draycott books (*Hour of the Rose, Bridge of Dreams, Bride of the Mist, Key to Forever* and *Season of Wishes*) are available. Each book is a haunting mix of danger, romance and otherworldly interference by Adrian and Gideon. Let me know what you think!

Ever since Adrian and Gideon swept into my life seven years ago, nothing has been the same, and Draycott Abbey just seems to grow more beautiful with every passing year. I hope Adrian and Gideon have brought a bit of magic and high adventure into your life, too.

Now it's back to work for me. I've got a brilliant heroine who has *completely* messed up her life and a man who is sensational at everything except what truly counts: believing in his own heart. What a roller-coaster ride this Draycott Abbey book will be, I promise you. Watch my Web site for more details.

Meanwhile, as the Wishwell sisters have foretold, "The page is turned, the mystery clear." Enjoy the Highlands and all the magic of Glenbrae. I hope you find every joy during this special and wonderful season.

With warmest wishes,
Christina Skye

Moonrise

PROLOGUE

Draycott Abbey
Southern England
Winter Solstice

MOON RISING.
   Darkness creeping over high stone.
   He could delay no longer....
   Shadows draped the parapets as a ghostly figure emerged from nine-hundred-year-old walls of granite. Fear followed him, coiled tight. Fear always hovered close on this night when he faced the thought of what lay ahead.
   And the grave harm he could cause.
   Yet no harm would come here on Draycott Abbey's high parapets. Never had a mistake stirred any creature in the night, alive or dead. So why this deep uneasiness?
   Adrian Draycott, the guardian ghost of Draycott Abbey, scowled at the mist that drifted over the crenellated towers. His duty was clear. The words were locked in his memory, and he was prepared for all challenges and intrusions. He had never failed before, nor would he fail this night.
   Yet his fingers trembled beneath the weight of his duty. Clearing away all distractions, he focused his will.
   The ritual began in silence, cast in images, framed by intention. As the working of his magic grew, Adrian took force from the very stones he had guarded so fiercely. As on every Winter Solstice, his words would soar, casting out

the old year's ills and then weaving an intricate new spell
of protection over all who lived within the abbey's walls.

Hold in the circle.
Hold to the light.
None to cut, none by might.
Fair winds before morning and bright dawn to follow.
Hold in the circle.
Hold to the light.

The words came low, chanted in the old Norman French
learned at his father's knee, chanted as Adrian had always
chanted to summon the full power of his being for the task
that was his alone. Every year the old vows had to be cast
away, and new vows reforged, woven with words of power
and protection.

Now the time had come again. Adrian raised one hand,
lace cuffs fluttering in phantom winds. The words filled his
throat, echoed over the cold rooftop. Power blazed.

Hold in the circle...

The energy rose from the stones, climbed through what
little physical body he retained. Sparks flashed. Silver
eddies crossed the roof, dancing in the purple twilight.

Hold to the light...

A bird called out over the rolling downs. The moon's cold
edge dimmed behind racing clouds. Without warning something struck at Adrian. He spun up, into the chill air, drawing
lines of power into a shield.

Too late.

A savage force slammed him back against the abbey's
cold stones. His senses screaming, he was tossed flat,

caught in waves of pain. Space seemed to bulge, then tear, while dark images streamed past, spewing from the middle of the parapets.

What had he done? Adrian thought wildly. How had he erred? Was some fine detail forgotten or a portal overlooked?

But no, every phrase and gesture had been offered correctly. The words were given, the four corners cleared. Old fires put to the damp and new fire lay ready to claim in the last minutes before the old year's gates closed forever.

Cold struck at the bone.

Too late…

Energy boiled up, swallowing Adrian. Vainly he tried to hold sight of the working of his magic, but his eyes were blurred. Mars trine Uranus was a difficult time, to be sure. Yet never had he expected this kind of violence. Something brushed against his booted leg and he saw the keen amber eyes of a great gray cat, face to the darkness.

"Gideon, do you feel it?"

The low meow was sharp.

"Aye, worse even that what happened in 1540. I'll need your help, old friend. This is something I have never—"

The stones of the roof shook. The abbey's great clock stopped in mid-peal, surrounded by yellow fumes. Cold gusted, filling the air.

The voice that rumbled through the darkness made Adrian stagger.

"Well met, my old friend," the harsh whisper came. "My liege. My deepest friend." The voice grew closer. "My betrayer." A figure in chain mail stepped through the hole boiling in the middle of the roof. His sword gleamed silver in the moonlight.

Adrian felt the whole structure of his abbey shift, time and space distorted. "Stay where you are. *Whoever* you are, you are not of this place. Not of this time. I order you gone with all the power of cross and fire."

"Cross and fire. How quaint." The figure's laugh seemed to play over the yellowing fog. "And you gave all the opening I required when you took down your old circle of the last year."

"Only for a heartbeat," Adrian whispered.

"But a heartbeat is all one requires to enter. A single heartbeat to whisper a lie and rip out a heart. To kill the thing you love best."

"Wild talk with no meaning." Adrian launched a spiral of silver energy, only to see it swallowed instantly by the noxious fog. "Who are you who treads on abbey ground?"

"What, no recognition? You've lost your skill at spells, my friend."

"What man calls me friend and then attacks my land?"

"You don't know this voice? You don't remember Navarre, who once ran fleet to your bidding, whose sword was your sword by blood oath?"

"Navarre," Draycott whispered, unable to believe the word. He had dreamed, just for a moment, but to see his oldest friend again seemed impossible. Navarre had vanished in the Holy Land, dead in battle.

"So many centuries have passed…"

The warrior removed his metal helm and their eyes met, hammered darkness to restless silver. Adrian saw limitless hatred in Navarre's colorless, cold eyes.

The Wolf of Navarre, the defender of Acre and the Crusade's most fearless fighter, stepped onto the abbey's roof, into the strangeness of the twenty-first century. Without fear, he stood straight and pulled the darkness around him like a cloak while he surveyed the abbey's distant moat. He faced the clean sweep of the wind, rich with roses, frowning. "My first smell in seven hundred years." He drew a long, savoring breath. "I should have known you would have your roses close by." A smile twisted his lips, as hard as the scar that marked his eyebrow from the final siege at Acre.

1291.

A year of rare courage and madness. Nights of brotherhood. But days that ran red with too much blood, Adrian remembered grimly.

Something dug at his neck. Moonlight glinted on cold Damascus steel where the point of the great broadsword traced his skin.

The warrior spoke harshly. "Do not move, betrayer. Not by nerve or muscle."

And it was so.

"Do not magick. Do nothing save listen and then obey."

Adrian tried to move, but to his horror he was frozen. "*Pie Jesu,* how can you—"

"Silence! How long have I waited for this sweet revenge." The black-clad knight turned slowly. "Your abbey will fall, stone by stone by my hand. Nothing will be left save ash and gravel. Not even dreams will remain to warm you. When I'm done, no memories will remain, nor a soul to enjoy them with, for I'll have your soul, too." The first limestone merlon quivered on the roof and then tore free. A gray parapet crumbled.

So much hatred.

But Adrian's harsh cry was blocked, soundless beneath Navarre's curse. Even the great gray cat pressed at his foot could not hold against the power of his oldest enemy. Dark waves poured out of the unsteady, throbbing hole.

The moon seemed to stop in its course, the wind howling.

Frost glinted, where none had stood before.

"You have one night to study on all I've said, Draycott. One passing of moonrise and moonfall to regret your deceit. Then I'll have this house and all inside it, including your soul. Everything that you hold dear will be scattered to the four winds."

Adrian felt the force of hatred seeping like smoke from the dark figure before him. *"Why?"* he growled.

"Because you took everything of worth from me, all that I loved and then even my life. Now I will return that favor."

The guardian ghost of Draycott Abbey fought to hold back the images streaming from the black hole that gaped above the roof. Directly over the abbey's heart, Adrian thought in horror.

Suddenly he felt his energy fading, the power of his attacker too great to measure. Yet he made one last effort to calm and convince. "I took nothing from you, Navarre. I looked for you without cease, but you were lost. I searched the waves of wounded and I searched every ship. Already on that last midnight your own anger had destroyed anything of worth in your life. You'd sent her away the night before, driven in anger to ask the help of strangers."

"Stay," Navarre hissed. "Not *her* name. Not from your lips, betrayer. I saw you with her that night in the old spice market."

"You are mad. I was within my household all the night, preparing for the desperate voyage home, just as you should have been." Adrian's voice was filled with reproach, but Navarre did not appear to notice.

"And you meant to take her with you, of course. While I lay half-dead, covered by sand that dripped with too many slain Crusaders' blood."

"This is a lie. I saw her not. It was you who had already cast her out."

"A fine explanation to cover your own rank sins, Draycott. But I've had enough of your talk. You have until moon's rise. Consider your perfidy well and all you will lose. When I return, I will strip everything away from you."

The knight raised his sword, icy in the moonlight. The wind howled. A black dome of space roiled above the abbey's heart.

And then the Wolf of Navarre was swallowed up by the night.

CHAPTER ONE

Eight centuries before...
Acre
The Holy Lands

PHILIP OF TYRE, bastard son of the King of Jerusalem, whispered to himself as he worked. The city was in a desperate mood, caught in a nightmare following the siege.

Now the Sultan's forces hammered at the gates of the stronghold.

But Philip had little interest in Crusaders or holy war. In his great stone house near the market quarter, all was still. His thoughts were on revenge.

On lust too long denied.

The only thing he cared about was her, unmoving under his hands. With deep satisfaction he retied the woman's knots, making sure they were secure. When the elixir wore off, she would fight him with all her strength.

But then it would be too late. None of her screams would pass from the thick leather box where he had locked her. For months he had labored over the details. Now before the next rising of the moon she would be his.

His and no other's. Her two champions gone, old friendships shattered forever.

"Three ships rock at anchor. Three ships grand. Fly with the wind and ever west."

He whispered the words as he smiled down at her, her

eyes opening in confusion from the drug that still had her locked in its grip.

So beautiful, he thought, touching the raven-dark hair that felt like silk. A full mouth to make a man harden in lust. Oh, how well he would train her, breaking her to his will.

How sweet to see her fear.

"You will not hate me soon, my sweet." Philip, the bastard son of the king, scraped her tender cheek with his nail, drawing a bead of blood. "You'll do all I ask and more." Then he closed the lid. "Soon," he whispered.

And slid the iron bolt home.

HE HAD FOUND THE MAN three fortnights earlier.

That night his plan had taken final shape. The traveler was a mere barrelsmith, but the king's hated bastard saw the potential in the stranger's face, with features so similar to that of Draycott's imperious lord.

Here lay his revenge.

Here lay the key to his feverish hopes for the past two years, a way to strike at the arrogant Navarre through his beautiful ward.

The traveler was pleased to accept Philip's summons and more than happy to enter into a small intrigue, at the price of twenty pieces of gold.

Well dressed with his head beneath a knight's helm, the traveler walked in the route specified, passing the woman in the market and entertaining her in warm conversation, also as planned.

Anyone watching would assume the proud Lord of Draycott was about his usual business, speaking with the ward of the Wolf of Navarre.

And that was just as Philip had planned that anyone think.

"So simple to see friendships torn apart," he murmured pleasantly. "So easy to see all hope trampled. Navarre will not be so haughty *now.*"

He watched his two oldest servants lift the heavy leather trunk. If something moved inside, carrying the muffled sound of a scream, the servants were far too well trained to comment or care.

The ship was waiting, face to the wind.

Tomorrow Marianne of Navarre would be his, body and soul, plundered as the Holy Lands had been.

He turned away, touched a white damask-cloth napkin to his lips. The night was filled with sounds of approaching looters. He surveyed the empty room and bade his silent farewell to a life that was no more.

He lifted his sword and his pouch of gold and followed the trunk down to the stinking waters of the harbor and a new life.

The desert
Half a day's ride south of Acre

THE GREATEST OF THE Templars, the finest warrior of Outremar, lay unmoving, covered by sand. His proud steed had been taken, his sword ripped away.

His body shattered.

And now the Wolf of Navarre opened his eyes to darkness— and agony. His left shoulder was broken and his sword hand...

Too painful to think of it.

Tendons cut.

Bones crushed.

Gripping his side, he took a wracking breath and staggered to one knee, feeling the hot wind whip his face. He was alone, both Hospitallers and Templars gone, swept away before the force of the Sultan Khalil. Navarre stared at the horizon, all blackness with neither star nor moon, a mute testimony to the evil of men's hearts.

He closed his eyes on a shudder, remembering how he had seen the woman he loved in warm conversation with his oldest friend. How his servant had seen them enter the inn just beyond the spice market.

And how she had emerged, flushed and disheveled, two hours later. Navarre's servant had heard her words of love with his own ears, then waited to see the Lord of Draycott emerge only five minutes later.

The pain of Navarre's shattered hand was nothing next to the torture of betrayal.

He struggled to his feet, cursing his friends, his life and all that he had ever loved. In his rage he had swept through the enemy ranks like an evil storm, cutting down dozens until a Mamluk sword had knocked him from his horse. Then had come the blows, the agony.

In the wild rush for the city walls, he had been forgotten, left for dead. And though he would have preferred death, Navarre found himself alive.

Doubled with pain.

Crippled with the loss of his beloved and his friend.

"Take me, if you dare." He raised one shattered hand in defiance. "And if you dare not, I swear to hunt Draycott down and make him taste my steel. A curse on him and a curse on the stones of the abbey he loves so well. May they all fall to darkness." His voice broke. "And may I fall also."

The sands did not answer as Navarre took a clumsy step, nearly swept unconscious from the pain. In the far distance he saw the hot orange fires where the city burned. How many had gotten away, he wondered, safe aboard ships bound for Cyprus or Tyre?

He cursed them all, along with this desert where he staggered. Pain walked beside him. Revenge burrowed into his heart.

And somehow Navarre sensed he was no longer alone. Something else stirred in the desert night, barely visible. He heard a low chattering and the click of sharp claws.

"You ask to be taken," the desert whispered. "You *dare* us. Puny human fool."

And then Navarre saw the darkness open, billowing wide. As a vast hole formed, it reached for him, greedy and relentless, swallowing his growl of surprise....

CHAPTER TWO

*Sussex, England
Present day
One hour past solstice*

A BIRD CRIED IN THE high wood.

The night seemed to press down, fearfully cold.

Curled up in a wing chair beside a long oak table, Sara Nightingale twisted, her body shaking in the clutches of a dream. Branches tapped at the window. Loneliness was a taste that clotted on the tongue.

She shot up, fully awake, shivering in the sudden silence. Something too dark to be a dream tugged at her memory, daring her to remember.

To remember what? she thought, rubbing grainy eyes. She had had enough restless nights since her arrival in this ancient house to make her swear off caffeine forever. Everything about Draycott Abbey seemed to stir memories, history beckoning from every room. And Sara could never say no to history.

Pulling on her sweater, she stared at the papers neatly spread over the polished mahogany table. Draycott's library was richer than any she had visited, and she had worked in all the great libraries of Europe and the U.S. during her professional career. On the shelves around her hundreds of fragile volumes and manuscripts held the wealth of Europe's history.

The pages before her were direct from the hand of Leonardo da Vinci, one small part of the abbey's priceless collection. But she hadn't come to savor the Italian masters. A decorated FBI forensics expert, Sara Nightingale had come to locate a priceless vellum map and a captain's scribbled logbook. The discovery would help her government pinpoint a missing treasure before it fell into the hands of those with hostile intent.

In a turbulent world, money would always be used to fund weapons of destruction and the forces of hate.

Sara stifled a yawn, trying to remember when she had last eaten. Six hours? Ten?

The great English house creaked, settling around her in that living way of all old places. Right now she was the abbey's only guest, while the viscount and his family traveled in the Far East.

But in reality, she was no guest. Her weapons were the rare documents arranged over the table. But the right document eluded her.

Her hand opened on the polished wood, worn beneath centuries of hands. Sometimes at night Sara sensed old secrets in shadowed corners, restless images always at the corner of her eye.

The history of this house touched something inside her, reaching through time in a way that felt odd.

Familiar, almost.

The very idea made the Washington law enforcement agent inside her scoff. This was her first trip to southern England and her first encounter with Draycott Abbey. Until two weeks earlier, she'd never heard of this great English estate.

But another part of Sara's mind reached out to sift the shadows, searching for the reason the walls felt familiar, and why she seemed able to find her way without once consulting any floor plan.

Closing her eyes, she leaned back, a hand pressed to the paneled wall. Her fingers curved, tracing the outline of what she knew—knew *without* opening her eyes—was the soft wing of a smiling cherub worked in gilt and Italian plaster.

She opened her eyes. The cherub smiled back at her.

Her hand clenched. A dozen times in the past week the same thing had happened. There was no possible explanation except that stress and jet lag had fueled her imagination.

Nothing else was logical.

Sara Nightingale didn't believe in coincidence or prescience. She was a seasoned professional with a focused, analytical mind. She did *not* believe in haunted houses or any other sort of hocus-pocus. There was a practical explanation for her sense of familiarity with Draycott Abbey, and eventually she would find it.

But right now her government assignment came first.

During a mission to Hong Kong three years earlier, Sara had located a thirteenth-century manuscript describing the route of a family of Europeans returning from the court of Kublai Khan.

The family had been called Polo.

Sara knew well that scholars had begun to question whether Marco Polo had really existed and whether he had truly visited the Mongol court. But she had found a set of captain's logs in a private maritime archive in Madrid. The journals provided ironclad evidence that Marco Polo had duly been escorted back to the West as a passenger, reaching Venice in the winter of 1295. The baggage of the travelers was said to hold a fortune in jewels, the gift of the great Khan for the Venetian family's work over two decades in China.

The captain's logbook, documenting the last segment of the journey, indicated that the Polos had vanished for three days while the ship made repairs somewhere along the thousand islands of the Dalmation Coast.

Sara's job was to discover where the travelers had vanished. She had her suspicions that they had gone ashore to hide part of their wealth, probably carried as jewels and gold. The most logical spot would have been an island in the north of the Dalmation Sea where the family had holdings.

Her search had focused there.

Sara had been awed by the meticulous maps in Lord Draycott's family collection. An avid historian and art collector, the viscount had given her free rein with the collection, as well as his own research on a set of rare thirteenth-century maps overwritten by drawings and notes.

Fighting the distraction of the beautiful view from the abbey's leaded windows. Sara rubbed her cramped shoulders. Before her was a bill of lading and a faded map. As sleep dug at her eyes, she stood up and stretched awkwardly.

Pain shot through her neck. She had a sudden, agonizing impression of being locked in a small space, feeling her muscles knot as she tried vainly to escape. *Darkness. Stifling heat.*

Sara dragged in a breath, forcing down her panic.

Just another bad dream. She had had too many of them in the past few months.

Squaring her shoulders, she poured herself a fresh cup of coffee, stretched her legs and went to stand at the window. She knew this assignment was meant as a gift, recovery time after a difficult field assignment had blown up in her face. But how did you forget difficult choices and a partner's mistake?

Sara worked at the knot of muscles in her neck. Going over the details of that night wouldn't help her forget.

No doubt the residual trauma was the source of her strange dreams here in the abbey. The Bureau therapist had told her not to fight the process, but keep a record and look for recurrent themes or symbols.

A dream diary. How wacky could you get?

Sara blew out an irritated breath. She'd had enough counseling and questions after the shooting. It was time to move on. She rubbed her shoulder carefully, feeling the burn of muscles that had still not completely healed.

Outside in the darkness a branch scraped at the window. Uneasiness whispered along her neck.

More imagination. More pointless fantasies, she thought. Cradling her coffee, she went back to work.

HE WATCHED HER from the shadows near the doorway, unmoving amid the silence.

He knew the name of the explorer Polo. A contentious man given to excess and exaggeration, from all that Adrian Draycott had heard. Their paths had crossed once near Constantinople in the sweep of times past, and the Venetian trader had been flush with pride even then. If half the man's stories were true, he had led a life beyond imagining. Most certainly there had been a treasure, lost through foul weather and the cunning of fellow travelers. The whispers had begun immediately after the Polo family's return to Venice.

But the abbey's guardian ghost had no interest in gossip. If a threat did not focus on the Draycott family or their holdings, Adrian was unmoved. Yet now, because of Navarre's appearance, this woman was involved in the danger. Adrian believed there was more at work here, something hidden in her past.

He sensed that she was a warrior in her own way, betrayed and wounded. Doubting her own courage. And beyond that something deeper…

But he could see no more.

Meanwhile, time was short. Already he felt Navarre's anger move on the wind, seething like smoke. There was magic to be made.

In the space of a heartbeat Adrian was back on the roof.

He flung back the lace at his cuffs. It had been years since he had attempted to make the change that twisted every molecule into physical form. But now it was time.

Adrian focused, stilled his mind, began to will the change. He pulled light from shadow. Sparks spun from his arched fingers, still not enough to draw in the density of human form.

He tried again. Failed again.

"Damn and blast. What torment a human body can be."

At his booted feet a low purr spilled through the night, followed by the press of warm paws.

"I know well that I must concentrate, Gideon. I managed it before, but I've forgotten how to—"

The cat's body moved. Tail flicking, he made a calm circle around his oldest companion. Light touched the tip of the gray tail, swirled slowly. As the circle climbed, Adrian felt the thickening, the density, the too-solid force of a physical body pulled up around him.

And then the change was done.

He drew breath, physical breath, as he had not done for a scattering of years. A mortal body now stood where ghostly light had played.

"Well cast," he murmured, feeling the sudden weight of muscle and human bone. "You've done it, Gideon." Adrian stumbled, awkward in the flesh after so many years. "Strange to feel my stones underfoot. Indeed, strange to feel the outline of my own feet." He pressed a hand to the parapet for balance, then made his way clumsily to the steps. "She'll not believe anything I say, you know. She wants nothing to do with anyone."

The cat meowed.

"Of course I mean *she*. The woman in the library. The one who's done nothing but pore over our books and maps since her arrival. And I'll need your help to make her leave in case we fail, Gideon. I do not want her shattered soul on my conscience."

The wind stirred with sudden violence. The abbey seemed caught in darkness. Slowly the cat circled the black dome. Across the fragile barrier shapes swirled with angry faces.

Their voices cried out for revenge.

"We must hold against it, Gideon." Adrian raised one hand and sent a bright spiral of energy by his will into the leaking wound of the Other Place, from where Navarre had emerged. But the light was swallowed up instantly. The hole seemed to seethe and grow larger.

The cat moved closer. When he raised a paw, smoky waves flowed down. Clean gray fur vanished beneath oily ripples.

"Stay, Gideon. No good to try. Not the two of us alone. We'll need more to help us this night." Adrian drew a harsh breath. "With three together we may hope to succeed. There is power in the woman. I can sense it clearly. But first, I'll need to convince her."

The cat meowed.

"Yes, she is still awake, hunched over a pile of dusty books, looking for more of her secrets. Something to do with travelers and maps."

Comparative document research. Forensic map analysis.

Adrian shook his head. She had it wrong. She rifled through old documents when she should have been searching for a deeper truth, something beyond words or paper.

Something locked inside her own heart, though she knew it not.

Adrian sensed her strong magic, buried in the past where it could not be reached. Her silent resolve came from the difficult work she did. A strong woman but also a stubborn one, used to making her own rules.

A *modern* woman, he thought irritably. Just his luck to be cursed with such on this darkest night of the year. Was she strong enough to face what waited?

He was at the door, about to knock, when he saw her stare up at the aristocratic portrait of the eighth Viscount Draycott.

His portrait.

Before he could do more, her small communication unit chimed on the desk.

SARA SCANNED THE SCREEN of her cell phone, surprised to see the number of her superior back in Virginia. Given the time difference, her boss was working very long hours.

She took a calming breath, then answered. "Nightingale here."

"Harding. Everything okay? We agreed you were to check in every day."

"My mistake. I planned to call you in two hours, sir. What time *is* it there in D.C., anyway?"

"Never mind the time." Edwin Harding, Special Agent in Charge of the Forensic Analysis Section, cleared his throat. "Something's come up here, Sara. Today we ran our usual security sweep of the unit offices and found a tap on two phones. One of them was yours."

Sara stiffened, working through all the things he hadn't said. "So someone knows what I'm working on."

"Almost certainly."

"And that same person knows…I'm here. Someone *outside* the Agency?"

"We have to assume that's the case."

Sara shoved down uneasiness. She'd faced killers with hollow-point bullets. This was nothing to spike her pulse. "I see."

"I want you to take extra precautions. If anything seems wrong, alert me immediately."

"Understood."

"Any developments to report?"

"I've found another log entry and some early port documents. So far nothing pinpoints a location."

"You are going to have some extra help. I've just had a call from Viscount Draycott, and he has asked his estate manager to see you. Draycott says the man is extremely knowledgeable about the abbey's document collection, and he will have information you'll find useful. Ask for any help you require. Lord Draycott regrets that his business will keep him out of contact for several days."

"Understood, sir. Did he give you the estate manager's name?"

"Mr. Adrian, I believe. The connection was terrible, but I think that's it."

Sara noted the information and waited. She had been out of her office for almost two weeks, between research and travel time, and the peace of the abbey was becoming dangerously seductive after the stress of her usual assignments.

Especially the last one.

"I want daily reports, Nightingale. And keep alert. If someone puts the pieces together based on your research, he could end up on your doorstep with no warning. A treasure of this importance would be a magnet to any of our country's enemies. Stay sharp."

Then the line went dead.

THE WIND HISSED in soft warning, full of images from the Other Place, where Navarre had been captive for almost eight centuries.

Not dead. Nothing so bearable. Simple death would have been a better fate than the torment he'd known in that place some called purgatory and others called Bardo.

He had been bound in torment, held captive until a solstice like this gave him the means to escape.

Now it had come.

Death was far better than what Draycott and its inhabitants faced now, Navarre swore.

CHAPTER THREE

BARELY TWENTY MINUTES had passed when a knock at the library door tore Sara away from a map of the medieval Venetian coast. She checked her watch, frowning, expecting to see the abbey's meticulous butler, Marston, with more coffee and excellent pastries. Though the hour was late, the man was attentive to a fault. The stories she had heard about English butlers appeared to be true.

"Yes?"

"I am sorry to intrude so late, Ms. Nightingale." The man in the doorway was half hidden in shadows. He looked determined but just a little uncomfortable. "My name is Mr. Adrian. I was told that you worked late and that I could find you here."

He wore a perfectly cut black jacket over a black sweater that looked like alpaca or cashmere. Discreet but expensive. Almost too expensive for some kind of estate manager, not that she knew what kind of salary an estate manager made.

He wore no watch. No ornament of any sort. Only black. As he moved through the shadows of the room, Sara had a glimpse of high cheekbones and cool eyes that flashed with intelligence. He glanced at the maps and old documents spread on the long table. "Excuse my coming so late, but Lord Draycott told me to help you in any way possible with your research."

"So you have a particular document to show me?"

The estate manager turned, trailing one hand reverently

over a shelf of leather-bound volumes. His face seemed almost familiar, Sara thought. But where could she have seen him before?

"I have a ship's navigator's records of an eastern voyage in the late thirteenth century."

Sara's interest was piqued. "That could be extremely useful. Where is it?"

The Englishman turned suddenly, his head raised as if he heard some unpleasant sound. Sara heard nothing but the rustle of the roses outside the library window. Someday she would have to ask him how they managed to have blooming roses in the middle of December.

His hand clenched.

"Is something wrong?"

"Do you hear it? Very faint. Up above us." He moved toward the window, as if following the sound.

"Only a light scraping. It's just the roses brushing against the window. I've heard it all evening."

"I wish you were right." He turned sharply and the light from the overhead sconces outlined his aristocratic face. He looked very upset, Sara realized.

She put down the map she had been studying. "You think someone is up there? An intruder?" This was serious. She closed her books and slid them into the safe beneath the desk.

"I'm afraid so." The estate manager strode toward the door, sliding back into the darkness.

"Where are we going?" Sara demanded.

But she was talking to thin air. The man had already gone, leaving the door ajar for her to follow.

ADRIAN SCOWLED.

He'd managed to take on physical form, thanks to Gideon's help, but using this tangible body was far more difficult than he remembered.

There was too much weight.

Too much delay of thought to movement. It was fortunate the American woman hadn't connected him with the portrait in the library yet. Fortunate, too, that she followed him without question.

Acutely aware of the moon rising above the dark woods, he stalked to the third floor and pushed open the door to the roof.

The woman raised an eyebrow. "You're sure you know where you're going?"

"Trust me."

"Just for the record, I trust nobody." She followed reluctantly, her body alert for signs of attack. She was used to danger, Adrian noted. And she would need all the courage she possessed to face what was waiting.

When he opened the door to the roof, the wind slapped at his face. The hole was exactly as before, black images swirling from its dark heart. The sight filled him with fury.

The woman walked beside him and scanned the gusting darkness. "Okay, this has been fun, Mr. Adrian. But frankly, I don't see any problem here. The only things here are stones." She frowned in distaste. "Stones that are pretty dirty."

The wind shrieked. "That is not simple dirt. Nor is the roof empty," Adrian whispered. He leveled one finger. "Do you not see?"

When she shook her head impatiently, Adrian sighed. He had forgotten that mortal humans had such a singular lack of vision.

"Am I missing something or is this some kind of game?"

"Not a game, Ms. Nightingale," the abbey ghost said gravely.

"Special Agent Nightingale." The woman stood taller, her eyes wary. "And if we're done here, I need to get back to the library."

"Your work can wait for twenty-four hours. I fear you have a far greater duty that will not rest."

Her impatience was turning to something harder. "I've given you enough time, Mr. Adrian."

Intractable woman. How could he make her understand? A demonstration was necessary.

"One moment." He ignored her frown and pointed to the center of the roof. "Stand by this chimney. Yes, just so. Now raise your hand. Slowly," he cautioned.

Looking irritated, she did as he asked. "Well? What am I supposed to see? There is nothing…"

Her eyes narrowed. Then the words trailed away. Her glare gave way to a look of confusion as a blurred shape drifted over her hand. "What's going on?" Her breath hissed from her throat. "How did you create that illusion?"

"What you see is not of my making." Adrian watched another dark shape writhe free. To his horror, the center of the hole tore wider with every passing minute.

Navarre's gift, he thought grimly. Soon that darkness would swallow all of his abbey.

"I only pray you will believe what I tell you, Agent Nightingale. Even as we talk, time is running out. Within hours this house and all within its walls may be destroyed."

She continued to stare at her hand. "Is this some kind of biological weapon? Is it Chinese? Russian?"

"You speak of things I do not understand." Adrian took a deep breath. "Listen well, Agent Nightingale. I have need of your help this night, from moonrise to moonrise. Otherwise all will be forfeit."

She made an irritated sound, but her eyes kept returning to the strange darkness that covered her arm. "If I believed you, which I don't, what kind of help would you want?"

"To oppose the man who did this."

"So he's a scientist?"

"Hardly. A…warrior. Once Navarre was the greatest of all. But now he is changed, and nothing is safe while he walks the night." Shadows seemed to gather along the stone parapet.

Adrian turned to face her, his body rigid. "You are a woman who can match him in wit and courage. There may yet be a way. I sense he may have one weakness."

She hunched her shoulders against the biting wind, her expression wary. "Tell me what to do and let's be done with it. Where is this man? I think it's time we met this infamous intruder."

"I am here." He walked out of the darkness, broad-shouldered, silent, his features blurred by shadow. His eyes held lifetimes of power, but no warmth lit them. Chiseled cheekbones rose above a hard jaw and his full mouth hinted at an equal mix of arrogance and sensuality.

He ignored the woman. His focus was all for Draycott. "She doesn't believe you, old friend. Not much help when you cannot win her trust." He cut through a wedge of moonlight that left his stark features in sharp silhouette. "Not that anything of mortal creation can help you. Even now your precious minutes dwindle."

"Moonrise to moonrise, that was your word. Or have you broken a promise already, Navarre? Just as you did long before."

The air seethed with old angers, nearly dense enough to touch.

"If so, I learned from you," Navarre snapped. "Or have you forgotten your tryst in the spice market? The way you left me wounded in the sands outside Acre?"

"How could anyone forget?" Adrian whispered. "There was blood enough for a lifetime of memories. But I did not leave you. We searched all day and most of a night. You were nowhere to be found," he said fiercely. "And I know not what you mean by a tryst. There was no time for such things with the Saracens at our gates."

"Even now you twist the truth." The tall Crusader flung out a dark cloak, fingers stretched toward the abbey's ghost. "Enough of your lies. You will stay here, feeling the weight of all to come. You will watch, helpless, until you are swallowed just as I was."

Light shimmered, driven before a wave of shadow that wrapped around Adrian Draycott's neck. Inch by inch his whole body was engulfed. "Moonrise to moonrise. Then you are Taken," Navarre intoned. "By word and act so do I declare."

Adrian tried to answer that cold, imperious face, but no sound came. Navarre's magick was beyond measure.

Within an instant, all movement was denied him.

CHAPTER FOUR

NEITHER MAN PAID ANY attention to Sara Nightingale. A relief, given all she had to process.

The sands outside Acre?

Something about the words tugged at her mind. Why did they stir her even as she recognized how impossible the scene before her was?

But the Draycott estate manager looked sick, so sick Sara grew truly worried. "What have you done to him? He can't seem to breathe."

"Nor can any ghost."

"Very funny, pal. Now tell me what you did to him."

The tall man turned at her flat command. Surprise stirred in eyes as cold as the North Sea. "You champion Draycott's cause?"

"That's right. So back off. Otherwise I'll have to alert the local authorities." As bluffs went, Sara had done worse. The situation required dire measures, even though she was way outside her legal jurisdiction. "Trust me, you won't like being arrested." Her weapon rose, level with his face. "They'll eat you up in prison with a costume like that."

The man's black mantle seethed in the wind. "Costume? I have fought the infidels from Acre to Syria. I have held to the Crusade at the will of my liege of Aquitaine and Anjou. But now I fight a different war. This man betrayed me and left me for dead, and he will pay for it now. Make no more feeble challenges, woman."

Aquitaine and Anjou?

Uneasiness filled Sara. Her knowledge of the Crusades was a little thin, but the parts she knew began to settle into a picture. Yet that picture made no sense. How could a living man remember events centuries in the past? Why did he maintain this fiction of having crossed through time?

Either he was a lunatic or a soldier with post-traumatic stress disorder. Barring that, she was watching a complicated vendetta carried out by two bright but highly unstable Englishmen, complete with costumes, historical references and theatrical boasts.

But the huge broadsword at Navarre's side was most certainly real. Moonlight glowed along its patterned length. Damascus steel, she recalled reading, was the finest of its era, forged in layers that gave legendary strength. Well-used, too. Not a theatrical prop at all. The thought made her uneasy. Again.

She kept her gun level, her hand steady. "Listen carefully, Mr.— Navarre. That is your name, I take it?"

"Gabriel of Montford and La Varenne, duc de Navarre," he said, cool arrogance in his voice. "And you may remove your weapon from my chest."

"I don't think so. And I repeat—tell me what you did to him."

She frowned at the Draycott estate manager. "He still looks bad. We have to do something."

"I *have* done something." The man called Navarre crossed his arms. "I have bound him fast just as he is. He cannot move until I will it."

Because her confusion was getting worse, Sara buried it with anger. "Oh, sure. I *completely* believe that. And unless I get some cooperation, you're headed off to jail."

"By all rights, you should be equally bound," Navarre said slowly. "Yet you snap and growl, unaffected. Most unusual." His fingers rose, outstretched.

Sara felt shadows deepen around her. "How about you stop the amateur-hour theatrics?"

"Are you a witch to block me so completely?" Navarre's eyes narrowed. "Did Ylaine send you?"

"No one sent me. Now move out of my way. Do it very slowly." Sara stepped around him, her weapon still level at his middle of mass.

But somehow the man moved without sound, and she was pressed to his thigh as an arm in chain mail and rough leather wrapped around her waist. Then her handgun simply...vanished. "How did you *do* that?"

"With the power of my intention." The madman held her still as she tried to dig her fingers into the small nerve at his neck. "Your fighting is useless. Submit."

Sara blew out an angry breath. "Sure. Perhaps I should just ignore all my training and bow to you. I'll crown you King of England, too. *With the power of my intention*," she said sarcastically as she twisted in his arms.

Navarre stared at her in amazement. "You truly are immune. This merits serious study. But perhaps Jehanne sent you. She was always the stronger enchantress and one step closer to the dark."

He was serious, Sara realized. This idiotic man actually believed she was some kind of witch. As she looked up, moonlight shifted, tracing gaunt cheeks, a scarred jaw, eyes filled with darkness without end.

She tried her best aikido move, knuckles to the radial nerve. She felt the lock of his muscles and his momentary surprise. Then she gasped in pain, yanked back against his chest. "You can't hold me. I'm a special agent of the U.S. government and—"

"Agent," he whispered harshly. "So that is your work. Not as a witch but a spy. But this world of yours holds no interest for me. My only task is revenge."

When she didn't move, he seemed to sink into deep

thought. Swiftly she drove one elbow into his kidney, an advanced technique that bought a second of distraction, enough for her to slip free.

Navarre cursed softly and eyed her with new respect. "So your minders teach you the arts of war. I will know in future to be prepared."

And in the space of a breath she was caught in the air, flung back against his chest. Chain mail dug at her cheek and she fought a wave of dizziness. This was no amateur theatrical. *Something* had jerked her through the air and was holding the abbey's estate manager in a kind of paralysis. She seemed to have no power to stop the man.

"By my order you will remain here until I choose to release you. Keep your friend, Draycott the betrayer, company in these shadows."

"You're wrong. This man's name is Adrian. He is Lord Draycott's estate manager."

Navarre's lips curved in the hint of a smile. "Estate manager. Seneschal to the viscount. How amusing. He was always an excellent liar." The towering warrior laughed coldly and Sara felt the sound rumble between them. She shivered, unbearably cold. Unbearably aware of the pressure of their joined bodies.

"Why would he lie, pretending to be an employee?"

"Because it suits his whim. Because he is arrogant as he ever was, both at court and in all Outremer."

Outremer.

Sara took a sharp breath. That was the Holy Lands.

In the Middle Ages.

Again she felt a cold flare of uneasiness. "None of this is my concern. Play at your twisted game of revenge, but I won't stay to be caught in the crossfire."

"Too late to run now. And even if you could—" As Navarre stared down, their bodies locked in struggle, something like surprise flared over his face. "There is a depth to you I did not expect, lady. A flame, well-banked. There is steel in you as well. A worthy opponent, in truth." His glove cupped her chin. Ignoring her angry struggling, he traced the curve of her lip with the rough leather.

Gentle, Sara thought. *Gentle for so much anger.*

"You're wrong," she rasped. "Wrong about all of this. Don't add to your guilt by doing more harm that you'll regret one day."

"Regret," he whispered. "Already it haunts every breath, every waking minute. The thought that I might have found her first and stopped her infatuation—" Torment darkened his hard features. "And you who are so different, opposing me as ever she did. Brave without measure." His fingers opened. The gauntlet twisted and slid free.

Suddenly warm skin touched Sara's mouth, and the roof spun dizzily under her feet. Despite the cold wind, her face flared with heat. His fingers were calloused, yet infinitely careful, and she felt his warm breath touch her hair. Her body seemed to come alive beneath that careful brush of his fingers.

Metal and leather separated them.

Just as it had separated them before.

Sara dragged in a breath, shaken to her core. His gentleness was her first surprise, but her swift response was the second. And now this deeper thing, a knowing. Almost like memories...

Fear made her clumsy. She jerked backward in his arms, her palm cracking against his cheek. She saw the imprint of her fingers in a welt on his skin. "Stop it. You have no reason, no right to touch me."

Or to make me remember...

She swayed and felt his strong arms grip her. A moment later she stood alone at the center of the roof.

Somehow Navarre was now six feet away, pacing restlessly. "Too late for all of us. You have passed into our crossfire, and at the next rising of the moon, you will be destroyed along with every stone of this house. No words or human tricks can change that."

She tasted his anger, felt the weight of his torment, heavy in the silence of the night. Then he flung out one arm, his cloak a slash of shadow.

Sara stared at empty space. Shock and confusion kept her rigid, trying to breathe, shivering in the cold wind. How was any of this possible?

Swaying, she turned toward the estate manager—or whatever he was. The man watched her but did not move, pale in the moonlight with no sign of response.

Sara closed her eyes. "I have work to finish. None of this makes sense."

She drove away a flash of memories, just out of reach.

Grim and determined, she strode through the dappled moonlight that now felt cold and threatening. The door was open. Light spilled from the narrow corridor to the floor below.

Forget the man. Forget his torment.

Abruptly her hand struck a pillar. Cold stone dug into her shoulder. Blinking, Sara looked into the shadows.

No stone.

No pillar within reach.

She touched nothing but empty space.

And yet not empty, because something held her where she was, five steps from the stairway down into the house and that invisible barrier was as real as granite beneath her fingers.

She heard the sharp burst of her cell phone where she had left it back in the library.

Useless to help her now.

Over the dark woods the moon crept higher, a cold disk against slate sky.

CHAPTER FIVE

FBI Headquarters
Washington, D.C.

EDWIN HARDING stared down at the number on his phone's
LED screen. Why in the hell wasn't Sara answering her
cell phone?

He dialed again, feeling a jab of uneasiness. She had had
more than her share of stress after her last chaotic field
mission. She still hadn't healed from that night—not
mentally, not physically. So when the call from a joint
agency task force had come in, he'd sent her to Draycott
Abbey on what should have been a relatively soft assignment. And Sara happened to be the best choice for the job.

But now she didn't answer her phone, and that wasn't like
Sara. Had something happened?

He glared out at the lights of the Washington Monument,
dim in the distance. It was hardly likely, not in that great
stone house built like a fortress. Special Agent Nightingale
was probably asleep at her work or she'd left her cell phone
in another room. Yet neither of those things sounded like the
woman he had observed closely for six years. He had
secretly cheered at her steady progress through the forensic document unit, noting her eye for detail, persistence and
relentless curiosity. She had excelled from her first day on
the job.

Harding made a mental note to locate their contact in the U.K. and have him check on Sara's status. Maybe then this odd uneasiness would pass.

He opened a locked drawer on his desk and removed a single file, code-named Traveler. Inside were six photographs of a set of worn Chinese ingots, each worth a small fortune because of their rarity and historical significance. There had to be hundreds more somewhere, equally rare, equally well-preserved, said to be part of Marco Polo's treasure conferred by Kublai Khan. Through steady work over the past three years Sara had found documents confirming that the Khan's treasure existed. Now she was close to finding their location.

But Harding worried about her state of mind and her safety. She hadn't yet recovered from the shooting. Though they were tracking the source of the recent bugs, it might take weeks.

He snapped the file closed and punched two buttons on his secure phone, drumming his fingers on the leather blotter. His Bureau contact in London answered on the second ring and immediately went into action. Harding's next call was to an old colleague experienced in electronics and surveillance. Izzy Teague was an independent operator who often handled sensitive tasks for Harding's agency. If anyone could stay beneath the radar, it was Teague.

He answered on the first ring. "Joe's Pizza."

Harding's voice was clipped. "I have a job for you. I've lost contact with one of my people in southern England. She's at a place called Draycott Abbey."

"I know of it. I was there not long ago. Any signs of foul play?"

Typical of Teague to get right down to the crucial details. "Just a precaution at this point. But my agent hasn't answered her cell phone, and that's not like her. Where are you now?"

"Outside London," Teague said.

That left most of England, Harding thought. Trust Teague to be as close as the grave about his current work, which was probably for another law enforcement organization. "How soon can you make contact?"

A car door closed. "Roughly ninety minutes."

"Do it. Call me on this number once you reach the abbey."

Papers rustled. A motor growled to life. "What am I supposed to be looking for?"

"Agent Sara Nightingale. She's there doing research. Find her and see why she hasn't answered her phone."

"Copy, sir."

No extraneous questions. No excuses. There was a reason Teague had a solid-gold reputation for success. But Harding still couldn't relax, not until he had a detailed assessment of the situation at the abbey and the status of his agent there.

AFTER HE CLOSED his cell phone, Izzy Teague sat for a long time without moving. Outside in the darkness a bus roared past. A crowd of noisy college students milled drunkenly at the corner.

It had been nearly a year since he had visited Draycott Abbey, but the beautiful, rose-covered walls were impossible to forget. Izzy had a great deal of respect for Nicholas Draycott, the abbey's owner, and he wondered what kind of research an FBI agent was doing there.

"Not your problem, pal."

Edwin Harding was a cool operator. There had to be a solid source of risk for him to call in Izzy.

Because he was a careful and meticulous man, Izzy continued to sit without moving, watching car lights flash past. He pulled out his laptop, found the wireless connection he had been using before the call had come in and coded his way into the FBI's personnel files.

He didn't like going into a mission blind, especially when the name *Sara Nightingale* rang a whole lot of bells. As he scrolled through her personnel records, Izzy found the profile of a dedicated overachiever with some of the highest forensic evaluation scores in Bureau history. Impressed, he kept on digging and turned up two notes of citation for excellence by her superior, Edwin Harding. Everything added up to the picture of an agent on the fast track.

Right up until the week when Sara Nightingale had been assigned to work on a kidnapping case in Maryland. After an impressive piece of forensic analysis of the kidnapper's notes, she had been shifted to surveillance. Then something had gone wrong.

Izzy reread the passages, scanning the pictures of the crime scene, seeing the rigid stance of the FBI agent in question. Sara Nightingale's partner had been badly wounded during the confrontation with a kidnapper. The details were not clear. Had she slipped up and brought her partner into harm's way?

After a long time, he powered down his laptop and punched in the main phone number at Draycott Abbey.

No answer.

Izzy knew there could be a dozen reasons why no one had answered, but a thread of uneasiness worked down his shoulders. He pulled out into the rushing traffic of the M40, headed southeast, already playing out scenarios in his mind. Edwin Harding was not one for bursts of fancy.

Neither was he.

CHAPTER SIX

GABRIEL OF MONTFORD and La Varenne, duc de Navarre, stared at the night, feeling the old betrayal as freshly as if it had happened yesterday. The air had been hot and still, the smell of the battlefield like a curse. All of the Crusaders' force had been hushed, as if all knew a storm was about to break.

The storm had come at dawn, when the first Turkish archers had loosed their poisoned arrows. His whole family had been taken that day while he was sent to fight. Brothers, sisters, mother and invalid aunt, all were butchered mercilessly, and Draycott had allowed it to happen, coveting Navarre's land back in France. Navarre had seen the written order with his own eyes, dropped from the hand of one of Draycott's knights.

Not content, his oldest friend had plotted to seduce his innocent ward, whom Navarre hoped to marry once the year's campaigns were done. But she was promised in marriage to an English relative of the king, and only by his exploits in battle could Navarre hope to win her hand for himself. Until the king's favor changed, they hid their true feelings carefully, scrupulous to preserve the proper distance of ward and guardian in public.

Draycott had acted sooner. He had lain with her the last night of the siege and then spirited her away to some hidden estate for his further pleasure, spreading lies about her real location. The mere thought set Navarre's blood to the boil.

So the greatest knight of Christendom had nursed

thoughts of his revenge through cold, harsh hours as he faced the invading army. Before the revenge could be worked, he had been cut down, outnumbered eight to one. His hand shattered, his body broken, all hope was gone.

And so began his long captivity, caught in the darkness between worlds, while his hatred grew. Now, by Adrian's slip and Navarre's own magic, revenge was once more within reach.

Before the next moonrise, house, lands and the man would be destroyed. Navarre had the power to shatter, learned over the long darkness since his death, while he was caught in the gray purgatory that stretched between worlds.

He had no regrets, no second thoughts. Revenge was all he had left. If the woman chose to stay, she would die, too. He had no thought of clemency.

Somewhere in the house a shrill ring caught his attention. Although bound out of time, Navarre had watched the change of centuries and the passage of war and kings during his captivity. He knew the ringing meant people could talk at a distance, though how he could not say.

The ringing began anew.

The woman would not answer the summons, Navarre thought. Not until he released her from the roof.

He remembered her heart-shaped face and the keen blue eyes. There was surprising strength in her slim body and though she wore ugly clothes in stiff fabrics that would have called forth wild laughter in his day, there had been a deeper force that touched something old and half forgotten inside him.

But he had no time for weakness.

Navarre cast a spell of forgetting. When that was not enough, he threw out one arm and drew a circle in the air, sealing away the past. And then he breathed deeply.

All emotion was gone. All he had left in his heart now was the vision of revenge.

SARA STALKED THE ROOF.

She scowled and cursed and searched vainly, but there was no way to push free and reach the steps, and no other way down except along a narrow drain pipe, which she was not foolish enough to attempt.

The moon rose, a thin crescent between swift clouds. In its pale light she saw the glint of the moat and the swans plying its curves.

She had stopped trying to rouse the estate agent. He stood still, saying nothing, and Sara was painfully aware that a heart attack had never affected a patient like this. She tried to believe that no magic was at work. More likely it was some kind of stroke or mental collapse, though strokes did not keep people frozen upright.

But magic might.

She shoved her hands in her pockets and turned to pace again, stopping at the far corner of the roof. Maybe she could find a way down. There was a narrow balcony fifteen feet below. Maybe she could…

She muttered and turned away. Impossible to try. She was in good physical shape, but no climber. One miscalculation meant she'd lose her footing and end up a bloody mess on the cobblestones far below.

For now she was caught here.

Something shifted at the middle of the roof. Sara realized she had seen the movement before—and from that space of shadow came other shadows. An oily shape quivered and slipped down onto the stones. Behind that came half a dozen more.

Fear twisted in her chest. As she backed away from the restless darkness, something slipped by her feet, turned and rushed back, cold against her skin, leaving a sick stench of death.

Fighting nausea, she kicked at the shadows, only to see

them climb higher, circling her legs. Gagging, she swept at the dark things, but her hands caught nothing.

A sound brought her around.

In the moonlight she saw movement, a shimmer of sleek muscle. She watched rapt as a great black horse sailed through moonlight and hit the stones of the abbey at the gallop. Head high and mane flying wild, he neighed, turning mere seconds from the roof's edge.

But the shadows had followed, clinging to his back, swarming over his legs and neck until he bucked skittishly, his flailing feet dangerously close to the roof edge. The creature would die, cast over the parapets any second.

Sara moved by reflex, lunging toward the twisting shapes, driving them away from the horse. But they were more shadow than flesh, more imagination than muscle, and her hands clung to cold tendrils, sticky and foul, with nothing to catch and fling away.

The great horse bucked again, his massive hooves inches from her shoulder. Sara flinched, but held her ground. "Still now. There's nothing to fear but shadows, and you're too big and strong to be afraid of a few wisps of nothing." She grabbed at his mane, whispered whatever words came to her mind, stunned when the huge horse nudged at her. Then he neighed, drew his head up and pawed the ground as if in some strange recognition.

Then he stilled, bowed, facing her as if he meant for her to mount.

As if she had mounted him this way many times before.

Her fingers closed over the black silk of his mane. When he nudged her side, she threw herself over the powerful back as if it were the easiest thing in the world. When the horse danced sideways in the moonlight, Sara steadied him with quiet commands, feeling the muscles tense and ripple beneath her. The oily things were forgotten now, the roof a magical place that belonged only to Sara and the great horse who strained beneath her.

Over the downs a clock struck twice, each peal echoing on the wind. Moonlight brushed the gleaming mane. Sara felt a keening in her blood, a wild exhilaration she'd never known before.

Free. With the power to match the wind itself.

She crooned softly to the horse in a voice that didn't sound like hers, with a touch that knew exactly how to steady and calm.

Impossible. She had only ridden twice in her life.

The mount shifted in the moonlight. Sara felt as if one step would send her sailing out into the air, out into the sky with the ground stretching away beneath her. The thought left her giddy with delight—and sweating with terror.

Madness.

Pain struck at her ankle, talons digging cruelly at her skin. The smoky shapes had flowed up from the roof. Now they bit hard, clawing everything in their path. Sara bit back a cry of pain, clutching at the horse while the powerful legs lashed wide. She was flung into the air, stone and moonlight blurring beneath her.

Pain cracked through her hip. She hit the roof, and the world blinked out.

THE NEIGHING WAS HIGH and wild.

Navarre had not heard that sound for centuries, yet it caught him cold. It was a horse's neigh, caught on the edge of frenzy, the same sound he'd heard in Acre as the infidels closed on the Crusaders' lines.

But the sight of the creature on the roof robbed his breath. The great destrier was covered with roiling shadows, half mad.

Navarre knew but one way to defeat the dark shapes. He drew his sword, placing the flat of his metal against the mouth of the tear between worlds.

Light glinted against shadow, metal against cold space. The shadows shuddered, stilled.

Navarre moved closer, close enough to feel the prick of small teeth and hungry claws, which he knew well. But the blade did its job. The shadows strained, then slid back and vanished.

The crack of hooves against stone made the Crusader turn. The great horse neighed, ready to bolt. Only now did Navarre see something between the horse's dancing hooves, on the verge of being trampled.

The shape moved and made a small sound of pain.

The woman.

He lunged for the destrier—his own great war horse, ridden in three countries over a decade of battle. The animal reared up, warning him back. The Crusader ground his teeth, but slowed his hand and offered low, murmuring words of comfort until the dashing hooves fell.

"No need to fear me, old friend. No need to move away. It is your oldest friend, Navarre." The horse calmed, listening to the familiar voice. Then he backed up, the woman safe beneath him.

"I never thought to see you again. By heaven, there's no need to pace away. No need to skitter now. All is safe." The horse paused, listening to the Crusader's voice. His tail twitched.

Navarre waited as the woman groaned, then fought slowly to one elbow, her face pale. "What happened?"

"Best not to move. The horse is skittish and you're lucky to be alive."

"He threw me when those things..." She sat up carefully. "It had to be my imagination. If I weren't a fool, I'd say they were some kind of sickening creatures." She caught a shaky breath. "I tried to stop it—them. Whatever they were, they wouldn't leave. The horse was too near the edge. I tried to calm him. I slid onto his back." She closed her eyes. "Then they were everywhere. All over us. That's the last thing I remember before I was thrown off."

"You rode him? He allowed you?"

"More than allowed." She knelt, wincing. "In fact, he nudged me until I had little choice."

Navarre was speechless. He stared at the great horse standing still, awaiting the touch of his master.

"What's the problem?" Sara eased out from under the horse, which obliged by stepping sideways, completely calm and obedient now. She patted the dark mane, then rubbed her hip, moving stiffly.

Navarre noticed that, too.

He shouldn't have cared if she'd been hurt. Her pain was of no import to him. She was going to die soon enough.

"I asked you a question, Mr. Navarre. Why are you staring at me like you've seen a ghost?"

"Because no one rides this horse. Not man nor woman." Navarre crossed his arms. "None save his lord, which would be me."

CHAPTER SEVEN

HIS MIND demanded answers. "Tell me this again. You *rode* my horse?"

"Yes." She snapped the word. She was pale. Irritated. Her fingers opened, tangled in the long mane as she swayed a little. "I already told you that. You act as if he's royalty."

Closer than she knew. His noble Ferrant came from a bloodline guarded by kings and caliphs, more regal in his way than half the rulers of France.

Then Navarre had his second shock.

His destrier, feared and renowned throughout Outremer, lowered his dark head and neighed softly at the woman, bumping against her hand as though they were the oldest of friends.

More than recognition was in that motion.

Almost obeisance.

The knight felt a wave of disorientation, images flooding his mind from centuries before. But too much had happened. Too many years lay in between the man he had once been and the gaunt shadow he was now.

"Ferrant?"

The horse turned, flicked his tail, and Navarre started to growl more questions, but in the light of the rising moon, he saw the woman wince, gripping the horse's side.

She had a bruise on her cheek, a cut on one hand. Navarre was aware of her sudden exhaustion. With an intensity he had never felt in his life, he sensed the chill of her skin and the broken catch of pain in her breath. Yet even in her exhaustion, she did not complain.

Perhaps he had misjudged the woman. Perhaps she was more than Draycott's minion or spy.

No more time for questions. Her hands clenched, she sank against the horse, one arm outstretched for balance. When Ferrant danced lightly, she swayed and would have fallen.

Something stirred inside Navarre, something he had not felt for too long to imagine. It was the first stab of need, and an almost unrecognizable tenderness. But these he could not allow. How could he, when his chance for revenge was before him?

Softness would not serve him. The warmth of a woman's skin was useless.

He ignored the hated Lord Draycott, still motionless. All of Navarre's attention was on the woman as she winced, rubbing her shoulder. "You have been hurt?"

She blew out a breath. "I've had better days."

"Yet you protected my horse."

"Anyone would."

It meant nothing. It changed nothing.

So he told himself. Then she staggered. Her fingers slipped down the horse's back.

"Go away. Leave us alone. You're…frightening the horse with your anger and questions." She closed her eyes, struggling to stand.

Willful and arrogant, Navarre thought. She had the bearing of a queen.

And he caught her as she fell. Lifting her into his arms felt utterly natural to him. She was warm, and her scent reminded him of all the things it meant to be a man. When her breath stirred on his cheek, it pricked more memories, more hungers he had thought long buried.

Not buried at all, it seemed.

Ferrant neighed and bumped his shoulder impatiently.

Navarre smiled just a little. "Demanding as you ever were. Very well, we'll be on our way. But not just yet." Pulling the sword from its resting place between two stones, he waved the silver blade across the restless place of shadows, cutting the shapes that trickled free. They skittered away from the bright metal, as dark will always withdraw from light. After that Navarre set the blade on the stones so that moonlight pooled from its surface, sealing the shadows into the Other Place.

For now.

With the woman still in his arms, he mounted his war horse. "I've found the way of Draycott's castle. Huge, by all the saints. We'll manage the stairs if I'm careful."

They were a strange sight, the dark horse stepping gently through the doorway that led down from the roof. Navarre guided the animal through the broad halls, over priceless carpets and through the front door. Once outside, he jumped down from the horse. "Stay near, old friend. I'll have need of you before this night is done."

He could not yield, Navarre thought, feeling oddly disoriented by the woman's heat as he crossed the courtyard. He would put her in one of the beds in the gatehouse. Then he would forget her.

He found his way to a room with cut-velvet curtains. She made a small sound of pain and confusion when Navarre put her down on the soft sheets. She was already half asleep. On the inside of her wrist was a fresh scar, the mark of a bladed weapon. A second scar crossed the back of her hand just above the wrist.

What manner of woman was she?

He forced his heart to harden, to ignore the scars and the bruise at her jaw. She was nothing to him, merely a pawn in the sweeping game played out between two warriors. It was his right to treat her as he liked, even to use her now while she slept, should he so desire.

Heat stirred at the thought. Lust coursed through his veins.

Silent, he turned his back, pacing the room. He must govern himself, putting away all distractions. Yet when she made a small sound in her sleep, something made him stop in the bar of moonlight and cover her, then slip one finger to check her pulse.

Fast but firm. She had strength to match her courage. There was no reason to stay.

No reason except to watch the play of her chest as it rose and fell. No reason except to savor the faint scent of roses and cinnamon drifting from her hair.

By the bones of all the saints, he was mad.

"No more of your temptation," he whispered harshly, crossing himself against evil.

Her simple white shirt parted, its odd circle closings awry. He saw the curve of one breast beneath a bit of white lace, and the dark outline of her soft nipple. The sight flamed in his blood. He could use her, treat her like a slave of war and teach her the pain that came with betrayal. It would have been a fine part of his revenge.

Yet Navarre's feet did not move. His hands were leaden. Furious, he listed the reasons why taking her was his right.

All were true. And yet he did not shift by so much as a hairsbreadth.

She whispered hoarsely, twisting in her sleep.

Nightmares, Navarre thought. The burden of a guilty conscience, no doubt.

But the words she muttered and places she named made no sense to his ear. As her restless movements drove her across the bed, he caught her when she would have rolled over the edge.

His skin met the warm hollow of her throat, and beneath that the curve of her full breast. His fingers burned. By blind instinct he could not name, he cupped her pale skin, reaching beneath white lace to trace her heat, his blood goaded when he felt her breath check in response.

Take her, by the saints. Use her for your needs. Too long has it been...

The hot lust rode him hard then, visions of wet, sleek skin and panting breath. The blind mating and then the silken release.

He pulled away, his hand clenched. He schooled his face to a mask, angry at his loss of control. No, he would go and wake the dreamer. Draycott would tell what the woman was to him—mistress or common harlot, though she seemed to have too much pride for either.

The answer was strangely important to Navarre now.

He had to know the truth.

Outside the wind was rising. As he turned, Navarre saw motion in the moonlight near the moat. In the courtyard he heard his horse whinny softly in an old sound of warning.

Two shadows moved over the lawn near the water, well hidden from all eyes but his. His awareness of danger, always acute, became a hammering in his blood.

Draycott must wait, it seemed.

CHAPTER EIGHT

OUTSIDE THE WIND was rising.

Branches scraped the abbey's stone walls, while leaves rained down like dark snow.

Exhausted, Sara was only dimly aware of noise and a sense of anxiety as she twisted in dreams that felt old and painfully familiar, too real for the world of sleep.

The street was crowded with travelers and traders, priests and knights, but she had eyes for only one among them.

The knight in gray, sitting on a horse that danced in the sunlight. She was promised to an old man of power and wealth who offered gold to finance the king's expensive Crusade. But the knight before her was all she saw.

They were forbidden. They had no future.

But three nights before, though it was dangerous beyond reason, they had found a haven for an hour. Their tryst meant death to them both if the truth were known.

Now they crossed on the road, and smiled, acting for all the world as simply ward and guardian, bound by respect and nothing more. She kept her expression calm and full of dignity and spoke politely. He nodded.

But their fingers brushed, just for a second, when her horse shied from the crack of a passing cart. His callused hand gripped hers, locked.

And then they were apart.

Two lovers, forbidden. Forbidden to the man she loved with all her heart and every singing surge of her blood, all hope of happiness lost in the ashes of war. By the order of the king, she must wed the man with rotting teeth and coarse oaths who brought valuable alliances and lands in the south of France.

Marianne, the ward of the duc of Navarre, tried to tell herself it was God's will, tried to believe it was her duty to be docile and submit. But she had never been docile or good at convincing herself of lies, and she would not begin now. She had tried to find an ally among those at the king's council, one who would speak for her to reverse the marriage. The Lord Draycott had offered his help, but not until the end of the campaign season. Her father and brothers were all gone, dead in the sands of Damascus. She had no allies, no wealth.

The ceremony was moved, now one month forward.

She closed her mind at the thought. She would give her body to no other than her knight. She would leave in the silence of night and flee....

To go where? Who would take her in once the truth was known?

A sudden premonition sent her back, trembling, one hand to her eyes. She saw not a crowded market and a sunlit road, but a broad avenue wrapped in darkness and shadows. English oaks lined the way. Before her stretched chill uncertainty and sure death.

But beyond that a slight flame, and with it perhaps something more. Perhaps hope.

NAVARRE MOVED LIKE A wraith through the oncoming storm, sure in his skill. At the edge of the green lawn he stopped, remembering the woman's devices and the strange powers they conveyed. If these attackers had the same...

If they could see in the dark...

Well, then, so could Navarre.

He chose delay over pursuit, letting the enemy come to

him. He dug a spot beneath a mound of leaves, covered himself completely and lay still.

His waiting was short. The first man crept out of the shadows fifteen minutes later. Navarre saw a mask across his face, with strange, misshapen eyes. The man moved at a crouch, turning his head to right and left, peering into the darkness. The mask allowed him sight, that much was clear.

Navarre let him pass, whispering a small piece of magic to make him confident that his prey was weak and would be easily taken. But what the attacker did next surprised Navarre. He opened a small sheet of rigid paper, watching a tiny light that moved against a small map.

So this intruder knew where he was going. He had a clear goal, some kind of old document hidden inside the abbey.

Navarre watched the man put away the odd map and then he sent out his threads into the man's mind. Thoughts were Navarre's special skill after centuries in the Between World, where thoughts ran with the force of physical things. He could shape them easily now.

The man in the strange mask didn't hear Navarre slide free of his hiding place, nor did he realize a blade touched his neck.

Only with the sharp pain did he begin to struggle, and Navarre planted the seed of fear into his thoughts, building the terror. Flailing, the man tripped on a fallen branch, his mask torn away. He lunged sideways, fell facedown on the muddy bank. In the space of seconds he dropped into the swollen moat, swept away downstream.

IZZY REINED IN his impatience, staring at the tangle of stopped cars.

Another fallen power line.

Half a dozen police were out directing traffic, but despite their presence this section of the A21 was a nightmare right out of a post-apocalyptic film.

As another crew attacked a second downed line, Izzy picked up his cell phone. The signal was erratic in the storm, but so far he was running fifty-fifty on his calls. Punching in the number for Draycott Abbey, he waited through six staticky rings, finally ending in a recorded message.

He scanned his written notes, found another number, and dialed with one hand, watching a new emergency repair crew dressed in black slickers grapple with a live line.

"Marston here."

"Same stuffy accent as ever, I see. I hope you'll remember an old friend."

There was a pause, then the sound of laughter echoing through the crackle on the line. "Mr. Teague, I take it? About time you contacted your old friends in England. We haven't heard from you in months."

"Life gets busy. You know how it goes, Marston."

"No apologies are required." By habit, Lord Nicholas Draycott's highly efficient butler kept any other thoughts to himself. Past incidents at the abbey usually indicated that Izzy Teague's presence in the area involved more than a social visit.

"Since you found my cell phone number, this must be important. What can I do for you, Mr. Teague?"

"Izzy, Marston. Don't start mistering me to death again."

"Of course, sir. Did you require Lord Draycott? If so, I'm sorry to tell you that he and the family are traveling in South America."

"No, actually I'm trying to reach someone doing research at the abbey. An American named Sara Nightingale."

"Ah. The woman from the Smithsonian Document Division."

The Smithsonian connection was Sara's current cover, Teague knew. She would be good at the role. He'd watched a video of her at a high-level forensics conference, and she'd impressed him with her calm, organized mind and excellent knowledge of chemistry. She had the kind of tunnel vision that made for an excellent FBI agent, Teague thought wryly. "I've called the abbey and her cell phone, but there's been no answer. You're not there now, I take it."

"Sorry, I was in town stocking up on supplies when the storm hit. Heaven knows how long I'll be stuck here now. There are trees down everywhere, and most of the smaller roads are closed. I take it you need to reach her urgently?"

"That's right." Izzy didn't offer details. Marston was smart enough not to ask.

"I suppose if you have a good four-wheel drive, you could take the road through the marsh. Nothing more than a walking trail, mind you, but it will steer you away from the traffic. Then you can loop north to the abbey."

With one hand Izzy brought up a GPS screen on his sleek laptop. "Sounds like it could work. Where do I pick up this road?"

"Watch for a green trail sign about ten miles out of Hawk-hurst. You'll see the entrance just beyond the stone cottage with the twin carved lions. Drive slowly past the hedge and you can't miss it."

As the butler spoke, Izzy cued in the location on his computer. "Excellent. About how long to the abbey?"

"In normal weather, twenty minutes. In this hellish broth? An hour or even more. Mind the washed-out track above Lyon's Leap though. It's a nasty go there."

"Will do. Stay dry, Marston. I'll see you…when I see you."

"Which will be as soon as I can manage it, I assure you."

The line crackled out. Izzy glanced at the stalled line of traffic and then back at the GPS screen. He was still twenty miles from the point that Marston had mentioned. Until the power lines were cleared, it was anyone's guess how long it would take him to cross that twenty miles.

Meanwhile, rain slammed against the pavement above the rising howl of the wind.

CHAPTER NINE

NAVARRE WAS NOT SURPRISED that the second man was more skilled in hunting than the first. Behind a bank of trees, the Crusader watched a dark figure crouch low in the mud. The man moved a small black wire at his ear, then turned and dug a spot into a wet mass of leaves, hiding just as Navarre had done.

Except Navarre had already seen him.

The storm hurled rain, and the ground oozed mud. Water spilled from the moat, which had begun to overflow its banks.

Patient, Navarre lured the second attacker out of his hiding spot with the imagined sound of clumsy, frightened footsteps running down the hill. It was a trick Navarre had learned well: *always give your prey the thing he wants most.*

Even if it was no more than an illusion.

And this man Navarre wanted alive, not lost in the flood like his companion, so he drew him on, making him feel confident. The force of the stalker's thoughts was nothing before Navarre's. The Crusader had come from a different world, where thoughts had physical form. He shaped them easily now: reckless confidence. Then a careful image of sleep. Finally Navarre drove the man up the hill toward the abbey's stables, which would make a safe cell for his captive until dawn.

Thunder cracked. Something made Navarre halt, his captive motionless and silent. A heartbeat later, lightning flashed overhead and a heavy branch hurtled down exactly

where the two men would have walked. Navarre's skin
prickled, little hairs rising at his neck. Something about the
maelstrom felt nearly familiar, as if he had met such
violence of nature before.

For all his effort, he could not remember when or where.
Even his magic had its limits. And more important than the
storm were the answers he meant to wring from Draycott now.

His patience was at an end.

RAIN POUNDED AT THE abbey windows. Sara did not hear,
caught in a bright, hot place where blood welled over desert
sand, where knights raced under the moonlight and her
death had already been written.

*Images ran like fog, slipping through her fingers. They
left her cold, trembling. She wanted to run from them,
though she had never run from anything in her life.*

*In this place there was blood and death, hot sand and a
wind full of strange spices. There was a sharp beauty that
called to her soul, but a greater calling came from the danger.*

*She had no one to trust. Even now Philip's men hounded
her, barely hours on her heels after her escape from the
nightmare of his captivity.*

The trunk. The terrible heat of her prison.

*Shuddering, she forced away the memory. If she could
only find a safe place to rest, even for an hour....*

Her eyes blurred. There was no rest in the night.

*Not for one who had disobeyed a king—and escaped his
mad son.*

NO LIGHTS BURNED in the stables.

Navarre opened the door to a windowless room near the
back and tossed his captive down on cold tiles. As a precaution, he picked up the small pack woven of black fiber,
which the man wore around his waist.

Then he probed the man's thoughts.

Why have you come here?

The map. Upstairs in the library.

What about the woman?

I will kill her when I have what I need. She knows too much....

Navarre's eyes hardened. *Who sent you to do this?*

His captive moved restlessly. *I do not know. It was arranged by phone. No names were given.*

Navarre shoved the man facedown. Then he sent a final thread over his captive's mind and barred the door from the outside.

At the stable entrance, his great horse waited, calm and regal. There was nothing skittish in his movements now, no sense of further danger.

"So the troublemakers are found," Navarre murmured. "But who sent them here?" He stood silent, testing the currents of the night.

No other attackers followed. Were they here, Navarre would have felt their traces. He was skilled at finding signs thanks to the Bedouins who had taken him in for nearly a year after he was lost in a caravan. After his return, some in Outremer had called him heathen. Despite his lands and titles, most had called him worse than that. Only one had accepted him for the man he was.

And that woman of flashing fire and rare courage was forbidden to him by the whim of a king.

Navarre shook away the images, feeling old despair mingle with new fury. Caught between two times, he felt past and present flow together, merged in the chaos of the storm.

The wind was like a fist, hammering the trees as he crossed toward the darkened gatehouse.

Trying not to remember...

But the scream of the wind brought another wave of memory and the vision of a woman lost to him for centuries. The pain nearly crushed him, but he strode on through the wind. Draycott had shattered everything he cared for in his life. Now Navarre would bring this great estate to rubble. After that would come the greatest blow.

Not death. Nothing so simple. Instead his enemy would be delivered through the barrier, taking Navarre's place in the twisted loop out of time.

He closed his eyes to lost joy and focused on revenge.

THE WIND HOWLED, driving sand into her face.

She struggled forward with the sure knowledge that her pursuers were a mere hour behind. Her cloak whipped at her head and she prayed the storm's fury would hide her steps.

Forbidden or not, her lover would come for her. She pinned her whole being on her trust in him. And if Navarre did not come, she would die here in the endless sand, suffocated and buried. At least she would be free of Philip's evil hands.

She closed her mind to fear.

Drawing her cloak around her, she struggled on through the storm.

DRAYCOTT WAS STILL ON the roof where Navarre had set him, rigid and unmoving. With a hissed rush of words, Navarre brought his betrayer awake and back into time, back into the fury of the storm.

"What—"

"Silence. You're here by my wish. Don't waste the little time I give you."

Draycott's eyes filled with fury, but there was cool intelligence there as well. He bowed his head by a fraction. "As you wish."

"I want answers. Who is the woman? What binds her to you?"

"She is a visitor to the house. Here for work and no more."

"Liar."

"My thoughts are open to you." Draycott stood taller. "Read them now," he snapped.

"So I will, betrayer. Your deepest tricks won't hold against my mind."

And Navarre probed deep, found layers of memory heavy with love for this great old house. The force of it set Navarre back. Love for a house was not what he'd expected to find.

Yet a woman held sway in that powerful, complex mind, too. A woman with gentle eyes and a calm voice by the name of Grey. Draycott had sent her away for her safety at the solstice, Navarre saw.

She was not the woman from the roof.

Other secrets beckoned, secrets from centuries past. Friends lost and grieved for. Battles won and lost.

Navarre cursed, pulling away. He would not risk the softening that came from longer contact. "Who is she?" His fingers caught at Draycott's throat. "What is her bond to you?"

"Better you should ask her bond to *you,* Navarre. Can't you feel it singing through your blood?"

"What bond?" Navarre took a sudden step back, feeling the hot fingers of memory strike his mind like a harp.

Soft muslin. Sweet lavender in her hair.

Her eyes full of trust and vast pride in his deeds.

Her love, given freely and without limits. Saints, how it hurt him, feeling as if it were yesterday.

"No," he growled. "A trick of your cunning. Marianne is gone, lost to me."

"You can lie as you wish to me, Navarre, but not to yourself." Draycott's eyes clouded. "I felt the weight of her past the second she stepped on abbey grounds. Though I did not understand all, I knew the danger of it. The rest is for you to find, because I have no answers. I never saw either of you again, though I searched from Jerusalem to far Damascus and sent couriers from one end of Outremer to the other. Not even the captains in the ports had news of you."

"Liar. Just as you always were." Navarre's voice was raw with fury. "I came here to destroy this abbey, Draycott. Not for a woman."

"What you came for, Navarre—man who was once my closest friend and the finest knight in the Holy Lands—is known only to yourself. The answers are locked in your mind. Only your key can reveal them."

Navarre raised a hand, fingers open on Draycott's neck. They closed, sucking out the energy, making Draycott sway. Even then the man did not ask for mercy.

Navarre's hold tightened, anger and misery driving the need to hurt as he had been hurt.

Somehow Draycott stayed upright against the unseen wave of Navarre's fury. His voice came in a mere whisper. "Hurt me as you will, old friend. But what you seek is not in me. You'll have to find the answers yourself, in your own heart and your oldest memories. You can feel them stir already."

"More lies." Navarre's grip did not soften though he felt the truth rise within him. He hid that awareness, summoning his old anger. "You'll watch your noble house fallen to rubble and no way to stop it. That is the only truth I have for you."

Somewhere a low ringing cut through the silence. Navarre remembered the woman's small silver device.

And he realized he had a faster way to find his answers. He would pick them like hard stones from the woman's mind, drawing them from the silk of her body.

Whether she willed it or not.

He took time to reset his sword over the roof stones to ward against any intrusion.

Draycott watched him, his eyes fierce. "*Don't do it. You'll lose everything you were, even your soul, if you persist upon this path, Gabriel. Only a fool would—*"

Navarre turned. "My soul is already lost." One toss of his hand, one whispered phrase and Draycott stood frozen, silent once more.

INSIDE THE SLEEPING house, all was in shadow.

Every room held old secrets, Navarre sensed as he strode through the dark halls. Great power and love remained, along with terrible dangers over long centuries. None of that mattered to him.

He *refused* to let it matter.

The gatehouse was still in shadow as he found his way by memory. In a room with blue curtains he saw the woman's shape beneath the coverlet on the bed. He caught the restless rush of her mind with all its confusion. So many layers, so much uncertainty.

He found his way to her side. The woman did not move, though he felt the chaos of her dreams.

He leaned down, close enough to smell the scent of apples and spring in her hair. His thoughts blurred at the smell, and for an instant Navarre was in another place of hot sands and hotter skin, feeling a woman's sigh as silks pooled.

He drove away the image. His hands trembled at what it cost him.

Too late, a knife drove into his side and he was thrown forward onto the bed. By a trick of rare cunning, she twisted up and dropped him swiftly, her foot against his back, her knife at his neck.

In that moment, captor became the captive.

CHAPTER TEN

SHE WAS STILL SHAKEN, caught blind from sleep. She'd heard a creak at the door and gripped the sturdy set of nail scissors she had found in the tidy bathroom. As he leaned down, her tae kwon do jab caught him by surprise. It had been easier than she'd thought to force him beneath her.

Or had that been his intention all along? Lying prone on the bed didn't seem to bother him. His soft laughter only made Sara drive her heel harder into his back.

She drove the point of the scissors at his neck and tightened her heel against his spine. "Who sent you here?"

"I sent myself. As I've told your Lord Draycott already."

He didn't struggle. Probably he was preparing a countermove.

"He's not mine. And he's not a lord. Where is he now?"

"Still on the roof, of course. A little rain won't hurt him. And he is most assuredly a lord, though he lies superbly."

The man was insane. She'd have to subdue this one and then help free the estate manager, who had looked sickeningly pale. Probably some kind of stroke or heart attack. If she locked this man, Navarre, in the closet—

"It won't work, you know. I'm stronger and quicker than you."

She glared at his back. Two fingers at his vagus nerve, in an old Chinese *dim mak* move, and he'd be out long enough for her to apply restraints.

She leaned down. Carefully, her fingers closed on his neck.

He didn't fight her, which was beyond strange. Something slipped into her mind, an image of a quiet garden, ringed with trees in bloom, and the sound of birds. Sara blinked. Where had that come from?

His body moved as if in slow motion. He rolled to his side, watching her with each movement, and somehow Sara was powerless to stop him; her mind refused to fight, even when he rose to his knees and tossed her back against the sea of cool white sheets.

Her hands fisted. Her mind shouted in fury.

No words came. She simply...

...collapsed.

Standard evasion moves flooded through her thoughts, but she could not bring her muscles to carry them out. "Let me go," Sara whispered.

"I have not bound you. Not with hands or ropes."

His eyes stripped her bare, keen and measuring. He found her palm and pulled back the cotton cuff, turning her wrist to his mouth. "So much anger. So much certainty and determination. I think you must be very good at your work. Tell me again what kind of work that is."

"It's secret," Sara hissed.

"Witch or spy. Lover or lord's harlot. Or all of those," he said quietly. "Name one."

"Damn you. Stop—"

Navarre raised his hand, almost casually. Suddenly he was in her head, a tall shadow Sara could not dislodge.

She stiffened, expecting fury and disgust. Instead she found curiosity and a stream of images personal enough to be her own memories. She saw their bodies, thigh to thigh, breaths caught as heat drove them together in blind climax.

"Now you see it, too." His hand opened over her wrist, fingers slow and gentle. The heat spread over her skin and into her mind as more hot images raced to life.

They had been lovers. There were no secrets between their bodies.

Impossible.

Sara struggled against the yielding, fought her way to one elbow. "More tricks. You don't fool me, Navarre."

"There's no point in resisting."

"If you think that, you don't know anything about me."

"It is a waste of your energy," he said roughly. "I will always win. I am more than mortal."

"Magic again? That's pathetic." But Sara knew her voice betrayed the doubt in her words. "You're doing this for a reason. What do you want?"

"Maybe I'll ask you to halt your trust in Draycott. You'll find me a better master. I'll give you the things you want." His whisper at her ear was low and soothing. "Name your price. Lands or wealth beyond measure."

Not that Sara believed a word of it.

She closed her ears to him, but in silence the visions grew, two shadows mating, sleek and perfect. "Stop."

"It troubles you?" His eyes were unreadable.

"Of course it does. It's...unnatural."

"Mating is never unnatural."

"You being in my mind like this...*that* is unnatural. I'm sure there's a satisfactory explanation—and until I think of it, get out of my head."

"I choose not." There was the faintest challenge in his dark smile.

"Why not? What does it gain you?"

He seemed thoughtful, then irritated. "It shouldn't matter. You shouldn't matter."

"Then leave me alone," she said fiercely.

"So I've told myself." He sank back on the bed, frowning. "Yet there are questions that remain." His voice fell. "You have the same scar, the mark of the waning moon." He traced the silver curve at the inside of her wrist. "It was given when your first horse threw you. You were barely nine, so you said."

The words fed new images, dim and grainy. Somehow they had the unmistakable weight of truth. She remembered the sharp terror and then the blood spilling over a child's small wrist.

Her wrist.

"No…"

He didn't argue. He was too deep in her mind not to understand her fury and confusion. "The scar is yours. You can see that now. Why argue with me? I prefer this instead."

His voice turned rough. His hand opened on her cheek. Images flowed as if a tap had been thrown open.

The moon rising. Hot winds over hot sand.

A man's touch like velvet in the night.

For a moment Sara dangled, caught on the edge of re-membering. But the memories carried more pain than she could bear.

"We've both seen it. He was right then. Damn Draycott for that."

"You keep calling him Draycott. He's not the viscount."

"Most certainly he is." He stood up suddenly, his posture stiff. "These memories change nothing. You will stay here." A muscle clenched at his jaw. "Until I decide what to do with you."

"It won't work, Navarre. People will come looking for me. I will be missed."

For long moments he didn't turn. When he did his face was cut from granite. "A lover?" His voice fell. "No, I would have seen him in your mind. No one has touched you in long weeks."

Sara flushed at the intimacy of his words. "You don't know that."

"No? Your mind is like water to me. You feel this tie as much as I do."

"I feel nothing," she said wildly. "Now—get out of my head."

"I don't believe I can do that. Not now." He seemed angry at the thought. He released her and stood up slowly, his eyes shuttered. "The noose spreads wide, and there's no going back."

Lightning flared through the tall casement windows. She felt the force of his gaze in the space of that brief flash. Amid the anger she sensed his infinite loneliness. And then he was gone.

Sara listened intently. There was no sound of a key being turned in the lock. No guards and no ropes to bind her.

She sat on the bed, staring at the door. She had never been given to wild imagination, priding herself on good sense and excellent reasoning.

And yet she didn't want to move. For long minutes after he was gone, the scents of cardamom and cloves drifted in the air, rich and earthy as his touch.

The line between reasoning and magic was getting harder and harder to find, she thought grimly.

CHAPTER ELEVEN

THE CRUSADER SEETHED.

Striding through the dark corridors, Navarre felt the pull of images that mocked him, seduced him. He saw a woman's face, pale and determined. Over that face were features from another time. A mouth of strength and gray eyes of rare innocence, the face of a lover forbidden to him, vanished and dead centuries before.

Her death was beyond changing, he told himself. Revenge for Draycott's treacheries had kept his spirit alive over the long centuries caught in punishment between worlds. His own death would have been a gift then.

He sensed that gift would come soon. As Navarre strode toward the moat, the wind fed on his fury, screaming across the abbey walls. Rain beat at his shoulders and he smiled, glorying in the weather's very outrage. But even then memories stabbed, sweet with trust and longing. Memories of a woman with eyes the color of a summer's twilight.

The memories left him weak, fighting questions he did not want to answer. His revenge would target Sara along with the abbey. Even if he somehow managed to draw this woman away from the danger, how would he begin to be free of her in his thoughts?

Strangely, Navarre had never planned what would follow his act of destruction. He had never hoped for a future of any kind as long as his act of revenge was fulfilled. The shattering of his own soul seemed a small price to pay for the torment Draycott had caused him and those he loved centuries before.

But now he paused, rain drumming on his face, cold wind digging at his shoulders.

He realized just how lonely those cold centuries had been, watching history unroll through a dim window, but forbidden from having any part in it. Now the window had opened, and that same magic might hold a life for him *here* in this world's future.

Not dead. Not cursed.

The possibility left him shaken.

The storm roiled over him, tossing up gravel and broken branches. In the storm of his mind, Navarre felt the prick of some other intrusion. He recognized Sara's thoughts. By all the saints, she was strong, and even now she sang in his blood, stormed through his head, twisted his will.

He wondered if she knew what power she held. He decided she did not. Like any mortal, she did not believe in her own magic.

But their contact could not continue. He had to drive her from his mind before their link was too deep to be broken. He could not risk weakness now.

Flinging up his cloak, he whispered harshly, sealing her away from his thoughts with the mark of his hand against air. Yet the silver cord of contact between them shivered and held, drawing him to her like the north-pointing metal he had seen direct caravans through the desert.

Through their restless link Navarre felt the fury of her thoughts. Beneath that lay the weight of duty that tied her to her work. But he also sensed her curiosity about him, mixed with the half-buried embers of desire. The knowledge made him whisper a protest. He was a warrior and a mage, not some boy to be swayed by the beauty of a woman. Furious, Navarre shoved her from his mind with a final spell, tearing away every thread of thought between them.

It was done.

Separate at last, he stood sweating, face toward the storm. A vast sense of emptiness engulfed him.

So be it. Empty he would be. Lonely he had always been. Either one was a small price to pay for his success. He had given up homeland and friends when he left for the Crusades. After a decade of fighting, he had lost his family and his own life on those hot, deadly sands.

He had no more left to give up.

THE WIND CRASHED and banged at the old shutters.

The *crack-crack* of wood hammering against stone tore at Sara's thoughts as she struggled to the doorway. She turned to walk outside—and her foot stopped in midair. Nothing visible blocked her, but her body refused, no matter how she willed it. There was no passing beyond the threshold.

Damned man. Damned house.

She closed her eyes and rubbed her face, struck by exhaustion. There was a sensible explanation here somewhere. She just hadn't found it yet. With all her will she fought her memories of Navarre's hands, surprisingly gentle on her face.

Her struggle brought more memories.

The moon like a sickle in an indigo sky. Hot winds, hot skin and a lover infinitely persuasive, all too gentle. She didn't want to remember *any* of that.

But suddenly her old world composed of task forces and document assessments seemed to close in on her like a tunnel. How long had it been since she'd eaten cotton candy with sticky fingers or walked barefoot on a white-sand beach? How long since she'd seen her own smiling reflection in a lover's eyes?

Her fingers clenched shut. When had she lost sight of her own joys? How had her life become so narrow and governed by routine?

And why had it taken Navarre to show her that?

Staring at the framed abbey maps on the wall, Sara thought of her assignment, but now the old maps and yellowing captain's logs seemed part of someone else's world. Some new part of her mind hungered for hot nights and soft sighs, her hands raking a man's skin in passion.

And the man in those reckless visions was Navarre, softer somehow, smiling when she least expected it, conquering her with his ability to see deep and true into her heart.

Sara bit back a soft moan. Had she gone completely mad, driven to the breaking point by the stress of the past months? Was everything that had happened at the abbey an intricate hallucination?

Navarre held the answers.

And he was the last person she could trust to tell her.

All thoughts of the Dalmation Coast and Marco Polo's family home on the island of Korcula seemed to bleed away to nothing. Even now some part of Navarre stirred in her mind, making everything else seem empty and without meaning. How had he shattered the quiet order of her life, reducing her to this creature who chased shadows?

The man was unhinged, and she would be unhinged, too, if she allowed herself to believe in these hot fantasies he had created so well.

She needed to leave. Sara reached for her coat, then froze. No coat. No briefcase. Her cell phone was gone, left back on the library table. Even if she found it, it would be out of power by now. She grabbed the phone on the nearby chest, but the line was dead.

She had to find a way out of this room. Wind hammered at the roof, and something pricked at her neck. "Is someone there?"

She heard no answer except gravel cracking at the window. She felt the weight of Navarre's anger, which seemed to be part of the storm outside.

And then…
Nothing.

All sense of the man seemed to drop away from her like a stone into a dark well. There was no feeling of contact at all.

She moved to the door, reached out a tentative hand.

His bonds were gone. Nothing held her.

Free, she swept up her blanket against the storm, then crept silently toward the gatehouse foyer, braced for the lashing rain as she ran across the broad courtyard to the main house.

CHAPTER TWELVE

SARA WENT FIRST to the roof. Struggling against the wind, she tried to rouse the motionless estate manager, but neither words nor gestures seemed to reach him. There was nothing else she could do except call for help.

Back in the library, she found a penlight in the desk and tried her cell phone.

A small bar marked only a little remaining battery time. The landlines were still dead, too. She would have to drive to the village for help.

The wind howled as she strode to the door. But something held Sara there, uncertain.

It called her to the last of the maps left for her by Nicholas Draycott. They were still spread out on the long table, clear in the beam of her penlight.

The fragile paper showed the outlines of the island of Korcula with a row of hills outstretched like the wings of a bird. Their curve was very clear in Sara's modern topographical map, kept nearby for reference. Then she saw the single word on the fragile paper, barely visible after age and handling.

Gerenge.

In Mongolian the word referred to a mark of protection given to favored travelers by Kublai Khan. The Polos, Sara had always suspected, had carried just such a token of favor on their return journey. The name on Nicholas Draycott's rare, fragile map could hardly be a coincidence.

This island held the Italian's treasure. She was sure of it.

Her heart hammering, she gripped her cell phone. After a long burst of static, she finally connected.

"SAY THAT AGAIN. You found…" Static hissed and crackled loudly. "…repeat that, Agent Nightingale. Your connection…terrible."

"I said, it's on the Dalmation island of Korcula. There's a hill called Gerenge on the northwest side of the island. Two historically dated maps from the abbey confirm details I suspected from the logs."

"You think…authentic?"

"They are definitely authentic. I needed them to fill in the missing pieces. My other documents were incomplete, but the Mongolian word was the link I needed."

Over another burst of static, Sara heard Harding's quick, sudden laughter. "Fine work…anyone else but you would have taken a month…." More static crackled. "…have a man there before morning. I'll need…calculations…pack up all the maps for safety." Static cut across the lines. "The storm…bad, I take it?"

"Conditions are serious, sir. The power is out and I expect there will be flooding all over this area."

"Let me worry about that. You get…sleep…whole lot of people will want to shake your hand. I'll be the first to…" His words were swallowed up.

"Sir, there's something else. The estate manager has been hurt. Things are—strange. I can't—"

Static filled the line and she lost the connection.

She rubbed her forehead, feeling frightened and seriously out of her depth. She was an expert at electrostatic document imaging and infrared luminescence. She had highest skill ratings in marksmanship and surveillance, but the things she faced in this ancient house were beyond her understanding.

A tree branch scraped against the library's front window. Wind howled, tearing at a loose shutter on a higher floor.

A branch broke free and shattered the big window, raining glass over the floor. Sara gathered the priceless maps and swept them into the safe beneath the desk as curtains of rain hammered the room.

Against the restless sky she saw movement. Oily, clawing movement. Darkness twisted.

In a second the shapes were all around her, sliding through the window, over the sill and across the floor. The phone was still in her hands with only a slight charge left. She redialed with shaking fingers, heard a burst of static and then Harding's voice, sounding surprised.

"Nightingale, why—"

She had to warn him. "They're all around me, dark things. Things that I can't describe. Tell whoever you send to be careful. Watch the roof and all the windows. They—"

Pain knocked her backward.

Her fingers opened and the phone fell.

STRIDING TOWARD the stables, Navarre felt a sudden sense of pain. A weight centered at his chest.

More intruders?

He opened his senses, filling his mind with the movements around him, from moat to towers. He found no men crawling through the mud and no sign of vehicles racing from the distant road.

He turned, looking back at the darkened house, and the force of malevolence struck him like a blow. Dark forms spilled over the high stones in a flood, focused on the shattered window of the second-floor library.

Lightning clawed through the sky. Navarre saw the outline of a woman caught in their demonic train.

CHAPTER THIRTEEN

IT WAS IMPOSSIBLE.

Nothing could cross the warding of his sword. His sword was Damascus steel, perfectly forged. There were laws to the dark world, laws that bound its insatiable inhabitants, and Navarre had learned those laws well during his sojourn among the shadows.

But the evidence of his inward eyes was clear, the roiling shapes growing. Even as he watched in disbelief, their malevolence seemed to feed on the storm's fury.

Suddenly the black wave twisted. He saw the woman shifting along the wave, and his heart dropped. He raised a hand, tracing a command over the storm, but his spell bounced back, rebuffed. In the cold flare of a lightning burst Sara looked out over the darkness, saw him, struggled to raise an arm for help. The force of their eyes locked and sent energy surging, strong enough to bind them close and free her.

She tilted and screamed, plunging to the ground.

Desperate, Navarre looked away. As soon as the bond between them snapped, she was wrapped up in the black wave as before, pulled roughly and inexorably toward the roof.

He could not do what he had to alone. There had to be three to work the circling magic. The woman would be one. The third would have to be his sworn and mortal enemy. But how could he release Adrian, even for the space of a few minutes, after so many years of waiting?

Hatred battled logic, spilling out to cloud Navarre's mind. What point in helping this world that was not of his time?

High above he sensed Sara's struggles, her broken sound of pain, and the black, churning entities that swelled around her.

Revenge called to him, part of his being.

But Navarre found he could not allow the dark its sway. With an oath, he ran toward the house. His revenge would wait.

NAVARRE FOUGHT his way through the storm, one more shadow in the swelling darkness. Finally on the roof, he found his footing on the slick stones and brought Draycott awake in a stream of words that left sparks of blue-gray energy.

The abbey's guardian ghost staggered, squinting into the rain, one hand raised in shock. "Who—"

"Navarre, that's who unbinds you. Now that you're free, don't waste our time with questions. They have Sara. If we tarry, they'll have your precious abbey too, along with everything else within eye's reach of this roof."

"They?" Draycott ran a hand over his face, staring at Navarre. "Those things like smoke, you mean." He muttered a harsh oath. "So many of them. I'll hold them back with a spell of shielding."

"No use. This storm feeds them, and we haven't much time."

"Then I'll call the cat, Gideon. Together we—"

"*No.*" Gabriel's face was grim. "It will take the three of us to block this power."

"Sara is a mortal. What power has she to offer?"

Navarre didn't answer for long moments. "Her power is to me," he said gravely. "She grounds me, if I will it. With her, my energy will be tenfold." His muscles tightened. "If I will it so."

"And what is the cost of this grounding?" Draycott asked, always astute.

"The link between us cannot be dropped afterward. Once bound, we will always hold the awareness of each other."

"Even in death?" Draycott asked quietly.

"Especially in death."

Navarre spun, watching the edge of the roof. "There's no more time. Once she is within their world, she will be lost forever. After that others will come, flush with their success. They will pour through and their energy will create…" he stopped, shook his head "…disturbances beyond describing. The loss of this place. Perhaps even of this piece of your world, and all souls within it. I won't have that on my conscience." He glanced at Draycott, his eyes unreadable. "Will you stand beside me at my right arm? As we fought those long years past on Crusade?"

"I will." Draycott watched black wraiths begin to swarm across the edge of the roof. "I trust your strength is as good as ever."

At the edge of the roof, the woman was lifted, her body caught on restless waves of shadow. Her eyes were huge, filled with fear as she tried to twist free. When she saw the two men, she lashed out with wild strength. "Stop them."

"We'll need your help," Navarre growled. "Raise your hand to me. Hold your eyes on mine until you feel my energy."

"Hurry," she rasped, struggling vainly. "I think I'm about to be someone's dinner."

Far more than dinner, Navarre thought. But he forbore to mention that.

"Keep your eyes on me. Heed only my voice. Let everything else fade, Sara. Only my eyes and voice…nothing else matters."

As he spoke, Navarre caught her gaze and let the force of his summoning link envelop her. Her face went paler still.

And then her body went rigid. The link snapped tight between them, and Navarre knew the wave of thoughts and sensation that raced along that binding way. With it would come the flood of memories from long centuries. "You," she whispered. "I remember. You and I— We were…"

He ignored her panicked look, intent on building the bond until it grounded him for what he had to do next. When the bond was tangible, a silver outline against the shadows, he reached out one hand to her. "Take it."

She took a sharp breath, her eyes huge. When she was close enough, their fingers linked, and the very air seemed to crackle between them. She swayed and lurched upright on the roof.

"Well met." He turned to Draycott and felt the man's strong, cool grip. "Do not let go," he ordered both of them. "No matter what you see. No matter what you hear. Close your hearts and minds to whatever things they offer, for they will offer you much."

Even as he spoke the true storm began, a rage of fury and longing as the beings sensed they were about to be denied their prey. Images rained down on the three bound together, images that tugged hard and called to the soul's deepest yearnings. Unlimited power. Unlimited life. Unlimited adventure.

"Come with us," the voices whispered. "Never alone. Never failing. Our power will be your power in worlds without end."

"Hold," Navarre repeated, his voice hoarse. "Only hear my voice. Feel the strength of our circle."

He was less immune than the others, for he had come from the Between World and he knew the taste of its power. The things of the dark crawled in search of any weakness, any hint of temptation. Navarre felt them skitter and claw up his legs, over their linked hands, hammered by rain and wind not of any mortal sky.

The three of them were engulfed in shadows. Sara shuddered, battered by the wind.

"Hold to me," Navarre said, his voice raw with strain.

Any weakness now would betray their circle.

The shapes swarmed over Draycott, then turned. With a low roiling hiss of glee, they swelled over Sara in a wave of oily black.

"I'M SLIPPING—" Sara grimaced, terrified as the weight of shadows moved, pushing her toward the roof's edge. How did the other two stand this foul sense of invasion?

"I can't hold any longer." She felt her fingers tremble, giving way.

With a rough phrase of reassurance, Navarre gripped her hand and pulled her toward him, while Draycott offered his counterweight. As the men strained against the unnatural wind, Sara felt Navarre tighten their bonding, letting his energy flood into her, making them one. His mind settled into hers, taking over every corner and secret place. Color washed her face as she felt their contact become total. Hot and intimate, his thoughts poured through mind and muscle, bone and spirit. Nothing was closed between them.

She saw through his eyes and her own, felt his arrogance and the edge of his fear. Through the link, she also felt the cool steel of Adrian's mind and the duty of long centuries in protection of this house. Now that duty was turned, forged into the weight that anchored their circle.

And over that rose the blue-gray force of Navarre, the fierce power that locked them together as one. Sara wondered desperately if it would be enough.

SHE WAS GROWING WEAKER. The darkness had centered its attack on her now.

Through the link, Navarre felt Adrian's arrogant strength. He felt Sara's growing fear, and over that her sense of uncertain wonder at the joining.

As the hammering force of the attack grew, he filled her mind with images of heat and joy, drawn from their past. The distraction would hold her against the dark things, he prayed. To his infinite surprise she answered with images of her own, sharper still. Rich and true, they were drawn from her own memories.

Remember, she whispered, brushing him with her thoughts.

Yes, he remembered well that particular night. They had stolen from the camp and found safety in the tent of Navarre's friend. Away from prying eyes they had learned the joy of each other's touch.

By the saints, he remembered too well, feeling his body grow heavy with desire.

"You learn swiftly," he grated.

"I appear to have an excellent teacher." But she spoke through gritted teeth, trying to ignore the howl of the wind and the gravel flung in her face. "H-how much longer?"

Navarre drew her mind tighter as she swayed in the rain. "I cannot see."

He said no more. It took all his strength to fight the temptation to slip just a little and become part of that swirling, infinite power that welcomed him so intensely. The call of the dark was sweet, so fierce he could taste the limitless corridors of the shadow world that welcomed him by name.

That knew his weakness and his deepest temptations.

Join us. Be at ease, Gabriel of Montford and La Varenne. Make your home here, great warrior.

How sweet to let go, to slip back into that infinite belonging.

Dimly he felt hands clenched around his. Someone called his name.

"Navarre, you're with us now." Sara's voice was strained. "Remember that. *Listen to me.*"

Then Draycott's low growl. "Hold as we are bound to hold you, Gabriel. Turn away from their promises."

Their words reached him at the very edge of reason.

Navarre stared across the roof, feeling the pull of power, vast kingdoms of energy and freedom.

Then heat poured through their locked hands. The power of its light cracked through him like a burning flame, joined in the force of the three. The dark temptations held, fought the light, and his body and soul shuddered, a battlefield for the greatest war souls could face.

Dark or light. Good against evil.

Either one was his, simply for the taking.

He saw Draycott's eyes, grim in their worry, his grip like granite on Navarre's wrist. He saw Sara, terribly afraid but fierce in her determination, and from her came a deep, intimate calling to his soul.

He took a hoarse breath, felt the lure of the dark. Slowly he pulled back from it while the storm raged in fury at his leaving. Closing his eyes, he wove together the force of the three. When the power was fully summoned, fully shaped, he drove it like a sword over the roof toward the source of the shadows, adding words that came from no mortal language.

A harrowing wave of cries and shrieks and curses seemed to darken the air itself, while the abbey stones shook. But the six hands held together as the fury hammered on beneath lightning that scraped the sky.

Time seemed to stretch out, and Navarre saw a cold eternity that held no hope of any release....

CHAPTER FOURTEEN

Four Oaks Hill
Fifteen miles east of Draycott Abbey

IZZY TEAGUE peered into the harrowing north wind. He had followed the small track Marston had suggested, but the countryside looked nothing like the terrain he remembered from prior trips to the abbey.

Twice he had circled, following the readings on his GPS. Each time the track had faded away into the marshes. His third attempt brought him over a slight rise. In the light of his night-vision glasses, he made out a black SUV stopped fifty yards back from a tiny path.

No lights. No motor running and no sign of a driver.

Silently he left his car, circled through the brush and approached from the back, only to find the big Range Rover empty. The car was locked, but picking locks happened to be one of Izzy's specialties.

Once he was inside, he found the backseat full of expensive, up-to-date surveillance equipment, the kind that required big money and big contacts.

Powerful directional audio devices were stacked carefully beside a laptop and two wireless transmitters. Both transmitters were brand-new. So what were they doing in a stormy corner of coastal England, five miles from Draycott Abbey?

Izzy made a quick search for identity papers, but found nothing. No personal material of any sort had been left inside the SUV. He scanned the area and saw dim footprints, nearly flattened by the rain. As he followed a set of prints up the slope, something cracked beneath his foot. Kneeling, he saw a piece of plastic jutting out of the mud. When he wiped it with his cuff, he realized it was a broken microchip.

Izzy Teague raced back to his car, certain that Harding's agent at the abbey was in greater danger than anyone had realized.

DRAYCOTT LOOKED ASHEN.

Navarre's face might have been carved out of stone.

Sara looked from one man to the other, feeling the force of their joined will and the protection that surged through their linked hands. She forced her eyes away from the darkness that seemed to boil at the center of the roof.

She could feel the power of those shadows, and with the power came a sense of longing and temptation. No death there. No loneliness or loss.

And power beyond imagining....

Hold.

She felt Navarre's mind, powerful and focused, slip through her thoughts. "It is nearly done," he whispered. "Three tries, that's all they are given."

"Fascinating." Draycott's eyes held a wild excitement amid the force of his determination. "I'd count one try spent already."

"And another far from over." Sara tried not to flinch as the claws scuttled over her neck and into her hair. Then softness. Warm words. Belonging.

She relaxed for a moment, feeling Navarre, remembering the dance of their bodies by lamplight.

Yes, she thought. *This is what she wanted most.*

Suddenly Navarre's fingers jerked on hers, his mind like

a sword cutting through her hazy thoughts. *No. It is not me you welcome. It's them. Hold, Sara. The way is but the space of a sword blade and on both sides is loss forever. Look at me. Look into my eyes and remember what I tell you.*

Gasping, she turned her head and felt the false images roil in fury. In that moment she saw the shadows for what they were. Not Navarre's mind, but something cold, endlessly hungry to possess.

How close they had come to trapping her forever....

The darkness hissed and screamed. Then, in a sudden burst, it turned. Furious, it began to recede, slipping over her hands, flooding onto the roof. The dark waves poured back into the gaping hole while the wind shrieked overhead.

And it was done. The hole shuddered and then disappeared.

Navarre didn't move.

Adrian didn't move.

Sara bent over and was violently sick.

When she straightened, Navarre stood grave and silent beside the place where the hole had been. Only a faint outline remained.

"I'll do one last warding for safety." Navarre glanced at Draycott. "My sword, if you would."

Draycott nodded slowly. "It will be my honor."

Many things were said between the two men without words then, Sara realized. She only hoped that the hatred had not stretched on too long to be overcome.

A FRESH FIRE DANCED in the hearth, lighting Draycott Abbey's magnificent library. Sara tried to focus on the flames as Adrian worked the logs with expert hands, prodding the fire to crackling heat.

Meanwhile, Navarre seemed to move his hands across the broken window. Somehow the glass rose back into a solid layer.

Her mind recoiled even as the sight fascinated her. Navarre seemed oblivious to her stare, his powerful hands smooth and sure as he checked the antique glass that appeared perfectly whole.

"Is there anything you *can't* do?" Sara muttered, exasperated by the man's utter confidence and the sight of one more example of the laws of nature and science gone seriously awry.

"There are too many to count," he said dryly.

"Name one."

"I…" He studied the fire. "I cannot forget."

Nor could Sara forget. Her memories were suddenly too intimate. When she turned to walk through the room, her legs trembled. As she swayed, powerful fingers gripped her shoulder.

"Slowly. The chair is just behind you." Navarre's voice was gruff.

She heard the concern, felt his mind probe hers, checking the extent of her fear and exhaustion.

Beyond odd to have a man's mind prowling restlessly inside your own.

Stranger still to be able to explore his thoughts in turn and feel another person's memories slip through your fingers like sand.

And since it hurt to focus on the night's terrors, she simply shut down. With a sigh of relief, she slid into the smooth leather chair and closed her eyes.

Bliss to relax.

Bliss to be warm and safe.

A glass met her unsteady fingers, and she heard the rush of liquid.

"The abbey's current viscount keeps an exceptional whiskey," Adrian said. "Drink it down, my dear. All of it."

Sara swallowed, savoring the slow burn that brought warmth to her throat.

When she looked up, Navarre was studying her. Gravely he brushed her cheek with a linen handkerchief. "Your face is cut. You held well against the attack."

She desperately wanted to lean. To be weak and glory in his strength. But leaning wasn't in Sara's makeup, not even after a night like this. "I thought you said there would be three attacks."

"So I thought. It appears that our joined power drained them first."

"Thank God." Sara stretched her weary muscles, then extended her hands toward the fire that was rich and bright, for all that she was certain it was a piece of magic. The lack of smoke was a dead giveaway.

She turned, slipping into Gabriel's mind. "Well?"

She saw the answer before he spoke it. "Magic," he confirmed.

The thought didn't bother her as much as it should have. "I thought we were…lost."

"And so might we all have been," he said grimly. "It was well done of you both." Navarre's face was lined in the phantom firelight. He ran a hand over his eyes and then took the glass Adrian held out to him.

"Real spirits?"

Adrian's eyes narrowed. "You question every detail, I see. Just as always."

Sara observed the byplay between the two men, sensing images of power and pride in Adrian's mind. "I see what I didn't see before. Clearly, you are *not* the estate manager."

Sara felt him consider his explanation carefully. "I am, you might say, the guardian of this place. The task has been my duty and my honor for years too long to count. You'll forgive me the lie." A faint smile played at Adrian's lips. "So few mortals can see me that I took the opportunity for a little masquerade. My willpower has always been weak."

"That much I remember full well." Navarre took a long

gulp from his glass and cleared his throat. "What manner of spirits have you poisoned me with?"

"Only the finest whiskey from Scotland. Too strong for you?"

"Hardly." Navarre glared at the amber liquid. "It tastes passing strange, for all that. So many things different in this time," he mused.

Draycott finished the last of the whiskey from his etched crystal glass. "Men pay a fortune for such spirits."

"Men have always been fools," Navarre said flatly. "Consider us. Consider our ideals. What good did our great Crusade do in the end? Dust and blood, that's what we left behind. Precious little else."

"Perhaps," Adrian mused. "But our ideals *were* high. There must be some power in that." The abbey's guardian leaned back in a deep leather chair, studying Sara. "I don't mean to pry, my dear, but after what happened on the roof, I feel a familiarity with your thoughts. This comes from the link you made between us, Navarre?"

The warrior nodded.

"You have no family?" Adrian continued.

"One sister. We trade cards at Christmas, but not much else."

"I see. And your work remains first in your thoughts. Something dangerous, I saw."

Sara shrugged. She wasn't in the habit of discussing her job or her personal life. "Mostly it's simple detective work."

"Not simple at all," Adrian mused. "I can see that from your mind."

"Hard work that has defined rules," Sara amended. "Work that is assisted by long hours at a computer. It's hardly glamorous and rarely dangerous."

"But there are times of danger," Adrian persisted. "One of them occurred recently, I think?"

Sara looked down at the drink forgotten in her hands. She

turned away the question and the memories that came with it. Instead, she picked an image from the bond that held her to Adrian, seeing the weight of old responsibility. Right now he was worrying about missing stonework on the roof and possible flooding of the moat. He was also thinking about a great gray cat and a woman with auburn hair. "The woman is very beautiful."

Adrian grinned like a schoolboy. "She is that most certainly. You saw her?"

Sara nodded. "The gray cat seems to belong to the abbey in a way that I cannot describe." She glanced at Navarre. "And you…brood deeply. I think your right shoulder hurts, too." She nodded when he rubbed a spot near his neck. "A little lower and to the right."

He muttered something.

"You've never had a real home, have you? Somewhere you truly felt safe."

Navarre made a noncommittal sound and looked down into the fire.

"A place with a stone hearth and a pair of gray hunting dogs. That was your dream."

"You see a great deal," he said stiffly. "That home is something I never experienced. But Draycott has asked you a question. What happened in this recent work of yours? There was something about a woman. Three children were involved."

Sara felt her face go pale. Navarre had seen too much. Even now the memories from that day scraped at her like a raw wound. "It was a kidnapping. I was called in to investigate the ransom note and provide forensic evidence."

"Forensic?" Navarre repeated the word. "Explain."

"Legal and physical clues that help to identify a crime or criminals." Sara stretched out her hands to the fire. "My expertise is paper and other writing media."

Navarre considered and then nodded. "What happened when you were called to perform this work?"

"The kidnapper broke through a roadblock. My partner and I were the nearest agents. The kidnapper had taken a minivan with a mother and three children as hostages." Sara looked away.

Her hands tightened on the arm of her chair.

Navarre leaned forward intently. "You told the criminal you would make an offer to him," he said slowly. "You proposed a trade—you in exchange for the children."

Sara could still smell the dry sage and creosote inside the narrow Utah canyon. She heard the crying of terrified children. "He said no. I was working my way down from behind, into a position near the children in the minivan. When I was halfway there, he shot my partner." Sara stared into the fire.

"And you feel you were to blame. You chose to protect those least able to protect themselves. It was the correct decision."

"No one else thinks so. My partner is still in rehabilitation. He may never be able to use his shoulder again."

Navarre shook his head. "That is the cost of his duty."

Once Sara would have agreed with him.

"Those you work with blamed you," Navarre mused, "because your partner was hurt, even though you did the right thing."

"I should have had a better plan." Sara stood up abruptly, pushing away the memories. "I'm very tired. Now if you'll excuse me, I have to—"

"No." Navarre blocked her way. "I do *not* excuse you."

CHAPTER FIFTEEN

SARA FLINCHED.

Navarre saw the reaction and hated the knowledge that he had hurt her, even a little, but he meant to know the full truth of what had happened. "They treated you unfairly." His voice tightened. "Despite your courage you were punished."

"I don't want to discuss this." Sara stared over his shoulder. "Let it go. This doesn't involve you."

She tried to turn away, but Navarre's fingers curved, tracing the scars at her wrist. "Your life and all your past involve me now."

"I said, let it go." Sara pulled against him, and the sharp movement made her wince.

Gabriel cursed. He lifted her in one smooth movement and set her in the chair before the fire.

"Gabriel, I don't need to be *babied*."

"I will try to remember that." Ignoring her frown, he swept her hair back from her forehead. "Just as I thought. You are bleeding."

Sara blinked at the blood on his fingers. "I—I don't feel anything."

Navarre knew it was a lie. She felt heat where his hand anchored her cheek and pleasure where his arm met her shoulder. She was desperately trying to close her mind to him, but their link made that impossible. She still did not understand this.

Adrian Draycott held out a heavy piece of wool cloth. "Use this tartan."

Sara was studying the fire as Gabriel slid the wool around her shoulders and raised a soft piece of cotton to clean the blood from her forehead.

"Tell me the rest, Sara. What did these men do to you?"

Sara listened to the fire, feeling the weight of memories bleeding still. Why wouldn't he let her forget?

"Why?" He picked her thought from the air. "Because *you* will not forget. It gnaws inside you," Gabriel said.

"Stop reading my *thoughts*." She stood up suddenly, stiff and weary. Even now the memories were minutes-fresh, bleeding-warm. "You're right, they did hurt me. I was shunned." She smiled wryly. "In your time, it would have been called excommunication, I suppose."

His fingers curved, gentle but inexorable about her wrist. He turned her hand and shoved up the cuff, muttering a long, harsh oath.

The scars were paler now. They didn't hurt Sara at all, at least not physically. Only her shoulder remained stiff, unhealed.

She tried to pull away, but his fingers tightened. They loosened immediately when he saw her wince. "How was this done?" His voice was soft and very dangerous.

"In the crossfire. It was chaos—my partner panicked. Things…got out of hand."

That was the official version that had gone in Sara's report. It was the version that her partner had forwarded directly to Harding after their return. At the time, while he lay bleeding from a gunshot wound, he had made it very clear he thought Sara was a detriment to the Bureau, and if he'd had his way she would have been gone already.

Sara had every word carved on her heart. But she only shrugged. "The details aren't important."

"Of course they are. Right now I hear every taunt this

partner of yours made. Every threat. All because you saved the innocent ones rather than protect an adult man."

She'd forgotten that she couldn't lie to him. Not while this strange link connected them. "I had…a choice. It's done. Old news. I'm supposed to put it all behind me."

Navarre's face was only inches from hers, and Sara thought she saw torment there. It was as if he had relived her own pain that long day and night. "The man was a coward. A pig. He should be punished. It will be my pleasure, in fact."

"It's my responsibility, not yours."

He lifted her wrist, studied the track of scars, and then kissed the skin very gently.

Sara closed her eyes at the touch of his lips. The air seemed full, almost dense with energy. "I don't believe any of this." She shook her head. "Magic is for children."

"Only because there is no wonder left in your world. A true pity, Sara."

She stiffened. "Oh, really? We have trains and airplanes and fax machines. Why would we need wonder?"

"Everyone needs wonder. If you believe anything, believe in this." Adrian Draycott turned from the fireplace, studying the two of them. "I am not needed here, but one piece of advice I will give you. Time has shifted in ways of great possibility this night. Do not waste the precious gift you have been given, because gifts may be taken in the passing of a moment."

The door closed softly.

"I'm going, too," Sara said stiffly. "I've shared my nightmares. What more is left?"

Navarre felt her anger, her confusion. He could not let her leave with so much unsaid and undone. "There is more to be faced."

"You mean the shadows that move like oil? Things that confound every law of science? No more. I've had enough for one night."

His fingers curled over her hand, a restraint for all that his touch was gentle. "You did not flee from the storm. You did not flinch from an attacker. Do not run now."

He felt her pulse begin to pound.

"Remember." He whispered the word, slipping over the link between them.

"No."

Gabriel felt the force of her resistance, tempered by fear and old pain. He felt every struggle her mind made.

"No more talk, Gabriel. No more magic spells and memories. I'm too tired."

He shifted, his fingers curving over her cheek. "I could change that," he said softly.

She made a broken sound and shoved him away.

The force of her indecision was like the cry of the wind and Navarre heard every note. "I know, Sara." His breath touched her cheek. "I can feel all of it."

She closed her eyes. "Are we always going to have this…awareness between us?"

"Once the link is forged, there is no way to sever it." He spoke slowly. "It was the cost of protecting you and your world."

"I don't *want* it." She spun, her forehead against the wall. "I don't want to feel you like this. Make it stop."

"I cannot. What has been freely given in the circling cannot be taken back." It hurt Gabriel to continue, but honesty demanded no less. "Yet I do have the skill of forgetting. If you truly wish, I can wipe all the memories away. A still, quiet pool, as if it never happened."

She didn't turn, her body taut as a drawn bowstring. "You could do that, make me forget everything that's happened here?"

"I could. If you truly wish it."

She wavered, turning her face toward the dancing fire. Such beauty and strength, the Crusader thought, caught by awe and something deeper that he had not yet put a name to.

"Everything gone," she whispered. "Good along with bad." Then she shook her head. "I won't choose forgetting. Just tell me how to accept what I can't believe in."

His fingers slid to anchor her waist. Navarre felt her shifting awareness of his body so close to hers. With his touch, images spilled into her mind, part new and part memories. In the newness of their contact, she had not yet understood how to separate the two.

"From moment to single moment, Sara. Feel us, skin to skin. From there we will knit the past together and knot it to the future. This we can do, I promise."

His hand traced her neck.

The bond between them snapped tight, dancing and shimmering with energy forged of old joys and older pain. Sara's breath caught. Navarre saw heat spill into her face.

She tasted the passion that had slept for almost eight centuries.

"This is insane. How can I believe any of it?"

"Believe," Gabriel whispered.

She started to pull away.

And then with a broken sigh she turned. Very carefully she set one palm against his chest.

The simple gesture was like the blow of a sword. Navarre flinched at the force of it, and she missed none of his response, her hand sliding up his chest. He read her emotion in her eyes and through the dancing thread between them.

Her eyes widened, dark with wonder. "So much is here. So much that feels real to me." Her fingers traced his locked jaw. Her heat was already seducing him.

She drew a low sigh and pulled him closer. "I want you touching me." Her mouth brushed his, loosing a wave of raw hunger. Time seemed to bend and the room seemed to stretch, vast with energy, rich with memories.

Navarre forced his muscles not to move, kept his hands at his sides so he would not take. Taking would have been easy, and he did not want the easy way. Not with this woman.

He drew his thoughts back, hiding the force of his temptation.

"I can see now." She moved closer. "You're afraid you will hurt me. That we will somehow be betrayed as we were in the past."

She shivered with sudden memories of heat and terror. "I remember he had ropes to tie me and a drug. He put me inside some kind of trunk."

Navarre's hands gripped her shoulders. "You remember this?"

She nodded blindly. "I fought, but he had two other men to help him."

"You see—and yet I cannot? You are certain?"

"The images are too real to doubt. It was stifling, Gabriel."

His body was rigid with tension. "Not Adrian? He did not take you?"

"No, another. The name Philip is all I remember."

Navarre whispered a graphic oath. "I should have known. What happened to you then?"

"My nails broke and my fingers bled from my fight to escape. How much I prayed for you to come—"

Her words broke Gabriel's heart. "And I should have, my love. I was a fool of the worst sort."

"This man had great power. A very twisted man. I can see his face now. He wanted—" Her fingers closed to fists.

Gabriel didn't need her to finish. The image of her captor was blindingly clear in his mind. "Philip, bastard son of the king. The craven blackguard. If only I had known."

He held her while she shuddered, his hand in her hair.

And then she pulled away. Her face turned up to his. "I want your skin against me, Gabriel. I want to feel heat, not cold fear." She bit her lip, uncertain. Her hand closed on the smooth wool of his cloak.

She took another slow step toward him. Their bodies met.

Dizzy with hunger, Navarre summoned the willpower not to grip and seize, drinking from the well of memories.

"You won't make this easy, will you?"

His hands clenched. "I think not."

"For a man who believes he is evil, you are full of goodness."

"What goodness?" The knight closed away the thought of her body, the scent of her hair. When her tongue brushed his mouth, he closed away that sweet heat, too.

The pressure of her breasts was beyond even his control to resist. Blinded by hunger, his hands speared into her soft hair.

Sara bit his lip gently and slid her body against his with a sigh. "I loved you then, Gabriel. I see it clearly, even if you can't." She pushed him back against the wall. "Now be quiet and I'll make us both remember."

CHAPTER SIXTEEN

HE WAS A MAN well versed in dealing out death but Sara had never felt safer in her life.

Through the link so much was clear now. The scattered images of horses and the smell of spices on a hot wind made perfect sense. They had been betrayed in an age of peril and war. Now they were given a second chance, even if it lasted only an hour or a night.

He didn't answer. His eyes were still haunted by what she had just told him.

She touched his jaw, forcing his gaze to hers. "I don't know if this is love, Gabriel. I don't know how we came to be here after centuries have passed or what the future holds. But I'm not going to play fair tonight." She let her desire spill between them as she explored the heat of his mouth. She found the taut muscles of his waist and slid her body closer, hearing his low oath. Her hunger became his, prowling and goading.

No going back.

She felt her buttons slide free, felt the tartan fall. Her damp clothes slid away without any help, tossed across the thick rug.

Her startled question faded into a laugh. "Magic? Will I ever get used to this?"

"I hope not. I hope it will always be a wonder to you," Navarre said roughly.

But it was not a magic of his working that bound them.

It was an older magic, cast up by desire worked in the truth of love.

Their love had been lost, blown through their fingers like sand. Now a new chance was given to them when least expected.

Though she didn't understand the forces at work, Sara wouldn't risk losing him again. She tugged at his clothes, unfamiliar with the ties and bindings of his age.

He spared them both, shrugging free of wool and linen with a muttered phrase of power.

Her breath caught when she looked upon him, hard chest and lean muscle. He was all planes and shadows in the glow of phantom firelight. Stirred by the sight, she leaned down to explore with mouth and fingers.

He whispered her name. His fingers opened, twisting in her hair. He pulled her mouth to his for a kiss that held an edge of violence. "You steal my breath."

She closed her eyes when his tongue found her tight, aching nipples. His hand moved over her stomach, tracing dark curls slick from desire. He pressed slowly inside and Sara felt the world blur.

Moving deeper, he lifted her, met her with his fingers. Her breath caught at a wave of sharp pleasure and a hot sense of remembering.

Coming home, she thought.

Finding his arms after so many years.

He bit the curve of her shoulder and Sara felt her body bow, nerves stretched to breaking beneath the certain fingers that slipped and teased. He watched her as his fingers slid deep. He whispered her name as he slid inside her again. Dizzy, she felt the hammer of his heart in response. And then he stroked her, fully sheathed inside her.

She felt his heartbeat as she came apart, locked in a breathless climax. He drove her up again, blood racing, skin hot. She gasped his name and drove her nails into his shoulders as he shifted to one knee before her, then leaned to taste her, slowly and well.

No more, she thought.

Far more, he answered, showing her a new heat beneath his lips and hot tongue, the world gone white and blind. He pulled her against his mouth, gripping her hips with his hands while she shuddered at the tracing of his tongue, sensing he would not be denied.

Trust me, Sara.

Strangely she did.

Feel this joining.

With every grain of her being, she did.

Come apart for me now.

That she did, too, shaken even as she was protected, caught against his body when she might have fallen. Her arms wrapped around his neck as she felt him lift her.

Soft carpet at her back. Skin to hot skin, naked on the thick wool.

And then Gabriel's body above her, tight with control.

The low whisper of her name. His heat at her thighs as he spread her. The first giddy shock of his slow, powerful entry.

His body rose above her. His rigid length pressed to fill her. Sara shot to another effortless climax, matched by every stroke he made inside her. She called his name.

Falling, falling.

There was no hurry in his taking, only certain familiarity, pulling the thread of thought between them so tight that it quivered. Over the hammer of her desire, she felt logic slowly return.

"Gabriel?"

His eyes were dark, his body rigid in the force of his control.

She slid her hand between them, feeling the outline of their bodies, and he shuddered at her intimate touch. Some part of her drew on memories, given in the wake of their binding on the roof. She had seen enough to remember how she had touched him long before. He had protected her, defended her and finally lost her through an act of betrayal. This much Sara had seen clearly.

She bit his shoulder, pulling him with her as energy coiled and snapped.

His hands tightened. His lips nuzzled her breast, and suddenly she tensed, caught in the sure rush of another climax. This time Sara slid her legs around his waist, drawing him down to her, welcoming his body and his need.

So much pain in him still.

She took him just as he was, with all his shadows and regrets. With her love she gave him back the man he'd been before his losses, whole again, perfect in her memory.

His breath came harshly. She drove against him, gripped him tightly, matched in spirit and flesh. Her legs locked at his waist, and her body opened to him completely as he threw his head back.

Engulfed in dark pleasure, bodies taut, they felt the shattering heat of their joining, denied them for long centuries. His name was on Sara's lips as she fell.

SOMEONE MOVED.

Someone sighed.

Dim sounds followed. Not English. She struggled to hear and understand.

"Dearest love."

She tried to move and found it beyond her. With great effort Sara forced open one eye. Their clothes lay scattered across the library's thick rug while the fire danced. Gabriel had the mark of her nails on his neck and the smile of a man well pleasured. *Gorgeous,* she thought, *with his long hair tangled and his eyes glinting with secrets.*

She caught a sharp breath to feel him harden inside her again. Her eyebrow rose. "That qualifies as impressive."

"No more than you, my heart." Gabriel withdrew and then traced the tight line of her pink nipple. His tongue followed the same slow path, then moved across her stomach and down to her thighs.

She shuddered. "You'll kill me," she whispered breathlessly.

Sighing when he came inside her again.

"Then we'll die together," he said roughly. The heat spun up, bright like silver, new like dawn, gripping them again.

MUCH LATER GABRIEL watched her sleep, thinking on the odd ripples of time and the strange, unpredictable network of life. He had thought his ward infatuated, betrayed into an act of wantonness by his oldest friend. Now Gabriel knew that was a lie. His ward had not betrayed him. Nor had his friend.

Instead a cunning man had taken her against her will. Gabriel suspected that Philip had worked evidence to suggest that Draycott had been involved, though he could not be certain of how it was done.

He closed his eyes. He had been so quick to hate, to believe the worst of those he should have trusted. Such a fool.

And yet…

She was here beside him. Possibilities were given, it seemed.

Miracles were granted.

She had been the daughter of a trader long centuries in the past. Before her father's death she had studied beside him, poring over maps of all the old caravan routes. Even as a girl she had heard legends of the wealthy empire that lay far to the east. Gabriel wondered how much of that knowledge had remained, aiding her search at Draycott.

Possibilities.

Miracles.

He slid a worn metal cross around her neck. "Keep this,"

he whispered, hearing her sleepy sigh. He kissed her hand. *Wear it and remember me, Sara.*

He felt her sleepy agreement, a warm sigh in his mind as she tumbled back into dreams.

Happy dreams this time.

He was content. Far more than content, the warrior of Outremer realized as her thigh slid across his and her fingers eased through his hair.

Love is here, he thought in wonder.

And love was a force to rock kingdoms and shift castles. More powerful than any skill of siege or sword.

After so many centuries, to feel her again, her breath against his chest, her hand curved over his. When all else ended, love remained.

He knew the nightingale, or thought that he had. A small, plain bird of little wingspan and power.

Yet now the mighty warrior knew how perfectly its song could break a man's heart in two.

CHAPTER SEVENTEEN

SARA WOKE TO FIND HIM dressed, looking out the window, his shoulders tense.

The wind still shrieked and she shivered beneath the warm blanket that covered her. Her body was sated, her skin flushed from all the ways she had taken—and been taken.

But she forced away the remnants of sleep. There were questions to ask and a future to explore. And something remained for him to do, something he might resist, even now.

She walked to his side and slid her arms around his waist, feeling his sigh. "You should have woken me."

"There was no need. You must have your rest."

"I will. First I have something to ask."

She felt him stiffen, picking up the determined thread of her thoughts. "Let him go, Gabriel. I can feel that some part of you resists, but let it be done once and for all. If you won't do it for him, do it for me. Remember the honor of the friendship you once had."

She felt him try to block her out. "Mistakes were made. How can either of us go back now?"

"Can't—or won't?"

"Is there a difference?"

"Of course there is. You are a man of strength, a man who can choose. Use your strength to choose the right thing. Set things fully as they were with your friend."

He looked at Sara and smiled a little grimly. "Do you control everyone around you so easily?"

"It's a request. Nothing more than that."

"Which gives it more weight than any order." He pointed to the leather chair beside the door. "Your clothes are dry."

She saw her folded sweater and on top of that her cell phone. "I will need some things from my room in the gatehouse."

He touched her cheek. "You will stay there and rest? No more work?"

She winced as she pulled on her sweater. "Agreed."

He muttered a little. "I will go with you."

Silent, he watched her dress, and then he opened the door. "After that I will go to find Draycott's lord." His coldness melted a little. "I do this because you ask me. And because it is, just possibly, the *right* thing to do. For what time I am given, I am yours to command."

His shoulders stiff, he walked her out to the gatehouse.

AFTER HE WAS CERTAIN that Sara was safe in the gatehouse, resting in bed, Gabriel strode grimly into the rain. Looking up into the sky, he summoned the man he had hated so long.

No one came.

Once again Gabriel issued the silent words of calling.

The storm answered, wind gusting fiercely.

"By all the saints, Draycott. Reveal yourself now. I have…amends to make. Questions remain to be answered."

Adrian Draycott walked out of the mist near a great fountain at the edge of the gatehouse. He was immaculate in white lace cuffs and a black velvet jacket, every inch the abbey's lordly guardian. "You have me all ears, Navarre. Amends, you say?"

Gabriel paced a little, rubbing his neck. "She was right, heaven knows. But how hard to begin." He cleared his throat. "She's a rare woman, Sara Nightingale. How strange that I should meet her now, when there is so little certainty to anything."

"Little is better than none," Adrian muttered. "Don't tell me you've managed to shatter that young woman's heart so soon."

"Never." Gabriel paced the abbey's courtyard, oblivious to the rain and wind. "With my heart, I vow it."

"I am glad to know you've got some sense left. So why this summoning?"

"I meant to demand answers," Gabriel said slowly. "And then I meant to argue and attack. But that way lies emptiness." He closed his eyes, feeling the rain on his face. Feeling the physical world with aching clarity. "Hear me well, Draycott of Outremer. I release my hold over you. Whatever you did or did not do those long years past, I—accept."

He held out one hand.

Adrian studied it, then crossed his arms. "Not good enough."

"Be cursed! What do you want, a papal decree?"

"Sincerity. An explanation. And we'll do it somewhere with a degree of comfort. Not shouting in the rain with a storm overhead, by heaven."

FIRELIGHT CAST A phantom glow over the old study above the moat. Adrian leaned one arm on the mantel, watching the restless patterns of the fire he'd made. "Strange to be in mortal form again, but I might as well enjoy it."

Reaching down, he found the singularly fine sherry that the current Lord Draycott had brought back from Spain several months earlier. He poured a glass and held it out to Gabriel. "In welcome to the abbey."

"None for me. My wits are all askew from that last brew you gave me."

Adrian hid a smile, then turned to stare into the firelight. "I will accept your explanation, when you give it."

Gabriel ran a hand through his dark hair. "They came to tell me my family was gone. Your cousin had the very document with your signature, ordering their capture. They were...killed. All of them."

"My cousin." Adrian spat out the word. "A viper if ever one lived. He hated me for my rank. And he hated you even more."

The Crusader's eyes narrowed. "I had no hint of it. But why?"

"Because you were the better man and the stronger warrior. Because we were closest friends. My cousin, I learned later, was also in the pay of the bastard Philip."

"Philip." Gabriel spat out the word. "Sara saw the truth, that Philip ordered her taken captive. His evil knew no bounds. Yet he was clever, leaving no evidence of his involvement. I believe now that he conspired to goad me, to make me think that you had trysted with my ward. And God help me, I believed the lie so easily." Gabriel's jaw clenched.

Adrian's eyes filled with anger. "He left the court in the chaos after Acre fell, and he was not seen for over a year. I found him in a muddy village near Arles, and he begged me for money." Adrian made a grimace of distaste. "He seemed half deranged. But even deranged, he would admit nothing."

"You searched him out after you thought I was gone, after my ward was long vanished?"

"Could I do less in the name of friendship when I had doubts of the truth?"

Navarre glared at the fire. "My apology to you now would come too late."

"Not too late."

The Crusader moved stiffly across the room and held out a hand. "I ask you to forgive me."

"We were both duped, but now we will put it behind us. The angry past will be sealed."

Their hands locked. The years peeled away, and a light of friendship filled Gabriel's lapis eyes. "I have her to thank for bringing me to this. A miracle, if I believed in them."

"You may learn to, my friend. Over the centuries this old house has seen many."

Gabriel took a long breath. "What happened to her, Adrian? Did you find a trace?"

"I sent runners from Acre to Jerusalem. They followed her into the desert. She wandered, but knew how to hide. A week later a great caravan passed on its way to the east. We believed that she tried to find it."

"And?" Gabriel's voice was raw.

"And…we found no answer. The sand swallowed every print in a storm. The next day I sent a runner to the caravan, but none there knew of her."

Gabriel turned, his face like stone. "So much treachery. If Philip and your cousin were here now, I'd quarter them with my sword."

"There is no need," Adrian said quietly. "They both suffered at the end. My cousin conspired with the king's high counselors. For that he was convicted of treason and hung from the city walls. Philip died by his own hand six months after that. It was whispered that he had the leper's disease."

"Too late to help her," Gabriel whispered. Then he turned, one brow raised. "Caravan? Bound for the east?"

"It went to meet an emissary from the court of the great Khan, escorting merchants home after their years in the Khan's employ. She might have found her way to meet them, who can say?" Adrian shook his head. "It would explain her persistence here."

"What do you mean?"

"Sara has found a great treasure, my friend. Its location was hidden in old shipping records and maps. Here at the abbey she found details that no one else thought to check. Most uncanny." He pointed to a book open on a nearby table. "You'll find an ancient copy of Marco Polo's book there." He raised a hand and the book's pages turned beneath his thought.

When Gabriel didn't speak, Adrian glared at him. "What bothers you now? That she is not only beautiful but ingenious in her work?"

Gabriel lifted the old book, his face lined and uneasy. "You think me a true fool? Not that at all. But great treasures bring great greed. There were intruders already in the darkness. I fear this news is known. Sara will not be safe here."

Adrian picked up his sherry and studied the fire. "At least here she will have two Crusaders to protect her. All in all, I think it will answer very well."

CHAPTER EIGHTEEN

EDWIN HARDING was tired.

The prior weeks after the kidnapping had been a nightmare, and now he was worried about his agent in England. Sara Nightingale's cell phone switched to voice mail with every call, and no one answered the landline at the abbey.

He checked his watch.

Teague should have made contact by now. What in hell had happened?

He looked up at the sound of a knock at his door. Raymond Doer, head of the Bureau's Office of Internal Compliance, stood in the hall, a folder in his hand. "Sorry to bother you, Edwin." He looked troubled. "But you need to see this before I leave. It has to do with Agent Nightingale."

Harding controlled his impatience. "Is something wrong?"

Doer moved inside. After a moment he closed the door behind him. "Her field laptop was taken in for routine security updates, and the tech in charge called me last night. He found two bugs. Someone has access to all the info in her laptop."

Harding felt a prickle at his neck. "How long have the bugs been in place?"

"According to the tech staff, probably three weeks. It had to be after their last security sweep."

Long enough to provide all the details of her current assignment, Harding thought.

Harding gave Doer a distracted wave and turned to dial Izzy Teague, praying he would reach Sara before things got any worse.

CHAPTER NINETEEN

TWENTY MINUTES LATER Sara sat in the gatehouse listening to the howl of the wind. A notebook lay open on her lap, but she was too tired to move.

Memories of Gabriel's rough hands and warm mouth stirred her memories, making her skin flush. She wanted him again. She wanted to make up for all the lost years and shattered dreams.

She closed her eyes, remembering the stunned look in his eyes when she'd told him she loved him. Did the man truly believe he was entitled only to hate and be hated? Anger could end, she firmly believed, and everyone had a chance for redemption.

She was determined to teach him how true this was, to make him laugh and remember how to dream again.

Fighting exhaustion, she pulled back the velvet curtain, looking out the gatehouse window at the stormy sky and hoping that Gabriel's errand of reconciliation was a success. Changing hatred back to friendship would never be easy, but it was the only way to free him from the past that still clung to him like an oily shadow.

Like the shadows that had nearly taken her.

Sara shuddered at the memory. In her job she saw evil, violence and greed every day, but never such evil as the things that had gripped her.

And yet the world remained, and her duties remained. Though she was exhausted, she needed to try to contact

Harding and check on the status of the man he had told her would be arriving at the abbey. She wouldn't be able to relax until her documents and information about the island of Korcula were turned over to safe hands.

But she couldn't stop thinking about Gabriel. She took a deep breath and tentatively reached out, following the trail of her memories. Feeling more than a little odd, she closed her eyes and tried to focus.

Warm skin. Callused hands.

Gabriel, where are you?

For a moment there was only silence. Then Sara felt the caress of phantom hands on her shoulders. His mind brushed hers. *We are almost finished. Yes, our breach is mended.*

I'm very glad. She put her smile into the thought she sent him. *And now, if you don't mind I have a call to make.*

Very well.

I also have important documents to check in the library. Other maps—my notes. I worry about another gust or a broken window.

She felt his resistance instantly. *Stay there. Do not leave, Sara. I will be—*

Their contact fluttered like a flame in the wind. Frightened, Sara stood up, her notebook dropping to the floor. *Gabriel?*

STANDING AT THE SIDE of the abbey, Navarre pointed up to the roof. "The gate is opening again, as I feared. I can feel the pull of the darkness. It's affecting us, too. I could barely reach Sara. Watch how the storm moves toward the abbey."

"I'm afraid it is so," Adrian murmured.

"This is no human storm, Adrian. It has already crossed between the two worlds. We have little time to stop what has begun."

Navarre heard the ring of hooves. Ferrant loomed up the muddy slope at the back of the abbey, eyes wild. "Yes, my friend. I can use your strength, too, if you will."

The horse threw back its head, pawing the wet earth.

"And so to war," Adrian said grimly. "As it was those centuries before. It must be so. No one will be allowed to destroy my abbey."

Navarre ran a hand along his destrier's mane. "One choice. One chance." His face was grim. "I must shift the dark gate to a place of hallowed ground. There it will be sealed forever. Have you such a place, Adrian?"

Adrian studied the shadowed walls and nodded slowly. "There is an old spring beneath the gatehouse fountain. Legend holds that St. Alban rested there and the fountain sprang up at his hand."

"For our sake, pray that the legends are true. Come. We will need St. Alban's goodness tonight," Navarre said flatly.

Adrian moved in front of him. "One thing you neglect to tell me. How do you intend to move this dark gate? It cannot be an easy thing to manage."

"With my body. They want me back, you see. Very badly." Navarre did not meet Adrian's gaze. "If I call to them with open welcome, they will come," he said grimly.

"The risk," Draycott whispered. "If we mistake by even a moment, you will be Taken…."

"There is no other choice. Someone has told me I am a man who should use my strength to make the right choice, so I make this one now." Navarre pulled his cloak back, revealing a tempered steel Crusader's cross at his neck, a larger copy of the piece Sara now wore. "If you have holy relics, summon them now. In this battle, every weapon must be used."

"What about Sara?"

"In her room," Navarre said. "She wants to help, but she will stay as I have told her. I feel danger all around us. We must *hurry.*"

SARA STAYED BY THE window, hoping for a sight of Gabriel or Adrian Draycott. The storm seemed to pick up force with every gust, and two trees beyond the moat had already snapped.

She had had no more contact with Gabriel, but she sensed him nearby. She could feel the deep force of his concentration.

Gabriel, what are you doing?

Static. Emptiness. *Gabriel?*

Soon...

With the touch of his thoughts, she felt a wave of relief. At the window, she eased back the curtain and then froze.

Two dark shapes moved along the side of the gatehouse. Both of them wore night-vision goggles and carried automatic weapons.

Sara struggled to take in this new threat. No possibility that these were friendly visitors. Harding's contact would not have arrived with such stealth.

Gabriel, be careful. There are men—

He was back in her mind suddenly, drifting like a warm wind. *We have seen them. Stay where you are.*

Sara felt the cold weight of his fear. And then his thoughts broke into a hiss.

What can I do to help? There must be something.

There was an echo. *Stay...stay...*

Sara was still out of sight at the window, hidden by the velvet curtains, when two more figures moved up the slope from the far side of the drive.

She leaned against the cold wall and forced herself to think calmly. To act like the professional she was trained to be.

Gabriel and Adrian had skills she couldn't hope to equal, and she had come to accept their magic as real. They had already seen two of the intruders, if she understood Gabriel right. But would the two of them be equal to four men, all well equipped? Modern weapons had power and range that a Crusader couldn't hope to understand.

She stood undecided, her heart pounding. She had told

Gabriel she would stay, because he feared for her safety. But she had also sworn to perform a job, and her responsibility was clear.

She couldn't sit passively and hope for success. Adrian and Gabriel might be outnumbered. Even with their magic their bodies were physical now. They could bleed and die.

She tried her cell phone, but the batteries were completely dead. Tossing the unit down on the bed, she tugged on her clothes, then searched in her drawer. With her service revolver loaded and holstered, she climbed a flight of stairs and inched silently outside. At the third floor of the gatehouse, a balcony overlooked the front and inner courtyard. Crouched out of sight behind its stone railing, she crept to the balcony's far side.

She made out one figure flat on the ground beyond the fountain, invisible to anyone on the first floor. The other three men had vanished.

Gabriel? Tell me what is happening.

Wait in safety, Sara.

Nothing more came through.

I'm on the third-floor balcony. There are two more men now. One is beyond the fountain with a rifle. You—

Sara froze at a creak below her. When she looked over the edge of the balcony she saw a tall figure moving through her room, one floor below.

How had they found her room so fast? It didn't make sense.

In the sudden flare of lightning she saw the man pick up her cell phone from the bed. Sara realized they had some kind of tracking device on the phone.

She was being tracked at close quarters. Her only hope of safety was to keep moving.

Carefully she drew back against the balcony wall. Over her head a narrow metal staircase led up to the roof. A stone arch connected the gatehouse roof to the main house.

Sara knew surveillance protocol. A sniper would search out the high ground and use a scoped rifle to monitor all activity while his teammates methodically subdued opposition in the terrain below. Sara assumed they had blueprints of the abbey as part of their careful preparation, which meant they had a route to the roof.

From her own mission preparation she knew there was only one door from the main house that led out to the roof. That was where she would be.

Panic sliced down at memories of the nightmare *things* that waited there, but she had no choice. With her gun holstered, she climbed the slick rungs of the ladder up toward the roof.

GABRIEL STARED AT THE man lying behind the conservatory. Twenty yards away, Adrian had dropped a second intruder, using a broken tree branch.

Neither man had suspected they were being watched, thanks to Navarre's skills. But this unholy storm had affected even his magic. And if the storm continued to gain power...

Suddenly Navarre froze.

Sara?

Something was moving on the roof. Dark and unsettled, the gate had roiled back to life, feeding on the storm's growing energy. He looked down at the man breathing haltingly at his feet, focusing as he drove his mind deep in search of answers.

"No," he growled. "Not Sara."

Adrian gripped his arm. "What is it?"

"They want what she has discovered. After they have the papers they will kill her and take all clues of the work she has done here."

"Not while I can draw breath," Adrian muttered. "They think to storm my walls?" His eyes gleamed with unholy fury. "Just let them try."

CHAPTER TWENTY

SARA FOUND HER VANTAGE point on the flat stone parapet overlooking the door to the roof. From the space where she huddled, she could see the front of the door, but she would remain hidden behind the stone panel.

Gabriel?

A surge of warmth. The memory of his hands.

Sara—where are you?

On the roof. I'm hiding above the staircase. Someone may come up to this vantage point. It's where a sniper would go first.

She felt his irritation and the weight of his fear. *Stay well hidden. Leave this to us. We are coming.*

Sara didn't respond. Her duty came before personal safety or comfort. If a sniper broke cover, she would see him and deal with him as she had been trained. Gabriel had his skills.

But *she* had hers.

FOUR MINUTES LATER, the door from the stairway creaked faintly. Sara squinted into the rain and kept her focus on the area where the man would emerge onto the roof.

Gravel hurtled past, driven by the wind, and her finger itched, but she forced her muscles to relax against the cold metal grip.

Not yet...

She saw the back of a head, the outstretched hand that held a scoped sniper rifle shouldered to fire.

Adrenaline pumped through her, blotting out the ugly kick of fear. Long months of weapon training held her dead-still, her aim steady.

The figure moved into full view, turning fast to scan the perimeter. Sara squeezed the trigger, felt the recoil in the same blurring moment that flame shot from the muzzle.

The black figure was thrown sideways by the round, but he spun awkwardly, sighted in her direction. Sara fired twice. He fell from her third shot.

As his rifle clattered onto the roof, a round burned through Sara's shoulder and she saw a second man in firing stance at the other corner of the roof. A round whined above her head, shattering a ridge of stone behind her. She dropped flat. A third round zigzagged across the parapet.

Something grazed her face as she hit the roof. The world spun, going black.

Gabriel's alarm crackled into her mind. *Sara—*

Hurt. Watch for a sniper—east side of the roof. Hurry.

She felt Gabriel's fury as she crawled painfully toward a broad chimney, the only cover close. Blood seeped down her right shoulder and every movement was agony, but she gripped her pistol, watching for a clear shot at her attacker.

Abruptly she felt a change around her, felt the weight of darkness and hunger. Shadows roiled up, pouring from the dark, shifting hole. She forced down panic as the nightmare began anew, shadow forms pouring out in search of fresh prey. Sara pressed against the tall chimney pillar. There was no more room to retreat, not with a sniper closing in.

Stay down.

She turned to see Gabriel striding through the mist, his cloak drawn about him. Adrian was near the stairs, gesturing toward her.

Sara, go to Adrian. I will deal with this cur.

Be careful—

Go now!

Wincing, she crept along the chimney, then sprinted toward the staircase, one hand pressed to her bleeding shoulder.

As wind howled over the rooftop, she heard a man's grunt and the crack of a rifle falling against stone.

Gabriel raced past. Her attacker cut in the opposite direction in pursuit. Sara realized the shadows had followed the men, boiling over the roof like smoke.

She caught back a sob of panic. "Adrian, help him—"

Adrian's hands circled her wrist. "Hurry. We'll meet them at the fountain."

She didn't understand but there was no time for questions. She followed Adrian down the narrow staircase and through the dark house.

"This way. Hold my arm."

For seconds that felt like an eternity she followed Adrian along a twisting maze of corridors through what was probably an old servants' area. They emerged at the far side of the house, facing the gatehouse.

Through a rain-streaked window Sara saw Gabriel backed against the fountain, parrying her attacker. Smoke writhed up like living waves around them. She couldn't imagine how they had reached the ground first, but she also didn't understand how her attacker seemed to rise and fall two feet above the ground with a spin of Gabriel's hand.

"Adrian, we have to go. We can help him."

His fingers gripped her wrist, holding her where she was. "We cannot. This is his work to finish. He opened the gate and now he must close it." His voice was rough with emotion.

Sara's fingers tightened on her pistol. "I'll help him if you won't."

Adrian pressed her back against the wall. "No. This is by his order. We may not interfere."

As she squinted into the rain, Sara saw the dark storm of figures above Gabriel's head. Too late she realized the danger he faced. She wondered if Gabriel had chosen this as a penance.

Be careful, my love.

He didn't turn but Sara felt his thoughts curl around her in warm solace. The darkness opened, enveloped the man from the roof, then seethed out toward Gabriel.

No!

This is my choice, Sara. For you, with all the gifts of my heart. Remember me and that this is the first good thing I do in too long…

And then the link between them was lost in a pounding wave of emotion.

The hole widened, surrounded Gabriel and his attacker like an angry mouth.

Nightingale. A small bird but its song will break your heart.

His last words.

Then he was gone, swept into the darkness. The hole seethed and then the dark shapes were swept back in its passing. Mist drifted slowly. Equilibrium was restored. Only rain and emptiness were left.

Sara cried out in disbelief, starting forward. This time Adrian let her go, and she felt the terrible weight of his sorrow as he followed her to the fountain.

Emptiness struck her like a blow.

She sank down blindly, rain in her face. Her fingers clutched at the rough stones of the fountain where Gabriel had been swallowed up without a trace.

WHEN IZZY TEAGUE reached the abbey's front lawn fifteen minutes later, he found Agent Sara Nightingale sitting in the rain on the edge of a weathered stone fountain.

She was oblivious to the downpour, and she didn't seem to see him cross the gravel drive.

Two bodies were stretched out flat at a side entrance on

the east of the house. There was no sign of anyone else nearby, although two fresh sets of footprints crisscrossed near the edge of the fountain, and another set of prints approached the front door from the gatehouse. In the pouring rain he might have overlooked others.

Oddly, a black horse had raced past Izzy in a state of frenzy only moments before.

Izzy called Sara's name, but she didn't seem to hear. When he leaned down and removed the gun gripped in her cold fingers, he heard her say a name.

It sounded like "Gabriel."

CHAPTER TWENTY-ONE

THE RAIN FELL HARDER.

Sara hunched over, trembling, dimly aware of the rush of the fountain behind her.

"Agent Nightingale—Sara, are you all right?"

She heard the man repeat the code word set by Harding. Now he slowly took her service weapon.

"You've got a good deal of blood on your shoulder, and I'd like to take a look at it. Why don't we go inside?"

Sara stared blindly at the blood streaking her wet jacket. How strange. After the first wave of pain, she hadn't felt anything at her shoulder. Right now nothing seemed to matter to her.

She took a hard breath and forced her attention back to the man's questions. "Mr. Teague, you said?"

"Call me Izzy. And I asked what happened to the men who came here. I saw their tracks."

"There is a man up on the roof. I shot him. There were others, but they—" Sara's voice caught. "The phone lines were down. My cell phone hasn't worked, so I couldn't make contact."

Izzy shone a small penlight on her shoulder, speaking quietly. "The storm has knocked out power lines all over southern England. There's extensive flooding, too. Sara, why don't we go inside now?"

His voice was low and compelling, but she didn't want

to move. Not until she could accept the things she had just seen and the loss that was too great to bear.

"I can't leave. Not yet," she said. She frowned at Izzy's rugged features—he was the spitting image of Denzel Washington. "The maps and my notebook are locked in the library safe. I'd prefer if you took possession of them for delivery back to the States."

"As soon as I finish here. Would you look to your right please?" His voice was pleasant but firm. He shone his penlight into Sara's eyes and kept talking quietly. "Must have been some firefight here. You held them off by yourself?"

There was no scoffing in his voice, no censure or disbelief. It was a simple question.

So different from the antagonism she'd faced back in the States.

"Only one. The others...got into some trouble with the storm." She couldn't find a clear way to explain what had happened, no way that wouldn't leave her sounding like a lunatic.

"But the two bodies behind the abbey show no signs of bullet entry points. Did you rig up some booby traps?"

Sara rubbed her forehead wearily. She was shivering and rain was seeping between her shoulders like cold fingers.

Like the cold brush of the things from the roof. The things that had ripped Gabriel away. "Can we talk about this later? I'll...explain everything then."

She'd come up with a story somehow.

"No problem. Let's go inside. I'll make a fire, then find something warm for you to drink."

"They already made a fire," Sara whispered. "It seems like a century ago."

"They?"

She stood up slowly. "It doesn't matter. Why don't you go on? I'll be in shortly."

"I don't think I should leave you."

"Please, I just need several minutes…alone. No longer."

He hesitated. Then Sara heard his boots crunch over gravel. The gatehouse door creaked open. She didn't move, feeling the weight of terrible sorrow. Blindly, she reached out to the emptiness, searching for the link that had bound her to Gabriel. Once, twice, ten times she called to him.

Nothing.

He was gone.

Her fingers met the cold outline of the cross he had given her barely two hours before. The metal was worn from the pressure of Gabriel's fingers for too many years to count. She slid to her knees, one hand outstretched. She felt the mist and the rough stone ledge of the fountain.

Gabriel…

Behind her the black horse emerged from the fog. He moved restlessly across the courtyard, neighing.

What would happen to him now? Sara wondered. Could she find a place where he would be safe and well taken care of? The horse nudged her hair, blowing noisily against her neck, but she had no energy left to smile. Her fingers rose, closing hard around the silky mane as she pressed her tear-streaked face to the horse's back.

Wind gusted up in eddies, churning through the gatehouse courtyard. Lightning speared the sky overhead.

Gabriel, what is there left without you?

Space tore open, hissing with the force of nature turned against itself. Inky clouds churned up.

Thunder rumbled as Gabriel plummeted to the ground, landing on his back with a groan.

Sara stared, afraid to believe the figure was real. Half laughing, half crying, she shot onto one knee beside him, touching his face and shoulders.

He looked dazed and confused as he tried to stand up. "Sara?" When she lifted his head, he couldn't speak. His hands simply circled hers and gripped hard.

The contact between them was dense and electric now.

"They—they refused to have me," Gabriel finally rasped. "They forced me back. I could not stay because of the choice I made. A pure gift, they called it." He lay flat in the mud, coughed once and rubbed his throat. "It appears that I am here to stay." He tried to sit up and landed back in the mud. "Here with you, Sara. If you will have me."

His hands closed on hers as if he wanted to be certain he would never lose her again. When she didn't answer, he pushed onto one elbow and raised an eyebrow. *Sara?*

His thoughts slid into hers, merged and raced, rich with the certainty of people who had known each other far longer than one day or even one lifetime. *Speak now. Will you have me, despite the harm I have caused?*

The rain had stopped. Over the abbey's wooded hills dawn was brushing the horizon. Through racing clouds the low moon gleamed silver, then vanished into the pink flush of the new day.

The first day in a new century for a man who had wandered too long.

Sara brought his callused hand to her lips. *I like to give orders. I think I should warn you. I won't be calm and subservient if you bluster and wave your arms around. Especially then,* she added.

Is that a yes, Sara, my heart?

I'm...thinking about it.

Gabriel stood up awkwardly, frowning down at her. *There is blood on your shoulder.*

Being shot generally has that effect.

By all the saints, you should be inside—

Stop blustering. She smiled gravely. *And I think I will have you, Crusader. Living with a battle-hardened knight may suit me very well. Although how I'll explain you to the IRS and the Immigration Service...*

Gabriel tried to walk and swayed sharply. *I seem to be*

weaker than I thought. There was a bit of a fight before I was thrown out of the Between World.

Sara didn't ask what had happened to the man from the roof. She could imagine the grim scenario well enough without details.

They've thrown you back, Navarre? Adrian Draycott walked out of the mist, a look of shock on his face.

So it appears.

Adrian pursed his lips, trying to hide his sharp relief. *So why are you delaying? Settle the matter with this singular woman before she comes to her senses and runs away.*

Gabriel slanted a look at Sara. *You're right. She might do far better than I, Draycott. Probably there are rich traders in her home city. Or maybe a prince who would woo her.*

Not too many princes hang out on my block, Sara cut in dryly.

She crossed her arms, frowning. Because it felt far too comfortable sharing her thoughts, she put those thoughts to words. "I'd appreciate it if you two would stop trying to organize my future as if I didn't have a brain in my head."

"He's right," Draycott said thoughtfully. "You could do very well for yourself, Sara."

"Depending on how you define *well*." She took a deep breath. "No, I've decided that living with a prince—or a rich trader—would be boring. But living with a black-hearted, bad-tempered, querulous Crusader? Now that's an interesting prospect."

Adrian studied the two of them and shook his head. *I warrant there will be sparks between you. Enough for twenty Crusades.*

Gabriel traced his cross where it hung over the collar of Sara's jacket. "I'd like to show you La Varenne. Both of you, in fact. If the walls still remain," Gabriel said roughly. "There are roses in summer, great banks of them. The Rose of Castile. The Rose of Four Seasons. The Hundred-Petaled and the Rosa alba."

Adrian looked interested. "Perhaps I'll go. I'm always in search of fine old blooms for the abbey gardens."

He glanced up as the sun burst gold and glorious over the horizon. Behind him Gabriel slid his arms around Sara and pulled her closer. She whispered his name. The Crusader's mouth closed hungrily over hers.

"I can see I'm not needed here."

Neither of the other two answered or appeared to notice his presence in the slightest.

Which was probably as it should be, Adrian thought, when two people were lost in each other's arms, weaving together dreams for their future.

Yes, it had been a fine night's work despite the violence and the danger. The old anger was cleared at last. Navarre had found a home in the arms of the woman he had lost.

The ghost of Draycott Abbey smiled. Smoothing the lace at his cuffs, he surveyed the oblivious couple at the edge of the fountain. Given that all was well here, he had a desire to see the rest of his house and grounds.

Would their link hold once Adrian returned to his phantom form? Would the other two even remember what had happened here? And how would a Crusader survive in the modern world?

He had no sure answers. Only the future would tell.

And now it was time to go. The abbey's guardian took a deep breath, staring out at the dappled sunlight beneath a clearing sky. He took a last breath, savoring the rich perfume of his roses.

The Changing was far easier this time, moving back into the spin of light and color he was most used to. The air quivered as he felt the density of his physical body fade.

Suddenly rose petals drifted down, brushing the surface of the fountain and perfuming the air. "Nicely done," Adrian said to the gray cat that stalked over the cobblestones.

Gideon's tail flicked from side to side. He looked a little proprietary as he pressed against Adrian's boot and showed no intention of moving away.

Adrian's hand rose. The words began, low and grave, taken from the old Norman French that he had never forgotten.

Hold in the circle.
Hold to the light.
None to cut, none by might.
Fair winds before morning and bright dawn to follow.
Hold in the circle.
Hold to the light.

Adrian smiled, staring up at the sky. The ritual was complete.

His work was done.

In the full glow of dawn cat and ghost walked calmly forward and vanished into the abbey's weathered granite walls.

* * * * *

REQUEST YOUR
FREE BOOKS!

2 FREE NOVELS
FROM THE ROMANCE/SUSPENSE
COLLECTION PLUS 2 FREE GIFTS!

YES! Please send me 2 FREE novels from the Romance/Suspense Collection and my 2 FREE gifts (gifts are worth about $10). After receiving them, if I don't wish to receive any more books, I can return the shipping statement marked "cancel." If I don't cancel, I will receive 4 brand-new novels every month and be billed just $5.74 per book in the U.S. or $6.24 per book in Canada. That's a savings of at least 28% off the cover price. It's quite a bargain! Shipping and handling is just 50¢ per book.* I understand that accepting the 2 free books and gifts places me under no obligation to buy anything. I can always return a shipment and cancel at any time. Even if I never buy another book from the Reader Service, the two free books and gifts are mine to keep forever.

185 MDN EYNQ 385 MDN EYN2

Name	(PLEASE PRINT)

Address	Apt. #

City	State/Prov.	Zip/Postal Code

Signature (if under 18, a parent or guardian must sign)

Mail to **The Reader Service:**
IN U.S.A.: P.O. Box 1867, Buffalo, NY 14240-1867
IN CANADA: P.O. Box 609, Fort Erie, Ontario L2A 5X3

Not valid to current subscribers of the Romance Collection,
the Suspense Collection or the Romance/Suspense Collection.

Want to try two free books from another line?
Call 1-800-873-8635 or visit www.morefreebooks.com.

* Terms and prices subject to change without notice. Prices do not include applicable taxes. Sales tax applicable in N.Y. Canadian residents will be charged applicable provincial taxes and GST. Offer not valid in Quebec. This offer is limited to one order per household. All orders subject to approval. Credit or debit balances in a customer's account(s) may be offset by any other outstanding balance owed by or to the customer. Please allow 4 to 6 weeks for delivery. Offer available while quantities last.

Your Privacy: Harlequin is committed to protecting your privacy. Our Privacy Policy is available online at www.eHarlequin.com or upon request from the Reader Service. From time to time we make our lists of customers available to reputable third parties who may have a product or service of interest to you. If you would prefer we not share your name and address, please check here. ☐

BOB09

In 2009 Harlequin celebrates
60 years of pure reading pleasure!

We're marking this occasion by offering
16 **FREE** full books to download and read.

Visit

www.HarlequinCelebrates.com

to choose from a variety of
great romance stories
that are absolutely **FREE!**

(Total approximate retail value of $60)

We invite you to visit and share the Web site
with your friends, family
and anyone who enjoys reading.

CHRISTINA SKYE

77307	TO CATCH A THIEF	___ $6.99 U.S.	___ $6.99 CAN.
77294	DRAYCOTT ETERNAL	___ $6.99 U.S.	___ $6.99 CAN.
77262	ENCHANTMENT &	___ $6.99 U.S.	___ $8.50 CAN.
	BRIDGE OF DREAMS		
77209	CODE NAME: BIKINI	___ $6.99 U.S.	___ $8.50 CAN.
77123	CODE NAME: BLONDIE	___ $6.99 U.S.	___ $8.50 CAN.
77069	CODE NAME: BABY	___ $6.99 U.S.	___ $8.50 CAN.

(limited quantities available)

TOTAL AMOUNT	$ _____
POSTAGE & HANDLING	$ _____
($1.00 FOR 1 BOOK, 50¢ for each additional)	
APPLICABLE TAXES*	$ _____
TOTAL PAYABLE	$ _____

(check or money order—please do not send cash)

To order, complete this form and send it, along with a check or money order for the total above, payable to HQN Books, to: **In the U.S.:** 3010 Walden Avenue, P.O. Box 9077, Buffalo, NY 14269-9077; **In Canada:** P.O. Box 636, Fort Erie, Ontario, L2A 5X3.

Name: _____

Address: _____ City: _____

State/Prov.: _____ Zip/Postal Code: _____

Account Number (if applicable): _____

075 CSAS

*New York residents remit applicable sales taxes.
*Canadian residents remit applicable GST and provincial taxes.

HQN™

We *are* romance™

www.HQNBooks.com

PHCS1109BL